Sunnyside

Joanna Murray-Smith

VIKING
an imprint of
PENGUIN BOOKS

VIKING

Published by the Penguin Group
Penguin Books Ltd, 80 Strand, London WC2R ORL, England
Penguin Group (USA) Inc., 375 Hudson Street, New York, New York 10014, USA
Penguin Group (Canada), 90 Eglinton Avenue East, Suite 700, Toronto, Ontario,
Canada M4P 2Y3 (a division of Pearson Penguin Canada Inc.)
Penguin Ireland, 25 St Stephen's Green, Dublin 2, Ireland (a division of Penguin Books Ltd)
Penguin Group (Australia), 250 Camberwell Road,
Camberwell, Victoria 3124, Australia (a division of Pearson Australia Group Pty Ltd)
Penguin Books India Pvt Ltd, 11 Community Centre,
Panchsheel Park, New Delhi – 110 017, India
Penguin Group (NZ), cnr Airborne and Rosedale Roads, Albany,
Auckland 1310, New Zealand (a division of Pearson New Zealand Ltd)
Penguin Books (South Africa) (Pty) Ltd, 24 Sturdee Avenue,
Rosebank, Johannesburg 2196, South Africa

Penguin Books Ltd, Registered Offices: 80 Strand, London WC2R ORL, England

www.penguin.com

First published in Australia by Penguin 2005
First published in Great Britain by Viking 2005
1

Copyright © Joanna Murray-Smith, 2005

The moral right of the author has been asserted

Printed in Great Britain by Clays Ltd, St Ives plc

A CIP catalogue record for this book is available from the British Library

ISBN-13: 978-0-670-91600-9
ISBN-10: 0-670-91600-5

To Raymond, Sam, Charlie and Lucy

Prologue

Molly McLelland had only just finished clearing away the breakfast things when she saw a tall young man in wet-weather gear striding across her lawn. She wiped her hands on a towel, turned off the kitchen radio and opened the French doors onto the terrace. It was almost spring and there was a faint smell of lilac and violets in the air. There he was, Mr Magnificent Swim, with his little containers of chemicals, surveying the murky green water of the pool. Summer would soon be here.

Molly opened the small gate at the front of the terrace and made her way down the stone steps. The tall young man looked up from the water and, on seeing her, his expression lost its look of puzzlement.

'You're new,' said Molly.

'Kevin's gone up north to his kid. I'm taking over his pools until after summer.'

'I'm Molly McLelland.'

Molly extended her hand and the young man shook it.

'Dan.'

They regarded each other for a moment. Molly thought that he looked like a surfer. Shaggy brown hair, streaked by the sun, strong arms, tanned even after winter.

'If it's okay with you I'll just come by every three weeks or so and do what needs to be done.'

Molly lingered.

'We're not very practical. My husband doesn't have time for a lot of things.'

'Well, that's not unusual.'

Behind him, the wisteria was dripping from the fence, cold blue tears.

'How is the pool? Is it in good shape?'

'It's a great pool. Nothing wrong with the pool.'

'You come on up to the house if you'd like a coffee. It's chilly.'

Molly had been a good wife to David. She had borne him a son, cooked well, kept the house tidy and carried off a part-time job as a publicist for a local vineyard. She was sexually obliging, a good decorator, rarely nagged and remained optimistic in the face of life's ordinary trials. David loved her, appreciated her and they enjoyed a happy, convivial marriage. Every Thursday night since Justin was born, they had hired a babysitter so that they could go out for dinner, just the two of them. They often said that this small dependable outing kept their marriage safe from fraying. At Christmas time or anniversaries, they gave thanks for the strange confluence of events that led to their meeting at a fringe theatrical production in a cold church hall.

Molly made fresh coffee in the dripolator and read the newspaper while Dan from Magnificent Swim surveyed and anointed the pool. In fifteen minutes, he was standing outside the French doors peering in at her. She got up and unlatched them. He slipped off his boots and pulled off his yellow slicker. He was wearing only a faded T-shirt underneath. Without saying anything, Molly poured him some coffee and put the tray with the milk jug and sugar bowl on the kitchen counter.

He said: 'Nice house.'

She said: 'I like it.'

He took her face in his hands and kissed her cheeks and then her forehead and then her neck and then her mouth. He tasted young. He brought the outdoors in, his face was cold and his lips were thick and hungry and he pushed his hands up inside her cardigan and undid her bra and felt her breasts and pulled off her cardigan and undid her skirt and pulled off her tights and her underwear and then he lifted her and placed her on the Persian rug and unzipped himself and pushed his way into her and she fell completely away, as if she had travelled to a place where no-one knew her. She wasn't elegant here, or beautiful, but she was unfinished and exciting. And he came inside her and then he touched her here and there, fast and slow, tenderly, and for the first time she came from where she was, instead of from some imagined story inside her head. For the first time in many years, she *was* the story.

one

Alice Haskins snipped the first white hyacinths of the season with the secateurs and laid them carefully in the basket. The basket she considered somewhat twee. But then life in Sunnyside *was* twee; one might as well embrace the tweeness. Here she was with her secateurs cutting white hyacinths, standing in two acres of whipper-snippered paradise. This was the life people wanted. This was the life *everyone* was supposed to want. In a few minutes, Alice would carry the hyacinths inside and arrange them in an Orrefors vase and place them somewhere in the house. In the beautiful house. In the house anyone would want.

After many years in the inner city, Alice and Harry had decided that they should embrace the kind of life where you could drive your station wagon all the way to the kitchen door to unload the Safeway bags. It was time to grow up. For the last few years in the city, they had been steadily noticing the advance of the young on their territory. The cafes were exploding with young people and their piercings, their infantile politics, their arrogance. And Alice's father had died, leaving them just enough to get something good on the Peninsula, although still with a hefty mortgage.

It was time. Harry was growing into himself, into manly middle-age, and wanted to announce it. It was hard to announce your manly middle-age in the city. The city was about reinvigoration, something Harry had given up without regret. From his mid-thirties, Harry had started to inhabit himself. With an advancing career, more money, his initially reluctant acceptance of membership of an all-male club (which gathered monthly to debate issues of social and cultural significance), and the awareness that he had, firmly and undeniably, a beautiful family, Harry had felt, at last, *grounded*. He needed a suburb to swagger in.

Once they had made the move to Sunnyside, Harry began to look like the big, strong-jawed men selling barbecues in mail catalogues. After their first month in Sunnyside, Harry had admitted to Alice that he *liked* having a mortgage, since it made him feel as if he belonged to the whole cycle of existence, an important treadmill of birth, jobs, acquisitions, debt and death. It was clear to Alice that Harry had become enthralled by his new sense of permanence. Alice, however, had been taking longer to accept the triumph of convention over her own self-image.

The house was set back on Carringdale Road in Sunnyside's 'golden mile', where a covenant decreed no further subdivisions could take place and all the blocks were on one or two acres. Beyond Carringdale Road, the roads leading to the village were filled with the terracotta walls of Tuscan villas, the glistening white columns of neo-Georgian homes and the rammed-earth properties that were Santa-Fe Eco. These were the residential medals earned by the corporate barons of the eighties, medals for having appetites beyond good taste, good reason, good ethics. In between were mock-Tudor cottages from the thirties, clinker-brick mansions from the fifties and even a few remaining sixties beach houses, paint peeling, roofs buckling, uncertain on their stilts but still effortlessly modern. Soon they, too, would be purchased for land value, for sea glimpses, replaced with some hefty show homes.

Alice and Harry's house was 'Old Sunnyside': a beautiful, sprawling, low-slung nineteen-fifties gem in white weatherboard and stone, set in two acres of established garden surrounding a pale-blue-tiled pool. Built as a series of wings, the rooms faced into the garden. Many of the walls were edged in glass, which met at right angles with more glass, so that the corners of the house were like verdant portals, welcoming inside the green tendrils of wisteria and clematis, the bouquets of lilac and jasmine and piles of crisp, singed autumn leaves. Because of this, and the pale wood and the abundance of sky which seemed to pass through the house as if it wasn't there at all, the building appeared to float, suspended several feet above the ground, hovering angles and planes of glass. Only the presence of two vast rock fireplaces, one in the sunken sitting room and one in the family room, stopped the house from ascending into the clouds.

Alice and Harry had been seduced by the huge elm trees and birches and liquid ambars throughout their property, interspersed with green lawn and beds of lavender and roses and hydrangeas and thousands and thousands of bulbs. Someone had planted the garden to erupt chronologically into rooms of colour: white, blue, pink. The highway to the city was only a few minutes east, but from where they stood they seemed to be in a private park, where their lucky, privileged children could climb trees and play tennis, where they were surely safe from the proliferation of weapons of mass destruction.

Alice carried the basket along the path between the hedges and through the sliding doors into the house. *Here I am,* thought Alice. *Here I am, Alice Haskins. Forty years old and still with the body of a young woman. Here I am with my hyacinths and my Scandinavian glassware and my house full of vistas.*

Alice felt light in the house, as if she were passing through it. It would exist beyond her tenancy. There was a certainty to the house that a human being could only pretend to. For now, as she traversed its rooms, putting washing away in drawers, straightening duvet covers, replacing books on shelves, she felt confused by her own belligerent temporariness. As she moved lightly, thinly, through space and light and form, she forced herself to repeat a little mantra of belonging: *all this is mine, it is mine, it is mine.*

two

The definitive humiliation of not yet being legally adult was this: Scarlett had to endure her mother singing along to Air Supply on the way to school. Her mother insisted on the Peninsula light 'n' easy radio station that featured DJs you just *knew* looked like games-show hosts and had polyester satin sheets. The only way to avoid this was to get her learner's like all the other girls in her class. But this would mean being at the wheel of a Daiwoo. Scarlett had seen the other girls crawling the boulevards of Sunnyside in their fathers' sparkling Mercedes convertibles, or their mothers' Mercedes station wagons, streaked hair flying, faces furrowed in concentration. There was no way in the world she would be seen driving a Daiwoo.

Scarlett allowed her mother to drop her off at school on her way to work in Seabank in order not to have another argument. Whenever she argued with her mother, her mother morphed into an *office manager*. She became all technical and started talking about rules and deals. *We made a deal, Scarlett. This home works on systems. It's a team effort and we're both part of the team.*

Scarlett leant against the school fence and watched her mother as she pulled out. Kids were hovering around the gate, gathered around the boom box. Ingrid Pettigrove, in some strange plaid skirt shaped like a poncho, was heading for the library where she'd been wearing out the furniture all year. The younger grades were playing four square before the music started over the loud speaker. Some clown in the office had been playing sixties hits all week. Probably the principal's PA, a fifty-something having trouble coming to terms with her mortality. These days it was hard to tell the baby boomers from the gen-xers *being ironic about the boomers*. Like Scarlett's chemistry teacher, who wore vintage cowboy shirts every single day like an ironic gen-xer should. On fancy dress day, he'd come dressed *as a teacher*, in a cheap suit and thin nylon tie. Maybe he was responsible for The Mamas and the Papas now foggily blaring through the loudspeakers.

As soon as her mother's car had turned the corner heading for the highway, Scarlett started for the bus stop on Ocean View. She'd be home again in twenty minutes. Her mother was at work until six. Now that Scarlett was in final year, none of the teachers seemed to keep track of attendance. As long as her mid-year marks were okay, everything would be all right.

When she got home, Scarlett changed into her cargo pants and lay down in the doll room, her mother's doll room, and scowled at the dolls. Sometimes she liked just looking mean at them. All those Princess Dianas with their plastic faces and big blue glassy eyes and blonde helmets made out of real hair, but presumably not *Diana's* real hair. Her mother's pride and joy. The newest one had come yesterday, registered post. Scarlett had signed for it. It was hard to believe that somebody somewhere was still cranking out those Diana dolls almost a decade after she'd gone to God.

School was a waste of time. The problem was that the teaching was aimed at the lowest common denominator, which left her and Ingrid Pettigrove *hungry*. And after a while if your appetite was neglected you just stopped wanting. She would pass the exams all right. She was fairly sure she'd get into just about whichever course she wanted, but she wasn't sure what that was and in any case, she'd defer. Because the world was out there. And there were things to do. And whatever happened, she was going to make a difference.

The thought of turning into her mother was enough to send chills down Scarlett's spine. That her mother had ever seen anything in her father was incomprehensible. Not to mention vice versa. It disgusted her to think that she was the product of two such ordinary people. *She was going to have to turn it all around.* She was going to have to ignore the whole concept of genetic inheritance. Her mother was exactly the kind of person the newspapers described as the 'average Australian'. She was the one the advertisers aimed for. She was the one high-rating bad TV drama series were produced for. She was the one who voted for this government, a government full of grey men making grey decisions. She was the majority. It was no good despising her taste because hers was the taste of the *majority*. However much she, Scarlett, considered herself better, smarter, more vigilant, you couldn't argue with the numbers. *Her mother had the numbers*. Her mother, an overweight para-legal, and her father with his slut in their town house up north at Rainbow Lakes with the man-made canal at the bottom of every garden. At least, since they'd split, she only had to live with one of them. One was enough.

Scarlett made herself an organic juice and then walked outside to the hole in the brushed ti-tree fence overlooking the Haskins' property. If she positioned herself properly, she could see over the vegetable garden and the lawn to the driveway and the house beyond it. This way she knew if Alice or Harry Haskins was home, because they hardly ever bothered to park their cars in the garage, despite the remote control. Right now, she could see Alice cutting flowers, Alice in her man-style pants and her skinny knits and her blonde hair pulled back just so. Like a model. Even at her age, she looked like a Scandinavian model, only Scandinavian models didn't usually write prize-winning books. A body like that *and* creative credibility. It was too much. There she was snipping flowers and probably deep in creative thought, working through some interesting *subtext* for her new novel. Scarlett took a long gulp of her juice. This would keep her going. It had ninety-seven calories but it was filling and it wouldn't create malignancies in her body.

At seventeen, it was a little weird to be spying. Ten-year-olds *spied*. With their little notebooks and their walkie-talkies. But sitting amongst the camelias in her mother's ultra-neat garden and looking at the Haskins' life was the only way Scarlett could fight the inevitability of being a Kornhaber. The Haskins were a *real* family. They were the best family. Alice and Harry were the kind of parents anyone would want. If she had Alice and Harry as parents, she wouldn't have the feeling, every single day, that life was wasted on her. That she, Scarlett, should never have happened.

three

Alice pushed her chair back from her antique cherry wood desk. When she had moved it in, set it up in front of the windows, its aesthetic charm augured well for the words that might be written at it. It was the first time Alice had had a real study, a room to herself. The old desk looked perfect in a nineteen-fifties house, mixing the decades up, very New York Eclectic. Outside, the pool glinted in the sun, a few oak leaves floating on the blue. It was too beautiful.

She hadn't written anything worth keeping for eighteen months. Even the publishers had stopped calling. When the words came out and hit the screen, they were stretched with artifice. She felt most of the time as if she were playing the part of a writer in a Hollywood movie. Hollywood could create all manner of types – crooks, informers, business executives, housewives, serial killers – but they just couldn't do artists. Artists always seemed fake, as if the production designers added just one detail too many to decree the occupation: the paint-splattered clothes or the empty bottles of wine or the sharpened pencils. And there she sat in the world's most perfect writing room, plate-glass windows looking onto elms and oaks, a swimming pool floating clouds across it, a perfect neutral canvas for her imagination. Perfection. Something her imagination had found too sleek and slippery. It seemed to Alice, finally, that the suburbs, lovely as they were, resisted commentary. They shrugged off the pretensions of those who sought to name them, hold them, look into them. The suburbs did not want to be looked at.

The last novel had not set the world on fire, but it had won three notable prizes, had sold steadily, including to three countries in Europe, and a high-profile film producer was nibbling for the rights. For literary fiction, it wasn't bad to have tripled the usual print-run, almost certainly due to the book's sudden popularity on book-club lists. Ironically, just as success tried to claim her, Alice found she had no follow-through. The suburbs had dried her up. The house, which they had bought partly for its wonderfully literary feeling, its quiet spaces and gentle outlooks, had offered Alice no resistance. And resistance, she had come to realise, was critical for the volatility of words. Resistance and freedom. The house, despite its loveliness, had not made her free, but fixed her almost bitterly to an overwhelming sense of ownership.

Rain pockmarked the surface of the pool. Soon it would be

summer, with children out there dive-bombing the blue. Perhaps summer would work some magic, with its louche, sociable mood.

Alice had deflected Harry's attempts to make love to her for almost a year, since around the time it had finally hit her that her words had dried up. For six months, she could pretend it was some kind of creative hiatus, a time of absorbing rather than producing. But a year ago it had become apparent that the disappearance of words was not a matter of choice. No words and no sex – some peculiar timing, some odd synchronicity. Harry had tried, in the nicest possible way, then let go.

A year sounded like a long time, but the months fell away. Children disguised things. Their insistence was more than occasionally useful to marriages, allowing things to vanish almost unnoticed. Perhaps Harry felt it was the way of marriages, that they let things slide, then picked them up, that fifteen years of good sex was a useful antidote to worry. A year without was not such a big deal.

But even before this strange passivity had overtaken her, when had she last sensed in Harry the flourish of something rampant, like a wild weed? Sex had once been that way, in the skinny house opposite the campus, the dollhouse, full of med students, a hundred years ago. There, sex had pushed past thresholds, lost its conviviality. It seemed to come from somewhere outside of them, a pure, discordant desperation that was both despicable and beautiful at once, intimate and unfriendly and sinister. It had happened. When they were young. It had happened. Many times and they never spoke of it, happy that silence protected the miracle of it, the miracle of their own strangeness.

Alice realised she didn't really know how Harry felt; couples were such genuises at privacy. The obviousness of coupledom trained husbands and wives to perfect secrecy so that, strangely, two people united became *more* individual rather than less. But the absence of .desire puzzled Alice, depleted her, since she had lately come to feel that she had exited her body, so surely had she pushed aside her physical identity. Sex, somehow, was connected for her with words. Words and sex. They fed into each other, breathed life.

Suddenly, Alice lurched back in her chair. A face had appeared at the window, huge and back-lit. Scarlett. Alice relaxed. Scarlett had the unnerving ability to appear and vanish at alarming speed.

'Hey!' said Scarlett, muffled through glass.

Alice pointed to her computer and mouthed, 'Working.'

Scarlett smiled and disappeared through the garden, a flash of red.

This was the third time in a week that Scarlett had appeared during school hours. This was what happened when mothers worked. They thought their daughters were safely ensconced in structures, *safe*, whereas they were running loose through gardens.

Alice looked across the room to the clock. Almost school pick-up and there was shopping to be done. Thank God, a reason to leave the room, a dignified escape.

Alice sat in the driver's seat, parked outside Melvin's Prime Meats, debating whether or not to buy a coffee. She missed her old mid-afternoon caffeine shot, with city people on a city street, a fusion of taste, adrenaline and smog. She was going to have to give up her coffee habit. No-one in Sunnyside seemed to be bothered by the lack of good coffee. Through the window, the school mothers were laughing together, a gaggle of suburban contentment, all blonde ponytails and clear skin and flat suede shoes. It was amazing how much better looking wealth made you.

The list of things to do stretched in front of her. All the shopping, at least, was done, but for the meat. Melvin sold the best meat in Sunnyside, everyone said so. On Saturday mornings, you could barely squeeze in there, with a line of customers hovering outside the window where the scout club had a sausage sizzle to raise money for local charities. But Alice felt incapable of getting out of the car. Sometimes she felt exhausted, not so much by the activity of normal life, but by the repetition. Repetition was exhausting, why was that? It was the feeling of not being able to extricate yourself from a set course.

A tap on Alice's window. Lily, smiling. Alice buzzed the window down.

'Shouldn't you be home cooking us something delicious?'

Alice smiled. Lily was one of those people her mother would have described as a 'tonic'. She was so here and now. She was one of Wilson Fenwick's best agents and Wilson Fenwick was one of the best agencies in a town that took property seriously. There wasn't much about Sunnyside that Lily didn't know, since, as she herself said, buying and selling was the number two hobby of locals *after* tennis and *before* golf.

Everyone was looking. Everyone was tallying their own worth. Everyone wanted something better.

'Eight, right?'

'Come earlier if you like.'

Lily let a little pause sit there, between Alice in the driver's seat and herself standing wedged between the parked cars.

'Have you seen Molly lately?'

Lily's eyebrows were raised. Lily had long maintained a vague suspicion about their closest friend, a sense that in her expensive habits, her spontaneous class-taking (Basque cuisine, nineteenth-century Asian ceramics), she resisted the ordinary effects of time, station, mortality.

'I spoke to her Tuesday to organise tonight.'

'So you haven't seen her embellishment?'

Alice smiled, puzzled. 'Embellishment?'

'A tattoo.'

Alice studied Lily's face to see if she was joking.

'You're telling me Molly has a *tat*?'

'A very small one on her left shoulder blade. I saw it at tennis. She had it done in *Deptford*.'

Molly, with her Louboutin heels and her well-cut suits, stained with ink. It was hard to imagine Molly driving her shiny new Golf into Deptford and queuing at Tattoo Addiction, the one next to the doughnut shop.

'What kind of tattoo?'

'A *dolphin*.' Lily smirked. 'I *know*. Don't say anything.'

Alice let the image sit with her a moment. Lily leant in and kissed her on the cheek.

'I'll see you tonight. I'm racing to an inspection. The hideous place with the columns on the corner of Ratcliffe and Fenston.'

Alice remembered it from family walks to the beach. When she had been a child, there had been a beautiful nineteen-twenties house on that corner, looking out to sea, with the house name written in the hedge: Bambra. Now it was some nineties nightmare with tinted blue windows and a six-car garage, a symbol of all that had gone wrong with Sunnyside, deluged by executives burying tradesmen's fees in their corporate expense accounts. The entire section of Sunnyside on the beach side of Fairmount Parade was an ant-farm of carpenters and tilers and stonemasons, building Disney fortresses with turrets and drawbridges.

'The Bentons are interested!' said Lily happily. She whispered, 'As I've always said: *no taste*.'

Lily waved and raced off.

Alice and Lily had been friends since university days. Lily had been in Alice's second-year English tute and Alice had been drawn to her for her vivacious irreverence. 'If they want to go to fucking Moscow, why don't they go?' Lily had announced one morning as they sat in their tutor's cramped room, discussing Chekhov.

She and Raph had married in the city but soon after moved to the Peninsula, shifting from year to year to bigger houses in better locations, aided by Lily's increasing inside knowledge and a genuine instinct for seeing the good bones buried in ugly properties. They had long ago made their peace with the suburbs. Lily had often told Alice she could never go back to the city now. She had adjusted too well to boredom.

Lily had told Alice that eighteen months was not enough. Alice herself was aware that you couldn't move from the city to the gleaming bayside suburbs without a little psychic push and pull. She missed stepping through the door and landing on the street. She missed the junkies and the alcoholics. She missed the Greeks and Italians and Jews and Asians. She missed everything she had thought she wanted to escape: she missed *variety*. She had been motivated, in part, by a desire for the outside world to be simplified; this and the colossal love for her children, which made an attraction of the blandness and sterility of the suburbs. It took only a headline, a TV trailer about a terrorism alert on a tabloid current affairs show to reassure her that they had done the right thing. When it got down to anthrax, hijackings, bomb warnings in city malls, Alice considered there to be no safer place than Sunnyside. This was the place to raise children.

Alice looked at the car clock. It was three-fifteen. If she hurried, she might just get a car park outside the school, instead of way down the street towards the sea. She drove out of the shopping centre and then through the Tiddesdale housing estate. Tiddesdale had been designed by Burley Griffin in the thirties and some of the elegant weatherboard houses had survived, their large green hedges squeezed by brown brick-veneer houses with ugly, straggly flowerbeds. The road curved up and down hills, alongside the bush reserve where tartan-pants-wearing birdwatchers could be glimpsed through ti-tree on fine mornings, and up to the cliff top that ran along the bay. Here the school sat, two elegant old buildings, one for the juniors, another for the seniors, surrounded by modern classrooms added over the years. Alice reversed into the last available space outside the school. *Molly with a tat.*

Some of the mothers sat in their cars, reading paperbacks or listening to talkback. Others hovered beside the road, arms caught tight under their bosoms, holding themselves in from the bitter winds whooshing up from the sea. They stood in huddles, giggling, teasing, sharing plans for the weekend: the good-humoured exchanges that protected them from loneliness. They had made for themselves a humour based upon a benevolent superiority to husbands. Alice thought it must always have been this way, women arming themselves against their aloneness by making jokes at the expense of their men.

Alice waved to Tabitha Arbuthnot's mother, who was sitting behind the wheel of her new Subaru station wagon. The word was that Tabitha's older brother was dabbling in drugs. Alice buzzed down her window and yelled over the street to the other side.

'How are things?'

'All right, thanks, Alice. Not too bad.'

'Grace told me you're running the class stall for the fete?'

'*Preserves*,' yelled Jenny.

'What about if I whip up some lemon butter over the weekend?'

'You have to label the ingredients,' yelled Jenny. 'It's the *law*.'

Across Sunnyside and further down the coast, mothers sat inside station wagons or houses, trying to be modern, to have careers or ambitions, private energies. Since the nineteen-fifties, when places like Sunnyside had first established themselves as affluent refuges from the real world, suburban women had lost their one great justification: the belief that they had no other place to be. Throughout the seventies and eighties, these women had lost their way, intent on finding purpose in the world beyond their fences. They had struggled against their own maternal urgings, their happy laziness, their pleasure in men, the perfect fabric for the slip-chair, the best strawberry shortcake recipe and, instead, made for the academies. They had short-circuited their own inner longings, trembling in the face of their own softness, pushing it away as if it were quicksand dooming them to the quagmire of Electroluxes and Singer sewing machines.

Alice was part of the generation to rediscover lemon butter, rediscover ordinariness, conscious of what she was forsaking. It was a liberation from liberation, although no woman seemed to sit easily in the strange mix of expectations that feminism had provoked. Real jobs in shiny offices had liberated women from things they came to realise they could not quite abandon: the mysterious reveal of seeing a child come into themselves.

The young mothers of Sunnyside had practised as merchant bankers and legal partners for a decade or so before the onslaught of OshKosh. They had cupboards full of Donna Karan's early nineties ranges – smart black suits and camisoles they could not quite bring themselves to take to the thrift-store bins in the village car park or the school jumble sale. They had old filing cabinets stuffed with old files, archives from a renounced life. They had photos of themselves at office Christmas parties, flash-framed ambition, flush with their own potential, with purchasing power, with the sexual charisma of nice girls on the loose with good university degrees and proper jobs. Alice had been one of those girls. She had spent three years in publishing, editing books on what to do in a bushfire, or the porcelain collections of the Hungerforth gallery. That was before she had written the first novel, the book that had surprised everyone, most of all herself. At the company, she had imagined a tight little life of bonuses and office politics and international book fairs. But with that first surge of hormonal lust for a baby she had been kidnapped by another instinct, and delivered herself into the relentless tidal clash between mothering and writing, both all-consuming, neither expendable.

The school bell sounded. At once children spilled out across the grass, helter-skelter noises, smiles, waves, an army of creatures certain about each day's destiny, marked so reliably, so depressingly, so comfortingly by a drop-off and a pick-up. Alice could see Grace down the slope, pulling on her shoes outside the classroom and chatting to Astrid, her new best friend. There was something disturbing about Grace. There was something disturbing about finding your own child disturbing. But Alice had to admit that Grace's self-sufficiency was unnerving and unlikeable. It was a girl-thing. Alice knew that she had been just like Grace at eleven, giving off a sense of impossible self-containment. It would be easy to dismiss such confidence as simply stupidity. But Grace was smart as a whip, not just intellectual but bright like an arrogant little star, gorgeous, capable of startling wit, but because of all of this, somehow inaccessible. It was hard to love a child who found being loved so unnecessary.

Through the crowd of schoolchildren, Alice could see Joe, an awkward, skinny frame walking alone up the path, his schoolbag heaved onto his back, his face so lovely that Alice had to consciously stop herself dwelling on it for fear of weeping. He had such a noble face, pale skin and large blue eyes, a mop of dark curls, thin and tall for his thirteen years, but somehow so young. Alice wished she had been a better mother, less intense, sweeter. She had made the mistake of hurrying Joe up, of willing him onwards. One day, when she had first gone through his baby clothes and put them into acid-free boxes with little stickers saying nought to one, she had realised that she was losing sight of him, and that perhaps he was even losing sight of himself.

A parent could look at an object in such a way as to be consumed by it. A baby shoe was, perhaps, the most potent object in the universe, a magical thing, capable of undoing those who were mostly done-up, a tiny relic of scuffed leather and laces that transported its witness into the heart of the matter, of birth and its compelling consequence, life. A baby shoe was a tiny voluptuous shrine to the panic of profound love. Why had she hurried Joe on so? Was it because she anticipated this pain, the sorrow of permanent evaporation, tiny feet tapping on wood floors, a call in the night, disappearing out of view? Perhaps she had known this and sought to rush through it, not dwell on what she was losing as time marched. Or perhaps it was the blinkered exhaustion, the resentment of a mother who wishes, at the deepest level, to be what she once was, innocent of childbirth, free to go to the movies. Why had she stared Joe in the face and willed him on?

Harry was a much better parent than she was. He was modest and calm, he was opposed to melodrama. He saw less. He was less observant, less sensitive and was given to simply forgetting about them at certain times. But in his favour, Harry had an innate understanding of when to leave well enough alone. Unlike Alice, he cared more strenuously for his children's feelings than for his own. Alice could not put a lid on her own tide of despondency. It kept her company, banishing the huge, grey sprawl of serenity which lapped at the edges of other women, women who forgot to want things.

And then. The symphony of car doors snapping shut, enclosing children into the worlds of their birth, for better or worse. The state was forgotten, banished until eight-fifty on Monday morning when it once again asserted its rights as guardian. For now, children seemed eager to be folded back into the place from whence they had come, the place of inexplicable tempers, of labradoodles and dead, floating goldfish, of late-return DVDs collecting dust in forgotten corners of the family room, of pantries with lovely edibles and mothers, mothers in all their sweetness and their horror and their secrets. The children clambered in, flung their schoolbags in boots, shrugged off the eager hands of knowledge and application, and readied themselves for home again.

four

His mother was driving and she was quiet. Usually, when she was driving, she chattered to him about nothing, some soundtrack to adult life about what to cook for dinner, about the third quote from the roof plumber, about the pool filter going. And Joe could sit there and not listen and kind of like it, because in its own way, it was comforting being able to move in and out of his mother's world, tuning out of her soundtrack and into the soundtrack inside his own head, more than a soundtrack, also a field of images, of skateboards and Cokes and teachers and friends and weird stuff, like how old he'd be when he died and how long the planet would survive if the sun went out and if you became your name or if your name decided who you would be. But he had given her his school report as soon as he got in the car, to get it over with, so she was not chattering. She was taking it in. She was brooding. Joe felt as if he was nailed into a crate, a crate from the greengrocers, one that let air in but didn't let things out.

29

Grace, in the back, was silent. As usual, she was analysing the jottings of Mr Polhurst in the margins of her workbook, endlessly combing his suggestions for evidence of stupidity on her part. Finally, as they came to the stop light at the edge of Sunnyside village, where the surf shop was, his mother said, 'You know, there is stuff in books, there are things, stories, there are things that are funny and weird and extraordinary and they can take you to places without you ever needing to leave your room.'

'You're just saying that because you're a writer.'

Joe could see the frustration on his mother's face, anger kept in check. Turning away, he noticed Toby Carmichael walking home down the hill, by himself. Lucky Toby Carmichael.

'If you'd just work at it, and I'd help you, you'd find, honestly, I'm not just saying this, I really mean it, you'd get so much out of it, and I'm only saying this because it is actually heartbreaking to me that you do not know the incredible, unbelievable pleasure of how it is to have books lead you where you didn't know you could go.'

'I *do* read,' he said.

'I'm not talking about skateboarding magazines. I'm not talking about the sports pages. I mean *books*. I mean, stories written by writers.'

'Well, okay,' he said, because that is what he said when he saw his mother struggling, seemingly at his mercy, at the mercy of his weaknesses. He couldn't stand to see her that way, to feel that powerful.

Joe had liked it when Alice read to him, when he was small, wearing those old red pyjamas; he never told her he had cried over them when she threw them out. The memory of them reminded him of when he was happy. When he lay in the bed and she lay next to him and read him the stories about mice in the paint puddles, about Max and the Wild Things, about Orlando the cat that went to the farm, and the Red Balloon, he loved the Red Balloon, especially the middle pages with the coloured picture of all the balloons against the blue sky. He loved the feeling those books gave him of being excited at the same time as being safe. But now he was too old. He should be reading himself, but at night when she left the room he turned off the lamp and just lay there in the half-light.

Some nights, Joe lay watching the clock on the wall at the end of his bed, thinking of strange things. Of how it would be to live out there, in that other place where there were suicide bombers and people exploded and things happened. How it would be to hate something that much, to give up on yourself in the belief that there was something so much bigger than you. To be the guy who kay-aked over Bass Strait, alone in the shipping channels in the dark knowing you only had fifteen minutes to get out of the way of the cargo boats. To be the kid he'd seen in the newsagency, the one who got caught stealing, and that look he had that made Joe think maybe the kid *wanted* to get caught, like he'd willed it. Lately, every time he tried to make himself read, he started seeing sheep. The contaminated Australian sheep stranded on the boat in the middle of the ocean, floating across foreign seas, nowhere to go. It was weird, but Joe felt he knew what it was like to be a sheep, there on the boat, barely able to move, waiting, waiting for something to happen.

Thing was, he *liked* stories, but when he saw the black and white he got tangled up in it. So many of the books they gave him didn't let him in. They used words to build fences, keeping Joe out, tricky words, full of trouble. But the slower he went, the further away the point got. He knew Grace could see pictures in the words. Grace looked at a page of writing and went to a parallel universe, with street maps and populations and things moving, things being said that changed everything, beginnings and middles and endings. There was a place, a place with detail like real life, Planet Book! And she just glanced down and she was there, inside it, vanished. But the longer he stared at the page, the more he felt like he was looking at one of those stupid 3D pictures where you were supposed to see something amazing but you never did.

It wasn't like the movies. The thing about movies was, they slipped you in. You went through the door before you knew it and you were inside, being carried along through the scenery, hearing without listening, seeing without looking. It was so easy it was scary. With books, it was about deciding, making a choice, *trying* to get inside. You had to want it. You had to know enough to know you wanted to be there, but books didn't give much away on the outside, so how could you know?

I have to want it, he had once said to Alice. Maybe last school report. Maybe at the same stop light, even. I have to want it. I want to want to read but I can't make myself. You can't punish me into it. You can't scare me into it. *You can't shame me into it.*

Sometimes he felt full of things, like kindling ready for a match. Like something was about to happen. He kept his face quiet. He kept his voice normal. He looked out of the window like he was now, looking at the neighbourhood, the kids in different uniforms, going back to different houses, some big, some small, some with pools. He wasn't going to give anything away, but inside something was mounting, something weird, like it was rolling, like it had its own life and there was nothing he could do about it. He feared that if he got inside those books that thing inside him would break loose, *be triggered*. Everything stupid he had ever done, all the great things too, the past, the future, every single thing that ticked over him at night when he pulled the blankets up, when he willed himself to be better at things, to be smarter, to be more good, to make his mother proud, to stop irritating everyone, to achieve something that made the world less mean, more useful. Books had that kind of creepy power. Stories could do that. Joe didn't know if that was something he should want to want.

five

Harry was at the Super-Savers roundabout, on his way home. Harry could bypass the roundabout by taking the back road to Sunnyside from the campus, and thereby avoid the edges of Deptford, but Harry liked the roundabout, *enjoyed* the roundabout, since it symbolised the vagaries of fate and confirmed Harry's sense of being on the right side of it.

Deptford, the nearest big town to Sunnyside, was only five kilometres down Freeman's Hill, but a million miles from Sunnyside's gentility. Sunnyside was all undulating rises and dips and views, while Deptford sprawled on the flats. Built on swamp-land one hundred and fifty years earlier, its concrete developments and redeveloped foreshore could not disguise its mosquito-ridden origins. At a time when bayside localities were tripling their property prices every twelve months, Deptford sulked and stalled, the heart of the suburban badlands: a whining, miserable repository of people so defeated they rarely seemed to stray beyond their car-yard fringes. This was old Australia, still living in the seventies, ignorant of the popular currents that had crossed over the global class divide: political correctness, modernist furniture, Pilates. People went out for milk at 9 p.m. in Deptford and never came back. Police crime-scene tape often surrounded the railway station car park. The dress code was slippers and nylon windbreakers. It was always windy. One miserable motel sat wedged between the bacteria-laden canal and the service station, with a neon sign of a windsurfer facing the highway. The sign boasted about a wedding reception banquet room, but it was hard to imagine anyone getting married in Deptford, or any other formal act of optimism. The contrast with Sunnyside up Freeman's Hill, with its gorgeous shiny people and domestic espresso machines, was accepted by both neighbouring populations as just the way things were. This tolerance was based upon a common belief that one created the other, that neither place would exist if not for life's inevitable need for contrast. Sunnyside had become itself in order not to be Deptford, and Deptford folk took peculiar pride in squatting within Sunnyside's view.

Harry acknowledged the vibrantly grotesque character of Deptford but, unlike Alice, he consciously enjoyed its proximity as a reminder of what he had avoided. It was important to remember what one had narrowly, or not so narrowly, missed out on. Otherwise, one might begin to slip into the expectation of eternal delight and find, at some point, that one had fallen flat, punctured by reality. Deptford's grid of bankrupt streets; the video arcades and the take-away chicken shops; the cheap hair salons offering bargain-basement peroxide jobs, synthetic nails and hair extensions; the cheap home loans and pawn shops – these gave Harry a frisson at life's variety. If everywhere were like Sunnyside, what would be the point of living there?

What Harry wanted, what he *really*, *really* wanted, was the new, wall-mounted Bang & Olufsen CD player. It was only five-and-a-half thousand dollars. Five-and-a-half thousand dollars was *nothing* to a lot of people. Those Sunnyside people in the houses with views on the other side of Fairmount Parade could buy it without even thinking. *Without even thinking*! With their Range Rovers and their huge fucking nineteen-burner barbecues and frameless glass pool-fences, their houses were probably *internally wired* with B&O. Harry had visited the city store seven times and just stood in front of the CD player. The gleaming stainless steel, the seductive black speakers, the whole Scandie charisma of the thing. It was sexy and it was practical and *he deserved it*. Once he had even taken Alice to stand before it, in the vain hope that she would become infected. If she could only *catch* it, the horrible lust.

Harry was trying very hard to philosophise his way out of his consumerist impulses, but he was fighting a losing battle. Sometimes he found himself daydreaming about those stupid weekend newspaper questionnaires in which celebrities were asked what was most important to them, what they wore to bed, what quality they most wished they had, and so on. He finessed his answers to present the version of himself he liked: playing with his kids, sleeping naked, the benefit of hindsight. Playing with his kids. As everyone knew, this was the only correct answer. All well-adjusted middle-aged men knew that Bang & Olufsen sound systems were meaningless yuppie props that could not compare with frolicking with the offspring. The trouble was, all too often, *Harry really couldn't be bothered playing with the kids*. He loved them all right. But by the time he got home from the university, having dealt with the students, the staff, the politics, the staff club wine tastings and so on, he was tired. They should have had their kids earlier, he and Alice. If he'd had Joe at twenty-three, he'd be running triathlons with him after work, bonding through physical exertion. His kids were important to him, of course they were. But he dreaded nothing more than the sight of a Cluedo box on the dining table after work. That, or one of Joe's ping-pong tournaments. And at least once or twice a month, Harry dreamt about the B&O showroom.

On the far side of the roundabout, a girl of about twenty with long stringy hair the colour of nutmeg was waiting for Harry to make his move. Her hands grasped the plastic handles of a pusher, and nestled within it Harry could see a toddler wearing a pink nylon hat with rabbit's ears. There was something positively medieval about Deptford's average age of reproduction. Did rich girls fuck later? Or were they just better protected, the reluctant recipients of ardent parental warnings, groundings and general vigilance? Deptford parents apparently let their young loose, providing ample custom for the plethora of bargain baby shops full of Made In China cots, keeping the social-security bureaucrats busy and the methadone programs full. In Deptford, thought Harry, the good folk of Sunnyside could glimpse the banality of their own optimism. The whole town shimmered with tension. Sunnyside folk made gags about their snobbishness, but Harry knew it was fear rather than superiority that fuelled their disdain.

Harry had reached the top of Freeman's Hill and he took in a quick glance of the bay. *Bellissimo.*

Harry had to be home early because the gang were coming over for dinner. The first Friday of every month, one of four couples hosted dinner, and the ritual of it was one of the comforting aspects of their Sunnyside life. Everyone lived in or near Sunnyside. Their friends Lily and Raph had moved down not long after their only child, Maisie, was born. David and Molly followed three years later with Justin, claiming city property prices had become too expensive, the traffic too clogged, the gardens too small, the drunks and junkies too prevalent. David had started a small bookshop in Seabank that had now expanded into the neighbouring shops and hosted the Peninusula book-signings for touring authors. Even Alice had signed there, when the last novel had started attracting a buzz, before her nerve had failed. Not long after, Tess and Jim and their twin girls had moved into a Cape Cod weatherboard with sea views, around the corner from Lily. Tess worked as a pyschologist at the university student health centre. Now, all of them were nestled within ten minutes of each other, connected by the map of cul de sacs.

Alice and Harry had made the move to the Peninsula after driving past the house on their way back to the city after an autumn Sunday lunch at David and Molly's.

The whole Sunday lunch thing was sitting sweetly in their guts, a few glasses of a Peninsula red, everyone in a nicely synchronised good mood, autumn sunshine, the bay glinting, winking at them as if in on the secret of their collective good fortune, ruddy-cheeked children happily occupied on the tennis court, obliging inheritors of their parents' friendships, and all around them the blossom and bonhomie of Sunnyside. It all came back to Alice, her own childhood, only instead of all that it wasn't, Alice was suddenly taken with all that it was. And Alice and Harry, together, looked upon the vacant house, drove around its desirable circular driveway and suddenly, deeply, irretrievably fell into another dream, another vision of their ongoing life together, the Sunnyside chapter, the soundtrack of which would be the gentle ploosh-ploosh of the garden sprinkler, the bark of the golden retriever, the burble of the coffee percolator.

Like so many others, Alice and Harry equated appropriate real-estate decisions with existential happiness. If the structure over them was fine and good, then so, too, would they be. The house would be their benediction and Sunnyside, with its whipper-snipping men, its book-clubbing women, its rollerblading children and cocooned, organically fed infants, would embrace them with its quiet, earnest hedonism. And so they had bought it.

Harry, who had been angling for assistant professor on the city campus, had been offered a full professorship at the local university campus. A less prestigious campus was made up for by the proximity to home and the more prestigious title. Alice had declared it the perfect place to write, far from distraction, bathed in prettiness, a retreat.

Now, some eighteen months later, Harry and Alice privately acknowledged that existential happiness had not been delivered along with the local papers amongst the agapanthus lining their driveway. Harry took this as a cue to give up on existential happiness. It had, in fact, been one of Harry's most comforting moments when Ed Mayhew, a mere acquaintance, had jovially observed in passing that *no one felt happiness*, just varying degrees of okayness. Ed Mayhew's hokey wisdom bathed Harry in a nectar of tender acceptance. Yes, Harry had thought. Yes, that is so. And yes, be happy with unhappiness, be settled with it. Happiness was a red herring, the point being *sheer endurance*. Endurance was what life was all about. How one endured with the least possible shame, the most possible dignity.

Harry let himself in and followed the cheerful sounds of domesticity, *his* domesticity, into the kitchen.

Alice was standing at the counter, pulsing something elegantly green in the Magimix. Grace was lying in front of the fire, flicking through a magazine. Harry kissed Alice on the mouth, touched her arse lightly, affectionately, packaged as it was so nicely in her favourite black pants.

'Dad! Tabitha's brother is going to a place where doctors put him in a room all by himself for a week!'

'What sort of place?'

'It's like an in-half house or a half of a house or something. He's a drug addict!'

'Nice,' said Harry.

'He *robs* people!'

Harry made a mental note to bludgeon Alice into using the alarm. What was the point of paying all those bills to the security firm if she refused to use it? On the television news, a furry image of another leaky boat full of Afghanis, intercepted off the coast.

'Where's Joe?'

'Next door. He's staying over with Monty.'

Alice had stopped whizzing, moved to the fridge and taken out a bottle of white wine. She poured them two glasses, handed him one. When things were good, when no obscene bills had arrived in the mail, when Alice was not slapped by misery or ordinary complaint, when the children were not ill, this was truly his favourite moment of the day.

'Everything okay?'

'One of the students is a bit of a handful.'

'Who is he?'

'*She*,' said Harry. 'Olivia Mathers. Nihilistic, acerbic, inattentive, obstreperous and contemptuous.'

'Of you?'

'Amongst other things.'

She smiled her clever smile.

'That won't do.'

'No, it will *not* do.'

He kissed Alice again. Her lips were soft and smudgy. She tasted of carrots.

Harry noticed the shopping bags from yesterday were still in the corner of the room. Once, Alice would have scurried to hide them at the back of a cupboard. Now, it seemed, she was flaunting them. Alice bought too many clothes. She looked good in clothes and Harry liked seeing her in nice clothes but the fact was, Alice only liked *expensive* clothes. David's words were still ringing in his ears about Molly buying seven-hundred-dollar shoes. *Seven hundred dollars*. And it wasn't like they stood on a pedestal in the sitting room attracting admiring glances until they could be sold in old age for a place in a classy retirement home. They were not a couple of

Jackson Pollock etchings. No. They were *shoes*. They were dragged through mud, smeared in dog shit, beaten on asphalt. These women simply didn't understand the terror. They were constantly trekking up to city boutiques to *consume,* returning at dusk, dragging from car boots handfuls of shiny bags spilling tissue paper. All the years of feminism they had endured and still it was only really the men who got it, who lay awake at night sweating. School fees. Credit card bills. The mortgage. New spouting because it *had* to be replaced. Car servicing. School camp (one hundred and eighty-five dollars for two days in a log cabin, what the hell was *that* about?). *Alcohol.* Sometimes it seemed as if the more Harry worried about money, the more clothes Alice bought.

'Tess rang to say that we'd be getting an invitation to a party at Minnie and Tim Staunton's. *Whips and spurs.*'

Harry savoured the warm rise of the alcohol. This would be the fourth time in eighteen months they were going to have to fork out for costumes at the tacky costume hire in Seabank. On the other hand, it could be worse. This time Harry could wear a cowboy out-fit, which would be much more fun than the Kofi Annan get-up he'd worn to Jim Baraldi's fortieth, a World Leader's party. Most people had thought he'd come as Sidney Poitier.

'And this is going to get you *very* excited,' said Alice. 'It appears there's going to be a mechanical bull.'

six

Around the dining table, Tess and Jim, Molly and David, and Lily and Raph were waiting for the main course. In the kitchen, Alice was putting the finishing touches to the salmon. Grace was finally, perfectly, adorably asleep. The first three bottles of wine were empty. The smudged martini glasses stood perilously on the edge of the sink, the fires were blazing, they were halfway through. Alice suddenly felt the familiar sensation of wishing she was in bed. She could imagine herself there, showered, smooth, accomplished, one dinner party down.

Alice could hear Tess through the swing doors.

'Gordon Stoddart told me at tennis that house prices are about to dip.'

'I should know,' said Lily, 'shouldn't I?'

'Well, I'm only reporting,' said Tess. 'Don't shoot the messenger.'

Raph said, 'Some geologist has been roaming around Sunnyside and making a song and dance about the fault line. Big deal.'

Raph, a sports journalist for one of the city dailies, had a happy demeanour like his wife. For Raph, all wins and losses were transitory. He had a high-turnover approach to life. Life was a fast dance of triumphs and disappointments, each with built-in emotional obsolescence. As a result, the minor catastrophes and ecstasies washed over him. He had a sweet, soft resistance to Lily's breathless updates on the only real business of Sunnyside: real estate.

'What geologist?' said Molly.

'Some government guy. There's a report. And the way gossip gets about, pretty soon everyone's going to be asking themselves do they want to lay out a couple of mill for a palazzo on Fairmount Parade when it could come crashing into the sea next week?'

'Crashing into the sea!' said Lily, contemptuously.

'That's all we need,' said Jim, quiet until now. 'What with the roadworks around Safeway and the council fighting over whether Christmas decorations in the village are a form of cultural bullying, all we need in Sunnyside is an *earthquake*.'

Alice fondly remembered when dinner parties acted on her bloodstream like an amphetamine hit, sending her into an irrepressible high of food preparation and home maintenance. Lately, she had started to wish that food was plainer, guests were fewer and nights earlier. Alice's friends had started to bother her and this absence of instinctive generosity was unnerving. These were her best friends. These were the people who were her buffer zone between private woman and public sphere, the ones who were able to explain the improprieties of the universe to her, correct her thinking when it was askew, exhibit tenderness when required. And yet, lately, the rituals of friendship, which she had hitherto been so sentimental about, had begun to seem more like some silent contract between parties intent on furnishing their lives with appropriate props. Dinner parties, after all, punctuated the calendar. They were almost the only pauses in lives rattling ahead with alarming and pointless urgency. Everyone was flat out. The months whirled past. Work issues were struggled over and resolved. Fashions shifted from season to season. Dogs were selected, washed, fed and put down. Jars of olive paste were purchased in a flurry of culinary endeavour, only to be dredged up from the back of the fridge and discarded weeks later.

Only the children actually *progressed*. Inside Sunnyside cupboards, ladders of dashes, Robinson Crusoe markings, climbed upwards, annotated with names and dates. In each of the houses was an ordinary archive sending terror and disbelief into the hearts of parents, who read into those notchings their own march towards the nursing home.

'The Bentons made an offer on the Ratcliffe McMansion,' said Lily. 'Not at liberty to disclose actual numbers but we're talking *well over* two.'

'The bubble's going to burst,' said Tess. 'It has to. I mean, a two-bedroom Edwardian on a quarter acre in the inner city is going for close to seven hundred grand. Remember when half a million stood for something?'

'The entire industry is built on the back of the human being's fundamental fear of death. We ward off the notion of our own mortality by ownership of the roof over our head,' said David.

'Really?' said Tess. 'I thought it was built on the human being's fundamental desire to make money.'

David shook his head. 'The entire concept of living with vast debt is built on *denial*.'

Alice wondered if David and Molly had had a few drinks before they arrived. They seemed sprung, as if they had arrived over-fuelled. Alice had been trying to catch a glimpse of Molly's tattoo all night.

She placed the platter on the table. The fish looked beautiful, succulent and pink, perfectly cooked, elegant with the herbs. A success.

'Yum!' said Lily.

David said, 'Nigella.'

'Thank God for Nigella,' Raph said.

'She's done for cookbook sales in the noughties what Xaviera Hollander did for the porn industry in the seventies,' David said. 'With basically the same technique.'

Harry brought in the glass salad bowl spilling curly shining leaves of butter lettuce. 'Didn't men in the fifties want to see Elizabeth David in nothing but an apron?'

'No,' said David. 'They most certainly did not. In those days they wanted to see the chicken in aspic, not the chef.'

Raph smacked his lips. 'Nigella in aspic.'

'Since when did the Bentons get so wealthy anyway?' asked Tess. 'I thought he lost everything in that internet thingy.'

'He started importing party lighting from China and he's made a killing,' said Lily.

'Party lighting!' muttered Jim. 'This is the thing. Some people wake up at three in the morning and think: party lighting.'

'You should hear the inventory of what Alison Benton just *has to have*: home theatre, tennis court, summer fucking house. I mean, for God's sake! A *summer house*.'

'That'll be a nice little commission for you, Lil,' said Harry, spooning salad onto his plate.

'Howard's trying to flog them a mansion on Merrivale Drive. He's probably couriering bouquets to Alison Benton as we speak.'

Howard Wheeler *was* Sunnyside property. His 'We Put the Proper in Property' signs were all over the village, alongside his smile, a sparkling billboard for cosmetic dentistry. Lily and Howard were rivals for every significant property in Sunnyside. To Lily's eternal chagrin, Howard had the edge. Sunnyside vendors still liked men to handle things.

Tess nibbled a piece of dripping lettuce. 'I want a new house.

I want one and I deserve one and if it means I'm in denial about death, David, so be it.'

'I'll buy you a new house, my flower,' said Jim, 'but first we need a cash-ambulance.'

'So who's selling the Bentons' old place?' asked Molly.

'Howard fucking Wheeler, that's who,' said Lily. 'I can't believe Tamsin's still with that jerk.'

'She's spending more and more time at the ashram, that's how. She heads up Mountain Road every morning with her yoga mat,' said Tess.

Alice had met Tamsin at school functions and tennis charity tournaments. She had watched her vague cynicism metamorphose into psychic dishevelment over a year. But in the last six months, Tamsin had discovered the ashram and her equilibrium and had lead the way for local wives and even a few husbands. Until Tamsin, only city-based hippies commuted to Sunnyside's own spiritual haven. Now the ashram car park was lined with luxury vehicles driven by disenchanted Sunnyside women caught between their conventional lives and their budding acknowledgment that those lives had somehow not *delivered*.

'The Italian Stallion at McLaren and McLaren sold Kirsty Forsythe's place right from under Howard. One point two.'

Alice realised her silence was becoming conspicuous.

'One point two!' she said. 'And no view.'

'No view *and* an asbestos roof. The new owners are going to have to call in the National Guard to get rid of that asbestos. Jackman's Road's going to be overrun with men in anti-plutonium body-suits. All that for one point two,' said Raph.

'The X factor,' said Lily. 'You're all forgetting the X factor.'

'And that's where you come in,' said Raph.

'And that's where I come in,' said Lily.

Harry returned to the kitchen, then came back carrying a new bottle of opened white.

Alice noted that Harry had started to swagger under the weight of his middle age. There was always something faintly ridiculous about these men. Here they were, Raph, David, Harry, Jim, at long last so thoroughly themselves. Until now, they had seemed not quite formed, struggling to reach completion with their smooth faces and rampant athleticism. Something had happened. They had turned the corner. All those years of climbing towards themselves and now, suddenly, they were facing the downhill run. Small imperfections, just faintly overweight, a creaky knee, high cholesterol. It was hard, sometimes, not to laugh at them.

None of the women seemed so at ease with where they were. It seemed to Alice that each of them still agitated against what they had, craved something either past or ahead, known or unknown, *difference*. They felt their own temporariness so keenly. Was it childbirth? Fertility? The chapters of a woman's life were so neatly marked by menstruation, pregnancy, menopause. It was hard to feel satisfied in a woman's body, since one was constantly forced to acknowledge some new obsolescence. The body was the smartest and most vigilant clock. Maybe that was the key to the differences between the sexes, thought Alice. Men belonged to the present much more effectively than women: they owned it. Women were always renting.

'He's so secretive. Not so long ago, he had no secrets, he was an extension of me. Now, he sits inside his own small universe.'

Molly was halfway through a story about Justin, at fifteen the oldest of the collective offspring and already showing signs of alarming self-sufficiency.

Alice and Harry privately thought that Molly and David were too relaxed about Justin. The previous weekend they had talked about it with Tess and Jim after tennis, agreeing that permissiveness had not been proven as an antidote to wildness.

'All the kids I knew who had permissive parents ended up as junkies,' Jim had said over a beer. 'The myth was that authoritarian parenting forced children into rebellion.'

Harry agreed. 'It's astonishing how often children who are brainwashed into conventional behaviour end up being conventional. The great lie is that it backfires. It hardly ever backfires.'

Alice had a sudden memory of visiting Molly in the hospital, when Justin was a small sleeping bundle in a plastic humidicrib. Molly in a pale-blue toile dressing gown, flushed with the beauty of birth, the miracle.

'The twins have too *much* perspective for their age. They want to see their lives laid out before them, all known,' said Tess. 'When we were their age, we were *playful*.'

'Justin's not playful,' said David. 'Nobody's playful.'

'Children are being forced into adulthood,' Harry said. 'How do you stay innocent with DVDs and satellite TV and high-speed internet access? Our children's childishness is evaporating under the weight of technology.'

'We have a problem our parents never had,' Alice said. 'How do we keep information *out* of our children's lives?'

'I don't know about all of that,' said Tess. 'What I do know is that we want compassionate children. We want children who will turn this country *around*.'

Molly helped Alice clear the plates into the kitchen and Tess helped organise dessert: various couplings facilitating the chapters of a dinner party. It's like a dance, thought Alice. Take your partner round and round.

'What happened to this country?' said Tess as Molly and Alice returned. 'What made us mean?'

'The relentless need to put oneself first is what allowed this country to find its feet,' said David. 'And now it's the reason this country is losing its identity. A nation finds itself through identifying *its best self*, not the path of least resistance.'

'Oh, for God's sake, David,' said Molly, throwing her hands up in exasperation. 'It's *best self*. Get with the real world! We're the *good guys*. Before you start sobbing into your sauvignon blanc about what nasty people we all are, why don't you spend a week-end with the Tutsis or the fucking terrorists or the ones who knife their wives for showing their faces in public?'

'I don't think we can escape culpability just because some people are worse. Maybe our moral inadequacies are less forgive-able because we can't blame poverty.'

'I don't believe it,' said Lily, 'we're not that bad.'

'You're the reason we're this way, Lily. You've trained us into thinking interest rates are more important than human values. You and your ilk,' said David.

'That's a lovely thing to say to our *friend*,' said Molly. 'Just terrific.'

'The last time I looked, it wasn't a crime to want a nice house,' said Lily.

David looked suddenly serious. 'There are refugees drowning off our coast and people like us are building fucking *summer houses*.'

Harry was thinking that David was right, but somehow it was hard to get behind him.

It was awful that refugees were drowning. Nobody wanted that. The government had lost its humanity, but frankly, despite it being wrong and selfish and mean-spirited, Harry wasn't so sure he *wanted* boatloads of swarthy foreigners flooding the border. They were almost certainly not terrorists. They were almost certainly regular people in dire straits looking for a better life. But what if? *What if?* America had billions of dollars poured into its security systems, its CIA and FBI and counter-terrorism, and it *allowed a bunch of Arabs into Florida to learn how to fly planes*! Liberalism had possibly run its course. Not that you could say that out loud. Jesus! If his friends knew what he was thinking . . . But through the whole September 11 thing, Harry kept thinking how obvious everything was. You'd think the terrorists would all look like Alabama beauty queens or mid-western mums. But no, if you looked at the photos, they all looked like Arab maniacs. The Arab maniacs *actually looked like* Arab maniacs!

Australia was this big exposed paradise. The biggest problem here was the ozone layer! Okay, so there were the Aborigines, they'd been treated shamefully. Okay, true. But things were getting better. They were on lifestyle shows these days and their paintings were all the rage at Sotheby's auctions. Basically, it was still a paradise, a Sitting Duck Paradise. It was all very well for Raph to talk about letting people in, but it was only going to take one bomb in the Sydney Opera House to change everything. Harry cared about people, of course he did. He wanted a better world. He despised the government too, with its lack of heart. But he could despise it and understand it at the same time. Life was complicated.

If he stuck to the back roads and avoided the highway, it would probably be all right. He could pretty much count on not being busted, but you could never be absolutely sure. In movies, the plots depended on the unlikely happening, because human beings always counted on the most likely. So plots and stories and things were often about how stupid people failed to expect the unexpected. So if a light from behind him suddenly turned the trees blue, he'd say he was on a joy-ride and they'd take him home and he'd tell his parents the same thing and that would be that, except he'd be grounded for about a hundred and eighty years. Still. It would be okay. He wouldn't go to jail or anything.

He had driven a ute around Will's dad's farm over the last holidays, got used to the pedals. Thank God Molly's new car was an automatic, so there was less to think about. It felt huge underneath him, even though it was a Golf. Maybe this was how it would feel for soldiers, driving a tank for the first time, like it was an extension of your body. If you drove all the time, like adults did, maybe you stopped feeling that way, it became ordinary. But Justin felt as if the engine had merged with his pumping heart. *No wonder everyone did it. No wonder everyone had one.*

In the shopping centre, only the pizza place and the Vietnamese were open. The coloured flags on the poles were blowing in the breeze. A few kids were hanging out in the shadows in the community square, which wasn't a square, more like a paved circle. It could be Mikey and Phil, but it was hard to see when you were in a car because things were over before they started. Maybe they'd been doing some graffiti behind the greengrocer, or they could be smoking dope. Justin didn't like dope, he wanted to, but couldn't. Mikey and Phil were smoking more and more, it brought them closer together. It wasn't like it used to be. It wasn't like it had been with Joe, either. His parents and Joe's parents were best friends and, not so long ago, he and Joe had been best friends too. He couldn't explain it to himself, but it was as if he'd left Joe behind. Joe seemed like a little kid now, something had happened to that good thing they'd shared. They had been great, those days with Joe, just hanging out. Joe liked him. It was good to be liked. Justin had felt comfortable at the Haskins. Things felt kind of normal there. But Joe didn't understand how bad things could get. Maybe that was it. Once you understood how bad things could get, you didn't really want to hang around people who didn't. Joe reminded Justin of who he had been before it all went wrong. He didn't want to remember because if he remembered, it made him cry.

He'd been scared about the shopping centre but now he was through it and moving up Ocean View towards the back part of Sunnyside. The street lights were scarce now and the sky a whole lot bigger. It was important not to go fast, not to attract attention.

Where the highway crossed Ocean View, he waited for the lights. There were cars streaming from Seabank and the Peninsula towards Deptford, bypassing Sunnyside itself, on their way to the city. People were going home from dinner parties. His parents would still be at Harry and Alice's because they always stayed late there. He had told them he was sleeping over at Will's but they wouldn't call him there, they never did. He was there so often that the parents had become super-casual about the whole thing. And Justin had told Will's dad that he had a headache so he was riding his bike home and Will's dad never thought to ask if Justin's parents were home, he just assumed it.

The bush got thick on the other side of the highway. He accelerated a little up Mountain Road, past Shellforth Academy where the football scouts came to check out the private-school players. He'd like to go there for that. But he hated the uniform and the whole fancy thing. He'd been arguing with his mum about it. She'd said it was fine to be all alternative about everything, but what happened if you woke up at twenty-five and decided you'd missed a whole lot of opportunities and it was too late to get them back. 'What if you don't turn out to be *that* alternative?'

Could that ever happen to him? Would he end up being normal? Would he be a regular law student or something and wish he'd been a Shellforth boy and done things that way, with a network of Shellforth old boys? It was hard to believe. All that stuff, the Shellforth thing and the prefects and the parents' fancy cars . . . it was as if people forgot they were going to die. Eventually. Sooner or later. They were just bullshit, these status symbols.

At the top of the hill, the housing developments turned into pasture. Justin took a right turn up the dirt road. The moon was just a sliver, partly covered by cloud. He stopped the car by the fence, took out the bolt cutters and applied his weight to the chain. It snapped easily. He dropped the chain beside the fence, pulled the gate all the way open and lodged a hunk of granite under it to stop the gate closing as he drove the car through.

There was the reservoir in the moonlight, the calm surface shining with a faint silver skin, like fish scales, and it looked big. There was hardly any wind. If it wasn't so cold, it would be inviting. The bush would normally creep Justin out, but having something to do saved him. He drove the car to the top of the earthy bank. He left the motor running in neutral and the parking brake on. He got out of the car. It was quiet.

He leant in and thought for a second about how fast he had to be. Then he clicked off the parking brake and lowered it, pulled the gear stick onto 'D' and backed his body swiftly out of the car. The new blue Golf moved down the slope slowly at first, then faster, sailed over the earthy bank and dropped almost silently into the water. The headlights tracked the impact on the surface, illuminating the beginning of waves, then they, too, disappeared and it was dark again. Justin stood there for a few moments, then he turned and started the long walk back to Sunnyside.

Alice passed around the tiramisu and the berries. They were tart, good for offsetting the dessert's sweetness. She chastised herself for her lack of generosity, her judgementalism. *These were her friends!* It was good to be here, in her house with her friends. It was good to know that she and Harry had created a world for themselves, populated by contemporaries and their children, furnished with belongings. *This was what grown-ups were supposed to have.* These were all good people and if they were good, there must be more out there. It suddenly seemed important to know this.

'There's no idealism left in politics,' David said. 'Either side. It's about sheer pragmatism. Public service has been sacrificed to personal ambition. Everyone keeps talking about *vision*. But vision is an obsolete word. Politics isn't about shaping a better world any more. It's there to perpetuate itself not to facilitate things for its society.'

'You're just a cynic. We have *enough* cynics,' said Molly.

Alice noticed Molly had not touched her dessert. Alice had the vaguest sense that her professed desire for more honesty in social circumstances was dishonest. It was easier if people behaved.

'I don't actually think I am a cynic. A cynic wouldn't care enough to notice.'

Raph said, 'I think our kids are idealistic. I think they will defeat the current political meanness. They are full of goodness. We *made* them good and in the end, they'll *win*.'

The phone was ringing in the kitchen. Harry looked at his watch and rose to his feet. As she watched Harry disappear, Alice thought about Joe. He was safe. He was at Monty's house. Grace was in bed. A mother never felt safe when the phone rang.

'This tiramisu was the best ever,' said Lily. '*Scrumptious*!'

Harry walked back into the room, his face washed out. Alice felt her blood hiccough.

'Justin's in some kind of trouble.'

David stared at Molly, faces looking for answers.

'He's at the police station at Deptford. You need to go and get him.'

Out of the silence, David stood. 'Is he okay?'

'What did he do?' asked Molly, pale and still.

'It sounds as if he's okay. If he's at the station, then . . .'

A tiny reverberation of relief: no ambulances, no hospitals.

Harry looked puzzled, as if he couldn't put this news together with all of them, Alice and their friends, assembled in this room.

'He drove Molly's car into the reservoir.'

The air had changed, disappeared, been sucked out.

'He's there? At the station?' said Molly, finally.

Harry nodded. 'They said to come and get him, so he must be all right, Moll.'

Alice looked at Harry. Harry disliked events, wanted only familiarity and ritual. But now it had happened, into their house had come trouble, trouble for one of their group, yet somehow belonging to all.

Molly said, 'He drove my car into the reservoir?'

In the sitting room, Miles Davis played on, oblivious to events. The gorgeous horn sounded through the house, reminding them that they were living only one small story. There were other stories, other places, other times. This is what music is there for, Alice thought. To reinstate scale.

'I'll go get him. I'll take him home,' said David.

Molly stood, suddenly animated, looking for her handbag, eyes bright, manic.

'No,' said David. 'Let me get him.'

'Shouldn't I come?' said Molly in a tiny voice. 'I want to be sure he's —'

'No,' said David. 'You make everything worse.'

The words hovered over the table, introducing something new to be recollected later. Later they would all recall how David had said Molly made everything worse. That had been the moment the benevolence of friendship had come undone, the unarticulated faith that what they all had to fear existed outside themselves.

David turned to Jim.

'Can you drop Molly home?'

'Of course.'

Harry said, 'I'll come with you.'

Molly stood still, watched David walk quickly to the door. Harry looked to Alice and between them they acknowledged that there was a crisis and in a crisis things had to be done. He grabbed a jacket from the hall cupboard and followed David out to the car. Inside, they were silent until they heard the double thump of the car doors slamming.

Alice poured Molly a cognac, handed the bottle around.

'At least Justin's all right,' said Alice.

'Although your car may be a little the worse for wear,' said Jim, looking for lightness.

For a moment, they all saw Molly's brand-new Golf at the bottom of the Sunnyside reservoir, a gleaming package of painted steel and leather, drowned.

'Listen, *kids*,' said Raph, trying.

They all nodded too quickly. A chorus went around the table: *Kids! Exactly.*

'Kate and Georgia are driving us crazy at the moment. They text-message all through dinner, for Christ's sake.'

'Oh boy, boy oh boy, *kids*. They *are* a handful,' said Lily.

Everyone was looking at Molly, who had covered her face with her hands.

'Well,' said Raph. 'It must have been a joy-ride that went wrong.'

They all tried to imagine a Golf accidentally ending up in the reservoir.

'No,' said Molly. 'It's not like that.'

She took her hands from her face. Her mascara was smeared around the edges of her lids. She swallowed her cognac.

'I'm having an affair.'

Alice started laughing.

'Right! With the pool man!"

'Yes,' said Molly.

She was staring at them blankly, her lovely eyes watering up.

'*What*?' said Lily.

'With the pool man. Don't even say anything. I'm ridiculous.'

Alice said, 'You're in love with the pool man?'

'I didn't say *in love*.'

Tess said, 'Does he look like Brad Pitt?'

'No. He looks like . . . a white Lenny Kravitz.'

Alice wouldn't have thought that a white Lenny Kravitz would work, exactly. The music had ended. A cold, ironic silence fell over the room. Molly sat still, composed, in the aftermath of a gunshot.

'He's the *pool man*?'

Molly nodded.

'Well,' said Alice.

Raph said, 'Does David know?'

Molly nodded. 'That's why . . . Justin . . .'

'Justin *knows*?'

Molly nodded again.

Alice said, 'When I called to ask you tonight . . . You never . . .?'

'We're trying to be as normal as possible. That's why we came. We don't know what we're doing yet. And we still . . . well, we still love each other. Of course we do.'

'For God's sake, Molly. The pool man. Couldn't you find a less clichéd member of the domestic support industry?'

'Well, what can I say, Lily? Next time, I'll try to be more original.'

Alice thought it was interesting that their men were not philanderers. These men that she and Lily and Tess and Molly had married, these men were steadfast. They aspired to 'family life'. They believed in the wife, the kids, the house, the car, as a conscious choice, rather than a natural inheritance. Plenty of men older than them had embraced irresponsibility. They were locked in custody battles, stung by alimony payments, lonely. They were no happier for having escaped the middle-class ideal, for thumbing their noses at good behaviour. Harry's generation knew enough about infidelity to realise that it was for losers. These men were lovely men, good men, kind fathers, keen providers, but their imaginations were threadbare. They were fearful. They were right to be afraid, thought Alice. Women's curiosity was awesome. It distracted them from the known. There was something undimmable about a woman's curiosity.

Molly's words had made cuckolds of all the men at Alice's table. The women did not want them there, hearing this, confessions from the other side. It was not good to allow men into that space, the space where women fuelled their actions. Men did not want to go

there and women did not want to let them in. Molly was disman-
tling, letting barriers slide, sledgehammering the necessary walls.

'I should go home,' said Molly.

'David and Justin won't be home yet. Why don't we have a coffee and then Tess and I will take you home,' said Jim.

Tess and Lily followed Molly and Alice into the kitchen, leaving
the men to discuss practicalities. They could talk about tow trucks
and insurance. They would make everything all right for themselves. It was unkind not to let them do that, find a way out of the
night that did not leave them frightened.

seven

Scarlett had been sitting for one hour and twenty minutes in the twelve-degree night with nothing more than a parka pulled over her nightie. She'd told her mother she was watching *Millionaire* in her bedroom, leaving her to her *Law and Order* re-runs in the family room, then pulled on her jacket and sneakers and snuck out the laundry door and around the garden path to the hole in the fence. Now, perched on the balcony of Grace's tree house, Scarlett could watch them at the dining table, knowing that she was invisible in the night.

The Haskins were entertaining. Harry was walking around with two bottles in his hands, filling glasses, and people were laughing. Scarlett could hear the vague notes of the music filtering over the garden towards her. They were grown-ups. Okay, so at seventeen she was technically nearly an adult but *these were grown-ups*. They had families, real families, not like the Kornhabers. *Why did they have to be called Kornhaber*? It was just so typical that she'd have such a bulky name. Alice and Harry had friends to fill their house, a real house, a house with books and art and Persian rugs. They had a family room for an actual family. Alice and Harry had friends who threw back their heads and laughed, who had things to talk about, who *got together*. Her mother never got together with anyone. Scarlett had noticed the way Alice Haskins talked to her mother. She bent over backwards to be nice, not to show her contempt. But Scarlett could read it. Scarlett could read Alice Haskins. Scarlett could read every word, every move, every glance.

If her father's stupid slut had not come along, things might have been different. Not that her father was any great loss. Sometimes the moment came to her, technicolour. Her father standing on their old cement driveway, the car door open behind him, his sudden, swift farewell and her mother on the doorstep in her floral dress. The belligerent, mundane detail of a final, unforgettable exit. Once, way back, Scarlett could remember a moment. Her parents in the front seat of the car and her in the back, on their way to a fete. Her father had made a joke, her mother had laughed and Scarlett could remember one swift flash of happiness.

Empty bottles were lining up on the sideboard, chairs were pushed back from the table, there was a general sense that the standards of early evening were collapsing in the evolving night. Scarlett wondered if she would ever be at dinner parties, places where there was a chair for her, an invitation. It seemed unlikely. No-one had shown any interest in her at school, and school was almost certainly a blueprint for real life. Intelligence was no password for popularity, that was clear. She was *tolerated* for her intelligence, but not *liked*. There were moments when Scarlett imagined trading her intelligence for popularity, making a deal with *the force* that decided things. But at the last minute, she resisted. What was the point in being liked if you did not like yourself?

Watching these adults at their party wooed Scarlett back into her dream, her little dream, that one day there would be a place for her in the scheme of things, a place that valued her mind but also gave her comfort. A dining room would do.

In the kitchen, Alice said, 'So, so *what*?'

Pots and pans were spread across the kitchen bench, jettisoned.

Tess said, 'Well is it . . . you know . . . is it serious?'

Molly said, 'I don't know! I don't know what's going on. I don't recognise myself. I'm sneaking around.'

Lily swigged from a leftover bottle of champagne sitting on the bench top, wiped her mouth on her lacy sleeve and asked, 'Where do you go?'

Molly blushed and took a sip from the large glass of white wine she had poured herself. Her face took on a tougher look. Alice felt as if she could see the compartmentalising going on, there in front of her, the way a woman could shift from remorse to revelry in the sweep of a single thought.

'The Deptford Motel.'

Alice and Lily and Tess pictured the sign on the highway, a sign that had hitherto indicated the proximity of seediness, of otherness so unlikely as to be unthreatening. Now the sign for the Deptford Motel took on significance, flagging the invitation to enter a new, exquisite realm, the universe of thrilling degradation. Running inside Alice's head was a projection of Molly with the white Lenny Kravitz's penis in her mouth, kneeling on the synthetic carpet of the Deptford Motel.

'When, for God's sake?'

'After I drop Justin at school. Sometimes I drive to school with no underwear on. I stand there on the lawn waving him into his educational facility without any knickers. And then I drive straight to the Deptford Motel. And if you're wondering why I would risk everything for the pool man, I'll tell you why. Because I'm as high as a fucking kite.'

Tess put the kettle down and stuck the plunger too forcefully into the glass container, splashing hot coffee over the bench.

'You're a professional, Tess, what do you think?' said Lily.

'I think I'm too professional to mix friendship and business.'

'There must be reasons,' said Lily.

Molly stopped pacing and sat down on a kitchen stool. Her strap had fallen over her shoulder and Alice could just make out a kelpy stain peeking out from the edge of her silk top. *Now the tattoo makes sense.*

'It's like everything I've come out of, all of it, childhood and parents and marriage, all those inherited and acquired things, they've just *gone*. I don't even want them back. In fact, I'm terrified they'll come back and *stop* me. Because I feel so unbelievably, incredibly *alive*. It's as if I've been fused. And now Dan has fixed the fuse.'

His name made things shocking all over again.

Tess said, 'Do you love him?'

Molly took another drag of her cigarette. She had to be the last defiant smoker in Sunnyside, thought Alice.

'No, I don't love the pool man!'

Alice felt the first electric shudder pass through her, the shudder of possibility. For a high-voltage second, she remembered the violence of sexual attraction, the potency of loveless physicality. There was nothing quite like it, the loveless fuck. Whoever said women's sexual thrill was located in deep emotion knew nothing. There was something fantastic about sex with a man to whom you owed nothing.

Molly's long legs were swung over each other on the stool. She had great legs, the best on the tennis circuit.

'How could I? He's not stupid but he knows nothing about anything I care for. But when he makes love to me, he *devours* me.'

She let that rest a moment, stubbed the butt out on a vintage Kosta Boda plate.

'I've never been with a man who gets so much pleasure out of my body and what I'm saying is, I don't love him but how do I *go back*?'

Molly's eyes watered and a tear spilled. She had switched again, the vixen banished. 'You know our mothers said the most important thing is to like them.'

'Pool men?' said Alice.

'Husbands,' said Molly. 'To *like* them. Because they are companions first and foremost. David is an excellent companion. We have a lot of fun together. But you know, that's good and lovely but there's something to be said for a guy who loves the taste of you, who's down there – *there* – for hours because he *loves* it.'

Molly's eyes were shining with juice, the juice from down there, she was awash in it. She looked at the women, head tilted, willing them to understand, knowing that unless you had been there, there in the full wild weather of it, of tongues and sweat and friction, you couldn't, you just couldn't.

'Once you've tasted *the other* you're forever in the sway of it.'

Alice thought about what she and Harry were in the sway of . . . nothing untoward. They were in the sway of ordinary expectations.

He hadn't been *down there* in a long time and he'd never been down there for *hours*. Was Molly exaggerating? Alice could feel the slow heat of relief seeping through her, that she and Harry had remained immune to the disease that had taken hold of Molly and David, and yet mingled in the relief was a yearning to know more about this *other*. Alice could remember the feeling of power she had possessed at university, the power of the desired. This was what had revisited Molly, the thrill of being coveted.

At the kitchen door, Grace was standing, sloe-eyed with sleep, in her blue penguin pyjamas.

Grace said in a slow voice, 'Where's Dad? What's going on?'

eight

On the way into Deptford, David said, 'It's not the sex, that I don't mind so much.'

David refused to allow Harry to drive. Harry thought that David probably needed to take charge of the car, since events were taking charge of him. It was natural.

'You know, they say that, don't they? In art, in books, in magazines, those talk shows. It's not the sex, it's the *closeness*. Sex really doesn't bother me too much. I never really understood why men were so possessive of women's bodies. It's just a *body*, right?'

Harry nodded. He was watching the road, which was wet. It had rained throughout dinner and now the roads were greasy. It was still spitting. Above them, a sliver of moon was covered in brightly lit cloud. Men had been there. These same men who had wives who slept around. These same men who drove Mercedes to police stations, who raised kids and tried to manage ordinary events. Guys like that had been up there, on that sliver of light; they had taken to the moon thoughts of unfaithful wives, of difficult, compelling children, the burdens of fathering, the pitfalls of husbanding, the whole shebang. Had Neil Armstrong's wife played around back on earth? Probably not, but who knew? She must have been alone a lot of the time, while Neil was doing gravity experiments at NASA, or public speaking at campuses around the nation. Mrs Armstrong (*what was her name . . . Peggy? Elaine?*) may have given Neil a lot to think about and he had taken it with him. The moon *had* to be different now, because of that.

David was driving erratically, alternating between a pensioner-dawdle and adolescent-bravura.

'It's knowing what you belong to. Snugness. That's love, no?'

'Snugness? I don't know.'

'I love her because she knows me better than anyone and I know her. It's the knowing. The knowing is exciting, even if what you know is not very nice.'

'I guess so,' said Harry. He wished David would slow down a little descending Freeman's Hill. On Harry's side, the cliff dropped away to the sea.

'I want to kill her,' said David.

'Sure,' said Harry evenly, trying to keep it light. 'We all want to kill them sometimes.'

'No,' said David. 'I *really* want to kill her.'

74

They were at the bottom of the hill now, where the road stretched out straight. White waves were pounding the Deptford beach. Across the four lanes, on the other side of the road, was the reassuring light of the all-night service station. How comforting it was to see people buying Cokes and filling up late at night. It was good to know that while he, Harry, was unconscious, other people were on watch. Through the long hours of the night, nature was not just left to its own devices, waves pounding the Deptford pier, the wind, the tides. On wild nights, it seemed to Harry, human beings needed to stay vigilant.

'I understand how it is that a man enters his wife's domain and *stabs her and the kids to death*. I'm not saying I'd do it. But I understand it.'

David's hands were white around the steering wheel, ghostly in the fluctuating moon.

'You're angry and that's completely natural. It's right that you should be angry.'

'I actually *understand* why a man likes to see that look of terror.'

David sounded surprised and happy to have discovered this.

Harry wondered how Alice was going. It would be good to see Alice again. It struck Harry that if everyone were subjected to even twenty minutes of another person's crisis, their lives would be immeasurably sweeter. David's intensity made Harry hot with happiness for his own placid plot, the waves of pleasantness radiated through him. For a few seconds, Harry believed he was in possession of The Perfect Family, the original example against which all other versions struggled to compete.

'Why should she have the power to wreak so much havoc?'

David turned sideways to look at him, seemingly impervious to road safety.

'Huh, Harry? Tell me that. *Explain it to me.*'

'Gee, David,' said Harry. 'Things sometimes get messed up. Maybe for no good reason.'

'Now she's screwing Justin up! Is that fair? I'm asking you Harry, *is it*? Is it fair?'

'Justin will be okay. He's a good kid. One miserable event is not going to cancel out years of good parenting.'

'This isn't an event. This is *the* event.'

'David.'

'No wonder so many Americans get fucking shot. If I had a fucking gun! Harry! Harry! Harry! *I'm crazy about her*!'

They had stopped at the roundabout. There were no other cars. The rain was falling on the windscreen, and for some reason David had turned off the wipers. There they were, Harry and David, walled in by rain on glass, on the way to the police station. David stared at Harry, glassy eyed.

'I used to be the one who knew her. It was me. Molly and *David*.

Now there's *this* guy. This guy I wouldn't even recognise! That can't be a good thing.'

'No,' said Harry, 'none of this is a good thing. That's for sure.'

David switched on the wipers and turned into Main Street. He pulled into a park right outside the station and rested his head on the steering wheel. Harry and David were swamped by blue light, the reflection of the neon police sign. Far down the street, Harry could see two kids in beanies on mountain bikes, not a parent in sight. Didn't anyone care any more? What had happened since Harry was a kid? Those forty years hadn't seemed so dramatic and yet things had altered dramatically. It was raining and kids in beanies didn't seem to have anywhere to be. It was enough to turn a man into one of those religious nuts.

'Who is he?' said Harry. 'Who's the guy?'

'The pool man,' said David.

'The *pool man*?'

'The guy who cleans the pool. A guy *I've been paying*.'

David raised his head and looked at Harry. Without warning, they started to giggle. David tittering, Harry too, little giggles erupting, building, eyes watering. They were caught inside of it, surrendered to it, tears streaming. Through the hysterics David said, 'The upside is, *there's not a leaf in it!*'

The Deptford police station pulsated with white light. Justin was scrunched up on a bench in the corner, sobbing into his body, face hidden. Next to him was a tall, uniformed blonde, looking bored. When Joe and Harry entered, she stood up.

'Who's the father?' she said, looking at Harry.

'Him,' said Harry.

'Can we speak alone?'

She took David into a glassed-in office and closed the door. Harry took her place beside Justin. He could see them talking inside, still standing. She had a poster on the wall that began in cursive writing, 'If I had my time again . . .' The first response was, 'I'd run through paddocks in bare feet.'

Justin was wearing a long-sleeved Eminem T-shirt. He was fifteen years old; it seemed so sudden to Harry. Joe would soon be here, here inside Justin's Grecian youth body with its huge feet in trainers. Justin had not looked up, his face buried in his arms, his back shivering with sobs. Around them, thin, pale people came and went, junkies, kids in hooded windcheaters. The police looked so robust amongst them, so solid in their navy blue, the authority of uniform. An old man with a sleeping-bag around his head sat in the far corner of the waiting area with a bottle in a brown bag. Where did people like that sleep? Maybe he was a human community-service installation, paid to sit there so that rich kids from Sunnyside could see where their bad choices might lead. When Harry had first taken the train to the city from the Deptford station, he had been surprised to hear Brahms being played over the station platforms.

At first he had thought this was for the listening pleasure of intelligent, well-rounded men such as himself. Then he had read in the *Peninsula Times* that it was a strategic initiative to pacify the rampant aggression of the typical Deptford commuter, a chrome-addicted kid looking to beat up Sunnyside commuters.

Harry touched Justin lightly on the back. Justin swung himself around and allowed himself be held, burying his face in Harry's chest. Harry had taken Justin to a football match once, when Alice was pregnant with Joe. Justin had cried at the end, overcome by the crowds and the noise and Harry had carried him on his shoulders across the park to the car. Before Harry had become a father, he thought that other people's children were essentially mysterious. Now he knew that your own children were infinitely more mysterious. Love clouded things over.

When David came out of the office, he looked down at them and said, 'We can go.'

Justin sat up and blinked. 'Where's Mum?'

'She'll meet us at home.'

'The car's gone, Dad.'

'I know, son.'

As they drove back to Sunnyside along the coast road, no-one spoke. This time, Harry drove. The rain had stopped, but there was a cold, dark wetness to the world. Justin had stopped crying. David stared straight ahead. Harry turned into Jackman's Road and then left into Boronia Crescent. The gardens of the half dozen houses in the crescent glistened as the car lights traversed them. The lights were on at Molly and David's house. Jim and Tess must have dropped Molly home. Harry parked the car in their garage. The three of them got out of the car, pausing on the pebbled driveway beneath the coach light. David's face was fixed with resignation. Out of nowhere, he had an adventurous wife. She was inside, probably making coffee and smoking a cigarette and they would have to find a way of getting through the night and then the next day and the day after that.

Somehow, thought Harry, it happened. Night passed into day and on it went, the relentlessness of nature confounding disaster, mocking it. The confusing thing was that Molly did not seem terribly apologetic. Now that he looked back on it, it had seemed, all through dinner, as if she was much the same Molly, only more so. She exuded an air of entitlement, which her long legs and symmetrical face only exaggerated. It was somehow typical of Molly that she could behave badly without appearing remotely petulant.

Harry decided to walk home. It was only a couple of kilometres. He had his coat. The rain had stopped. It would do him good. He shook David's hand. Justin had already started walking slowly towards the house, a young man moving towards the inevitable.

Husbands carried quite a load. It wasn't anything to complain about, really, since women were worth it. They were tricksy and pulled all kinds of things out of the hat. But that was part of their charm. Molly was a handful, no-one would wish for it. But you had to admire a woman who could all but persuade you that an affair was her due. Harry had never really thought about Molly in a sexual way but as he walked he realised that this was only because he had short-circuited any such reflection. Maturity had armed him with a vaguely depressing ability to suppress the random wanderings of his imagination if they gave off the faintest suggestion of trouble. Now, however, the spectre of the pool man was forcing him into those thoughts, fast, slippery images of Molly in places he had never seen her, dexterous and undressed. Were Raph and Jim thinking the same way? Had he just drunk too much?

Molly had tilted them all into those usually neglected recesses of eroticism, not that they'd asked for it. At a certain point, couples just seemed to let go of appetites, lose them inside prejudice, monotony and fatigue. Everyone agreed to this, the banishing of the wilderness, the dark woods, where things were savage. It was a pact. In its place came things and diaries, pruning hydrangeas, theatre premieres, trips to the tip. It wasn't bad, not a bit of it. But then someone like Molly did something foolish, and put wilderness back on the agenda.

The sky had cleared and Harry could see the Milky Way. The great thing about the outer suburbs was that you could actually see the sky, the biggest outer suburb of the lot. The wind was coming up off the bay. The air was icy. The deciduous trees in the front yards of the houses were still bare. In a couple of months, they would be covered in masses of green leaves. Rows of agapanthus lined the footpath along the fence-lines, white azaleas forming little clouds in the darkness. Harry enjoyed being out. He rarely walked in Sunnyside. It was hard to remember the last time. Certainly never at night. No-one really walked in Sunnyside, only teenagers who had exhausted their parents' chauffering goodwill.

The night had started so well. Now, across the township, friends had disbanded, dishwashers been turned on, leftovers sealed beneath little tarpaulins of plastic, half-empty bottles of wine corked and good silver counted before the rubbish went out. All that promise had been fulfilled or disappointed; either way it was over. Couples were returning to coupledom, houses reclaimed, electric blankets switched on, children re-swaddled, babysitters released. The cars of Sunnyside had returned to their garages, all but Molly's. It seemed to Harry as if a spring shower of sadness had rained over the neighbourhood, a late-night melancholy. Change had crept into the night. It was the job of the suburbs to withstand change, to be small pockets of resistance. Alice was always saying how little Sunnyside had changed since she was at school. The children of the past had grown into their parents, younger, perhaps, in their appearance, but wishing for much the same things. The curve of the bay had not changed, nor had the cliffs edging it. The fences had gotten higher as the residents barricaded themselves in, but the trees that Harry passed had stood forty years before, and inside the houses similar lights had been on, holding out the darkness, allowing residents to savour both their distance from their neighbours, and their closeness.

The suburbs had surely got this right. A little distance around one's family was a good thing, making it special and defined, binding its members in some inalterable way. But too much space was dangerous, giving a family a sense of separateness that might make it think too much of itself. Harry hoped that David and Molly and Justin, inside their house, were able to look about them, down the cul de sac, through the yards of elms and gums, the scattering of scooters and pool scoops and trampolines, and see that, really, they were not too special, not unbearably special. They had as much and as little happiness as their neighbours.

nine

'She's behaving like a teenager. She even *looks* like a teenager. She's got that glow you get when all you think about is sex.'

Lily had snuck in a quick coffee with Alice in the chaotic choreography of Saturday morning inspections. They had spoken on the phone at eight, agreeing that they both needed desperately to *debrief*. Alice wanted to say something that would allow them to believe such an event had never happened before. *But this happened all the time*. Not just infidelity, but the sudden impact of involuntary occurrences. Money was there to protect you, Sunnyside money, the unseen notes that floated freely over the suburb, unseen but worshipped, the confidence of affluence. Yet as it turned out, money really was *not* everything. It could not save them from these small, unheralded comets, landing unevenly on their irrigated lawns.

'Do you think she realises what an impact she's having?' said Alice. 'Do you think she realises what she's doing to David and Justin?'

'*Of course she realises*,' said Lily, taking a sip of her caffe latte. 'On some level, this is just a major attention-getting exercise. She's saying: "Look at me, I'm still young, I'm still wild!"'

'She *is* wild,' said Alice. '*Can't* we be wild? Being white and middle class? Does that cancel us out automatically?'

Alice and Lily pondered this for a moment in silence. You couldn't have everything. Maybe what they had sacrificed in embracing good fortune was the ability to cut loose. Molly was an aberration. Alice wondered what she might have chosen if the choice had been offered to her, like a job position or a place at a university. What would she have chosen if the choice had been laid out before her: surrender or struggle? Was the forfeiting of sensual abandon the price she had paid for order? All of them, Lily and Raph, Tess and Jim, made a good go of pretending they still led interesting lives. They subscribed to the *Guardian Weekly*, attended arts festivals, even went on the odd adventure-travel holiday. But was the stirring of the soul really answered by a two-week hike in the Himalayan foothills? Maybe there was no way you could lead a safe life that was also interesting.

'There are times when I want to be wild,' said Lily, 'but it's hard to sandwich an intrepid spirit between school drop-off and pick-up. Three-thirty in the afternoon just isn't the appropriate curfew for the vixen within.'

Alice laughed.

'The truth is, Alice, *I'm jealous*. Who *wouldn't* want what Molly has?'

Joe kicked the football high in the air and it slammed into the tennis court fence right between the imaginary goals. It was possible that he would make the draft one day, but it wasn't very likely. He was one of the best footy players in the school, but he wasn't *the* best, that was Monty Hargreaves. Also, what happened if he was sick the day the football league scouts came recruiting? He might have a cold. And then what? His entire destiny would be obliterated by an act of God. This week was the end-of-season pie night and Harry still hadn't said if he was going. Harry had been vaguely promising all season to do something, to actually *do* something, like be a boundary umpire, which anyone could do, at Wednesday night training or at a Sunday morning game. But in the end, his father had not taken up one single voluntary position. It would be great to have a dad who coached. Like Monty Hargreaves's dad. It would be great to have Monty Hargreaves's dad as a dad.

It just wasn't possible to communicate these problems to his parents because his mother would just tell him to stop worrying, like it was that easy. She was always telling him that he worried for nothing, that he had 'an elevated sense of the rules', that he needed to relax. She always said he could tell her anything, but she made it impossible. He only told her the tiniest part of what he worried about, the top layer, and she thought *that* was ridiculous. She would freak if she knew what really went on inside his brain. Why couldn't he be more like the boys in his class? *They knew how to be kids.*

Joe stood back and lined up the goals in his head. He positioned the ball and kicked it again.

A year ago, when he had these thoughts, he could tell Justin and Justin, being so cool, could make them vanish in a few words. Now, Justin was definitely weirding out. Grace had woken Joe with the news about Justin and Molly's car. The entire morning had been spent with his parents speaking some kind of code to each other about everything that had gone on the night before. Things had suddenly got very strange. Lying in bed after Grace had delivered the news, Joe felt ashamed at his first thought that Justin was now well and truly unavailable to him. He should have been thinking about Justin, about the trouble he was in. But all Joe could think about was that he was even more alone than before.

It was probably okay to be this alone. Most people didn't realise how alone they were and it would be quite a surprise to them to discover this fact as adults. At least Joe knew right from the start how separate a person was from the next one. Most of his thoughts were not things that could be shared. Other people would think he was nuts and maybe he was. Maybe his endless, repetitive thinking was a sign that he *was* nuts, the thinking that ran over the top of everything, even here playing football alone on the tennis court. Lately, he couldn't get those sheep out of his mind. Every day that passed, every hour, the sheep were still there on the boat. *They were still there!* Nobody would save them. *They'd asked nearly sixty countries so far and none of them would take them!* Joe couldn't help but put himself there, inside a sheep, looking out of a sheep's eyes at all the other thousands of sheep. There were fifty-seven thousand on the boat. There was no space to move at all. If he moved one tiny bit, he jostled up against ten other sheep, who jostled against fifty more, and so it went, all of them trying to keep their heads up in order to breathe. They didn't even know they were on a boat! All they knew was that their life was hell, *they'd rather be dead.*

The weekend had been spent dissecting Molly and David's marriage, when opportunity allowed. By Sunday night, Harry thought it conceivable that there was nothing left to say, but Alice was not done.

'The problem is that people want more than they have a reasonable right to expect,' said Alice.

Harry said, 'The problem is, she doesn't have enough to do.'

'That's it?' said Alice.

Harry was buttoning up the fine navy linen pyjamas she had

bought him, because she thought he'd look like George Clooney in them. He *did* look like George Clooney in them. They were worth the money. Harry was aware that he always slowed down when he was shocked. He became physically lethargic, as if he was absorbing a blow but didn't want to appear to be. He started sounding like a newsreader. His voice became extra modulated, not giving anything away. He didn't want to register change. He didn't want to give it room to move. If he kept his voice quiet and unexcited, unexcitement might restore itself. News might recede.

He pulled back the bed cover and got in. He drew the doona up under his chin and put his arms straight down the sides of his body, a horizontal soldier. What would Harry's father have done if, as an aggrieved adolescent, he had wrecked his mother's car on a whim? The thought was inconceivable. Harry's father, a history teacher at a country high school, had been a salaried man, his expectations firmly contained by his income. Moderation had been the watchword of that generation. His mother, a nurse before having Harry and his sister, had budgeted the week with uncomplaining resignation. The thought of what he had, of what his children had, by contrast, gave Harry simultaneously a sense of shame and pride. The luxury not only of their material lives, but of their emotional lives, too. For his parents extremes of feeling belonged only to artists and the mentally unbalanced.

Harry didn't want to turn to look at Alice. At this moment, he didn't really care to take in her expression, no doubt one of those female expressions assuming a mutual wonderment at the world. Harry didn't want to wonder, especially mutually. He wanted to stamp out everything that might be described as befuddling. If he looked at Alice, he knew the whole conversation would rapidly get out of control. They'd be locked into some conspiracy of witnesses, going over hypotheticals *('He'll find someone too', 'She'll come to her senses')* until the early hours. Harry had to teach tomorrow. He had that girl to contend with.

Harry only used the word 'girl' inside his head. It could be wrongly construed. Ever since Howard Woodbridge had gone up in front of the Ethical Standards Committee, the campus had become tightly wound. Harry thought it a shame, because learning had always seemed to him to be a sexy thing. The giving and gaining of knowledge was a sacred transaction between teacher and student, and capable of triggering something special, something cerebrally erotic. Surely there was a world of difference between the thinking and the doing? In recent years, the *imagining* of a blow job from a succulent nineteen-year-old in a tartan mini in a dimly lit tutorial room had become as criminal as *doing* it. Just his luck to be teaching in an era where the imagination itself was permanently apprehended.

'You know, we all strive to have a life like Molly and David's,' said Harry, already knowing he didn't believe what he was saying as he said it, but compelled onwards by the pleasant sound of his own voice, 'but once such a life is achieved, there's nothing left to wish for so they have to fuck it up.'

'Is that what Molly's doing? Trying to fuck up her life?'

Alice was sounding the way she did sometimes, like there was no available rational reason why she was married to him, like she had just landed here in this bedroom next to Harry, fallen from the sky. Harry could either try to win her over by agreeing with her or he could just keep going on the same tack and bludgeon her, conversationally, into the refuge of sleep.

'I think it's sad,' said Alice. 'I think it's sad that you don't find it sad.'

'Me?' said Harry. 'Don't think I'm not sad. No one likes a broken marriage, especially two people so well suited.'

'Do you think they're well suited?'

'Don't you?'

'No. No, I don't. I never have.'

'You don't think David and Molly are well suited?'

'He plods. She sprints.'

Was he a plodder too? Alice certainly looked like a sprinter. Maybe sprinters *needed* plodders. Until they didn't.

'Molly has always been impatient with things that came easy. She *likes* difficulty.'

Christ, thought Harry. Now every sentence has to go through

91

a thorough workshopping. Women always needed to make everything *interesting*. They had a natural intolerance for letting things go. The female sex mistrusted the concept of experience without analysis. Worryingly, this lead Harry to ponder whether there might be certain pleasures in living intimately with another man, or were gay men just like women? Maybe what Harry really wanted was to be married to another heterosexual male. They could sit around watching prison movies on the weekends eating toasted sandwiches or visit Bang & Olufsen showrooms and not talk at all. Two plodders in no particular need of a sprinter. Attractive, non-drug-addicted, cello-playing callgirls with law degrees could pop over every so often. It was a thought.

'Okay,' said Harry, giving in. 'You tell me what this is about.'

'*The resurrection of impetuousness,*' said Alice.

Harry was going to respond to this as if it were a story they were reading, not a life they were living. If he said what ought to be said, that love was over between their friends, or if not love, then innocence, everything would collapse. The walls would start to tremble. The roof would cave in. It couldn't be simple.

ten

The week had passed so slowly. Scarlett had made it through school on Monday when they'd had history revision, skipped Tuesday and Wednesday, gone Thursday and now it was Friday and she couldn't face another day. Her mother had not caught on that Scarlett was turning around and going straight home after drop-off. Her mother seemed consumed by her recent promotion to office manager. Office *manager,* when there were only six lawyers in the entire firm and three assistants!

Scarlett looked out of the car window. It was weird to think that real things were happening somewhere else. The President of the United States was asleep in his bed. Julia Roberts was making a herbal tea, terrorists were target practising in some desert in Afghanistan.

'To tell you the truth I'm a little worried you're not focusing, Scarlett.'

Scarlett had the overwhelming desire to say: Who *gives* a shit? *Why* do we care? What am I working for? *This* life? *Your* life?

Her mother was wearing a new apple-green pencil skirt. The body of a jumbo marker and she was in a pencil skirt!

'You know what, why don't you concentrate on what *you* do and I'll look after myself.'

The village traffic lights turned red just too soon. *Bummer*. Scarlett's mother looked at her.

'Why are you so hostile to me?'

'You're paranoid.'

Scarlett could see Mrs Bailleau from the yacht club coming out of the milkbar. That reminded her, she had to wash the waitressing uniform she'd kicked under her bed. It stank of festering kitchen smells.

'Scarlett, I'm doing the best I can.'

Scarlett wasn't interested if this was the best she could do. The best! Living in an ugly house with shiny furniture. The two of them!

'It's not *my* fault Dad left, is it?'

Scarlett's mother looked straight ahead. 'Is it *my* fault?'

Her mother pulled up outside the school. Scarlett looked at her mother. For a moment, she felt not in control.

'I know you're not happy, Scarlett, but it's not really so bad. You think I'm pathetic, but I'm not that pathetic. I'm not as pathetic as you think I am.'

Scarlett said nothing. Her mother reached over and touched her cheek with the back of her hand the way she used to when Scarlett was young.

'Scarlett, I know you can't bear to hear this, but I have to say it to you. There isn't a day that passes that I'm not angry with you and there isn't a day that passes that I don't think you're the best thing that happened to me. I know I disgust you. I know you hate this. I'm not what you want. I know we fight a lot. But still, I love you. Through everything. Despite everything. You are the only great thing in my life.'

Scarlett got out and shut the car door hard without looking at her. When she glanced back, her mother's car had turned the corner. The thought of entering the school building nearly killed her. She could do more work at home, away from all the idiots. Scarlett lifted her laptop strap onto her shoulder and started walking quickly along the footpath. Kids were arriving, passing her on their way into school, avoiding their parents' waves. She tried to look casual, head down, skimming the pavement as if she'd dropped something and was backtracking. She turned the corner towards the bus stop and stopped. Her mother's car was parked by the side of the road. Her mother's shiny Daiwoo. Scarlett quickly crossed the street and hid behind the bus shelter. She peeked around the edge of the advertising sign. Her mother was crying. Scarlett hadn't seen her mother cry in a long time, not since he had first left. That was three years ago. A quick tide of anger rose up in her. Mothers had a responsibility not to cry.

'I know what you're going to say. You're going to say I could do better. We don't need to have this conversation. I can imagine it.'

Olivia Mathers was sitting across from Harry in his large office, leaning back on a low-slung Knoll chair from the seventies, upholstered in oatmeal wool. The office was on the third floor of the humanities building, the P J Krappworth building, known to students simply as The Krap or Krappsville. Harry's office was level with the top boughs of a large elm tree that, in combination with the office furniture, gave him the illusion he was teaching somewhere in Scandinavia. During dull tutorials, Harry entertained fantasies of the timber summer house in the Swedish woods where his long-limbed blonde wife was playing the lead in an Ingmar Bergman movie. In breaks during filming, he would frolic amiably, lie her down on the banks of the brook and ravish her amongst the perfect Swedish wildflowers.

Olivia Mathers was just a little too skinny. Girls had gotten so skinny lately. Harry was capable of thinking that she'd be pretty near perfect with an extra ten pounds and bigger breasts, without taking it any further. He appreciated women. When he met a woman whose demeanour or glint suggested possibility, Harry sometimes imagined a ripe encounter – a broom cupboard, a hotel suite – but in general, Harry got more sexual excitement from denying himself other women than he ever could from bedding them. Fidelity gave him a charge. Bad behaviour was so rampant these days, decency had an aura of exoticism. He could feel the beginnings of an erection just thinking of Alice at home, peering at her Jamie Oliver behind the perspex of her new recipe holder from Abode. Knowing she was there. Was Harry alone in finding the quiet collusion of marriage a turn-on?

Contrary to popular myth, the matter-of-factness of marriage was not what made it dull, but rather what made it so enthralling. In his twenties and early thirties, it had exhausted Harry not knowing who and what he belonged to, so unutterably dull living life without any degree of formality. It had been an amorphous endurance test full of exams and football matches and pubs with hairy musicians playing music you had to pretend to like. It had been so depressing sleeping with women who had no manners and no taste. Having grown up with images of Ali McGraw and Katherine Ross, he'd spent an entire decade looking for a great-looking girl in cotton underpants with ideals, and found she barely existed outside of the movies. There was a world out there of women who wanted to be property managers and lawyers, hard-faced girls whose sexual allure was dulled by their prosaic plans for the future. Not one of them could recite poetry. Not one of them dreamt of lying in a field of mustard flowers in Rajasthan. He had fallen in love with Alice, dreamy Alice, whose dignified beauty caused his friends to joke that when she rode her bicycle on campus, angels sang. For Harry, the state of marriage had made everything more piquant. At last he had something to give, something that time had made honourable and proper; he was a husband, a fixer, a provider, *an authority*, the kind of man who could sign a school excursion form or query a plumbing bill, the kind of man who could open jars.

'Your assignment was due Thursday. It's eight days late.'

'The thing is,' said Olivia carefully, 'I *did* it. But I misplaced it.'

The same thing. Every term. One hopeless excuse after another. Did she think he was an idiot?

'Olivia, the fact is, you could do better.'

'What makes you think so?'

Alarmingly, she was wearing a pleated miniskirt, no tights and long socks with the chunky black shoes old ladies used to wear with flesh-coloured support hose. Her thighs were so white, they looked mint-green. She was also wearing a T-shirt with 'If you can read this, you're too close' written across her breasts in tiny letters. Her long straight hair was loose and dyed black. She had a permanently superior expression, an asymmetrical contempt that gorgeous young women felt it necessary to assume in order to defy their own perfection. Harry found it hard to tell if it was physiological, or whether it was because she felt permanently superior to *him*. Next time they were out on campus, he would make an effort to see if she wore the same comely sneer while speaking to her other tutors.

'Well, for starters, your essays demonstrate occasional flashes of real insight and I can tell, just from our little exchanges, that you are engaged with the world even if you try to appear not to be.'

'So we're talking about appearances?'

Harry decided just to let that one go by. Leaning back in his chair and looking down through the branches of the elm, Harry could see Rohan Beaumont-Smith, the Vice-Chancellor, talking to Quentin Trilby, Associate Professor of English and Number One Pain in the Arse, on the pavers outside the portico.

'Olivia, I think you know very well that if you do not improve your attendance record and if you continue to ignore my warnings about class submissions, you are going to get kicked out. You need to think about whether this is what you want.'

'You think I *want* to get kicked out?'

'Don't you?'

'So, like what, I can become a dental nurse? Or a beautiful wife?'

'There are worse things.'

Harry had to consciously avoid using the phrase 'little lady'. Harry very rarely felt physical, but he would have liked to give her a good slap. Was this what Grace would be like one day? A savagely beautiful combination of resentment and impertinence and ego, desperate to be recognised as *something, anything.* Olivia uncrossed her legs and slumped down lower in the already low chair, so that only the tilt of her head stopped her from being actually horizontal.

'I guess you *have* a beautiful wife, right?'

'Yes. She married me right after completing her qualifications in dental nursing.'

For a moment, the air hung loose in the room, like after a bar brawl. Olivia looked out from under her fringe.

'Are you trying to frighten me?'

'Yes I am,' said Harry.

Why couldn't she just take her damaged psyche and long socks into someone else's office and drive *them* nuts. On the other hand, he had to admit there was a kind of pleasantness, too, a pleasantness to do with her awfulness and his ability to manage it, to assert himself against it. Later, he could have a glass of that nice new merlot from the staff-club list. Merlots had come up *a lot.* Once upon a time they were not taken seriously, but all that had changed. It was worth having this little encounter just for the pleasure, later, of knowing it had been and gone.

'You are very close to sabotaging a promising future. You think things should just be delivered to you. That's not realistic. Nobody owes you anything.'

'Ain't that the truth.'

'You can piss it all away, Olivia. There are plenty of other students just busting to inherit the world. You want to deny yourself a place in that, be my guest.'

Changing tack, Olivia shook her eyes free of the fringe, sat up, looked sideways at him.

'I'm really, really, really curious about you, Harry.'

'*Professor* to you.'

'I really want to know what rocks you, you know what I'm saying? I mean, what makes you get up in the morning?'

'Can we cut the bullshit? We can act out the cliché of the rebellious student and the uptight teacher all term if you like, and at the end of it you'll be kicked out of school and working in a chicken shop in Deptford and then, if you're really lucky, you'll have four kids and sit around the food court at the mall eating potato wedges despite being *very, very fat*. We can do that. Or we can stop wasting time and you can get me your assignment by Friday week. A two-week extension. You tell me what you want.'

Fantastically, wondrously, she started to cry. Harry felt magnificent. A big tear dropped from her eye and splashed on her huge pink-lilo lips. Harry felt better than he'd ever felt. His penis began to harden. No girl-power politics could dampen it. No legislation could counteract it. Biology was still one step ahead of ideology. He had to think about something sobering, otherwise he'd just be some ordinary prick who got off on humiliating women. To subdue his throbbing penis, Harry thought about the Vice-Chancellor and his wife, Moira, eating cheese twists at last year's staff-club Christmas drinks.

Olivia was really crying now, pulling her woollen sweater sleeves over her hands and allowing her thumbs to poke through two hacked holes in the end. She used her sleeves to wipe her wet nose. Harry passed her the box of tissues, which she nursed on her knee.

'Professor is so formal,' she said sulkily. 'I *can* call you Harry, right?'

'I'd rather you didn't.'

'Why are you picking on me?'

Harry took a breath. Olivia was looking better after crying. Her eyes had been washed over and her sneer was missing. Harry found it thrilling to think that women Olivia's age were dancing – even as they spoke! – on tables in bars. Girls like this. A long way from Alice and her scallop and ginger hors d'oevres, her masters in fine arts, her French T-shirts. Really, when all was said and done, what a man needed was one of each.

'I like you.'

Olivia looked up at him, smudged eyes, girlish, the vamp banished.

'You do?'

'Yes, I do. And to be honest, I respect your intelligence. I actually honour your talent, Olivia.'

Olivia's face crinkled in disdain. 'What talent?'

'You could do exceptionally well. But you have to stop showing off as a way of masking your insecurity.'

'Is that what I'm doing?'

'Is it ringing any bells?'

'Jesus, you're a tough bastard when you want to be.'

'*I want to be.*'

Harry stood up. Somehow he'd gotten through it. It hadn't been that bad. He seemed to have come out of it quite well, actually. Tough but caring. And in control. They could make a song and dance about sexual liaisons in education, but things happened when you put people in a room. It might be stated or unstated. It might be graphic or subtle. But things just did happen. He was feeling more successfully a man than he had any right to feel. Because this little girl was in some way in his grip. When all was said and done, he was going to *mark* her. Harry realised, suddenly, why it was that some men wanted to be traffic cops or customs officers. There was something horribly thrilling about another person's nervous gaze.

'My parents have fucked me up.'

Olivia had not moved. Harry had been hoping not to get onto the family background. He didn't want to hear about bad parents. He'd never had one. He didn't plan to be one. He didn't really know any.

His world was the world where parents were basically okay. They made mistakes. They occasionally attempted to camouflage emotional reticence with material purchases – Barbie ski-chalets, Duplo car-washes, Thomas the Tank Engine station furnishings, Sims City software – giving their children what they wanted, which was to have the accoutrements of adulthood in the silky soft hammock of childhood. As parents, his friends and associates sometimes came down too hard on unimportant errors. They occasionally embarrassed their children by wearing leisure suits at weekend football matches or even appearing, on occasion, on television current-affairs shows. But they were not the kind of people whose children took semi-automatic weapons into school cafeterias. He didn't really want to know anything about those people. There were some things better not to know. He started shuffling papers on his desk and putting some in his bag.

'Well, I'm sure it's not easy,' he said, making a show of buckling his satchel. 'But there's a statute of limitations on fucked-up parents. I want to see that assignment Friday week. I'm glad we've had this talk.'

Olivia pulled herself to her feet and threw her backpack over her shoulder. It had a button saying 'Men are from Mars, Women are from Shopping Malls'. A minute ago a guy would have been branded a sexist pig for coining such a phrase. Now girls sported them on their bosoms. It was so confusing, the way feminism had finally cottoned on to irony. Harry held the door open for Olivia.

He hoped that he was not being unduly insensitive. He could have stayed and listened. He could have taken her out for a beer. But at all costs, Harry's mission was not to provide any ammunition to God, any chance at all to upset the balance of destiny, destiny as defined by a really lovely house and family in a really nice neighbourhood. The trees outside his office had been whispering *Stay on track*, and he was listening.

Some nights, Alice had the annoying habit of watching the five o'clock news, then the six o'clock news and then the seven o'clock news. She had to watch the seven o'clock news because it was non-commercial, and therefore the only *reliable* news. But she watched the commercial news shows anyway, because they happened to be on while she was preparing dinner. And every time the sheep came on, Joe insisted on turning up the volume. She could go to her room, Alice always said so. But sometimes Grace just wanted to be in the middle of things, of family, of noise and dinner preparation, of Bamixes and newsreaders, of Joe saying stuff, of Alice saying stuff, of the phone going. There was something comforting just being in the mix of it. But since the five o'clock news had shown the sheep and Joe had started up again, she'd begun to feel the pinched thing around her eyes.

When things got too much, Grace could feel her head get tight, like a belt was strapped around it, and a weird chemical buzz. She could usually feel it coming. Doctor Vanderlay had recommended that at the first signs, she should lie in a darkened room. Last year Alice and Harry had taken her for a series of tests and she had actually had her head *inside a machine* to try to get to the bottom of the pain, but nothing had shown up. Grace could feel the pain now, beginning to take hold of her.

Grace ran back through her thoughts, trying to work out the starting point of the pain. She'd been thinking about the sheep on the boat because of Joe. Before that the Nigella ad had come on and and she'd been thinking that maybe instead of being a celebrity chef, it would be better to be an investigative reporter, one of those ones who sneak past librarians in city buildings in order to rifle through top-secret files in the pursuit of truth. They were always very attractive in an unshowy way and headstrong and *they made a difference.* And if she became a reporter she'd find out why the prime minister made stuff-ups, she'd get to the bottom of these *puzzles.* And Grace had been thinking about journalism because before that she'd been thinking about a magazine she'd read at Scarlett's, and *before that* she'd been thinking of the article about beauty and how if the left and right sides of your faced really *matched*, everyone thought you were gorgeous and did Grace's left and right sides match? Did Tabitha Arbuthnot's? Possibly. Grace had tried to imagine a photo of Tabitha's face. Inside her head, she folded it down the middle to see whether or not each side was a mirror image. *Before that* she'd been thinking of how Harry had played golf with Tabitha's dad, Ted Arbuthnot, at the St Merry's golf course and how Harry had described Ted to Alice as 'ordinary' and how that was just how Grace felt about Tabitha, which was weird, and she'd been thinking about golf because before that she'd been thinking . . . golf? . . . Golf? . . . *Why had* she been thinking about golf? . . . *That's right*! Molly's Golf. Molly's Golf in the bottom of the reservoir only now, since Monday, lifted up and out by a tow truck and some divers, according to Joe. Molly's Golf. Molly and David. And what was *that* all about? Molly had done something with the pool man, kissed him, *or worse* – yuck! Which was wrong, *way way wrong*. And *that's* when the pain started, right then, thinking about Molly McLelland who was her godmother! *This* is what had given her the headache! Thinking about Molly McLelland, who could not control herself. Molly McLelland, Alice's best friend, Justin's mother and until now, nice person.

eleven

Harry liked going to the supermarket. He loved its affordability. Walking into Safeway was not like entering a Bang & Olufsen showroom, all look but don't touch. Here, everything was possible, from the cereals aisle all the way through to the newly acquired rambutans and custard apples in the 'Gourmet Greens' section.

Harry also appreciated that the supermarket was the contemporary house of worship, the one place that most members of society routinely frequented to improve their quality of life, sustain their families and even mix and mingle. It was clean here. The staff were neatly attired, the men sporting white short-sleeved shirts and red ties. The customer, generally speaking, was 'it' here. They wanted you. They wanted you badly enough to sell you a jumbo-sized tin of Milo for $4.99, and after a hard day's dealing with recalcitrant young women, it was a relief to stroll beneath the neutral glow of the fluorescent lighting.

As Harry made his way past the oils and vinegars (balsamic, balsamic everywhere!), he could see a young couple up ahead wearing Peruvian goatherding hats, those brightly striped, ear-flapped beanies that had been such a hit at community markets in the seventies. Assorted followers of 'Swami M' up at the ashram were sprinkled among the traditional Sunnyside population of navy-clad little old ladies in fuel-efficient cars, giving Sunnyside the most unusual demographic in the state. Tamsin Wheeler had fallen so deeply under the swami's spell that, according to Molly, she had donated to the ashram a fair chunk of the inheritance she had received from her father, the millionaire importer of ChupaChup lollypops that had proven such a hit with heroin addicts. Swami M had Tamsin to thank for the new renovation of the sprawling white weatherboard building in which devotees did yoga, meditation and general spiritual intercourse with the guru from Queens. Said Alice, via Molly, the swami had re-invigorated the Wheelers' marriage and Tamsin had dropped eleven kilos.

Slowly, the image of Olivia Mathers was fading from Harry's mind. When strolling the Safeway aisle, it was hard to feel vulnerable to anything really perilous.

The problem, if he would admit it, was that the apparent aggravation Olivia had introduced to his life was not entirely unwelcome. Harry had been pretending to himself (and to certain colleagues in the department) that she was simply a blip on the smooth plains of his professional existence. But the truth was that he felt a strange buzz whenever she was around. She was irritating and yet he found himself strangely elated after their confrontations. It was his own reaction that was unnerving.

Harry moved down the aisle and attempted to distract himself with the plethora of choices offered up by the refrigerated section. *This* was therapy, the happy muzak-infused atmosphere of a grocery emporium. He could feel himself moving back into the domestic sphere. Only vaguely buzzing at the edge of Harry's contentment was the awareness that since their dinner party, the sweet dependability of this world had been compromised.

Harry chose a large pack of skinless chicken fillets on red-spot special. It was a pleasant sensation to find that your one designated purchase had the red sticker attached, although this could be counteracted by his memory of reading somewhere that there were so many hormones pumped into chickens these days that six-year-old girls were growing breasts. It was almost enough to send you running for the dried pulses aisle.

A disembodied voice said loudly in his left ear, 'Don't tell me, Nigella's Green Curry?'

It was Colin Vintner, the annoying American rich person. Harry and Alice kept meeting him and his wife at other people's parties. They were approaching the social crisis point of having to invite the Vintners over themselves, to camouflage the fact that they were only friends by proxy. Harry had the distinct feeling that while he didn't much like Colin, Colin quite liked him, an act of resolute superiority.

'Hello Colin!' Harry's voice boomed, amplified with artificial goodwill. It wasn't exactly that he didn't like Colin. He was just so unbelievably *nice*. To be that nice and that rich could only be read as an act of aggression. Colin and Rita were originally from California. In fact, the first time Harry and Alice had met them, Rita had said, 'We hail from Santa Barbara', a phrase so buoyantly offered, so uppity up!, that Alice and Harry used it on each other as a private joke. Colin and Rita had somehow made their way from Santa Barbara to Sunnyside some ten years earlier and started up Vintners Paints, a boutique heritage paint company that sold shades such as Sage Twist and Autumnal Soiree. The last time they had met, at the Mayhews' Easter drinks, Colin had told Harry that there were now thirty-six official shades of white. On the way home, Harry had said to Alice that there were also thirty-six official shades of rich arsehole.

'Listen, Rita and I are having drinks tomorrow night. Nothing fancy. If you've nothing else on, you should come.'

You *should* come. Not, Harry noticed, 'we'd like you to come'. You *should* come, as if there was something in it for us. Still, they did have nothing else on, as a matter of fact, and only last week Alice had said she thought it was time they had some new friends, 'broadened their circle', she had said. And Harry realised he was beginning to sound pathetic, even to himself. It was the paranoia of a middle-aged academic living in the midst of people who thought less and earned more, and knowing this did nothing to assuage it.

The only reason he and Alice owned such a great house in Sunnyside was because Alice's father had left them a few hundred thousand at the right time. Whereas the reason Colin and Rita Vintner owned an even better house was because they had sold several thousand vats of Oatmeal Crumble, aka fawn, to fancy housing developments in the eastern suburbs, inspiring a wave of changing domestic palettes. Paint was the business to be in. Bored housewives, magazine stylists, gay men . . . they were paintaholics. The whole feature wall thing was undergoing a revival, too. Entire communities were rushing out to buy a tin of Hazy Shiraz.

'That sounds great. What time?'

'Say, seven? You know where we are? Right around the corner from the Club. Big hedge. You can drive in.'

Big hedge. Big house. Big fucking car. Harry had to resist the temptation to unload on Colin, deposit before him the full contents of his afternoon. Harry wanted Colin to know that, despite comparative impecunity, he held the future of young women in the palm of his hand.

'We'll look forward to it. Say hi to Rita for me.'

'She's at Dunes with the girls.' Colin just perceptibly tilted his head and raised his eyes as if to say, 'Women!'

Rita. Rita reminded Harry of some actress, some actress who was moderately famous and had recently 'gone off' in the attraction stakes. Like that one Tom Cruise was married to before Our Nic. Big hair, big jaw, earthy. Rita Vintner. No doubt throwing down a cosmopolitan at this very moment, surrounded by other Sunnyside forty-something yummy-mummies at Dunes by the Beach, making cynical asides about their men, possibly even discussing what they were like in bed. What a salad-fest that would be. Rocket coming out of their diamond-studded ears. How many decades had it been since grown women ate something cooked?

Harry rolled his eyes companionably back at Colin, uniting them for just a moment. He found himself wondering what Colin was like in bed. Almost certainly incredible. Viagra-free and not a care in the world. Certainly, the biggest aphrodisiac for a man was money. His own. If Harry banked Colin's profits, he'd have a permanent hard-on.

Harry dawdled over the salad leaves as Colin made his way towards the checkout. Baby spinach, wild rocket, baby Asian, pre-mixed Caesar . . . Things had really got out of hand. Once upon a time, Iceberg had said all there was to say. Eskimos had four hundred words for snow or something and Westerners had seventy-three words for lettuce. Harry looked up for a last glance, somehow wanting to capture the moment . . . Colin Vintner from behind, making his way across the wide expanse of shiny white linoleum.

Harry noticed, with satisfaction, that Colin was carrying a large frozen pineapple pizza. You couldn't buy taste.

The front door slammed behind Harry as he walked through the hall and into the family room.

'Hello, hello.'

'Daddydaddydaddydaddydaddy!'

Grace hurled herself towards Harry, arms askew, sending the chicken fillets across the hall. From the kitchen, Harry could hear the distracted tones of Alice on the telephone and the muffled rhythmic sounds of the television. He bent to kiss the top of Grace's head.

'How was school, Gracie?'

Grace let go of him. As he retrieved the chicken and entered the kitchen Grace returned holding the large red cardboard project on nutrition she'd been working on. It featured a collage of magazine photographs of food stuffs and Grace's spidery handwritten 'Suggested menu from the five main food groups'.

Joe looked up briefly from the television. 'Hi Dad.'

Before Harry could respond, Joe's gaze had shifted back to the screen. Harry put down his satchel and coat, took his sweater from the chair and pulled it on. Alice had lit the fire. The redwood was tinder dry and putting out enormous heat. Home and hearth. Cooking smells. Wife on phone. Lawn newly mown by hired help. Children bouncing and welcoming. He leant over the armchair and kissed Joe on the top of his silky head. Alice was looking at him, rolling her over-large eyes conspiratorially as she said, 'Uh-uh . . . Oh, absolutely . . . Absolutely! . . . I know . . . That's exactly right.'

Harry flicked through the pile of mail on the kitchen bench and noted an invitation to a new show by his sister, Rachel. Luckily, on the other side of the country and therefore avoidable. The work featured on the invitation appeared to Harry to be a front-loader washing machine three times larger than an actual one, with a realistic papier-mâché three-dimensional girl inside it, peering out of the circular glass door. *What a waste of time*. As an educated liberal he had no choice but to defend contemporary art, but really so much of it was astonishing shit. Did the artists actually believe in their work or was it just some colossal hoax? It was a crying shame all those bad artists hadn't gone into medical research. Surely the world would be a better place with a few less decapitated cows in formaldehyde lying around the public art galleries.

Harry noticed that Alice had already opened the bottle of wine. That was something only forty-something women did. Not wait. He poured himself a glass. On the television, the hard-faced beauty who had reputedly been flown one night by Greg Norman to his penthouse in Queensland on a private jet was aggressively interviewing a woman accused of shooting her plumber. Harry felt cosy. Outside their house and down the street and out of Sunnyside and up the highway and through the city and beyond the airport and over the seas was a place where modern life ran rampant, where people shot each other in drive-by shootings and neo-Nazis daubed swastikas on synagogues. Guiltily, Harry was aware that the older a man got, it seemed, the higher he wanted to build his fence.

At forty, Alice sat awkwardly in the final days of imagined youth. Middle age could not really be delayed any longer. Harry looked over at her still hovering by the sink, peeling a potato with the phone receiver wedged between ear and shoulder. She looked great, but she looked forty. Frankly, she looked better now than she ever had, except for her breasts, which were smaller than they had been in her twenties, shrunk by breastfeeding. One good thing about being American, reflected Harry, would be that your wife almost certainly would have raised the topic of implants by now. A smart man would know how to diplomatically acquiesce to this, while appearing to be opposed. But still, Alice was beautiful. The beauty of young women was over-subscribed. Ironically, it was in mothers that beauty seemed undiscovered. Harry had always found experience sexually exciting. The deepening of a woman made her more of a conquest. All these years later, it still seemed a miracle that he had won her.

Grace had joined Joe in front of the TV, lying flat on the carpet, her legs raised at right angles, leaning on the chair. Harry thought about telling Joe that this program about the sheep was not appropriate viewing, but frankly, it would draw attention to the fact that Grace, despite being younger, was more than able to handle the brutality of the current-affairs world, where kleptomaniacs and shonky builders and paedophiles stalked the streets. Grace seemed to have no innocence at all. Joe stood up and threw down the remote control. He was a self-censor, knew well how much he could stand. Next to him, Grace seemed like an unempathetic little minx, nothing much bugged her, nothing much got to her. You couldn't help but admire her.

The receiver slammed down and Alice exclaimed, 'It's over. David's exploded.'

Grace's attention was diverted from the television. 'Who's exploded? David who?'

'Nothing,' said Alice.

'*Actually* exploded? Which David? David and Molly David?'

'Can I talk to your father in peace?'

'Why shouldn't I know? *Which* David?'

Alice looked at Harry as if it was all his fault that Grace had aural comprehension, that David knew, that Molly had something to tell.

'*Je pense que la mariage est complètement finito*' said Alice, taking a sip of her wine. '*Il dit que* she could just get out and take her *vêtements* with her. *Il est très, très triste.*'

'*Bien sûr, il est triste*,' said Harry, because he could.

'Why are you speaking in French? What can't I know?' said Grace furiously.

'We are discussing private matters, young lady. And I would appreciate it if you got into the bath, which is getting cold as we speak.'

Grace flung the remote down and ran out of the room. 'Is this *our* house or *your* house? Are these public spaces or what?'

Harry looked at Alice. 'How does she know about "public spaces"?'

Harry was frightened of Grace. Females were utterly and completely mysterious. It wasn't their chaotic, whimsical creativity that Harry found so frightening, but rather their excessive rationality. The whole cliché of women being instinctive weirdos, full of their own crazy logic, just didn't add up. The terror of women was that they were so switched on.

'Why were you so long?' said Alice, drizzling the potato chunks with olive oil.

'Colin Vintner stopped me at Safeway. Invited us for drinks tomorrow.'

She threw in a handful of rosemary leaves and swivelled the baking tin. 'Obviously someone couldn't come.'

'What?'

'We're the B list. You're not invited the day before a party unless several bus-loads of A-listers have declined.'

Harry nodded. As usual, Alice was way ahead of him in social code-breaking.

'Do we care?' asked Harry.

'B-listers can't afford to care,' said Alice. 'What was Colin Vintner buying?'

'Frozen pizza.'

'How's Rita?'

'She was at Dunes. With the girls. Eating rocket.'

'Which girls?'

'He didn't submit a list. Would you like me to ask him to fax one over?'

Alice passed Harry a serving plate with pâté and rice crackers.

'What did women eat before rocket? Answer me that.'

'So we're going?' said Alice, eating an olive.

'It would be rude not to. I said we would.'

'Great, okay, fine, all right, but then we'll *have* to have them back. Just so you know.'

Harry still had difficulty with the dinner-party code. He could endure some people in a passive kind of a way (their house, their catering), but they were not necessarily people he looked forward to entertaining on his own terrain and at his own expense. Even the thought of the Vintners coming over sent Harry's mind into a frenzy of prospective home-maintenance projects.

'So that means we're getting on the circuit with the Vintners?'

'Correct,' said Alice as she refilled her glass.

'So that would be: us, them, us, them, until . . . ?'

'One of us dies,' said Alice.

Harry flopped into the armchair in front of the fireplace. It was like some horrible treadmill. Once you got on you were trapped for a lifetime, sharing tapenade and sparkling shiraz with people you had not much more in common with than a neighbourhood.

'What happened with the obnoxious girl? Did you talk to her?'

'Yes, I did.' Harry bit into some pâté on a cracker. 'I actually think I handled it rather well. I was firm. But I was fair. Turns out she's got some hard-luck story. The usual. She's one of those good-looking girls who actively try to uglify themselves. Someone needs to get her into a pink cardigan and heels.'

'You're showing your age.'

Harry smiled pleasantly. 'All men like girls in pink cardigans. A man wants to see something he can mess up.'

'Do you want to mess her up?'

'And how, baby.'

Harry felt a sudden wave of uncensored desire. He and Alice hadn't made love for . . . what was it? Months. They had fallen out of the pattern. Tiredness. That day in the rain changing the tyre, when he'd asked Alice to marry him, who knew that fatigue would be the biggest threat to a marriage? That dopey little aggressor was love's number one enemy.

'Are you kicking her out?'

'She's got one last chance. If she blows it, she's gone.'

It was important for a man to be occasionally tough, intractable. Most husbands could no longer display authority with their wives or even their children. They were too frightened they'd be laughed at.

twelve

Harry poured himself a quick second G-and-T while waiting for Alice. Waiting for Alice was a necessary ritual, the preface to any social event. Scarlett and Grace were playing Connect Four on the rug in front of the fire. Harry felt awkwardly well-dressed and shiny. The Vintners' place would be full of well-dressed shiny people, so he should relax. In order to relax, he needed the gin and tonic. In the back of his mind was the irritating hum of medical warnings about alcohol becoming a prop. Harry was still of an age where he worried more about fat than illness. As long as he didn't develop a gut, that was the main thing. In the distance he could hear the click-click of Alice's heels on the timber floor of their bedroom.

Scarlett puzzled Harry. She was to all intents and purposes an excellent babysitter, since she was cheap and smart and required no chauffeuring. They had known Scarlett for eighteen months, since they had first moved in, and she had always impressed them with her academic achievements and her air of quiet intent. She was nobody's pushover. Somehow she had managed to avoid her appalling mother's air of suburban vulgarity, expressed largely in her twee domestic accessories, the hedges clipped into the shape of reindeer at the start of the festive season, the Diana dolls, the Swiss-chalet birdhouse in the front yard. There was no signs of twee-ness in Scarlett. On the contrary, she was twee-free.

And yet there *was* something a little unnerving about her intensity, her combination of silence, intelligence and proximity. She was *always there*. Every time Harry came home, Scarlett seemed to be arriving or leaving, having a hit with Joe on the court, showing Alice her exceptionally original English assignments. They had become her home away from home, only her own home was barely twenty metres away, over the ti-tree fence. Harry kept waiting to find out something else about Scarlett. That she was a scientologist or a haemophiliac, or something Not Very Sunnyside. Presumably there was some piece of information that would *explain everything*. The other disturbing thing about Scarlett, long documented in the Haskins household, was her apparent disdain for eating. And sometimes Harry found her staring at him or at Alice, a stare that seemed, somehow, *analytical*. It was not right, thought Harry, for a man to be analysed by a seventeen-year-old babysitter. This would not be so disturbing but for the fact that whatever Scarlett was thinking about him was almost certainly accurate.

Alice arrived in the kitchen looking good and clutching a small beaded bag. *New and unremarked upon by Alice and therefore almost certainly very expensive.*

'*Who* are we wearing?' Once, Harry and Alice had laughed together over a *New Yorker* cartoon of a heavy breather asking the woman on the phone who she was wearing. Now Harry always invoked it before they went out.

'We are wearing Martin Grant,' said Alice, unruffled.

'Doesn't sound very *haute*,' said Harry, 'he could be a geography teacher.'

'Yes,' said Alice, 'but he isn't.' She surveyed the room, blew a kiss in the direction of the television.

'We're late,' said Harry.

'Molly called right when I was getting in the shower. She wanted to know who I was wearing, too.'

Harry smiled. His clever wife.

'You guys be good for Scarlett, okay?'

Harry kissed Joe on the forehead.

Alice said, 'There's stuff in the pantry. Be sensible. Scarlett, help yourself to anything, you know that.'

Scarlett waved from the sofa. 'I'll be fine, I ate before I came.'

'*Right*,' said Grace.

Alice said from the doorway, 'The number's by the phone. The Vintners. But Harry has his mobile. We won't be late.'

Grace ran to Harry and hugged him. 'Daddy, please, please, please, PLEASE can I ride my bike to school?'

'Haven't we already had this discussion?'

'Yes, but you told me to talk to Miss Pressfield and she said I could sit for the bike licence next Thursday. And that means it's all right by the school. Why do you want to hold me back?'

'I don't want to hold you back, Gracie.'

'Yes, you do! You do! You *are* holding me back! My own school principal says it's all right and for some totally incomprehensible reason you will not let me grow up!'

Harry smiled. 'Don't tell me I'm incomprehensible!'

On the sofa, Joe was rolling his eyes.

'Honestly, I know what I'm doing, Dad!'

Harry looked at Alice, who shrugged.

'Well, I guess if you get it Thursday you could ride on Friday. But if I find out that you have not followed the rules I will be very unhappy.'

'OH MY GOD OH MY GOD OH MY GOD OH MY GOD! I CAN RIDE I CAN RIDE I CAN RIDE!'

Grace was spinning around the room, like a dying bee. As Alice and Harry made their way to the car in the drive, they could still hear her shrieks of happiness.

Alice was wearing a becoming little black dress with pleats that had cost roughly the equivalent of a discount fare to Europe. She was running her finger around her lips, checking for smudges in the car mirror, as Harry drove through Sunnyside. Harry hoped they weren't overdressed. He was wearing his blue suit and a good thick weave blue-check Italian shirt, but no tie. He looked good in a suit and there wasn't much call to wear them on campus.

'Don't say anything to Molly about what she told me,' said Alice. 'I don't want her to think that everything she tells me I tell you.'

'But you do tell me everything.'

Alice said nothing. Harry wondered what Alice didn't tell him. Was it stuff he wanted to know? Should know? Probably not. Women just didn't believe in filters. They wanted the full experience, short black. A man's wellbeing depended on a good filter system. Happy marriages knew this.

Harry was driving at the speed limit, passing through the village and up Mountain Road towards the Club. The oval of Shellforth Academy was empty. All the boarders would be inside drinking hot chocolates and drawing swastikas on their forearms in felt-tip. The immaculate grounds were a constant reminder to less affluent parents of exactly what they were denying their offspring. Club Med with a curriculum. This was where little Sunnyside folk ran around with hockey sticks and basketballs, on their way to careers in law or medicine and blue-chip share portfolios.

The houses were starting to get bigger, the blocks wider, the fences more elaborate. There were more and more hand-built stone fences. Stone masonry must be on an upswing. Harry wondered what it would be like to be out all day, laying rocks. No campus politics. No interminable meetings. No Olivia Mathers with her long knee-socks. Just sky and rock and fresh air. A man and the eucalypts. It would be nice to feel you really *deserved* that alcohol at the end of the day.

The Vintners' driveway was circular like their own, only the Vintners' was *perfectly* circular. At its centre was a cast-iron fountain of two dolphins that appeared to Harry to be mating. The garden was so over-landscaped it was hard to think of it as garden, exactly. Even the borders had borders. It looked like some kind of horticultural boardgame.

Around the pebble driveway was an assortment of European vehicles. Harry thought about the Ford Falcon station wagon his parents had owned, state-school green and seatbelt free. Alice's parents had had the same, one of those spooky coincidences which furnished their union. Those were the days. Excellent for the drive-in. They'd all pack in, Harry and Rachel dressed in flannelette pyjamas with space rockets. Now you couldn't see the screen for the front seat headrests. Obviously, the drive-in was not big in Oslo. Now, they all drove cars with electronics designed by NASA. Last year, when their locking mechanism had broken, they had been told that a new alarm system had to be flown from Sweden. Globalisation had a lot to answer for.

Harry backed the Saab out and parked on the street, ready for a fast getaway. There were at least twenty cars parked in the environs. Quite a little shindig. Their own Saab, Harry noticed, was a good three years older than the rest.

'My God, if someone cashed in these vehicles, we could feed Sudan,' he said.

'He says driving a Saab,' said Alice.

'An *old* Saab. It had already done thirty thousand ks when we bought it.'

'Oh, okay,' said Alice. 'That makes all the difference.'

Rita Vintner was wearing a short, red, strapless cocktail dress, which revealed a tanned chest just noticeably starting to pucker. It looked as if she'd ironed it on too hot a temperature. Beneath her armpits, little folds of skin flopped over the edge of the dress. Harry could see the pointless excitement of a sixteen-year-old in Rita's face, now looking positively Botoxed, all smooth and vaguely masculine and tanned like a famous Belgian tennis champion. Despite the dress, she had the sexiness of a woman who looked *vigorous*. Harry wondered if she and Colin still excited each other. Something invisible, unplaceable about their energy together suggested that they were still trying to please.

Colin was upon them, kissing Alice on both cheeks, taking their coats and handing them to the hovering staff, ushering them into the sitting room, which stretched backwards through a large tiled atrium to the back garden, technicolour green, with matching vine-clad pergolas at either end, painted, clearly, in Vintner's paints. Harry heard Alice say, 'What a gorgeous place!' as Colin whisked her off towards the bar. Alice didn't consider social lying *lying*.

The sitting room was French Provincial. There were earthenware pots on either side of the huge fireplace holding cumquats sculpted into lollypops, and the room was large enough to take several group-ings of sofas in blues and yellows, huddled cosily around coffee tables that had no doubt been fashioned from authentic French agricultural equipment – grape tubs or harvesting implements. Sometimes, dur-ing the Sunnyside festive season, Alice wondered if there was actually any French Provincial furniture left in the French provinces.

The parquet floor shone with wax, the champagne bottles clinked, the sound system was blowing something mellow for forty-somethings. Fresh-faced young women in ponytails and long black aprons bearing trays of oysters with ginger and lime juice in Chi-nese spoons glided amongst the fifty or so animated and mostly familiar faces. The women were fit from Pilates and tennis, the men less so, but the guests had in common a generic attractiveness, which, Alice reflected, was more about good dentistry and a sense of effortless entitlement than genetic good fortune.

Jim Pickworth, Harry's squash partner, was in a huddle with

Dale Carmichael, famous for the theft of two small Picassos from his Sunnyside den by his mentally imbalanced socialite daughter-in-law, and Alistair Wigg, who had started with the Rock Ridge drive-in and was now building a twelve-cinema multiplex in Deptford. Alistair Wigg had a Mercedes four-wheel drive with a sticker that said: 'The only true wilderness is between a Greenie's ears'. Harry made his way towards them, collecting a beer from a passing tray.

'Just talking about the property prices,' said Jim. 'You know Dale, don't you?'

'Yes,' said Harry, 'Toby and Joe are in the same year.'

'Can't believe what that double-storey fifties weatherboard got down the beach end of Ocean View. I remember we looked at it when we moved to Sunnyside. They wanted three hundred then,' said Alistair.

'Nine-fifty,' said Jim. 'And that's just for the land. Posy and Redmond Gullifer bought it and they're demolishing. They're doing something in mudbrick. *Oxagonal*.'

Harry felt good to be there, to be included. It was socialising Business Class. Only once in a while did he have to shrug off a vague sense of defensiveness when surrounded by people who asked, several times a year, whether he was 'still teaching?'. It seemed crass even to acknowledge it, but here your worth was directly assessed by the income you generated. Ten years before it would have applied only to the men, but the women now counted; in some cases they kept their husbands in ski trips. There were a few corporate lawyers amongst the hausfraus, the odd celebrity interior decorator, even a cosmetics queen.

Alice had moved off towards the huddle of women talking by the fire, including a furry little woman in a purple smock who, Harry vaguely remembered, taught yoga. Or did he make that up? The purple smock was confusing. She was either one step ahead of all the other women, or twenty years behind. Next to the smock was Molly. Infidelity was clearly not going to cramp her social schedule. Maybe David was at home, nursing his wounds, cleaning the pool now that the pool man had better things to do, like screw his wife. But Harry scanned the room and saw David in the corner talking to the short guy who did something with office furniture. Built it? Sold it? Something that had bought him a BMW convertible with a lot of leg room but, happily, could not furnish him with five more centimetres of leg. David was holding his glass of beer as if it were for someone else. It was hard to know if he and Molly had come separately as independent acts of social defiance, or together as a possibly overambitious show of civility. Molly was wearing a short blue dress that showed off her excellent legs. There was something about Molly that reminded Harry of a French political wife. She was so small and dark and well put together, as if she'd just been removed from packaging. Harry remembered when he and

Molly could have conversations about the European Union or Kazuo Ishiguro. Now, it was impossible. Now, Molly's tanned shoulders and swollen lips removed her from the world of unexcited friendship. It was impossible to ignore the insistent thought that Molly was distinctly fuckable and sexually *busy*.

Harry lifted a spoon from the tray and gulped down the oyster – slippery, salty – replaced the spoon and grinned at the pretty waitress. Across her apron top was embroidered the name of the catering company: Little Red Courgette.

'That must be heavy!'

Harry saw David extract himself from Mr Office Furniture and move through the room towards him. He felt a momentary panic, trying to recollect how much he was allowed to know about Molly. What had Alice told him to pretend he didn't know? Harry wished that he could avoid the whole subject. If David didn't raise it, Harry would just behave as if everything was hunky-dory.

David's face was stricken. He still had something of a surfer's body though, good biceps, relics from youth. He'd been trying to get Harry to go on a surfing holiday for middle-aged men, their original orange-kombi vans now replaced by Audi station wagons. Now that old people stayed young, surfing had become the new golf. Harry had declined. He had no desire to reclaim his youth or smoke pot with a bunch of barristers in boardshorts.

'Well,' said Harry.

The two men paused, giving the weight of marriage its one-minute silence. Around them, the room seemed to sway with ignorant happiness, something Harry desperately wanted, in this moment, to be a part of. But friendship required certain tedious compromises. Not knowing what else to do, Harry clapped David on the back in what he hoped was a sweet, blokey kind of way.

'You holding up?'

'Well, you know,' said David. 'It's. Hard.'

Harry realised he had to rally. Friends had to offer comfort, offer salvation, but by God it was difficult when you were surrounded by trays of canapes, by tinkling music, by fake fires, by women in high heels. Life just kept moving on. Wives waited for no man. Pool men overran the suburbs, pool men and garden maintenance guys, they were everywhere. An army of tanned, ordinary men kept eggheads like Harry oblivious in their towers. Pools got cleaned, edges whipper-snippered, roses pruned, filters replaced. Things were humming. The stay-at-home wives sat in their family rooms looking out of plate-glass windows at men with machines, foreign men, paid men, crossing their green lawns, issued with visas to the family compound. They could say what they liked, but in the end, women liked it when men tackled problems, took responsibility. Women liked men who could start chainsaws, who could fix a tennis net. You couldn't reprogram the human race, the biological imperative.

'She's going to come to her senses.'

David took a long gulp of his beer. 'I'm in love with her.'

'Of course you are. *Of course you are!* She's a great woman. You're a great team!'

David looked as if he was about to sob.

'You two are going to get through this!'

It came out sounding like an order. Perhaps that was what Harry was doing, ordering David to uphold the institution of marriage lest an epidemic of infidelity run rampant over the lanes and courts and crescents of Sunnyside.

Across the room, Harry could see Alice staring at them. Her eyes were round and agitated, sending a query over the room, not exactly sympathetic to his plight, more suspicious. What did Alice want him to say? He wondered what would happen if he told David to just chuck Molly in, put her down to bad luck, move on. I mean, plenty more where she came from, no? Campuses were full of young women who would eventually want to mate. Young women liked men like David, men like Harry, middle-aged men, just old enough to make boys look stupid, just young enough to still have promise. Frankly, this whole scenario was back to front, thought Harry. It was women like Molly who should require comfort, who should need to be talked out of paranoia. Throughout the Western world, wasn't it the women who were weeping over vanishing husbands? Wasn't it the men who, after lying dormant for years, suddenly sniffed death one day, mingled with the scent of backyard jasmine and heat beads, and set off in search of a comely antidote? He should shake David by his tweedy shoulders and tell him to get a life! Be a man!

Over David's shoulder, Harry noticed that Alice had repositioned herself, so that she could keep her eyes on him.

'No,' said David. He had an unsettling intensity in his eyes. 'No, we won't get through this, Harry.'

David's eyes reminded Harry of that other world, the world of Serious Incident. He had visited the world of Serious Incident a few times in the past – his mother's death, those moments when a tiny mauve Grace had the cord wrapped around her neck, an early, seemingly final fight with Alice – and he had no desire to return there or even to be reminded of its existence. That world, with its blood-pumping speediness, its wakefulness, its lack of hunger, was simply too invigorating. Far better to live in the half-light of ordinary contentment, even if it meant boredom. For Harry, boredom was, in its own way, enchanting.

'I'm *fucked*.'

'You're here together. That's something,' said Harry lamely, wishing he could be outside with the smokers, whose yelps of laughter he could make out over the music. They were obviously laughing about something delightfully meaningless, thought Harry, or if not meaningless, then at least abstract. Abstraction was really the name of the game when it came to having fun. It was really bad luck to belong to the age when the personal was king. Once upon a time at social gatherings, one could successfully depend upon the personal being avoided at all costs. Now, unfortunately, it was a wellspring of intercourse.

'You know she's still seeing him.'

Harry had to make a split-second decision about whether he was allowed to know that or not. Suddenly the two beers he had drunk quickly and the gin he'd had before leaving the house caught up with him. He was too tired to lie. Alice was at least five metres away and it was a relief just to accept the consequences of his own possible social breaches.

Harry nodded. He was in danger of coming across as disengaged. It was almost certainly bad to eat in the middle of David's confession, but in the throes of spontaneous self-approval, Harry grabbed a fresh asparagus roll from a passing tray.

'It's a real shame,' he said, launching into it.

Harry wondered if Molly had fucked the pool man in the house, in David's house. Presumably, yes. The convenience factor. And women could be tough. One minute they were buying expensive fabric to recover the ottoman, their houses their temples, the next minute they were defiling their interiors with aroused members of the service industry. How did it ever happen that women got the high ground?

'What kind of action can a man take?' said David. 'What's left?'

'My guess is, that it'll all blow over by Christmas. She'll realise that she's just . . . bored. That you and she share something that can't be . . . extinguished.'

'That's a good word,' said David miserably, 'an excellent word. Extinguished.'

Harry thought that it was possibly a mistake to use a word that poetic. David needed real advice. Solid advice. Who knew, maybe Harry would need advice one day. He wouldn't want to hear words that evoked the soul . . . extinguished.

'Harry, this is the thing. We understand that anything can happen, that things just come right around the corner and slam into us. We're not stupid people, any of us. We know that breast cancer or a car smash or a retrenchment or a plane in a tower is only a heartbeat away. We understand that in just a second, everything that feels steady and complete can be pulverised. *But the understanding doesn't change anything!* You'd think that the knowledge of this would lead us all into other kinds of lives, appreciating, you know, *stuff*. The way the buds emerge this time of year. The way a baby starts to talk. The way your wife looks in a normal moment, beautiful. These things should be at the heart of our experience, *but they're not!* Why is that? What's wrong with us, that we slip into greed and banality and prejudice and superficiality *at every available opportunity*?'

David lowered his voice and moved so close to Harry's face that Harry could smell the strangely pleasant whiff of wine and mints.

'Look at this room, Harry! The party's been thrown by two

137

people who love each other! What do they need caterers for? *Why do they need a forty-foot pergola?*'

To Harry's discomfort, David hugged him. Over David's huge shoulder, Harry could see Alice looking at him, perplexed. Harry managed to put his beer down on the side table behind David and return the hug. Clearly, the only way to end the hug was to recognise it. Suddenly the music became softer and Colin Vintner's voice punctuated the buzz of the room.

'Folks! Gather round if you please!'

Thank Christ, thought Harry. Conversations drifted off into giggles and anticipation. David set Harry free and the room shifted its focus onto Colin, a medley of cashmeres in earth tones, who had positioned himself beside the fire.

Alice suspected that Harry was getting quietly drunk. She had seen David hugging Harry. Hopefully, it was under control. This was not the right place for an epiphany. Molly had moved off to talk to Alistair Wigg's wife, Julie, who was wearing the famous pearls, the ones Tamsin Wheeler had told Lily that Alistair had *bought from eBay*. However annoying Harry might be at times, at least he didn't buy her jewellery on the internet. Laura McIlroy, the local yoga teacher, who had spent the last fifteen minutes attempting to lure

Alice to one of her yoga classes, had now moved on to Justin.

'Do they eat with the TV on?'

'Do *who* eat?' said Alice.

'The McLellands,' said Laura. 'What I'm saying is, studies have shown that seventy-five per cent of young adult serial killers in the United States eat their dinner in front of the television set.'

'Right,' said Alice. 'Uh-huh. Well, I guess.'

'A family needs to sit down and eat together and *talk*. Those kids shooting up classrooms . . . they're assembling their arsenal in their bedrooms while their parents are upstairs eating by themselves.'

'Well,' said Alice. 'I don't think Justin has an arsenal.'

'I know Molly McLelland is your good friend, Alice. But driving your mother's car into a reservoir is not within the parameters of conventional teenage rebellion.'

'Things like that don't happen here,' said Melissa Wu.

Alice was trying to keep an eye on Harry over Melissa Wu's shoulder. Melissa Wu, the only Asian in Sunnyside, and that was a fact. Did living here make her feel more or less Asian?

'It's all about eating together,' said Laura, refusing to let it go. 'My guess is that Molly and David and Justin McLelland don't eat together *as a family*. I could be wrong, but something has to be done about Justin McLelland before he gets himself a weapon on the internet and takes out Sunnyside village.'

'I'm going to win!'

'Miss Grace, do not be so presumptuous.'

'Whatever *that* means!'

Joe used to like it when his parents went out, because Scarlett would do stuff with him, playing memory or even sardines, hiding in cupboards, tricking Grace. Scarlett hadn't seemed so much a girl, as an accomplice. Some nights, Grace would go to bed and he and Scarlett would eat chocolate biscuits and watch talent shows on TV, voting on the contestants. She was tough, he respected her opinion, it was fun. But in the last few months, Scarlett had gone all weird. She seemed bored with him and Grace, with babysitting, with everything. Alice said that Scarlett was probably under pressure at school now that she was in final year, but Scarlett didn't seem to be under pressure. She didn't bring homework with her, only books with weird names. Right now, a book was sticking out of the top of her slouchy tote bag – *Alpha-Chicks*.

Scarlett was now playing checkers with Grace. She had her elbow on the table supporting her head, which was tilted to the side. Her long red hair was untied. She looked loose and sort of not present, like she was here but not. Grace didn't seem to care, as long as Scarlett kept letting her win. Grace was stupid when it suited her, which only confirmed to Joe how smart she was. When she wanted to think she was winning, she was just a kid, just a dumb kid.

'You are really bad at this, Scarlett!' said Grace, happy, pouncing on Scarlett's black discs, jump, jump, jump.

Scarlett smirked lazily, said nothing, just had her go, then took a sip of water. Plain water. She used to drink Diet Coke, back when she was fun.

Scarlett even looked different. She had grown so pale. She seemed to be shrinking. She didn't eat any of the treats Alice left out. As Grace and Joe devoured the Tim Tams and snowballs, Scarlett would flick through Alice's fashion magazines without interest. She didn't wear trendy clothes any more either. Just oversized cardigans and baggy no-colour pants. Joe thought Scarlett looked more and more like a ghost.

Sometimes Joe could see in Scarlett someone who was one step ahead of him on the way to adulthood, right in the middle of it, awful. He didn't want to be thirteen, he wanted to be where you knew what it was you were. Then you could just be done with it, just learn to be satisfied with what you were. Harry and Alice wanted things for him but maybe he was just programmed differently; deep inside his head, where no parent could reach, a fuse was ready to blow. He had to find *discipline*. He had to be able to control himself, control the outcome of things, not give in so much. Grace just ploughed ahead, forced her way through things, got what she wanted. It worked. It worked to be strong and annoying. The world rewarded people like Grace, people who whined until they got what they wanted, who were always jumping up and down saying: Give me!

'I won I won I won I won!' said Grace, jumping up and throwing herself over the back of the sofa. 'I'm the winner!'

Joe watched Scarlett pack away the game. She was switched off, somewhere else. Scarlett was living her life inside her head, just like him. Maybe Scarlett was trapped inside thoughts that had no place to go. Maybe Scarlett worried about the same things he did.

'Scarlett, do you know about the sheep?'

'The sheep on the boat,' said Scarlett distractedly. 'Oh yeah.'

Scarlett had vanished to him. She had gone. Joe had a sudden vision of Scarlett disappearing behind those electronic doors at the airport. Scarlett and Justin. Both of them had once been allies. Now even Justin was slipping away from him. Once, he and Justin had been practically brothers. They had slept over at each other's houses a million times. They had their own stupid games, Mr Ratchett's Toothbrush and Dead Zombies. They both liked football. When they were little, they used to like the Wiggles. When the Haskins moved to Sunnyside, he and Justin would sit in Grace's tree house and try to scare each other with creepy stories. Their mums were really similar. Between them there was a closeness that came from having parents on the same wavelength. They broke the same rules, obeyed the same rules. But something was changing – *Justin was changing*. There was the car thing, Joe didn't even want to *think*

142

about that. And now Justin was hanging out with different kids, the McLaine kid, who all the parents said was *no good*, and Will Roberts, who was tough. They were into graffiti. Justin wasn't that much older than Joe, but Joe felt like Justin had suddenly gained five years. Once, Joe had snuck out late and watched while Justin and Will signed their names on the newsagency's back wall, giant curvy letters in day-glo. Justin's handwriting stood out. He and Will were good at it, the words held together, looked kind of exciting there on the wall. Next to the proper signs, *Buster* and *Judgement Man* looked mad and real, like they were busting out of something. Joe wanted to like being there, but the night had closed in around him and instead of feeling one of three, he felt separate and cold. He couldn't stop thinking of Mr Perry the newsagent coming to work in the morning and seeing his back wall. He'd be mad. He'd have to get one of those scrapers from Bunnings to get it off, or paint over it. It would be awful for Mr Perry because what could you do? Security cameras would be expensive. He could light it with automated lights, but there were no security guards in Sunny-side village.

Justin's mum and dad were busting up, he'd heard Alice and Harry talking. Stuff about Molly, her going off somewhere, Joe didn't want to know, didn't want to think about Justin's mum that way. He liked thinking of Molly toasting them crumpets after school in their kitchen and teasing Joe in that nice, funny way she had about the size of his feet. If Joe felt that way, imagine how Justin felt. *Molly was his mum.* You believed they'd always be there, toasting crumpets, and then suddenly it was over, they were over, they were *over you*, over the whole thing. What was the point of a kitchen without them, these mothers? The mothers were the lights in the houses. The kids and dads switched them on. Without the mothers, the houses would just be dark and weird. *It would be so totally weird to have your parents split!*

Justin hadn't really talked about it, that was another thing that made Joe feel that Justin was slipping away from him. He wanted to say to Justin: Come back. But he couldn't. Justin would think he was nuts. Boys had to watch what they said.

Joe had gone into his room to reorder his football cards in the new plastic folder that Alice had bought him, which left Scarlett to Grace. When Scarlett was babysitting, Grace wished she didn't have a brother. As things were, Grace felt she had to wait until Joe was out of the picture before she could really, *really* talk to Scarlett.

Scarlett was different. She was not like the girls from the nanny agency, the soft girly-girls her parents occasionally used when Scarlett was unavailable. They were so ordinary with their neat blonde hair and their schoolbooks. They were so respectful of her parents, in that horrible, fake way. Grace knew that Harry and Alice actually liked Scarlett much more than girls like that, because she was *not* so sucky. Scarlett was very smart, Harry had said so. Alice thought Scarlett was beautiful in a strange way. It was hard to know exactly what she meant by that. Alice always saw beauty in faces that were not magazine faces. Sometimes Grace could feel Alice working inside her, feeding her opinions that swallowed up her own. It was hard to know whether to be happy or mad about this. To Grace, Scarlett was magically, mysteriously *herself*.

Grace had fetched herself an icypole from the freezer and they were sitting in front of the television when Scarlett started talking to her properly, the way Grace loved.

'This is for your own good, Grace. I'm telling you something right now. You have to find your passion and then you have to pursue it and don't let anyone stop you.'

Grace was a little confused. What *was* passion, exactly?

'It's something that makes your blood speed up. It's the reason you get up in the morning. It's the thing that goes round and round your brain at night when you're trying to get to sleep!'

'I *know* that feeling!' said Grace.

'You've got a lot to give, Gracie. You can't turn your back on that. You can't let anyone water you down!'

'Why would anyone *do* that, Scarlett?'

'Because some people are threatened by people who have energy, who want to do things. They're jealous. They'll try to drag you down. Especially *men*.'

'Why would men want to drag me down?'

'Because a lot of men don't like women who *do* stuff. They think women should just be quiet and in the background.'

Scarlett was lying on the couch. She was staring straight up at the ceiling. She had beautiful hair, thought Grace, beautiful hair that streamed golden red. She was beautiful without make-up or hair scrunchies or pierced ears.

'You know, my food group project got twenty out of twenty. I was the only one in the class,' said Grace.

'That's really good. But I'm not just talking about your *brain*,' said Scarlett.

Grace was disappointed. She hoped that Scarlett would some-how react more to the news. It seemed to Grace that the invitation to participate in this conversation was proof that she was what Scarlett was wanting her to be. But what did Scarlett mean?

'I'm talking about your *soul*, Gracie. I'm talking about the part of you that is you alone. About knowing what's important. About judging what is right and what is wrong. You have to *own* your own belief system and fight for it.'

Grace had never heard of a belief system before, but it sounded impressive. She didn't know exactly what Scarlett meant, but she *felt* it. Grace knew that greatness was not an easy thing, not always welcomed. It was true what Scarlett said, that sometimes people did not seem to like specialness, it upset them. But that was no reason to give it up. Anyhow, Grace suspected that she could not give up being special even if she wanted to. Like Scarlett, it had a hold of her. She and Scarlett were not so very different.

'I'd like to say how great it is that so many of you folks could make it tonight. Rita and I wanted to have this little get-together as a kind of a thank you . . . well, a kind of *thanksgiving*, to be honest.'

Colin Vintner was glowing in the light of the artificial fire.

'Several years back, Rita and I came to this country looking for a challenge, looking for a new life. Before too long, we managed to put together a little business, a silly little dream of mine. *Paints*. And not just any paints, but paints that gave a hue to the variations of a good life. Paints that didn't just see a blue as a blue, but as an infinite collection of small, individual blues with small, individual meanings. Well, gosh, I don't want to go on about it . . .'

Here Colin looked at Rita and Rita looked fondly at Colin.

'But Vintners Paints has come along nicely since then and we feel that Sunnyside has brought us good luck. Good luck and good fortune. And you all have made us feel right at home. So anyhow, here we are. Rita and I want to say thanks! And here's to more good times! And well, we didn't want to make a big deal out of it, but twelve years ago tonight a different bunch of folks stood in a different room and said, "What the hell does a girl like that see in a fool like him?" We had every damn fight we needed to have in the first twelve months and tonight we've been married twelve years!'

The room swelled with gasps and claps. Everyone was thinking how great it was that they hadn't known it was an anniversary party, since it avoided the usual last-minute dash to Gardener's Paradise for a Japanese maple in a pot with a giant bow. Rita was looking fantastic, swishing through the room to Colin's side. Colin clasped her and kissed her magenta lips. Everyone clapped. Harry suddenly wanted to kiss Rita Vintner on the lips, to have that robust body in his hands. Not so much for the sexual gratification as for the security. She was so optimistic. It must be nice to be physical with someone that sunny. It must be fun having someone that big and cheerful around all the time, like having a golden retriever that could bake.

Down the back, Harry saw Molly whisper something to Alice, who smiled. They could be so superior those two. They were such private-school girls, when you got down to it. Of course that's what Harry had liked about Alice to begin with. Liked and hated.

'Anyhow, it's been a great twelve years and we look forward to the next twelve surrounded by our good friends. Now, keep drinking!'

Everyone laughed and clapped and turned back to their neighbours. The music swelled up again, the trays danced, the anecdotes resumed, the jokes built. Women's make-up started to melt. Straps were falling off shoulders. Harry looked past Alice and suddenly took in the silvery shape on the far wall. At first he thought it was some kind of intercom. Sleek metal and black. He peered harder. The Bang & Olufsen BE984! Harry felt something die inside him, some small light he'd been carrying around, the light of imagined entitlement. Harry had no right to a B&O sound system. Only Colin Vintner had the right. Colin and his Burnt fucking Sienna, his Daydream Moss, his Amber Dawn. Harry looked at Colin Vintner. He was so well groomed, Harry felt he might smudge him just by being near him.

Harry wished, for a moment, that *he* was American. Americans like the Vintners had a core of tight-fisted self-belief. They had a sense of themselves *at the centre* that no Australian could ever have, except perhaps in a pro-tennis championship.

Harry envied this. He envied Americans their *volume*. It seemed to Harry that Australians just didn't quite belong to the land on which they trod their first steps. They tried, but it never felt convincing. Americans, on the other hand, had forgotten that the land was anything *but* theirs. That nation filled the cities and the fields and the suburban malls and the dust bowls, it wrote 'America' across the whole of it. Americans had claimed their land the way a people

149

could only claim territory after they had fought for it. A war cemented things. Maybe blood had to be spilt for the earth itself to be paid for.

Alice looked over at Harry, who seemed to be deep in thought. Alice could tell he was drunk by the way he had abdicated from chitchat. It was poor form, not to say plain *weird*, to stand alone at a cocktail party. She turned her gaze back to Molly who, looking tipsy herself, said, 'What am I going to do? Wake up at sixty and wonder where the hell my life went?'

Molly was beginning to sound repetitive, a missionary for infidelity. She was starting to mythologise herself, thought Alice. She was writing herself a script. The affair had lost its raw energy, the raw, awful energy. It was astonishing how swiftly new news became worn, over-told. Over her shoulder, Alice studied the clusters of Sunnyside men. For just a second she wished she could see, somehow, *into* them: the fledgling dreams, the unspoken sexual predilections, the unforgotten ghosts of their childhoods. It would be thrilling to see beyond their steadfast affability.

There was a vague fixed smile on Harry's face, the implacable smile of resistance, of holding oneself up against an unstoppable force. At one point in Colin's speech, Harry had looked over at her, and for a second they had merged. That was the great comfort of marriage, the agreement to find in one another the collusion that kept you safe, made you feel somehow simultaneously in the minority (special) and authoritative (the last word). A glance between them was enough to furnish them with a pleasant buzz of security, as if the world sat between them, as if the whole world was collected in this coldly perfect room. There they were, each covering a hemisphere, contained and containing, part of it and yet above it, their separateness bearable because they were separate *together*. No matter how trying things might be at home, to venture out was the safeguard of marriage, since in venturing out, one reconnected with ancient intimacies. The strangeness of other people, of other rooms, was enough to persuade a couple of their own belonging.

Moving toward her with a glass of champagne outstretched was the girl who used to go out with Angus Wilstruther, the handsome one who liked sporty girls. *The netballer.* Why was it that Alice could remember Angus Wilstruther after twenty years? There she was, the netballer, right in front of her, a smile stretched tight across her face, a blonde mane layered, and suddenly the name emerged out of the recesses of Alice's mind: Maddie Ridgeway.

'Alice! Alice Beaufort! You look *exactly* the same!'

The two women attempted a small embrace, arms outstretched around the curve of each other's back, the cocktail-party embrace that attempted to hold champagne glasses straight while maintaining warmth and friendliness.

'Hello, Maddie. You look terrific.'

And Maddie did look terrific, even in pale apricot.

'Well, well, well. Don't tell me you're back in these parts!'

'Like everyone else,' said Alice brightly. 'We made the big move back.'

'Well, I never really left,' admitted Maddie. 'I married Angus, a Tintagel boy, more fool me!'

Alice hoped Maddie had at least slept with a few other boys before getting married. Angus had always seemed forty, even when he was sixteen. She wondered if he still looked forty and scanned the room quickly.

'Oh no!' said Maddie. 'He's interstate at a golf masterclass. I'm a golf widow and *loving* it!'

Before they had both gone co-ed, Tintagel had been the brother school to Baybridge Hall, Alice and Maddie's alma mater. Alice had been in the musical co-productions, usually as a milkmaid or a governess. Maddie Ridgeway had been a large but colourless Auntie Mame in one production. Alice could recall her in a leopard-print jumpsuit with a boa, belting out a number. Angus Wilstruther had been her Tintagel equivalent, although there had always seemed something vaguely unhinged about him. In their senior years, there had been an unspoken belief that Tintagel boys and Baybridge girls were the halves of a perfect whole.

'A few Baybridge girls have come back to the nest,' said Maddie, happily. 'Vanessa Banks – *Vanessa Wilkie*! – is teaching PE at Tintagel! Andrea Fidgett – she's Andrea Wigglesworth now – she has Wigglesworth Country Interiors on the corner. Donna Richards is living here, too.' Maddie opened her heavily mascared eyes theatrically and peered around at the groups of men gathered around the room. 'Hoodja Marry!'

'Was she the Indian girl?' said Alice.

'No!' said Maddie with a smile that was positively bi-coastal. '*Who'd you marry?*'

'Oh,' said Alice, 'Harry Haskins. Not a Peninsula boy,' she added apologetically.

Maddie said, 'Clever girl! I always knew you'd catch one outside the pond.'

Alice had a sudden vision of Harry as a small brown frog, one of those sweet ones Joe caught in the swimming pool over winter.

'You had *possibilities*,' said Maddie.

'I don't know about that,' said Alice, embarrassed. It was coming back to her, Maddie Ridgeway's ability to flatter condescendingly.

'You had real possibilities ohyesyoudid. Now where is the handsome Harry?'

'That's him over there talking to David McLelland.'

Alice nodded in their direction. Maddie opened her eyes wide. '*Hello George Clooney!*'

Alice attempted a polite laugh.

'What line is he in?'

'He's an academic,' said Alice.

'*Typical!*' said Maddie. 'Typical Alice Beaufort would get handsome *and* brainy!'

'Do you know David?' asked Alice.

Maddie raised her eyebrows. 'Angus sold them the original Golf. We've got the Seabank dealership.'

The original. The drowning of the Golf had already passed into the domain of the anecdotal. Alice thought she'd somehow known that Angus Wilstruther had sold Molly the Golf. Known and forgotten, as it should be.

'She's already called to price a replacement. She's getting the same model, only in *Arctic*. That lady knows how to move on.'

'I guess she needs a car,' said Alice, feeling that she needed to defend Molly, despite thinking that she *was* moving with unseemly haste.

'After she called, Angus said to me if I get any big ideas, he'll shoot me. He has a licence actually. I said, "I'd shoot you first, honey!"'

It made perfect sense to Alice that Angus Wilstruther had a gun licence. He probably had a shed full of anthrax, too.

'Frankly, I think Molly's a pioneer around here. She's sending a message to the husbands that we can mess with them the way they mess with us. You know what I'm saying? I'm no feminist. I can't stand those women who think holding on to your facial hair means you're not a walkover. But in the end, men need *us* more than we need *them*. And anyone thinks any differently just needs to take one look at David McLelland.'

They both turned to take in David's face across the room, at that moment uncannily, perfectly desperate.

Maddie moved closer to Alice. She stared at Alice as if she was trying to read her. 'How about lunch some time? But let's do it. Let's *really* do it!'

Alice made her way across the room towards Harry. It was always around this time that her mother's words came to her, words about getting out before things started to fray. Arrive on time. *Leave early*. Alice moved past the huddles of laughing guests delaying the inevitable return trip, the loneliness of coupledom. Edging past them, Alice was enveloped in the surreal poetry of collated, random conversations: *Palermo was terribly sinister/The Chinese kids leave ours for dead/Just for starters, six airbags*. Harry was leaning against the bookcase, all alone and smiling at her, a tipsy, roguish smile, as if he'd known she was coming before she did.

'Frowsy Suburbanites,' said Harry.

'What, us?' said Alice, removing the glass from his hand.

'The colour of the walls,' said Harry, 'Frowsy Suburbanites. Fawn with an edge. And the skirtings are in Gruesome Affluence.'

'You really don't deserve me, Harry.'

'Believe me,' said Harry, taking her hand, 'I'm the first to agree.'

thirteen

Grace had fallen asleep with her lamp on. In Joe's room, Scarlett lifted the yellow eiderdown that had slipped onto the floor and covered him. Joe was getting that musky smell that took hold of kids flirting with the teens. His eyelids flickered, long lashes trembling. He was travelling to places Scarlett couldn't visit. People never knew what they looked like, asleep. It gave Scarlett the creeps to think of someone looking at her sleeping. How could married people bear it?

Scarlett turned off the light, left the door ajar and walked into Alice and Harry's bedroom. It glowed with bedside lamplight. Everything was in its place. *Harpers & Queen* on Alice's bedside table and a copy of Vikram Seth's newest novel. Classy. On Harry's side there was a book by a handsome French guy about philosophy and a *New Yorker*. Scarlett was careful to replace things just the way she found them, she wasn't stupid. Sometimes she fingered Alice's clothes, because the fabrics were so incredible and pure and real.

Alice colour-coded her wardrobe. It was all fawns and navies and blacks and browns with just a couple of really wild multicoloured silk cocktail frocks like the ones you saw those rich English girls in *Harpers* wear at Lord Feathersport-Lockbridge's twenty-first. Girls in two-thousand-pound dresses staring at the camera with that ecstasy glaze. Scarlett wondered how different she would be if she'd been born one of those Charlottes or Sophies, with a pony or six. Would she still be Scarlett?

Alice's shoeboxes had polaroids of the shoes attached so she knew how to find them fast. It was hard to put them together with her all-cotton undies, but then, on thinking about it, all-cotton undies were actually incredibly stylish. Hanging in the dressing room was a fawn cashmere robe with a hood. Scarlett had seen in it on weekend mornings. Alice in her robe, somehow graceful and unencumbered. She had managed to escape that haunted look that mothers often got. Her own mother tried to disguise it with Estée Lauder foundation, but Alice was often make-up free and somehow still smooth and beautiful. When she had been flicking through a *Who* magazine with Grace one Saturday afternoon, they had studied a pictorial essay on celebrity tattoos and Alice had said, *Scarlett, never get a tattoo. You have a beautiful body, do not defile it.* Scarlett had been shocked to be told she had a beautiful body. But Alice seemed to mean it and Alice would know. Now whenever Scarlett saw Alice, every time she babysat, or saw her pulling the rubbish bins in from the street, *every single time*, she remembered that Alice thought she had a beautiful body.

Scarlett put her face into the downy folds of the cashmere robe and closed her eyes and smelt Alice.

The television at the end of the bed in specially made built-in shelving, the dressing rooms – these were the things that made adulthood look extremely attractive and well organised. It must be great to get into that bed and watch TV, children asleep, food in the fridge, parties to plan for at the weekend, nice clothes in the dressing room, on properly padded hangers. For these things, Scarlett admired Alice and Harry. They had made a nice home, they had made a life. They had got there.

Scarlett had been working for them for eighteen months, since the first week they had moved in, and they had offered her all kinds of things: loans, a bed for the night when she fought with her mother, career advice, books, references for the waitressing position at the yacht club. Alice always made sure there was food for her, not that Scarlett would eat it, since it was full of additives and preservatives, even good food, like the hummous and the other dips Alice bought. Some people didn't understand that the poisoning was incremental. In ten years, the newspapers would be full of articles about how food additives were responsible for cancer. Food additives and chemicals, even the stuff they put in toothpaste. You could taste the cancer in toothpaste. How come no-one did anything about that?

Scarlett walked down the hallway to Alice's study. She pushed open the door. The desk was facing the window that looked out into the garden. There was nothing sentimental in this room, no photos of the children or Harry, no paintings, just books and stationery and the view onto the pool. The computer was closed, but on the desk was a neat pile of white printed sheets, annotated in inky longhand. Scarlett picked one up and read: *a tendency towards melancholy. Was this the way it had to be for her?*

The rest of the paragraph had been crossed out.

Scarlett closed the study door and walked back down the hallway and into Harry and Alice's bedroom. There she studied the photos of their wedding day. Alice was wearing a slim-fitting white dress with an empire line that showed off her long, thin neck, and her hair was back in a loose bun. Alice's eyes looked so sure, so certain. There was some trick Alice had of being *at peace* with her decisions. How did you get that?

There was a photo of Alice at night, lying in a hammock under some big tropical plant on a beach. She was wearing a blue sarong and her hair was loose and she was smiling at the camera, at Harry, flash-framed. You could tell from the photo that Alice was having a lot of sex. How amazing it would be, to let someone into you, *the right one*, the one who knew you best, who stretched you into the furthest corners of yourself. All those years of living inside your own outline, and then suddenly to feel that space around you dissolved, someone arriving at you, with their flesh and their touch and their lips! Harry must have put his lips to Alice's skin, travelled up her long brown limbs, moved around her neck, behind her ears, drunk her in. Did Harry understand what Alice had given to him, not just her physical self, but her separateness, her aloneness? To give that up, that was no small thing. There was Alice in the hammock, looking so directly at the camera that it seemed for a moment as though she was looking at Scarlett herself.

Scarlett went back to the kitchen. She took an apple from the fruit bowl and carefully washed it, peeled it and cut it into slivers. This was her reward for not eating any poison since lunchtime, for avoiding dinner altogether, her mother's dinner, derived from products that had been through at least forty different industrial processes before they got to your mouth. Scarlett sat down on the sofa and put her feet up on the seat of the armchair. On the TV, a rich ugly American bachelor was sitting in a spa tub surrounded by six human Barbie dolls in string bikinis. Only three of the Barbies would make it on to the next episode, and one would eventually become his actual wife. They were going to live in a castle that looked like it was built out of cereal boxes. Everyone knew that America didn't have any castles. Scarlett couldn't believe how much the women wanted him to pick them. They were all variations of the same stupid look, bleached-blonde, bronzed automatons. They didn't have the brains to realise they were victims of an entire universe conspiring against them. Or worse, they realised but didn't care.

Scarlett fervently hoped that *something* would happen before she was old. That she would make something happen or something would happen to her. It was pathetic enduring life, just doing what had to be done. Her mother was a classic example of wasted space. It wasn't that she was a bad person, it was just that she *added* nothing. Surely there would be some occurrence that would liberate Scarlett from simple inevitability. She had to have more faith, faith in herself. You couldn't make change without faith. At four or six or ten, she had faced the day with physical courage, just like Grace Haskins. She had confronted space as a dynamo, whirling, twirling, dancing, spinning, somersaulting. Now, she was tired the moment her eyes opened. Her mother's voice calling her to get up made her tired. Breakfast exhausted her. The school day stretched out interminably because attendance itself required such reserves of strength. Talking, walking, writing . . . everything demanded something of her. Even *thinking* exhausted her because there was no thinking without problems and so few of the problems that came to her had solutions.

'Why don't I know who I am?' Scarlett wondered. It had started to bug her, not that she didn't have a boyfriend, but rather that she appeared unable to get close to another human being. *Closeness*. It was such a dazzlingly complicated word, discreet, but promising so much. The girls at school could keep giving her a hard time. It didn't bother her that much, it was just another annoyance. But it bothered Scarlett that she didn't know how it felt to be up close, to give something away or get something back in skin and breath and taste. It sounded daunting and ghastly and miraculous all at once. It wasn't sex, it was knowledge . . . or surrender. But boys didn't care for girls who shunned sparkly lip gloss. Boys didn't care for girls who failed to jump up and down salivating at the sight of them. So, was she gay? She tried to think if she'd ever been actually attracted to a girl, but anyone she could remember had attracted her through something hazy and unnameable. Their voices. Or the way they brushed their hair in public. Alison Allsop flicked her long brown hair over the top of her head at the end of lunchtime and brushed it from the neck down with a proper Mason Pearson hairbrush. It was beautiful, the long strokes, her neck, the colour of the hair and the static from the brush.

Alice drove home. The night was icy for spring. The pasture land at the top of the hill looked pale and wild and lonely, like heathland. It was amazing how the furthest suburbs still tolerated these last tracts of pasture and bush, interrupting the sprawl of neo-Georgian homes built to within an inch of their blocks. At least they lived in the good part of Sunnyside, with large acreages dictated by the covenants of the original families who had owned vast tracts of the Peninsula in the nineteen twenties.

Sunnyside village was deserted, the bright little flags on the poles down the main street were blowing in a bitter wind. All over Sunnyside, women like Alice took pleasure in the thought that soon they could slip out of their cocktail dresses and their cocktail faces. On the side of the bakery wall, Alice read the graffiti: *Judgement Man*.

Suddenly Alice felt exhausted by the party, by trudging the topography of small talk. It seemed, driving home, as if she had lived a long time. There were times she could now barely remember, details blurred, vanishing from her. She was finally old enough to forget things that had once been crucial. Even facts were evaporating. A few days ago, she had found herself wondering if she had ever been to Geneva. Once, she could have given dates to her foreign travels, recollected hotel names, friends met and jettisoned at railway stations. Now her past was misting over. Did Harry feel that way? She could ask him as he sat beside her, tensely keeping an eye on her command of the wheel. She could ask him. But they had stopped philosophising together, just as they had stopped doing so many other things. He would probably make light, yawn, ignore it. Or was it that she did not want to risk a real response, a conversation that might, in its realness or urgency or depth, contrast too markedly with the vacancy that had overtaken them?

Alice *liked* Harry a lot, as well as loved him. He really was incredibly handsome and getting better. He still looked after himself, unlike most of the other husbands who had just subtly let their standards slip, believing that more expensive clothes could compensate for a less athletic body. Harry's body looked pretty much as it had at thirty: tall, solid, not too muscly. He had a slightly feminine cast to his face because of those electric green eyes, elegantly catlike. He wasn't vain. Also, he believed in what he did. He had conviction. He genuinely believed that good teaching was the foundation of good people and that with application he could make a difference. Whether or not Harry did make a difference wasn't the issue. Alice suspected he was just a little too reasonable to be charismatic.

Reasonableness, and its off-shoot *fairness*, had been what attracted Alice to Harry. Fairness was, perhaps, the most instinctively beguiling aspect of human personality. People were nervous that rightness was the guiding force of destiny, that it could be counted on to prevail over the chaos of greed and selfishness. So a person who exemplified justice, in the simple manner of their being, had a particular glow. And he had good timing, another underrated attribute. Fifteen years before, while fixing a tyre in the rain on an unmade road on the Peninsula, Harry had asked her to marry him. Water streamed off the canopy of eucalypt leaves above them, making tiny torrents. It was getting dark. There was no street light, no other cars, they were slightly drunk. They had driven down to the beach to have lunch with friends and on the way back to the city the storm had started. They were out there in it, Harry using the jack, Alice with Harry's raincoat pulled around her, bedraggled, and he had looked up at her mid-crank and said, 'Marry me'. She laughed and said, 'Why now?' And he had said, 'Because people in movies always propose when caught in the rain,' and she said, 'But we're not in a movie,' and he said, 'But we are, this is it, the movie of us.'

Now each of them was living their own separate life, joined only in the pages of the family diary, the schedule of events, a shared calendar, bathroom, anniversary. In the silence and absences lay the ruins of a love affair. Did he feel that? Did he know that? She had so successfully learnt the art of adaptation. Put her in a room full of successful buoyant people and she, too, would be successfully buoyant. Somehow, fitting in had become a mission in itself. But part of the process of being chameleonic was to sacrifice your nerve endings . . . to give up the sensations that were particular and peculiar. She disgusted herself. The pasture in moonlight summoned up nothing in her. Even lovemaking had become too much trouble. Lovemaking. Could you love someone just by not not-loving them?

In her last novel, Alice had written as if she were inside the story, the words had cured the disease of fear. She found herself in her writing, fixed herself to the page and thereby to the world itself. The certainty this gave her lent her generosity, the will to love. If she found the writer in herself again, maybe she would find the lover, too. If she could lose herself in words, she might re-find Harry. In so doing, she would re-find the point. The point of everything. The reason.

Harry wondered if he had eaten enough. It was impossible to know with finger food. Maybe when they got home he'd make a sandwich with some of that nice ham and mustard. Hopefully the kids would be in their deep sleep. Maybe Alice would feel like channel surfing with him. Sometimes they just got onto the same wavelength and rode the channels with perfectly synchronised boredom thresholds, moving from old movie to music video to some tennis match in Paris. It was great. *She* was great. He looked at her, the way she really concentrated when she drove even though both her feet hovered over the pedals and ruined the brakes by braking and accelerating simultaneously. It had cost them hundreds, probably thousands in repairs, but she was unapologetic and he liked that. She said there were some things she was too old to unlearn. A wisp of hair fell over her eye. She pushed it back. Her arm had goosebumps. Silently, Harry started to cry. Tears brimmed, spilt over and slid down his cheek. Things were so good. His wife was magnificent, his kids were true and kind, his work had meaning, the stars were out, there was good ham in the fridge. Things were so miraculous, how dare they ever change.

fourteen

Going to the party together had been a bad idea. Not that they'd gone together, but they'd agreed to both go. It might all have been fine if Molly hadn't lingered outside on leaving, trapped in a boring conversation about taking out subscription tickets to the theatre for the following season. That meant that when David left the party, Molly was still there, opening her car door. An open invitation to talk when, really, they weren't *capable* of talking.

David had started out by suggesting they go to Justin's parent-teacher interview together the following Wednesday, and ended up accusing her of behaving like a *whore*. Nasty. Molly had never heard David use that word before, not in all their years of marriage, and now he was using it about *her*. It was true what people were saying behind her back, it was actually true, that in having an affair Molly had not fully realised the consequences. A marriage break-up was a conceivable thing in the big picture. But it was the detail that made it catastrophic. It had always amazed Molly to see how marriages, once unstuck, descended into such incivility. Now she understood. The commitment of marriage took a kind of energy, the energy required to stay on track, not looking too much to the left or right. Once the terms of that contract were breached, that energy had to find another expression and there was nowhere for it to turn but vicious. David using the word whore frightened her. The bareness of it. They could be cynical about the suburbs, she and Alice and Harry and Tess and Raph and all of them. They could laugh at their own little pocket of privilege like all nice small-L liberals embarrassed by their choices. But the truth was, it was a comfort to live in a place where no-one used the word whore, where monotony was a small price to pay for general *niceness*. They could laugh at niceness. But perhaps niceness was as good a thing to aspire to as any. It was about *decorum* and when all was said and done, decorum suggested a kind of pattern to things. Patterns were important.

As Molly drove away, leaving David standing there beside the dolphin statue blank with rage, she realised she was going to have to find scale again, the scale that put her firmly in her place. Infidelity made you the star attraction in the movie playing inside your head. That was the appeal of it. But you couldn't live your life that way indefinitely. Somehow or other, she was going to have to rediscover modesty. And that was why she now found herself, the following Saturday, driving up Mountain Road on her way to the ashram.

Molly parked beside the main building, which was nestled in amongst the eucalypts. Around the house stretched paddocks with horses and a large kitchen garden enclosed by a picket fence. It had taken Tamsin Wheeler's recommendation to fast-track an audience with the swami before his annual trip home to Queens. Molly had rung Tamsin at the crack of dawn to ask her what to wear. Tamsin had laughed.

'The swami's not interested in externals, Molly. That's not what he's about.'

Before Molly could meet with the swami, she was obliged to take a yoga class and a stillness meditation class. Molly had been perturbed to find that she could not do this with Tamsin, since Tamsin was now advanced at stillness. First, Molly had to sit in a small purple room with a teacher who looked like Joni Mitchell *now*. Molly had seen Joni on TV singing with Sting at a concert for Guatemalan rainforests or something. *Not looking good, despite the cheekbones.* Through the windows, Molly could see a woman tending the horses and another woman weeding the kitchen garden, both of them normal looking. She had to divest herself of prejudices. What was the point in coming if she was going to be sceptical? The problem was, she simultaneously distrusted spirituality and yearned for it. The avaricious taste for deeper meaning which monied Westerners had adopted since the sixties had always struck Molly as vulgar. And yet she, herself, had been drawn to psychic remedies around the same time she realised that while a Prada frock helped mitigate the blues, it could not banish them. Tamsin had said, 'Spirituality is just the capacity for asking questions and not only the big questions, Molly. *The little questions.*'

The yoga teacher was unexpectedly tough. Molly had detected a note of disapproval in her voice as she told Molly to leave the external world in the background and to focus on oneness. *Focus.*

Forty minutes of stretching and bending later, Molly was desperate for caffeine, but knew she was unlikely to find it here, despite the fact that the ashram's cafe in Sunnyside village did, in fact, serve coffee. They had obviously made certain compromises with the real world. Now there was only time for a quick glass of water before the stillness meditation class, for which she had written a cheque for sixty-five dollars on top of the fifty for the yoga. So far, her spiritual morning had cost her over a hundred bucks.

Molly was shown into a bare red-walled room with polished floorboards. Four other people were in the room, two cross-legged and facing the front and two stretched out on their backs with their eyes closed. They were all younger than Molly, noticeably younger, and very serious. It was a hell of a lot different to Pilates, that was for sure, with the ubiquitous Joe Jackson CD playing in the background and the social chat on the reformers with other mothers. A very thin thirtyish man in cotton pants and a Swami M T-shirt sat up the front and bowed his head. Molly waited for the welcome speech, the explanation, but after ten minutes or so it became apparent that nothing was going to happen.

Molly felt a rising tide of panic. The other four participants were still in their original positions, all of them with their eyes closed. She cleared her throat. The young man at the front of the class opened his eyes and looked at Molly indicating that *verbalising was off the agenda*. Molly closed her eyes and tried to think about nothing. It was actually pretty difficult to think about nothing because the more you tried to think about nothing the more you thought about something. In Molly's case, sixty-five dollars. Molly tried very hard to clear her thoughts but every time she visualised sweeping away the contents of her mind, something new would pop up, something inevitably controversial. In what class did the swami travel when he flew back home? It was hard to think of a swami flying economy. On the other hand, it didn't seem right that he'd fly business with all those middle-management types.

Molly told herself to *focus*. Tamsin Wheeler had dropped eleven kilos. There had to be something to this stuff. But before she knew it, Molly was wondering if the pairing of her new brown twin-set with her new tweed skirt would be Katherine Hepburnesque or just plain dowdy. It was hard to know. Pearls would clinch it one way or the other. A twinset and pearls were so exaggeratedly *trad*, it could *only* be read as ironic. There was nothing more chic than Bourgeois-Chic.

Finally, Molly heard shuffling and opened her eyes. The young man had stood up. Molly pulled herself up, feeling dizzy. The others in the room bowed and Molly hurriedly copied them before following them out of the room. As the others scurried away, the young man approached her with a smile.

'How was it?'

'Ah, terrific,' said Molly. 'But to be honest, I'm not sure I was doing it right.'

'There is no *right*,' said the man. 'There's just the way that you do it.'

'Oh, okay,' said Molly. 'I get it. It's just the way that you do it.'

'There's no *right*. There is just *what is*.'

The young man lead her down a corridor to a small waiting room with a banner on the wall saying 'Leave it behind'.

'When you hear the bell, just enter through that door,' he said.

Molly nodded. She wished she hadn't brought her handbag with her. She hadn't really thought about it. Mostly, a woman just took her handbag everywhere as a matter of course. It hadn't even occurred to her to leave it in the car. It would have to be her new Gucci one. *Fuck*. Maybe *that* was what she was supposed to leave behind. Maybe Swami Marvin knew that Sunnyside women brought along their Gucci handbags and had an existential crisis in the waiting room about what to do with them. On the other hand, it *was* the new Gucci ball-bearings bag, the one Kate Moss had worn to Sadie

172

Frost's birthday party, the one she had coveted ever since she had seen it in British *Vogue*, the one she had paid well over a thousand dollars for and, ashram or no ashram, she was not leaving it unattended. Molly took a few deep breaths and tried to talk herself out of her tension. The swami wasn't interested in appearances. Molly suddenly felt foolish. *What was he? An accesssories expert?*

Molly heard the bell and leapt up, tucking her handbag under her arm. She opened the door. The blinds were drawn in the room and several candles flickered in a semi-circle on the timber floor. Swami Marvin must have been in his early fifties, guessed Molly, and she was taken aback by how un-swami-like he looked. A short, weedy, unprepossessing fifty-year-old schoolboy was kneeling on the floor. He gestured for her to sit down in front of him.

'I'm Marvin,' he said. 'And you must be Molly.' The way he said Molly came out as 'Marly'.

Molly sat down with her legs folded under her at an angle. But then she felt like some preppy mother on the floor at a baby shower, so she swung her legs around and awkwardly attempted to cross them, tucking her bag behind her.

They sat in silence. Molly wondered who went first, the *seeker* or the *guide*.

'You're on a journey, Molly.'

'Yes, Marvin. It appears that I am on a journey. But I'm not sure I've taken the right path, so to speak.'

'Where have you been and where are you going?'

'Well,' said Molly, confused, 'I've been in Sunnyside and I'm not sure where I'm going but possibly no further than Seabank.'

'I'm talking about the overview, Molly. I'm talking about the real journey, the *difficult* journey.'

'Of course!' said Molly. 'I left my husband David. He's a very good person. I've entered into a relationship with my . . . Well . . . another relationship. I've hurt my son, Justin. And for no good reason.'

'There is a reason, Molly. The reason exists and it is waiting for you.'

'Where?' said Molly.

The swami smiled. 'You need to take time. You need to come back and do the full stillness meditation course. Eliminate the distractions of life. You need to ask yourself where freedom truly lies.'

'Aha,' said Molly nodding. More stillness meditation. At sixty-five bucks a pop. 'Where *does* freedom lie, Marvin?'

Swami Marvin tilted his head slightly to the left side and then the right. It was hard to know if this was part of a mystical thought process or just a neck ache.

'Only you know that, Molly.'

Molly nodded. There was something strangely charismatic about him. Otherwise why would grown women in tennis bracelets be out there in the kitchen garden picking organic zucchinis?

'Freedom lies somewhere different for each of us, Molly. Perhaps true freedom lies in discipline, in constructing fences. Tell me, Molly, where are you happiest?'

'Happiest?' *In a department store*, thought Molly. Women's imports. 'I'm not very spiritual, Marvin. I'm very confused. To be honest, I'm not really sure this can help me.'

'We're just here to help you help yourself.'

Molly nodded. 'And I'd like to help you help me help myself, I really would, but I think there are two parts of me in conflict. The unhappy, unresolved, interesting me who wants to try to find meaning, and the selfish immature hedonist who just wants to try things out. She's right here in this room and she's whispering at me.'

'What is she saying, Molly?'

'She's saying that the spiritual search is so damn unoriginal. She's saying if shopping makes you happy, there's nothing wrong with that. She's saying you've been a good, organised, responsible person all your life and now is the time to find out what else you are. She's saying that maybe it's not such a bad thing if sometimes your conscience gives way to your imagination.'

'You're going to be all right, Molly McLelland,' said the swami.

Molly got to her feet and turned towards the door. Where *did* freedom lie? It wasn't such a stupid question. Maybe true freedom lay in no freedom. Maybe too much freedom just led forty-something women to look for pool men when they should have been at home tending their loved ones.

Molly had reached the door when the swami spoke.

'Isn't that the Gucci ball-bearing bag?'

Harry was judiciously dodging his fellow residents carrying vast tracts of newspapers stuffed with lifestyle sections. Around him, a Sunnyside Saturday morning was in full swing. Pre-ordered lemon tarts were being picked up at Tiggy's delicatessen and men were buying meat, queuing outside Melvin's where the scouts were busy sausage sizzling. Saturday mornings around the nation, *men bought meat*. Women had manicures or hit the ground running at the greengrocer in preparating for that night's entertaining, filling their trolleys with things Harry had heard of but had no idea what they looked like: fennel, tamarillos, rambutans.

Harry noticed the crowd gathering outside the newsagency. Barriers had been erected at either end of the street alongside the shopping strip. It was an annual event, the Sunnyside Real Estate Agents' Race, the equivalent of the inner-city waiters' race in which hot-footed young turks from the hip cafes attempted to sprint with trays balancing caffe lattes. This being Sunnyside, the waiters had been supplanted by agents attempting to run with Open For Inspection boards.

Harry could see Jim and Tess in the crowd and beyond it, Joe talking to Monty, no doubt about the football end-of-season pie night. *He had to go*, there was no way around it. He'd promised Joe. Ashamed, Harry realised he had managed to avoid every conceivable volunteer position this season, from writing the match report to time-keeping.

Howard Wheeler was at one end of the line-up, with Lily at the far end, sandwiching eight other agents. The fat guy from McLaren and McLaren, the one who had approached Harry offering a free valuation on their house a few months before, was standing on the podium with a megaphone.

'Ladies and gentlemen, I welcome you all. What a fine day we have here and what a great turn-out! I'm here to remind you on behalf of Sunnyside's property professionals that *we care*. Buying, selling, renting, we are committed to *property done properly*.'

The renting was a bit rich, thought Harry. The only renting done in Sunnyside was of marquees. Harry remembered one under-12s football match against Deptford that had ended badly. A Sunnyside parent had yelled at a Deptford parent, 'We'll put your rent up!'

'Following the race, Glanville Perry of the newsagency, our sponsor, will be serving refreshments in the square and all profits will be donated to Horse-riding for the Handicapped. Agents, *are you ready?*'

The crowd cheered as the agents readied themselves, feet forward, bleached smiles fixed, eyes taking in the finishing line up ahead outside the dry-cleaners. Teenagers attempted to camouflage their interest with sardonic smirks. Small children clutched balloons sporting the names of the agencies.

'On your marks, get set, *go*!'

The crowd yelled encouragement as the army of navy-blue suits careered down the street, clutching their boards. Outside the liquor store, Harry could see Raph leading a young man with a trolley laden with wine boxes. Harry peered closely, trying to read the label. What was Raph stocking up on? Something for their newly excavated, humidified wine cellar. Wine cellars were the new carports. He turned back to the crowd. Somewhere, Alice was waiting for him. Watching from the sidelines was the geologist Jim had pointed out to him at tennis, the one who was supposedly tracking the faultlines running through the Peninsula and who appeared to be reluctant to leave. Harry had the sudden vision of the beachcliffs toppling into the sea, carrying with them all the mini-Versailles marking the Sunnyside coastline.

Howard Wheeler, as expected, passed the finishing line first, some cute Mia Farrowish blonde from McLaren and McLaren a hair's breadth behind him. A manufactured cheer went up from the Jespers team. And then Harry saw her, standing back from the crowd, beyond the finishing line. Olivia Mathers, leaning against a tree with her arms folded, smiling at him.

The three of them lay in the sun beside the court. They had collected about four thousand cumquats between them and were playing their favourite old game, the one where they tried to throw the cumquats to the far fence of the tennis court. Before they went inside, they would have to clear the court of the squashed fruit, but that was later. They hadn't done this since last summer. Everything had changed since then.

Over the orchard came the hum of the pool filter. Grace thought it was weird the way water looked blue automatically in a pool, but when it came out of the tap it was clear.

As he threw his cumquat high in the air, Justin said, 'I'm getting two of everything.'

Joe asked, 'What does that mean?'

They were keeping the rhythm up of the throws, Justin, Joe, Grace, a perfect pause between each attempt. Grace sailed her cumquat high in the air and it landed near the net. Nowhere near good enough. She was out of practice.

'When Mum sets up her new place properly, I'm going to have a room there *and* my normal room and I have to get two sets of everything.'

'What? Like two tennis racquets? Like two sets of clothes?' said Joe.

'Victory!' yelled Justin and they all stopped to watch his cumquat hit the fence, as predicted.

'Everything,' said Justin.

'Cool,' said Joe.

'I guess,' said Justin. 'Whoa! Double victory! You know, they found this fossil with a backbone,' he went on. 'It's like our original ancestor. Some guy in South Australia dug it out of the ground.'

Grace was still thinking about having two of everything. Of how badly wrong David and Molly were getting things. She had one ear on what Justin was saying. Something about a fossil.

'The blueprint of us.'

Justin ran his finger up Grace's spine and she giggled.

'Everything with a backbone came from this little guy and it's five hundred and fifty million years old.'

Grace lay on her back and looked at the clouds, doing the maths. She could still feel the imprint of Justin's finger on her vertebrae.

'That makes it five hundred and forty-nine million, nine hundred and ninety-nine thousand, nine hundred and eighty-nine years older than me,' said Grace. 'Creepy!'

'How can you say that about your cousin?'

Grace whacked Justin on the shoulder and laughed. He and Joe started throwing the cumquats again, a new round, the pile of fruit dwindling between them and the tennis court polka-dotted in orange.

Grace couldn't believe that Justin was just *accepting* things. If this was happening to her, she'd be fighting it. She'd be doing whatever she could to make it all *go back*. It wasn't right to have two of everything. Just thinking about it made Grace's blood go cold. The idea of having two new bikes was horrible. The special-ness of the bike was in its oneness. What was the point of having two rooms? It just meant that neither one of them was your real room, and having to move every week – what a nightmare. Some-one really ought to speak to Justin, to give him the strength to do something. Would he listen to her? Most girls were nothing to Jus-tin, nothing to Joe, they just didn't figure on their radar. It was hard to tell if Justin just put up with Grace, or if he actually liked her. He didn't tell her to get lost, that was something. Maybe he *would* listen to her. On the other hand, she could imagine Justin telling her that it was none of her business. And technically, it *was* none of her business. But somehow, something just made it seem like it was central to Grace, it was right at the heart of her. Molly and David were not her parents. But they could have been. They so eas-ily could have been.

fifteen

David McLelland was staring at the boxes of the Booker Prize winner in the storeroom. They had put in a massive order after the announcement, but no-one was buying. The reviews had all emphasised that it was about a high-school massacre, they hadn't convincingly conveyed that it was *funny*. David had felt confused himself, when he had read it. Of course it had taken an Australian to write a funny book about a high-school massacre. No American would have the *guts*. Even so, the book wasn't selling, he'd miscalculated. Lately all the books about horror and evil and terror had been sitting passively on the shelves. All the post-September 11 analyses had failed to sell well. It was as if consumers had just said: *Enough*. On the other hand, anyone who felt like writing a book about females struggling with femaleness was onto a good thing. Searching for men, orgasms, career fulfilment . . . watch the royalties pile up. This raised the very interesting but thoroughly unsayable question: *When were women going to go out of fashion?*

It was a relief to have the weekend over with. Saturdays were no problem since he could camouflage his solitary status at the shop. But he spent most of Sundays pretending to have things to do. When Jim and Tess asked him for meals, he found himself lying to get out of going, because he could not risk revealing the desperation he in fact felt. Monday mornings were now immensely cheering. In half an hour the staff would arrive, the doors would open and McLelland's Books would be once more open for business. David McLelland was going to have to be the lovely bookshop owner, the reliable adviser, the no-problem-too-hard-to-fix nice guy all over again. In would come all the old ladies of Sunnyside with their incomprehensible requests. 'It's a book about a man. It's written by that girl from Canada, or Sweden, the one who wrote that other book about the people in the war.' He would nod kindly and turn to the computer screen, book detective.

Right now, Molly was no doubt drinking her first cup of coffee for the day, liberated from the demands of wifing and mothering, a naked slattern perusing the headlines, luxuriating in her liberation from decency. *Bitch*! Quite possibly that pubescent little blond-tipped arsehole was lying next to her tracing his tanned finger along her hip bone. Molly's hip bone. He loved that hip bone. *He, David McLelland*, husband, *loved that hip bone, had cared for it, it was practically his!*

David thought about going to the petrol station and buying a few containers of petrol. He would take off his shoes, sneak around the side of the newly rented unit (*unit!*) and liberally splash the petrol around. They would be lying in bed, Pool Man and Cunt Face, his cock inside her, banging away, Molly getting her rash, the rash she got over her chest when she was on the way to an orgasm, and the flames would start to lick the building, lick at it, then *take*.

He would be caught. Of course he would, he was a bookshop owner. Bookshop owners do not get away with murder. Someone would ring Tess and Jim and Alice and Harry. The word would go around. Justin would have to live with Molly's sister Hannah and the stupid Airedale in Byron Bay. Byron Bay wouldn't be so bad for Justin. He could surf all the time. He'd like it. In a few years, after a lot of grief counselling and therapy, he'd get over the fact that *his deranged father had burnt his whore mother to death in a unit.*

David made his way to the self-help section, which had been pushing its way bossily into gardening and performing arts, edging them out. At the top of the section, David saw three copies of *Making Good Choices: smart love for smart women* and threw them on the floor. Then he reached for the ubiquitous *Men are from Mars, Women are from Venus* and threw them down. Eight copies of *Women Who Run with the Wolves* hit the floor, along with *Don't Beat Yourself Up: strategies for female survival* and two copies of *Ouch! That Glass Ceiling's Gotta Go!* by Myra Hirsch. *Don't*

*F**k with me, I'm Smarter Than You: new tactics for damaged females* landed on the pile with a thud. Further down, David threw out *Grrrrl-Power!: a guide for teenage girls* and *Clit-Happy: how to fall in love with yourself.* With a sweep of his hand, he knocked to the floor *You're Okay but I'm Superior: self-esteem for the modern woman* and *The Vulnerable Vulva.*

From the shelf at the bottom, tucked away in a tidy corner, David extracted *The Proud Penis* and *Male Bonding: a lost art refound.* The men's section had lost ground over the past few years. In the seventies, when David himself had belonged to the local branch of 'Males Against Sexism,' male literature of the self-help variety had exploded. He had spent long hours in the campus bookshop working out the best way to shoplift well-meaning guides on how to find the feminine side. Balancing the books in one arm, David reached for *Male Oppression: self-help for the selfless and helpless*; *Snuff the Snag: how to eliminate the cissy within* and *The Masculine Arts: barbecuing tips for true believers.* The latter had a photograph of a happy bearded man in a chef's hat and apron holding a pair of tongs in one hand and a Budweiser in the other. He pulled out *Loving the Enemy: how a man can learn to love again after divorcing the bitch*, a title David had hitherto questioned but now saw the merits of. He moved them to the prime position now vacant in the centre of the shelf at eye level. There was a half-metre gap on the shelf, but not for long. *Oh no, not for long!*

David surveyed the pile of books on the carpet with satisfaction. He could put them in the dumpster out the back of the fruit shop, but that ran the risk of them ending up in the tip, where some mad female could resurrect them and stick them up on her bookshelf with her *Bridget Jones Collector's Edition* and garage sale relic *Everywoman*. At all costs, these books were going to go. They were going to burn.

The problem was in the *publicity*. Committing adultery was dishonourable, no question about that, thought Alice. *But what if no-one knew* . . . that was the question. If things had gone differently. If no-one knew, and if it made Molly somehow . . . *complete* . . . then perhaps, just perhaps, it could be seen as something, if not good, then at least purposeful. So long as David did not know. And Justin did not know. And there was no gossip. If things were kept quiet, then who was to say that Molly might not have an adventure, a small adventure?

Of course, Alice had not put this to Harry and nor would she. A wife couldn't condone the infidelities of another wife. No-one would relax.

Perhaps infidelity was without purpose if it stayed private. Maybe the whole thrill was in the publicity? Alice tried to imagine her way into it. It kept coming back to her that if it was the act itself, and no one knew, did it really exist? Perhaps the existence of things could only be measured by their impact.

Alice liked this time of day, right after the kids had gone back to school and Harry was gone and it was quiet. She missed silence. Once a mother, there was never silence any more, not in the house, not even inside one's own body. Even when the children were absent, her mind cruised through disasters, her heartbeat giving syncopation to anxiety.

It was beginning to rain. The swimming pool was dimpling, the trees bowing. Alice thought to herself: here I am in my house, here I am, what am I? From the side gate, Alice saw her own pool man in his Driza-Bone stride across the lawn. Alice felt a wave of aggravation. If anyone else was on the property, that airy, light feeling of peace evaporated. These days, it was so rare to have no-one there. If it wasn't the gardener, it was some tradesman or other doing a quote for a pool fence, which the previous owners had failed to install. Or the roof. Or an electrical problem. There always seemed to be a bunch of Blundstones at the front door.

Alice had once known how to find stillness, how to transform it into words. She had travelled deeply into it in order to write. She had misplaced the art. Misplaced or lost it? The suburbs, perhaps, had stolen it from her. Suburban life, a kind of psychic kleptomaniac, stealing the personalities of its newcomers, the talents, the small eccentric ways. She *was* a writer. She had been claimed by the sensitivities of a writer and even when she was not writing, they would not let her go. Writing was not something that she could give up. The reverse was also true: *it* could not give *her* up. She had to stop measuring the days in terms of production. Perhaps her present inability to write was just an instinctive, righteous resistance to the insistence of crass symbolism, the vulgarity of *tracking things*. A writer needed to live in order to write, and if every aspect of experience was constantly monitored and made concrete in an alphabetical straightjacket, then what chance did life have? And yet, if this were so, why did she feel so life-*less*? Why had the blood drained from her, leaving her only the faintly piquant memory of her own eroticism? Did writing deliver life or reduce it?

It was strange the way things kept shifting. One moment everything seemed in order, the next she felt as if she were losing control of things. Ever since the dinner party, it seemed as if the world was slightly off kilter. If she looked at the big picture fair and square, things were not too bad. Her kids were not heroin addicts, her husband was loyal and kind, they were rich enough. But so much was unseen, unsaid in the overview. If you looked up close, things were not quite right. Joe didn't read, that wasn't good. Harry had said to relax about Joe, but the reading was only a part of it. He was becoming unfathomable. A mother needed to look inside the head of her son, needed to make sure his mind was ticking over the right way. But Joe had kept the heart of himself silent. Years ago he had lost the baby exuberance, that sweet mad spirit of the toddler, with its hotline to absurdity. Now, Joe let life worry at him. Alice couldn't see him, couldn't get near him. He was her darling. Sometimes she felt so in love with him, she wanted to consume him.

Then there was Justin, Justin showing Joe just how things might be done, a nerve-racking adolescence. Alice had always liked Justin, which made things worse. It was Justin's sensitivity that was causing the problems and who could argue against sensitivity? It seemed wrong, but Alice wished that Justin was not *there,* right there, drawing attention to new choices that were also available to Joe, most specifically the choice to fuck up.

Alice thought about Tess and Jim's neighbour, a lovely woman who was always baking cakes and spring-cleaning in the service of her husband and four children. One day, she had left. Gone to live in the city, taken up with a new man, abandoned the family to whom she had previously enslaved herself, including two four-year-old girls. Alice sometimes saw the stoic husband, left in a wife's wake, as he dropped the younger children at school. Perhaps it was all his fault for believing in the Martha Stewart version of his wife. Perhaps he should have been wise to the fact that anything so perfect had to be false and the more frenetically his wife had baked, the greater the ballast to her precariousness.

The thing about mothering was that it was so consuming, it was hard to do moderately. Women supplicated themselves before their families and when they could bear it no longer, there seemed nothing to do but flee. Were there signs? Did Tess's neighbour leave small, pertinent clues preceding her flight: panic attacks, whimsical extravagance, disturbing dreams? Perhaps even she had not seen the clues of her own growing panic. Alice needed to be vigilant of her own behaviour. Was her discouragement of sex with Harry the natural ebb and flow of marital spice or the harbinger of something catastrophic?

Why did any man or woman want more than what they were rightfully entitled to? It was so hard for a married woman to feel adored these days. Even good husbands, like Harry, like David, could not adore their wives day after day, year after year. And real life, the ability to simultaneously breastfeed, peel asparagus and fill in the weekly diary of family commitments (children's violin lessons, dentist, school picnic) – this kind of real-life logistical know-how was never going to make a woman more adorable. *It ought to, but it didn't*. Alice had never met a man who adored a woman for what made her truly great – the simple ability to withstand the pressure of motherhood without taking out her frustration and exhaustion and anxiety on everyone else. Some women even managed to do this and pull off a job at the same time. Graciousness in the face of the greatest endurance test of life itself: the test of loving too much, the mother's test. This was what made a woman great. And who knew?

So a quick roll in the Deptford Motel was possibly the last ticket to transcendence and, looking at it this way, who could blame Molly McLelland? The ease of this thought frightened Alice. How fast things could come undone. Virtuousness fell headlong into passion, as if it had been waiting for years to escape itself. A small fuse of love burnt deep inside Alice, buried under layers of marital bureaucracy. She hoped that Harry wouldn't stop loving her.

Love, thought Alice, sighing. It was astonishing how many different tones one word could express: beautiful, insincere, poetic, kitsch. It was a word Alice didn't like using. Once, Alice had embraced the word as a fully subscribed, paid-up member of romance. When Harry had wooed her and she had felt the sweet, full purpose of reciprocation. With children, the word had shifted from the present to something vaguely historical, something that had become, in part, a memory. Only sex could really defeat the dissipation of newness that all relationships had to overcome. Somehow, sex kept things on edge, reasserted the fact that she and Harry were two separate entities, rapturously unified. Without sex, every part of their union had become dulled. For the first time, Alice felt frightened by what she and Harry had become. The precariousness of their life was camouflaged by the rituals of domestic cohabitation, the presentation of their life had become everything. But underneath the order was the loss of something and that loss was the engineer of catastrophe. She could talk herself into believing it was not that important, but Alice knew that somehow everything came back to sex. It was a mistake to think it the crude by-product of love. Sex was actually love's currency.

The pool man was fiddling around the filter, bending over the pool, enduring the rain, which was getting heavier. She stood up and opened the sliding door a little.

'Do you want to get out of the rain?'

He couldn't hear her. What was his name? Something unusual. Magnus.

'Magnus!'

He looked up.

'Want to get out of the rain?'

He shook his head and waved, then stood up and walked up the lawn towards her.

'Hi!' said Alice.

'You've got a leak.'

It was an old pool. They had suspected something when the water had dropped beneath the tile line.

'So what happens?'

'We're going to have to drain the pool, check it out. We can leave it, but if you want it ready for summer it's going to be better to do it now.'

'Well,' said Alice.

The pool man peered out from under his Driza-Bone hood. With his pointy nose and chin, he reminded Alice of a badger peering out of a burrow. Drips were falling from the peak of his cap onto the terrace.

'You sure you don't want to get out of the rain?'

'I'm fine. Really. Do you want to think about the pool?'

'No,' said Alice. 'Go ahead and do it.'

'I'll be back tomorrow,' said Magnus. 'We'll get started then.'

Magnus turned and walked back to the pool. Alice closed the doors and sat down again.

If her pool man looked like Brad Pitt instead of a badger, if she was not fearful of her body, ashamed of what time had done to her, just these last five years, if things were slightly different, would she have embraced that dazzling, gorgeous, terrifying, show-bizzy word: *infidelity*? Was it vanity that made women loyal? Was it the thought of breasts like punctured souffles, of slack thighs, that made women behave nicely? Perhaps the whole concept of a woman's faithfulness was based on another sin: pride.

In the sunlight, with the pool man off the property and many hours before husband and children would push her back into the outline of a wife and mother, Alice had a stirring of an idea.

Tess stared at the photograph on her desk: Lily and Raph, Molly and David, Alice and Harry, herself and Jim, standing on the summit with their skis on. Two winters ago. They had had their own small controversies – the time Raph accused Molly of being supercilious or when Lily told David that Justin was non-communicative – but overall they were steadfast. When she was young, she had believed that friendships would always be made with the velocity of youth. It had surprised her, in her thirties, to find that the ability to make friends slackened, along with bodies. Now, in her forties, it struck Tess that real friendships were serendipitous and valuable but could not overcome the enigmas of personality. She studied Molly in the photo. *Who was Molly?* Beneath the collage of acquired characteristics, human beings sheltered inconsistencies and perversions. If friendship was based on this undergrowth, what a comfort it might be. What tenderness might be offered, and received. The receptionist's voice crackled though the speaker phone.

'Your next one's here, Tess.'

Tess got up and opened the door. The student entered, unsmiling. Sometimes Tess had to fight the urge to tell the students to simply lighten up. Anorexia. Depression. Exam anxiety. Phobias. Talk about youth being wasted on the young. Occasionally, she had found herself fantasising about shaking these beleaguered kids and shouting, *'You're young, what more do you want?'*

The young woman sat down on the armchair facing her own and Tess took up her file from the top of the pile on the floor and opened it.

'What's happened?' said Tess.

'It won't go away,' said Olivia.

'Did you think about what I said last week?'

Olivia nodded. 'I don't know what I'm doing here. I'm play act-ing. I'm trying to make myself more important. I'm turning myself into a story.'

'Perhaps,' said Tess. 'Only you know that. But perhaps you're just trying to work something out.'

'I thought I was in love with him. But maybe I'm in love with what he does to me.'

'What does he do to you?'

'He sees through me. I create this performance, this version of myself. Out there. I'm acting. I can hear myself. I think to myself: Is that me? And everyone buys it. Except for him. He sees what I'm doing. It's as if he can see past it. He sees *me*.'

Tess said, 'And you want this?'

'It's like I'm waiting for someone to say: *Stop. Be real.*'

Tess nodded. She was one of those girls who put all their intel-ligence into a public performance, trying to convince others of their own invention. Put them in a small, quiet room and they were capa-ble of genuine insight. She had started out so angry, this one, for everything she had been denied. Sometimes it happened that way. But the angry ones usually had better outcomes than those who came in, at twenty, with clear maps inside their heads of the lives to come, dismal maps of pre-destination.

'But maybe I just want to put my mark on someone. I don't know. Maybe I just want to feel *recognised*. Is that love?'

'You're talking about what he does *for* you, what he does *to* you. Is that your measure of love?'

'What I want is for him to want me.'

'Well, that's not love. Is it?'

'How do you know?'

'Do you think love is just about being recognised?'

It was always unnerving when a client reminded Tess of herself. She could remember that feeling, the need to stir something in another, the need to figure in somebody else's story. It was hard to know if it was a female thing, the sense that only another's gaze awakened you, made you real. To be young. What mystery there was in the young's insecurity. It flew in the face of their arsenal, the arsenal of beauty.

Here she was, this young woman. A student. A married man. The Greeks covered everything. There were really only about four stories that human beings acted out. The truth was that youth was repetitive, middle age was repetitive, old age too. We were all destined to tackle the same terrors, the terrors that accompanied the different stages of a life. Every age was desperate, craven in its own way. The old were so stupendously self-involved with their endless medical appointments, their tiny journeys to pathology clinics and hairdressers and bridge games, their agonising over tedious schedules that meant nothing to anyone but themselves. Clawing for more time. But were the young any less miserable, with their panic and their ruthless need to know who they were becoming? Here was another young woman who needed to be sanctioned, who looked to compose herself in the shadow of an older man. And who were these men, these married men dallying with little girls? Who were these restless creatures who could not get succour from loving well, from steadfast love, love magically conjured through the structure of passing years, children's births, through trudging amiably, resignedly, through the foothills of domestic mountain ranges? Married men, who so often tried to catch the baton of youth in these pathetic assignations. They'd rather live nine lives badly than one life well. The relentlessness of human frailty exhausted Tess. She should have been a ski instructor, they way she wanted to. She could be up there now, swishing through the last of the spring snow, in a little fur-lined parka. Was there any point trying to intervene when humans were so doggedly tragic?

'Where did you meet him, Olivia?'

'He's my teacher. Harry. Harry Haskins.'

Tess didn't raise her eyes from the page. She wrote his name in the notes. And then again. And then again. Harry Haskins. There it was. In front her. On the page. A clinical note. Harry, whom she loved not least for how he loved Alice. Harry, whose charm lay in the beguiling combination of handsomeness and imperviousness to female seduction. There was nothing so beguiling as a man with beauty who did not use it. Surely not. And yet, how simple and how ordinary and how perfect, in a way. The final confirmation, as if she needed it, that there was no longer any such thing as honour. It had gone the way of all those things that she had foolishly assumed were permanent: typewriters, record players, honour.

Tess realised that the image of Harry that came to her was a mad close-up from last Christmas, when she and Harry were acting out 'Primal Fear' in Charades at Molly and David's. Harry, goofing around in a Hawaiian shirt, everyone shouting 'Film!' as Harry made the little wind-up signal of a hand-held camera in front of his face. In all the archive of Harry moments, this was the one her brain selected. Silently, Tess bid him goodbye.

Tess said, 'What do you want from me, Olivia? What do you want to find here?', but she was already thinking of Alice. Alice, who was too beautiful and clever to be spared.

'Hope,' said the girl, softly.

sixteen

It was a fine spring morning, the last day of the school week, and a perfect morning to ride to school. Joe had already left early, for football practice. Alice stood by the front door and cautioned Grace.

'Remember what Dad said. You have to be responsible. You have to keep your wits about you.'

'I will! I will! Okay, I have to leave *now* or I'll be late!'

Alice kissed her. In the basket, Grace had stowed her schoolbag. Alice had insisted she wear a mac over her uniform in case it started to rain, but above them Grace could see only brilliant blue. She lifted her feet from the ground and began to pedal down the driveway. The pebbles were slushy and trying to push the pedals reminded Grace of skiing in spring snow. At the end of the driveway she looked back briefly and waved to Alice standing and watching her. It looked to Grace as if her mother might stand there all day, a beacon of departings and homecomings.

Grace turned into the road. It had dips and puddles in it, and was strewn with gum leaves. It was amazing how when you were nervous you noticed everything. Grace had never seen the ground so clearly before, how it was scattered with objects, fine red mottled leaves from the eucalypts and wattle blossoms knocked off by the rain and gum nuts and tree burrs and bits of sweet wrappers and the odd milk carton escaped from the rubbish trucks. Her new bike felt beautiful beneath her. It was bright blue, a Raleigh, and just a little too big. But she had mastered it on the tennis court, Harry helping her on and off. And this was her first big ride, her first solo ride, and she had been dreaming of it for months.

Grace stopped on the corner of Ocean Crescent and turned hard left onto the bike track beside the road. Cars seemed to sneak up close to her then speed past, as if they were playing some kind of a game, but Grace knew that was just nerves. It just *seemed like* they were sneaking up. But all these cars were set on their own course, delivering people to other places, to schools and work and shopping centres, they were not really interested in Grace on her bike. She relaxed and sped up, anticipating the drop of the road down towards Sunnyside village. Some of the senior kids on their own bikes crossed her path at the lights. She hoped they had seen her, Grace Haskins on her new blue Raleigh, what a bike! They were going some fancy way through the housing estate but Grace was going the direct way, the way Alice drove. Maybe in a few days she'd start to explore other routes. She could get the street directory out of Alice's car and trace the courts and streets with her finger to find the best way. This would be the smart thing to do. She made a mental note.

When Grace was older, she planned on looking beautiful but in a strong way. She didn't want to look like a pop star, all blonde and stupid, dumb show-offs. She wanted to look like an adventurer, a long-distance swimmer, or the woman who climbed the seven tallest mountains. One day, she would share a very modern apartment somewhere like Zurich with a French industrial chemist, whatever they were, or a spy from Siberia. She'd forget all about Sunnyside, never come back, not until she was seventy, when she'd visit from out of another life, in a Rolls Royce. She'd drive around remembering things, like in a movie. She would look at her house in Carringdale Road, where another family would now be living and another Grace, Grace of another age. She would return to Sunnyside when it was all but gone from her, a vague collection of cul de sacs and incidents: the corner where she had fallen off her bike, the beach track where she and Caroline Forsythe had encountered a flasher one wintry Sunday. She would have lived a life, and Harry and Alice would be minor characters in the biography, the big hardback biography, of Grace Haskins's life.

Once she was through the roundabout, Grace started to feel as if she had always ridden her bike to school. It was so easy and nice to be out in the day early, to feel it on her skin. It was hot work riding, but from the roundabout to the school, the wind lifted up off the bay and brought cool air up and over her. She could feel the chill of the sea cut through her sweat deliciously. Now it was just a matter of five or so more minutes winding her way through the Tiddesdale streets, past the nature reserve and up to the clifftop road. She had the distinct feeling that she looked beautiful on her bike, she *felt* beautiful. Around her she heard the bright caw of the magpies as if they were cheering her on. *Come on, Grace! Come on, Grace! Nearly there!*

Through Sunnyside village, Grace only had to stop three times at the crossings. She was extra, extra careful to stop in time, to look both ways as she turned the corner into the maze of streets leading up to the bay. There was a small roundabout she had never really thought about before, but roundabouts were tricky, you had to use your *judgement*. Harry had reminded her about three thousand times that the cars on her right had right of way. She had to be absolutely positive that they had made their choices before she entered the circle and she had to be aware that other people made mistakes. *They don't always indicate*, Harry had said. *It only takes one second for your life to be over.*

Grace turned right into Baybridge Road. Way down the end, the grey sea shimmered. The traffic was heavy now as cars converged on the school. Yesterday she had been one of them! One of those poor kids locked behind metal and glass, forced to cooperate with adults and their adult things: cars, jobs, schedules. Now, she was free of all that! For sure, they were looking at her on her Raleigh, talking about how great it was. *Did you see Grace Haskins on her new bike?*

If only Justin could see it. There was something about Justin that . . . Well, what was it? A sort of stirring, a kind of beating wing in the pit of her stomach when he was around. Which wasn't that often any more. Joe and Justin were no longer best friends or at least they didn't act like they were. Alice and Harry used to joke that Justin was practically a resident. But now he hardly ever came over. For some reason, everyone was sorry for David, there was a kind of soft feeling around whenever his name came up. Molly had left him. How terrible for two adults to do that to a child. Adults were supposed to *look after* kids, to protect them from bad things. *It seemed insane that no-one actually oversaw parents!* If Alice and Harry ever said they were breaking up, Grace would kill herself. She had thought about it. It wasn't just that she didn't know who she'd live with. It was more that she *was* them. If they ruined themselves, they would ruin her. She would be finished. Her luck would have changed and Grace knew that luck was her number-one ally. She was a lucky person and luck brought luck. She had a kind of shine around her, like shiny mist.

Grace arrived at the bike path at the top of the school and

hopped off her bike. Tabitha Arbuthnot was walking down the path to the office building.

'Is that your new bike, Grace?'

Grace nodded coolly, wheeling it over to the rack, slipping the lock around the spokes and tugging it twice. Tabitha stopped for a moment to take it in.

'Has it got five gears?'

'Yes. And it's aluminium. That makes it light and fast. It took me hardly any time to get here.'

Tabitha looked surprised. 'Are you allowed to ride now?'

'I certainly am.'

'My dad won't let me. You're lucky, Grace.'

For a moment Grace entertained the thought of sympathy. It was generous of Tabitha to acknowledge her own envy. The moment passed.

Grace flung her schoolbag over her shoulder and made her way towards her classroom. She couldn't wait to get the day over, to ride home. She couldn't wait to see Alice at the doorway again. She couldn't wait to push the bike back over the last stretch of white driveway pebbles, to show Harry she could do it.

Alice had about a half an hour left before she needed to get ready for lunch with Maddie Ridgeway. The sun was shining and it was beautiful. The earth was sandy and tough going, but the herbs had to go in. They'd been sitting in their plastic trays for two weeks now, since she had made that expensive trip to Gardener's Paradise. Alice had become carried away at the nursery, by far the most expensive nursery on the Peninsula and a success because everything in it was big and beautiful and nobody wanted to wait for their garden to grow. Alice, too, had fallen under its spell with its majestic birches and lilacs, its old-fashioned roses. Initially, she had felt like a spectator of her garden, entitled only to watch it. Now she was beginning to feel responsibility, and with that responsibility, a kind of love, a fast, headlong kind of love. The garden had become the release that writing had once been. Was this where she placed her feelings? Here, digging into the earth her fears, camouflaging her needs amongst the helleborus?

There was something sensual about this garden. It was a *real* garden, not like the Vintners' with its impersonal, dial-a-designer feel, as controlled as its owners. Surely a garden should mystify its owners rather than reflect them. Surely, a garden should allow you to become lost, as Alice did, in the buzzy perfume of the jasmine and clematis, the meandering pathways.

From behind her, Alice heard the crunch, crunch, crunch of the driveway gravel. She swung around and saw Scarlett walking towards the front door.

'Scarlett!'

Scarlett stopped and looked around.

'Over here!'

She caught sight of Alice and switched course, walking across the lawn towards the garden bed. Scarlett was wearing those horrible grey cargo pants and a khaki long-sleeved T-shirt and trainers. Alice continued to push the earth back around the base of the basil, pressing it down, willing the basil to take to the earth.

Alice said, 'No school today?'

'Curriculum day.'

'Lucky you.'

'Need some help?'

'Actually, I just put the last one in. All I need to do now is water. What do you think?'

'I think it looks . . . good.'

Alice stood up. There was something vague about Scarlett. Maybe she was ill. There was always something unnerving about her, skinny to begin with but then everyone was skinny. And yet with quite shapely breasts she couldn't quite camouflage. Part girl, part woman, not quite belonging to either and knowing it. There was an obstinacy to Scarlett that sat alongside her fragility. She was one of those daughters who spent every waking moment resisting her mother. She reminded Alice of a small fighting bird.

'Are you feeling okay?'

'Oh yes,' said Scarlett, 'I'm feeling fine.'

Alice walked up the slope and pulled the hose down from the tap to the garden bed. Scarlett stood still, watching her as she began watering in the new herbs. Little rivers started to form in the earth.

'You want to talk to me about something?'

'No,' said Scarlett. 'Just thought I'd say hi. I'm working tomorrow night at the yacht club, but I'm free the rest of the weekend.'

'We don't have any plans right now, but I'll let you know if something comes up.'

Scarlett said, 'My father wants me to visit him on the holidays but I'm not going.'

'Why not?'

'Because he's a selfish arsehole, for one. And I'm not going to come running just because he's decided it suits him. And my idea of a great time is *not* accompanying him to a Wet and Wild theme-park with his plastic girlfriend.'

'Okay,' said Alice, spraying the herbs.

'I hate him,' said Scarlett.

'I'm sure you don't mean that,' said Alice.

'Actually, I do,' said Scarlett. 'My genetic stumbling block.'

Alice felt a chill pass through her. Scarlett was capable of the most savage truthfulness.

'You're the only person who means anything to me.'

Alice let go of the trigger and looked at Scarlett.

'Me?'

'I don't mean that in some sucky way.'

Alice studied her.

'Scarlett, you know we're all very fond of you. And I think you're a very bright girl who is going to have a very interesting life. But right now, you're still at home and everything can seem limited. You'll feel differently in a couple of years.'

'I don't think I'll ever meet anyone like you. Like you and Harry and the kids. The world's a really shitty place. It's full of unoriginal people who want to *take* something from you.'

Alice walked closer to her. She wondered if Scarlett's mother knew how alone Scarlett felt.

'It's really not so bad, Scarlett. I promise you.'

'Oh, don't worry about *me*!' she said, laughing. 'I won't let anyone take *anything* from me.'

Alice was there first, so she took the seat the waiter showed her to, facing the entrance. The restaurant was filling up, Alice was surprised. Lots of people went out for lunch. While she was at home, *being* at home, submerged in the vaguely comforting buzz of white noise purring under her, there were people eating their lunch in company every day.

For a moment, Alice felt a wave of simultaneous envy and annoyance. Within her walls she allowed herself to forget that another life existed. The life, in fact, that Harry belonged to for most of his twenty-four hours. It wasn't exactly that she wanted to be a lady who lunched so much as she wanted to feel one of many. In the house she felt at the centre of a small universe and therefore of too much importance. Peace came from being part of the unimportant generalised mass, where all problems were merely duplicates, and the ecstasies too. To feel ordinary was to feel convivial. It was *significance* that made life bleak with its alarming highs and lows.

The world seemed so much about herself. The starving children seemed, at times, to be starving so that Alice could eat. The suicide bombers seemed to be exploding their bombs out of hatred for Alice herself, for all that she was and all that she came from. The air was poisoned in order to poison Alice and her offspring, the apples demented by pesticide swelling over their cloudy flesh. The symphony of cancer-causing agents playing over modern life – the chemicals in house cleaners, the gas fumes, the asbestos on the wind, tiny particles of death-dust – all part of a mission to ruin her own small world. The writer's inelegant ego, always to see herself as the protagonist of every story.

Out of the window, Sunnyside business was being conducted: young couples envisioning happiness in real-estate windows, women in salons with bits of foil through their hair, looking like kindergarten Christmas trees. It was impossible to come to the village and not see phantoms of her mother, Louisa Beaufort, forty-five years old and lovely in tweed pants and cashmere twin-sets and huge sunglasses, sweeping into the shops with her air of urgent domesticity. It was five years ago that she had died. Alice felt both reborn and depleted by her death. Modern life meant ghosts inhabited the most unromantic of locations, strip-shopping centres and supermarket parking lots.

Louisa had applied herself to the ironing and school lunches, the sport and music lessons with the organisational zeal that women now used in high towers with personal assistants. In those days women channelled professional appetites where they might find some legitimacy. Even now, Alice admired mothers who made lists.

Alice remembered sitting in the back seat of the car, thousands of miles from her mother in the front seat, who was fixed permanently in Mothers' World. Mothers had to keep on top of schedules. They had diaries and calendars. Things to be paid for. Things to be collected from the cleaners and cake tins to be loaned to various neighbours. Books were launched somewhere in Mothers' World. Cocktails were drunk, children whined or whirred about good-naturedly. Men had to be pleased, or at the least cooperated with. God only knew how it all worked, Mothers' World. Far better to be a child, to just react. Kids really only had to decide one thing: to react well or to react badly. Alice mourned this.

How had she passed from daughter to mother? Such a transition defined a lifetime, but it seemed hard to believe that a lifetime was long enough to effect such a radical shift. It seemed somehow wrong, that a woman could still recall her childhood in detail whilst simultaneously becoming a mother. If life had been better designed, motherhood would only become available to a woman when all memories had neatly faded. It seemed cruel that a woman could recollect the pleasure of all she had relinquished, the sweet passivity of accepting experience as it was ordained by others. The sloth of daughters, that was something to regret the loss of, the feet on the sofa, sucking on a milkshake, yapping on the telephone. A mother remembered this as life on some curious other planet.

Perhaps this was why, so much of the time, Alice felt as if she were faking – acting the mother rather than being her. *Perhaps that's why I can't write*, thought Alice. *Perhaps I've become a professional actress.*

The waiter brought the wine list and a small white dish of warm bread rolls, disappeared, then came back and deposited a puddle of olive oil and black balsamic in another small white dish. Alice missed the comfort of butter. On the other side of the restaurant, a local real-estate agent was having lunch with a woman in a blue business suit. Now she came to think of it, he was the agent who had sold them their house, Franco something or other, swarthy and possibly no older than mid-twenties. The one Lily called the Italian

211

Stallion. He drove a shiny black car that Harry had scoffed at, too new, too crass, fat wheels, too clean. Franco Feltrinelli. They had laughed to see that the houses he represented were known as the 'Feltrinelli Portfolio'.

Behind them, against the wall, were two men, also in suits; and in front of them two women with blonde-streaked hair, laughing over white wine. In the other corner, four men in suits had napkins tucked into their shirts. They were all eating the same pasta dish. An American girl's voice sang through the sound system as if it were sucking on mangoes and light streamed in through the plate-glass windows. It was an elegant spring day, a day when people were finishing off the week's business, but leisure was in the air. The day's mood smacked of release, gave off a prophetic whiff of weekend tennis, of summer around the corner.

Alice ordered a glass of sauvignon blanc. She didn't know if Maddie Ridgeway was a drinker. A year ago, Alice would have waited to find out, opting for mineral water if Maddie did. But lately she had begun to get impatient with her own conformity.

The door opened and Maddie Ridgeway entered cheerfully in a pale yellow pants-suit and matching slingbacks. She looked put together and Alice appreciated it. It was nice the way women prepared themselves for other women. It meant more than men's efforts, because it was a gesture complete in itself, not requiring a response: flattery, blow-job, clean house, whatever. Maddie wanted nothing more from Alice than her approval and the mere act of soliciting it was a gesture of female friendship.

Alice leaned upwards, they pecked each other on the cheek and Maddie plopped down into her seat with a bounciness that made Alice realise she did this often, met other women for lunch.

'The phone went just as I was halfway out the door . . . Don't you hate it! Oh, goody, you're drinking! I'll have one of those.'

She indicated Alice's glass to the waiter, who was spreading the napkin over Maddie's lap.

'Have you looked at the menu? I tell you, the salads are excellent and the fish is very good, very fresh, nicely done; the chef's from London.'

Alice said the menu looked very nice, she was hungry, hadn't been here in a long time, had come with Harry months ago but he had been so busy lately that at night they were too tired to go out, children cramped one's style.

Maddie said, 'We've got our life back. Just. Tom is fifteen. He has his own life now. It's got so easy.'

'I'm still in that blur,' said Alice.

'Oh, it's not long now,' said Maddie. 'Anyway you look fantastic, you don't look like you have two children, you always did look wonderful.'

Alice wondered if it were true.

'Anyhow,' said Maddie, taking a roll and breaking it between pearly varnished fingers, 'who knew, back then, that we'd both be here in Sunnyside. It's so nice.'

Alice thought of Maddie twenty years ago, of how unalike they had been. Having children edged people closer together because the childless receded from view. It was a terrible thing, but inevitable, that people with children lost their appetite for the childless, whether it was from envy or boredom it was hard to say. Simply having a child gave you the opportunity or encouragement to fall into a kind of love with people you might not even like. Somehow it was enough. The giant step forward in evolution, the sheer energy required to follow through the consequences of reckless conception, was enough to unite you, at the very least for a lunchtime. Both of them had relinquished the night-time peace of oneness, oneselfness. Vanished forever. However different Maddie Ridgeway and Alice were, they shared *this*, an increased capacity for suffering and a cold certainty that there was *no going back*.

'It's so nice to catch up!'

The waiter brought Maddie's glass and they clinked, sipped, replaced their glasses at exactly the same moment, mirror images. Alice had the sudden urge to keep going, keep doing exactly what Maddie did a split second late, like that dreadful game Grace played when she sort of talked on top of you, saying the same thing you said. In fact, thought Alice, she and Maddie weren't catching up at all, there was nothing to catch up on, because there was no shared friendship, no detail. Clouds crossed the sky and made the sunlight flicker in the room, on then off, off then on, changing the mood instantly over and over.

They both ordered a salad and the grilled whiting. There was a pause as they wrestled with the right conversational strategy to bridge twenty years.

'Are you writing?'

Alice shook her head. 'Well, with the move, you know, I felt we all needed me to be available. Someone has to hold things together.'

Maddie smiled, happy at this. 'And it's always us! Good old us! The whole thing would just hit an iceberg if we girls didn't do our stuff!'

'Exactly.'

'You know, Alice, I'm kind of surprised you're here. When your book came out – the one that won that prize?'

'Well,' said Alice, feeling that familiar tide of shame welling up that she had not delivered to people like Maddie what she had once promised. 'That was a while ago, now.'

Alice momentarily considered telling Maddie about the film offers, but she had heard nothing for months. She could not face talking herself up to someone she barely knew.

'I saw you on TV. I said to Angus, "That girl always had fish to fry. Big fish." But seeing you back here in Sunnyside makes me think that even girls like you, the smart girls, realise that *security* amounts to something.'

'Absolutely,' said Alice. She had that vague hollow feeling she sometimes got when depression swerved around a corner and came bearing down on her from nowhere.

'At a certain point we say to ourselves: Okay, I either work for the UN and kind of speed through my life feeling clever and alive and at the centre of things – not to put it down or anything – or I commit to the simple order of things, the ordinary old order. A nice house. A nice neighbourhood. It's so easy to make fun of them, but actually there's a reason why women like us gravitate towards these things. You know what I'm saying?'

'I think so, Maddie.'

Alice suddenly felt like ordering a martini. A large martini.

'The ordinary old order. It's not so bad. The kids. The man. The station wagon.'

'Yep,' said Alice.

'In the end, who really wants to work for the UN?'

Alice did. Alice suddenly felt the wave of ambition that had flattened out inside her surge back into life. Maddie Ridgeway, sitting before her, extolling the virtues of resignation. It *was* resignation, wasn't it? Maddie trying to paint defeat as somehow a *choice*. Had Alice really chosen this? The whole shebang: marriage and Harry and the garden with its irrigation system and the discount vouchers for Video Ezy and the commute through Deptford to the city to go to productions of Chekhov reconceived in abattoirs? The thing was, certain kinds of women fell into this life. It was the life they automatically had if they failed to resist it. Had Alice just failed to resist?

This was it, thought Alice. *The mid-life crisis. This was it!* The single cerebral sprint from the starting block of what you once imagined for yourself to the finishing line of what you had actually become. Here. At Dunes by the Beach. The finishing line. Here it was, the moment of recognition, the big one, in a suburban bistro. *All I am.* Until this moment, Alice realised she had clung to the tiny insistent belief that, at some point, greatness would embrace her. But it was all over. The next thirty years would be about accommodating this, in the dining rooms of friends, or the waiting rooms of psychotherapists, or in churches, the churches one sought out or constructed. Perhaps Sunnyside was her church.

'It's all about kids, isn't it?' said Maddie, with a performance sigh. 'There are no U-turns on the freeway of parenting.'

Alice knew the truth of it, the banal truth that kids were the final, unequivocal alteration to who you might have been. But was it wrong to quietly wonder, as she did in bed at night, about lives not lived? Were mothers allowed to sneak surreptitious peeks at their own historical potential?

Maddie smiled and raised her glass. 'So how is life treating you?'

Alice struggled to put a positive spin on things, something that would make Maddie smile her million-dollar smile and suggest they make this lunch the first of many. Perhaps Maddie's friendly gaze would bestow on Alice some acceptance of how things had turned out. Maybe she just needed to be sanctioned by other Sunnyside mothers in order to feel as if she belonged. Lately, she felt old. Once things came and went, moods and worries arrived swiftly and then somehow left just as fast, banished by the sheer effervescence of youth.

'I just feel . . . well . . .'

Maddie replaced her glass and looked concerned.

'Gosh, we've known each other a long time, Alice. You can say anything to me.'

'Well . . .' Alice trailed off.

'I promise, I'm unshockable,' said Maddie.

'Well, the thing is, we made the big move. We thought things would feel . . . *right*. But mostly I wake up and I feel . . . *sad*.'

The word sat there between them, flat and heavy. Maddie took a sip of her wine.

'Sad?'

'Well. You know, yes. Yes. Nothing urgent. Nothing desperate . . . Just. Sad.'

Maddie rushed to make this all right. 'Listen, it's a lot of pressure, holding a family together. I mean, kids! And you're probably missing yourself, the part of you that is you. The "You" part of you.'

'The "You" part?'

Maddie said, 'We all need to find time for it and we hardly ever do. Because we're running around looking after everyone else. No? No? Isn't that so?'

Alice could see that Maddie was on a roll now, latching on to reasons as they flew past, in order to take charge of Alice and her unbearable sorrow.

'We are wives and mothers and nurses and teachers and mentors and we are also *goddesses*, you know what I'm saying?'

Alice thought it was hard to look at a woman in a yellow pants-suit and think Goddess. There was just something about the pants-suit, as such, that resisted transcendence.

'I don't feel connected to things, Maddie. I feel as if I'm floating. Don't you ever feel like that?'

Maddie Ridgeway stared at Alice with an enigmatic expression ... irritated? Found out? Possibly Maddie Ridgeway had never felt sad, raised by parents who did not suggest it, married to a man who did not evoke or permit it. Maddie Ridgeway, whom Alice had never liked and still didn't really like, although she was trying. It had all been clear, there on the school oval twenty years ago, that Maddie Ridgeway would make the ordinary work for her. She was a pragmatist.

'Floating?'

'Don't you feel that way, Maddie? Don't you ever feel that it's only your own vigilance that stops you disappearing? You stand there in your house saying, "I am here. I belong here. This is my life." And if you didn't do that, you'd just vanish?'

Maddie said, *'That's how you feel?'*

Alice looked at her. What perverse inclination had prompted her to speak this way to Maddie Ridgeway, netball captain, Auntie Mame, *prefect*?

'Maddie,' said Alice, quietly. 'Don't you ever feel that?'

Maddie enclosed Alice's hand lying on the table, the way a lover might. The waiter set their food down, reminding them of who they had been only minutes ago. Maddie Ridgeway had finally surrendered.

'I have those thoughts. But I try not to notice them.'

She looked at Alice sadly.

'Maybe you just notice too much.'

seventeen

'And so social changes would be drastically affected by these shifts in technology. As I have argued, this would be both a good thing and possibly a bad thing.'

Tabitha Arbuthnot was reading the final page of her essay on Life in the Future and Mr Polhurst was watching her in that way that he had when he was not overly impressed. Grace could read Mr Polhurst *like a map*. His flat brow had a tiny furrow in the middle which appeared whenever he was trying not to be annoyed. It was clear to Grace that Mr Polhurst's mind was made up about Tabitha Arbuthnot and Grace would like to bet that both she and Mr Polhurst were at one on this. Tabitha was the kind of person for whom *satisfactory* was the best she would hope for. It was what she expected that made Tabitha what she was, not what she achieved.

Tabitha's voice was starting to sound robotic and Grace could feel the air in the room shift from curiosity at how Tabitha would shape up, to confirmation of the expected (diligent, dull). There was a dead feeling in the room, as if the oxygen had come to rest on the window sills and blackboard ledges.

'As I have argued, our increasing power in terms of technology could very well lead us into more wars and greater harm to human kind. In summary, and between you and I, the present looks better than the future.'

Somehow, Grace was going to be beautiful and casual and glamorous and very, very famous. Fame was the essential thing. What she coveted was the collective sway of heads towards her as she walked through airports and shopping malls, a swaying shift in her direction. It was important to be *public*. Grace knew how it felt when the teacher's admiring gaze was on her, the attention of her classmates, the sense of warmth. It *was* warmth, a fast rising tide of warmth flowing through her, she felt herself light up.

Goodness alone was not rewarded. Goodness was its own reward, but fame was another kind of goodness, since one's own fame was, in a certain way, a gift to others. When Grace looked at Joe, she could see that he did not see the world this way. Joe, with his weird obsession with the sheep. Of all the brothers in the world, she had to get Joe. He'd come into her room the night before and started going on about the sheep and Grace had agreed that something must be done, but that hadn't seemed enough for Joe. He'd said: *Imagine being with a hundred kids in this room for fifty-six days, Grace!*

Imagine that! Shitting and pissing and breathing. It's not just a horri-ble thought, Grace. It's actually happening. Grace knew that Joe was always going to be more lovable than she was. Everyone liked Joe but their liking had the tiniest hint of sympathy.

The room shuffled into lacklustre applause lead by Mr Polhurst, whose solid, slow clap was distinctly, perfectly, a *teacher's* clap. His bottom rested on the library table, half sitting with his feet still on the ground, arms folded that way that he did, somehow *superior*. There was a look of contained irritation on his face. Mr Polhurst had become paunchy over winter . . . too many jam doughnuts from the canteen. Grace had noticed them during lunchtime 'See Me' sessions, when she had to go over work with him in his tiny office. Jam doughnuts spread out in a sugary puddle on the brown paper bag. It had been seeing this that had made Mr Polhurst no longer seem God-like.

'Very nice, Tabitha,' said Mr Polhurst. There was a bee in the room, buzzing somewhere over Tabitha's shoulder. She hovered uncomfortably in front of the class. 'You can sit down now.'

Tabitha, suddenly confident in the relief of her dismissal, straightened up and flicked her brown hair over her shoulders and took her seat.

Mr Polhurst moved from the side of the room to the front and perched on the edge of his table. He was wearing green and gold socks. *However this country got green and gold as its national*

223

colours was a total, total mystery, thought Grace. Who was going to take Australia seriously as a nation, with colours like that? Not to mention the national anthem, what a joke! The real anthem nobody could sing because no-one knew the words. The song everyone liked was a *story* about a guy and tucker bag. *Our national song* was about a sheep jumping out of a knapsack, for God's sake.

Mr Polhurst said, 'Tabitha, congratulations on some very solid work there,' but Grace noticed that his mouth was tight.

Tabitha smiled like someone was pinching her.

'But, there are a couple of grammatical things I'd like to go over. "Between you and I." Not good.'

The air in the room jumped just a little, a flurry of dust. Heads looked up from doodles, legs uncrossed.

'*Between* is a preposition which means it must be followed by the objective case and I as in 'between you and *I*' is *subjective*. The objective of I is what?'

Grace noticed that Tabitha looked irritated. She'd written the damn essay. She'd done the presentation. She had no idea whatsoever what the objective of I was. What did it even mean, *the objective*?

Grace raised her hand. Mr Polhurst's eyes scanned the room and finally, defeatedly, came to rest on Grace.

'Me is the objective of I.'

'Thank you, Grace. Between you and *me*. That is correct. Similarly, between him and her not he and she and between them and us, not they and we. Are we clear on that?'

The room nodded. There it was again, that tiny tickle of self-pleasure. There was absolutely nothing wrong with wanting to do well, it was just that for some strange reason, nobody was happy for her. Grace had something grand within her and grandeur was really not very appealing because it made other people, *correctly*, feel small.

Grace made her way up the stairs to the teachers' gallery. The building had been erected almost a century ago as the boarding house. The teachers' tiny offices had once been bedrooms, little cells each with a small window looking out onto the oval. From outside came the symphony of after-school noises, farewells, laughter. On Mr Polhurst's door was a fake road sign of a mobile phone with a line through it and another sticker saying 'Forewarned is forearmed', whatever that meant. Grace knocked and opened the door.

Another doughnut! Someone really should tell him that he should be eating more from the bottom of the pyramid. There were papers spread out over the desk, around a silver plastic lunchbox. There should be a law against selling lunchboxes to adults.

'Sit down, Grace.'

Grace sat on the student chair which, due to the confines of the office, meant her knees were yuckily only a few centimetres or so away from Mr Polhurst's knees.

'You completed a very fine paper, Grace.'

'Thank you, Mr Polhurst.'

'You're really applying yourself this year. We're all very pleased with the work you're doing.'

'Thank you. I want to do well. I *like* to do well.'

'I'm sure you do, Grace. I think we're all aware of that.'

Grace was confused. Why the 'See Me'? Maybe this was some new *building self-esteem* thing that Miss Pressfield was always writing about in the newsletter.

'Is that it, Mr Polhurst?'

'Yes, Grace. That's really all I wanted to say . . .' but he didn't close the sentence, Grace noticed. The 'say' was left hanging as if there was something more, something he was having second thoughts about.

'You know, Grace, you could try to relax a little more in class.'

'You want me to *relax*?'

The word sat in the air sounding somehow indecent. Mr Polhurst looked worried.

'What I mean is, you could try to enjoy it all a little more and not push yourself so. You know, you still have a few years before the pressure really starts. I'd just like to see you have a little more fun.'

'I *am* having fun, Mr Polhurst. I'm having a *lot* of fun.'

'Well, okay then. My mistake. You run along now. I'll see you on Monday.'

Grace stood up and moved towards the door. She opened it. Someone way down the corridor was singing 'Red! Red! Red is the best! Put our champions to the test!' Grace turned around. Mr Polhurst was bouncing a collection of papers on his knee, straightening them up, a farewell to the moment.

'Mr Polhurst, you know Shakespeare used "Between you and I" in *The Merchant of Venice*.'

'You've read *The Merchant of Venice*?'

'My dad took me to see the play. We read it together first. Is grammar the most essential thing?'

'Grammar?' said Mr Polhurst, blinking.

'Great writers make their own rules, don't they? Things don't have to be correct if they're astonishing.'

Mr Polhurst rested his papers on his knee. He looked so sad Grace suddenly felt her feelings of revenge fade. Really, it wasn't worth it. He had once been a kid too, her age, everything up ahead. Between then and now, something had happened to Mr Polhurst. *Life* had happened. The buzz of wanting badly, that buzz which gripped her, had once been part of him, only it had given way to nothing exceptional. A teacher with a doughnut habit.

'It seems like we have to make that choice, Mr Polhurst. Do we want to *become* the rules or do we want to change them?'

'I think you've already made that choice, Grace.'

Back at her bike, Grace threw her schoolbag into the basket and worked at the combination on the lock. What an annoying day this had been. This morning, riding to school, everything had seemed so great. She'd *looked forward* to school. And slowly, through the course of the day, her enthusiasm had got crunched. By the final tally of the inter-house athletics, her house, Green House, had been placed an outrageous last. *If they'd only let her run last in the relay.* And then there had been Mr Polhurst and his weird 'See Me'. What was *that* about?

Grace got on her bike and clicked her helmet into place. Miss Pressfield, the principal, was standing at the top of the path, chatting to parents as they herded their children into cars.

'Grace Haskins, is that your new bike?'

Grace felt a wave of velvety pleasure wash through her.

'Yes it is, Miss Pressfield. Isn't it nice?'

'It's terrific. Now, you'll remember your road rules, won't you?'

'Yes, I will.'

'Grace, I wanted to talk to you anyway and now's as good a time as any.'

Grace looked up at Miss Pressfield's strange, dry face. It had lines running deep across it, like creek beds.

'Baybridge is competing in the inter-school public-speaking competition next week. We were only going to have the seniors take part, but a few of the teachers suggested to me that perhaps you might like to enter the junior competition. It's completely up to you.'

For a moment Grace thought she might drop the bike. The inter-school public-speaking competition, oh boy! Grace had attended the year before when Astrid's brother had competed. He had spoken about the Australian film industry, but failed to qualify for the finals. Now, the school principal was asking her, Grace Haskins, to compete. This was incredible! The whole day was saved!

'Oh yes, Miss Pressfield, oh definitely!'

'Well that will be you and Tabitha Arbuthnot. You're the only two.'

Tabitha Arbuthnot! Didn't they *realise*? Didn't they *understand*? Tabitha wasn't in Grace's league. Tabitha Arbuthnot was never going to be extraordinary.

'So you'd better put your thinking cap on about what you want to speak about. You should submit your idea to Mr Polhurst by the end of tomorrow. If he thinks it's appropriate, you can go ahead and prepare your speech. No more than ten minutes long. And if you get into the finals, you have to speak impromptu for five on the judge's topic. We know you'll do your personal best for Baybridge, Grace.'

Speaking 'impromptu'. Grace had heard the phrase before but couldn't remember exactly what it meant. It was amazing how things just happened. One moment, you were getting on your bike to go home and watch TV, and the next, everything was different. Anything was possible. It was magic!

The wind was behind her. By standing on the pedals she found her legs could work harder going uphill. All the tiny turns and choices of the morning seemed aeons ago. She was doing it all again, only backwards. The school traffic had cleared while she was speaking to Miss Pressfield and it was a straight run past the nature reserve and through Sunnyside village. She wasn't even going to stop to buy sweets with the change from her lunch order. She just wanted to get home and tell everyone. Harry and Alice would be so proud. First the bike ride, now this!

The school bus passed her and, through the back window, Tilly Rogers and Jessica Peterson waved at her. They were both wearing plaits with ribbons threaded through. The bus climbed the hill in front of her and soon dropped down the other side, out of sight.

Grace turned into Ocean Crescent and then allowed the bike to sail to the left into Carringdale Road. As she came off the asphalt onto the dirt, the bike bounced around, and for a second Grace thought she might lose control, but it righted itself. It was fun doing things just a little more wildly.

Grace leant her bike against the walkway. Pinned to the front door was a note from Alice saying that she would be back by four-thirty and Grace was to let herself in and call Alice on her mobile.

Grace was furious. This was the one day! The one day she really cared that her mother was there. Her first ever day riding home! Didn't anybody care about that? All those safety warnings and stuff, what were they for if no-one was even going to make sure she got home okay? There was *no way* she was going to call Alice. *Let her worry*!

Grace walked around the house to make sure no-one was out the back. There were giant hoses leading out of the pool like fat white worms. It was half empty. The white pool walls looked weird. There was no sign of the pool guy. Grace thought about going next door to find Scarlett. But it was Friday. Scarlett worked at the library after school.

Grace went to fetch the spare key from under the gardenia pot at the start of the walkway. If only Harry were here. If only she could get to his work somehow, to the campus. She could ask him about the public-speaking competition, about *strategy*. It would be fun to see her dad in his office and there wouldn't be any distractions from Joe or Alice. She could get a headstart on her topic. It had to be the right one. It *had* to be. Grace knew that if the topic was the right one, she would just fire. *She might even win!*

Grace stopped at the gardenia, turned around and looked at her beautiful new blue bike. *I'll ride.* It was practically all downhill to Deptford. There was a bike track along the stretch of highway and then there was the coast road, the roundabout and from there it would only be about fifteen minutes to the campus, most of it foot-path. All up, it would take her about forty minutes. *Imagine saying she rode to Deptford!* The image of herself on her blue Raleigh sailing down Freeman's Hill pushed everything else out of Grace's mind. Imagine arriving at Harry's building and him seeing her there and saying how did you get here and Grace saying: *I rode!* Alice *deserved* to worry.

The first thing David noticed was that the air was thick with some-thing familiarly musty. Musty and dense. The collected smell of men.

Around the walls of the small hall was a continuous mural, painted by children in neon colours, depicting the street life of Sea-bank. David knew for a fact that the street life of Seabank ran to the Wednesday main-street market, with canopied stalls selling hand-carved wooden tug-along toys or paper-towel holders and granny-knit toddler jumpers in football team colours. You had your retired folk clasping single geranium pots they had got for a snip and the odd blonde mother up from Sunnyside for her Pilates session, but street life in Seabank was not awash with *diversity*. In the absence of anything more multicultural to draw on, the young Seabank muralists had chosen to depict kite flyers, yachts and the gelati-hued facade of the Seabank ice-cream parlour, a few doors down from his bookshop. Against this mural were a collection of faces united in their pallor, the pallor of men who had been betrayed.

Glanville Perry, the Sunnyside newsagent, was the group leader and initiator. It was he who had first contacted David, diplomatically dropping him a line to the bookshop saying that he'd heard David might need some support and enclosing the group's flyer, which featured a line illustration of a smiling man kicking a football to a smiling small boy while a smiling woman with a baby in her arms watched on. It was captioned: 'Remember when life was like this?'

At first David had thrown the leaflet and the letter in the rubbish bin, but found himself extracting and decrumpling the leaflet an hour later. *Other* people had to salvage their lives. *Other* people went to AA meetings or anger management or therapy. Why not him? What made him so goddamn special? All his adult life, David had nurtured a snobbery about self-conscious life-improvement, as if something would be lost by acknowledging that things could be better. He did not belong to the masses with their ordinary tastes and flaws, their Japanese cars and tabloid newspapers and bus tours through Europe. He was smarter, more tasteful, more sophisticated. He'd sell endless copies of Bryce Courtenay or Danielle Steel, nursing a private consternation that popular taste was so disappointing. And yet, what made him feel so superior? There was nothing sophisticated about suffering. There was nothing grand about going home to a son he didn't know and a ghostly wife. And so, when picking up his order of the *Spectator*, David, adopting the humility of an abandoned spouse, found himself chatting to Glanville and allowing himself to be talked into going along to the Seabank men's group the following Friday afternoon.

Sitting in a semicircle enclosing David was Bill, a chubby bearded man in jeans and an orange polar fleece; Des, a tall, youngish yuppie in chinos and a pink Polo shirt; and Terry Polhurst, the teacher from Baybridge, whom David had met at school functions in the past. It was cold in the hall. David pulled his jacket tight around his torso.

'Good to see you all here and a special welcome to our new member, David.'

The others nodded in David's direction. Glanville Perry gave him a big smile. He was holding a clipboard.

'Okay, so,' said Glanville. 'All right then.' Shuffling as Bill pulled out a cigarette packet from somewhere inside his polar fleece.

'Sorry, Bill,' said Glanville, still smiling, 'we're a drug-free environment here. Remember? No props. Let's spell it out again for David's benefit.'

In unison, Glanville, Bill, Des and Terry murmured, 'Embrace the pain, don't deny it. Release it like a dove and watch it fly from you.'

Glanville looked at David, content. Everyone had remembered the words. It was feeling like a *group*.

'That's what we're on about, David. We believe that it's important to acknowledge the pain. Now, we're all here because we share pain. And this is a particularly *male* pain. Which is fine. It's good. A lot of men never truly "know" their pain. They sense it. They fear it. They push it away. They . . .? Des, can you help us out here?'

The others turned to look at Des hopefully.

'They *deny* it,' said Des.

'And that's the triple truth,' said Glanville, nodding. 'We need to know our pain in order to give it away. And we *will* give it away. But you can't give your pain away if you have not truly *owned* it. Am I making sense, David?'

'Sure,' said David. 'I guess.'

'All of us have been, okay, let's get down to tintacks. All of us have been *left in the wake of another's wilful actions.*'

Terry nodded at this.

From the room next door, David could hear the sounds of a female judo class – the thump of bodies on mats and the occasional Oriental exclamation. David realised that tonight would have been his and Molly's turn to host the first Friday of the month dinner with the gang, already a rusty relic of an abandoned social calendar.

Glanville looked at Bill. 'Bill, can you summarise for David what has brought us here together?'

'We were all left in the wake of some cunts. Blonde. Brunette. Fat. Skinny. Whatever. Cunts,' said Bill.

Des sighed loudly. Glanville looked displeased. 'Now, Bill, let's make that anger *useful*. Angry words are a refuge from feelings.'

Des said, 'I really object to that terminology. I don't see why a group of guys can't hang out and salvage something good out of the wreckage without being sexist arseholes. Okay? I mean, just because we've been dealt a bad hand, doesn't mean we should revert to being cavemen, right?'

Glanville nodded. 'What do you say to that, Bill?'

'I can't speak for all of you. But my particular story stars a cunt in the leading role.'

Des sighed theatrically. 'You know, Bill, maybe that kind of attitude has something to do with why women behave the way they do.'

'What's that supposed to mean?' said Bill, still holding his cigarette between his fingers as if, possibly, there might be a change in policy coming.

Glanville said, '*Guys*. Let's give Bill a little room to move on this one, Des. Remember, this room has a glass bell over the top of it.'

Glanville looked towards the ceiling, willing the vision.

'What's said in here is between us. We can experience a *process*, without worrying about what others will think. For the purposes of the group, we are the only people left on the planet.'

A loud thump from next door and a woman's full-throttled yell of triumph.

'Here, here,' said Terry. 'Can I just add, for David's sake, that while we are all about solidarity, we're not trying to be a *movement*. This is not the eighties. We are not out banging drums in forests. We're just a bunch of guys recovering from some pretty savage personal circumstances. Marriage was the ocean. And now we're all together in the lifeboat.'

'The cunts threw us overboard,' said Bill.

Des turned his back to Bill and looked at David. 'Maybe you'd like to share with us something of your personal story, David?'

'My wife. The pool man,' said David.

Silence.

'I know, I know, what a fucking cliché.'

'Life *is* a cliché,' said Bill.

'You bet it is,' said Glanville.

'It's such a cliché that even *acknowledging* that life is a cliché is a cliché,' continued Bill, pleased with himself.

'Right on,' said Des.

'She's going through something,' said David.

'She's not coming back,' said Glanville.

'Well,' said David, 'I don't know.'

'She's not coming back, David,' said Glanville sternly, tapping his biro end on the clipboard.

David was confused. 'Well, I really don't know that.'

'*We* know that,' said Des.

Terry, Des and Bill nodded.

'We all have our Mollies, David,' said Des. 'We look out for their return. But they don't return.'

'I don't know that,' said David, beginning to feel irritated. '*You* don't know that.'

David saw Terry and Bill and Des and Glanville share a silent glance.

'Hey, hey, hey,' said Glanville. 'Think about it, David. Molly's moving on. She's moving on. It could be the pool man. It could be the guy who sells her the next Golf. It could be just about any damn fella in a convertible at the traffic light. The point is, she has thrown your marriage in the dumpster and you don't care to know it.'

'It's in the dumpster, Dave,' said Des.

'Think about closing the lid,' said Terry. 'Picture the lid coming down on the dumpster.'

Bill was nodding sadly in the background. There was an expectation in the air. They were waiting for something. David wondered if they were right, if wives, once gone, never returned. One thing was sure, they never returned in the same way. David felt a wave of superiority flow over him. He wasn't like these men in their mottled milky humiliation. In their company, David felt a kind of communion with the wives. Women *could* do better than Bill and Des and

Glanville and even Terry Polhurst. Women had a *right* to expect better than these slack-bellied losers, whining about justice. They had no right to women, women who, while hateful and strategic, were also long-legged and sweet-smelling, temptresses, baby-makers, secretarial geniuses, CEOs, sex kittens and counsellors. This motley collection of the charisma-bypassed had no right at all to complain about their loss.

Glanville broke the silence.

'What we're doing here, the purpose here is simply to say, "Hello *life*".'

David realised that he didn't really like men very much. What would it be like to be one of those women next door, flinging each other down on the floor, *powerful*.

'I need to leave now,' said David, getting up.

'Dave,' said Bill, *'mate.'*

'Face it,' said Des, 'we're all you've got.'

David's shoes made clack-clack sounds in the echoey space. As he walked through the door, he breathed in the salty spring air.

It was all getting too much for Grace. She had fallen twice along the highway footpath, even though it was straight, because several of the driveways had steep gutters that she couldn't see until too late.

Then, on Freeman's Hill, it had been hard to get the gears right. She couldn't remember which way to move them for going downhill, was it up or down? Then those cars had tooted her at the bottom of the hill and some stupid boys stuck their heads out of the window and yelled something she hadn't understood. Boys could be so unbelievably dumb, Scarlett was right. *It was like they just didn't think*, just did the first thing that came into their heads.

Grace hadn't brought a water bottle, which was stupid. She tried to drive her thirst out of her head, get on top of it, but Grace knew the more she tried to forget it, the thirstier she got. She thought about the African man in the Olympic marathon who had come last but kept going until he entered the arena *days* after the winner. Some people could play tricks on themselves, knew how to fool themselves for a purpose. The whole point of achieving rested on caring too much, caring beyond normal limits. She knew that the way she wanted things was not the way most people wanted things. Her wanting had danger to it. Everything special in life was dangerous or oversized. *Push, push, push away the thirst like the African runner*.

Grace got off her bike to cross the highway because it seemed too creepy riding across three lanes. She was pretty sure that was David McLelland passing her in his blue Volvo, heading towards Sunnyside or Seabank. She wished he'd seen her, but he was staring straight ahead, looking kind of *mad*. Then some maniacs tooted her from a car with surfboards on the top, even though she was back on the footpath before they even reached that section of the highway. Grace was disgusted to find that she was crying. It was just that she was so thirsty! And hot! And she wasn't there yet! If it weren't for her thirst, she wouldn't let those stupid tooters get to her. Some people just liked to show off. Some people just didn't like kids. But this was a *mission*. It was important to set yourself challenges, even if it meant breaking rules. Up above her, clouds flitted across the afternoon blue. Usually Grace would be in front of the fire now, chatting to Alice, or doing homework on the kitchen table. The thought of this gave Grace a final intense blast of courage. She had escaped the *usual*. She had broken free.

Finally, the clock tower at the centre of the campus appeared in the distance. Grace's shin was bleeding from where she had caught it on the chain guard. She should have changed out of her uniform. The hem had ripped when she'd fallen and now it was half hanging down and there was a huge ladder in her tights. That was the price you paid for going where you had not gone before! Grace sped through the boomgate with a final, triumphant surge into the university grounds. It was hard to tell exactly where she was. She seemed to have come in through a different gate to the one she'd been through before with Harry. She'd sailed past the security box and now everything looked familiar and unfamiliar at the same time, as if it had been rearranged. Grace slipped off the bike and took a long drink from the water fountain. Bells pealed above her. She glanced up at the clock tower and saw that it was already five o'clock. It had taken her nearly an hour and a quarter!

Grace wheeled her bike around the corner of the staff club. She had been in there, through the ivy-covered doors. She'd had dinner there with Alice and Joe and Harry a couple of times. Veal schnitzel. Joe had tried to talk her out of it by mooing plaintively at her as she ate. Harry had let her go up to the bar and buy her own lemonades. Outside the staff club, a sign pointed the way to the Krappford Building.

Halfway down the paved walk, Grace's shin finally gave out and she started to limp. It was humiliating. People were looking at her. There was blood dripping down over her ankle and her hair had come loose from the elastic. With a terrible, singing clarity, it occurred to Grace that maybe she wouldn't be able to find Harry. She willed herself not to panic. *Grace Haskins stay calm*! He didn't usually get home until after six, so he must be here somewhere. Unless he had a conference. Unless he was teaching. Unless he'd gone to something at the staff club, some farewell drinks or whatever. She should have called him. She should have warned him that she was coming, to be waiting for her, but that would have ruined everything. *The whole point was to show him what she was capable of.*

Grace reached the Krappford building, which was actually two eight-storey buildings, linked on the third floor by a walkway. She could tell Harry's office, because the window was shrouded by the big tree and he had a small stained-glass picture in the corner that Grace had made for him in first grade for Father's Day. He often told Grace that he looked at it every single day and how nice it was with the light coming through making patterns in the room. Grace looked up now and saw it there, just visible. His blinds were half-way down.

What was she going to do with her bike? She couldn't take it in the building. Bikes wouldn't be allowed in the lift and if she just propped it against something in the lobby, it would certainly get stolen. She'd never survive it if she lost her new bike on the day of her very first major ride. She couldn't risk losing just about the best thing she had ever been given, *ever*. Besides which, her parents would be furious. They were always going on about her taking responsibility for her possessions. They would never give her anything ever again if she let her bike get stolen.

Grace yelled up towards his window.

'HARRY HASKINS!'

She had made her voice as loud as it could possibly be. She took a deep breath and pushed the air down, down into her chest.

'HARRY HASKINS! HARRY HASKINS!'

But Grace could hear how her father's name broke up into fragments of wind and was carried off. A few students cast glances her way as they entered and left the building, but no one offered to help her. Grace thought about asking a girl sitting on the grass to keep an eye on her bike while she ran up, but maybe the girl was only going to be there for a couple more minutes, maybe she didn't want to hang around, or maybe she would steal her blue Raleigh, take it straight down to the part of Deptford where stolen goods were bought and sold. She had long black hair and spooky black eye make-up like a bat. Like a female bat. She didn't look like a thief, but thieves didn't look like thieves. The guy from Sunnyside who just had his face on the front page of the newspaper, he'd looked just like a school principal in his shirt and tie, he looked like a regular Dad and he stole *literally millions*. The Female Bat was almost certainly the member of a bike-stealing racket. Grace absolutely, absolutely couldn't risk it.

But there was also no way that Grace could ride home. The thought fell over her like a shroud. What was that word Harry always used about her? She'd had to ask Scarlett what it meant after listening to Harry and Alice discuss her in the bathroom one night when they thought she was asleep. *Impetuous*. Acting without caution. But what could be done, what could be *great* if approached cautiously? And yet . . . here she was. In a mess. And annoyed with herself for not *thinking through*. She was a disappointment *to herself*!

Exhausted, Grace sat down on the bank of grass facing the

doorway. Maybe Harry would just come out of the door, with his coat and his satchel, and she could yell to him and wave and he would look astonished and then embrace her. Grace would tell him all about her ride. He would inspect her wounds and kiss her and then he would call Alice to say she's okay. He would put her bike carefully in the back of his car and together they would drive home, in the warm, cosy vehicle, and Harry would give Grace a list of brilliant topics for the public-speaking competition. When they walked in the door, Joe would say: *You rode to Deptford*? He would be amazed, impressed. And Alice would pretend to be annoyed, but hug her with relief and love and pride. Then they would all sit down to a delicious pasta dinner, a happy united family that survived the ups and downs of children's remarkable efforts, and Grace could go to sleep in her beautiful bed with the starry sky doona cover. Grace closed her eyes to see it there, beckoning her.

Miraculously, when Grace opened her eyes again, the door of the Krappford opened and Harry came out, carrying his coat and his satchel. Around him, students swirled and separated, waving goodbye. Harry looked over to the lawn on the other side of the quadrangle, where the girl with the dark eyes was slowly rising to her feet. Grace opened her mouth to call to him, but no noise came out. Down inside her throat, her father's name stalled. He waved to the bike thief, who made her way towards Harry with long loose strides. Grace had missed her moment. Harry was now locked in earnest conversation with the girl. What did he have to say to her that was so important? It struck Grace that the girl had been waiting for him all this time.

Harry put his hand on the girl's back, to draw her along with him as he walked. Grace pulled her bike up and followed. Her father and the girl were slowly walking towards the car park. Harry was no longer touching her, they were just side by side. Just a regular teacher and student, thought Grace. She's asking him something and he's giving one of those long, don't-know-when-to-stop answers that he sometimes gave her and Joe. When the girl went her own way, Grace would surprise Harry. She couldn't appear now because she wouldn't have Harry's full attention. The glory, the double glory of the ride and the public-speaking competition, wouldn't have its proper recognition because Harry's reaction would be tilted towards the girl. That's what happened when another adult was around. Your own mother or father always seemed to think the other adult was more important.

Grace followed them past the Union building and the campus bookshop to the car park. Surely here the girl would leave. What was she going to do, get in the car with Harry? Into *their* car? The *family* car? That wasn't possible. But when they reached Harry's Saab, that was exactly what happened. Grace watched as Harry fished around in his pocket for his keys and clicked open the central locking. The girl went around to the passenger side and got in.

Some girl was getting into their car! What was Grace going to do? If she rode up now, it would be a total mess. There was the distinct possibility, only just now occurring to Grace, that Harry might in fact be *annoyed* with her for riding to Deptford, annoyed at being snuck up on in his place of employment, a place Grace had no business to be. Why this should be so was not a question Grace wanted to think about.

Grace felt tears welling up. What was he doing with a student in his car anyway? She was ruining everything! Grace had to admit it, everything *was* ruined! The whole day overwhelmed her, an exhausting marathon of highs and lows.

Harry started the car and was backing out of the car park. Grace put her helmet on. It was peak hour around Deptford. Maybe if she rode really hard, if she just pushed through the pain the same way she did at the inter-house athletics carnival (to win a gorgeous blue first ribbon), she would be able to follow Harry, at least into Deptford. Then she would be able to work out what was going on. Why the student was in *their* car. Students belonged on campus and then in beer gardens and messy student houses. She was angry with her father for letting things get confusing. Jumping on her bike, she turned right, out of the car park, and onto the pavement that ran alongside the main road leading into Deptford. Up ahead, she could see Harry's car at the stop light, sandwiched between two red cars.

Grace was feeling dizzy; a wave of lightness came over her. The mystery of the student and the fumes from the car exhausts and the throbbing pain in her ankle were twisting around each other, making a weird jarring sensation inside her head. Grace wondered if in a minute, in just a minute, everything would suddenly be okay. Sometimes, that was all the time it took. She remembered getting lost at Safeway when she was four and how her whole life seemed like it was about to explode when there she was, her mother, smiling at her at the end of the aisle near the cereal boxes and everything was wonderful. From one second to the next, things flipping over. Maybe that would happen this time. Maybe there would be a perfectly reasonable reason why her father had a girl student in his car. Maybe she would vanish and Harry would see Grace and everything would get back on track, the pasta dinner, the starry sky doona cover, *ordinary rightness*.

The lights changed and the cars ahead of Harry started to cross the intersection. Grace was gathering speed. She pushed her way past some students on the crossing and got to the other side. The cars were moving faster now and she was going to have to exert herself to keep up. Harry's car was still visible, but it was getting further away from her. Grace put her head down and willed herself to go faster. She had to find every tiny last bit of strength and use it. She had to go back inside the Ethiopian marathon runner in the Olympics who used his pain as fuel.

Then suddenly, about twenty metres before the roundabout, Harry's indicator went on and he pulled over to the side of the road. Grace rode on closer, then stopped. She was near enough to see their two heads in the front seat. The traffic had thinned out. Most of the cars were passing Harry now, and making a right at the roundabout into the main street of Deptford. Grace rode closer, using the scrubby bushes that lined the footpath as camouflage. She was only about five metres from the car now and her father's face, turned towards the student, was bizarrely clear. Grace saw him place his hand on the student's shoulder. They looked at one another for a moment, their faces in clear profile. Then the Female Bat opened the passenger door and got out, hauling her patchwork bag after her. Harry watched her walk away, then pulled out.

Grace could probably get his attention now. All she had to do was ride right behind him in the middle of the road and he would see her in his rear-vision mirror. But it was too late. She had left everything too late. It would probably have been better to have jumped right in when she first saw Harry coming out of the Krappford. It would have been better to interrupt the student and her father, that way maybe the girl would never have gotten in their car. Or maybe they all would have gotten in the car and everything would be explained and it would be okay. But now, Grace felt the day had become smudged, ugly.

Grace got back on her bike. She couldn't ride up Freeman's

249

Hill now. Not with it getting dark. Not with her ankle. Failure enveloped her. *Failure*. In a couple of minutes she would be at the Deptford police station. They would call Alice and in half an hour she would be home. There was no way she could tell her parents she had ridden all the way to the campus now.

eighteen

As David drove back down Main Street, he glanced into the shop and saw Trudy turning off the lights, ready to lock up. He could go in and start the stocktake on his own, get a head start. Or run through the orders and call customers to let them know their books were in. There was no shortage of things he could do in order to avoid going home. The house was dead. Quiet, closed, dark. Justin would not be home from school camp until the morning. Molly was probably at some unknown charming beach shack eating Chinese take-away straight from the container with the pool guy. By candle-light. He could lob into Alice and Harry's, but after a few glasses of red he'd inevitably confide in them about the men's group, which he had no wish to do. Besides, it was a Friday night. They were prob-ably out at some faculty thing or a movie. The creepy red-headed babysitter would be in residence.

He'd just have to deal with it. Go home, get some take-away

himself. Start a project: alphabetise the CDs, write a memoir. *Be a grown-up.* Dread filtered through him, a vague shivery tug, like the start of a virus. It was getting dark. The spring fog had enveloped the higher parts of Sunnyside, settling down over the reserves, the bushland, making civilisation cloudy. He took the turn-off into Sunnyside and tracked the house lights just visible along Mountain Road, each one designating *a place to be*, a tender meeting place of shared histories, lasagnas baking in ovens, spaniels lying by fireplaces, kids in dressing-gowns. People *loved* each other. It was important to remember that. All around, down those driveways, beneath those slate roofs, were human beings who saw in one another their own completion. *Whatever happens to me, remember that.* Despite everything, people knew that it was better to be together than alone.

Twenty metres up ahead, a car had broken down. *A Beamer,* David registered with satisfaction. It was getting dark, but the car had no flashing lights. *Idiot.* He'd give them a piece of his mind. A dead car in the middle of Mountain Road at dusk and the imbeciles hadn't put on their hazard lights! This was how disasters happened. David checked in the rear-vision that there were no cars behind him and slowed the Volvo to a stop beside the stalled car. He buzzed the passenger side window and leaned over. A woman looked up from the opened bonnet with a small torchlight. Blonde hair, big jaunty face.

'David McLelland!'

David peered at her. She shone the torchlight under her chin to illuminate it.

'It's Maddie Ridgeway.'

'Hello there, Maddie.'

David felt his fury check itself. Maddie Ridgeway, wife of the car dealer, *their* car dealer, a known person. If he yelled at her there would be repercussions.

'I can't find my hazard lights!'

'Hold on.'

David parked his car in front of Maddie's. He vaguely knew Maddie Ridgeway but only in passing. She always seemed to be there in the background of social events, a perky Zelig. The husband was an edgy guy, regular looking but giving off a sense of being not one hundred per cent stable. David walked around to the driver's door and leant in, pulling the hazard light switch. The bush pulsated with an orange glow. What was difficult about locating the hazard switch for Christ's sake? Typical idiot Sunnyside female. She didn't *deserve* a Beamer. None of them did. David had a sudden happy vision of a new law that forbade women from driving anything more significant than beach buggies. Two peddles: slow, slower, a magazine holder and a make-up mirror.

'Thanks! That's so nice of you. I know it's stupid, but I kind of panicked. I couldn't find the right switch. Typical female, right?'

'You called the RACV?'

'They're very busy. Friday night. They said it could be at least an hour.'

'I'll wait with you.'

'Oh, I couldn't ask you to do that.'

'You don't need to ask me. I wouldn't feel right leaving you here. I don't need to be anywhere.'

Maddie said nothing. In the pause David knew she knew that he didn't need to be anywhere. There was no-one waiting. Her husband was selling the McLellands multiple Golfs. Of course she fucking knew!

'Well, it's chilly. Shall we sit in the car?'

They walked over to David's car and got in. David sat behind the wheel. Insects chirped in the final twilight. Through the gums lining the road, the house lights struggled through the mist to resurrect suburbia.

'On your way home?'

'Just shut up shop. Yep. End of a long week. How about you?'

'Oh, I'm on my way home from squash. Hence the sweats. I play up there in Seabank with Jenny McAllister on a Friday evening.'

'You need to call home to tell them what happened?'

'Everyone's away. Angus has taken Tom on their annual boys' weekend. You know, campfires and fishing down at the cape with another dad and his boys. I think it's good for boys to have special alone time with their fathers.'

David let that sink there, into the darkness. Justin was going to be having a lot of alone time with him, but it wasn't quite the hokey bonding thing Maddie was referring to. He skipped through this thought to the somehow unforgettable fact that nobody was expecting Maddie Ridgeway home.

'It's awfully nice of you to rescue me,' said Maddie, smiling.

'Is that what I'm doing?'

'I don't like the dark,' said Maddie. 'It's ridiculous, I know, what ever happens in Sunnyside?'

Death. Debt. Disease. Envy. Greed. Isolation. Misery. David felt the words stretch within him, struggling to the surface. Lots happened in Sunnyside, but only to the upper-middle-class, so it didn't count. On the other hand, it was not altogether unpleasant sitting next to Maddie Ridgeway in a stationary car.

'You know, David, I hope you don't mind me saying this, but I heard about you and Molly and I'm really sorry. No-one likes to hear about a marriage break-up.'

David looked at her. She was really quite attractive, especially in sweats. She looked a whole lot better than the last time David had seen her. At the Vintners'. He had a dim memory of her across the room. She'd been wearing pastels and too much make-up, that frowsy, tropical look that suburban women were into. In sweats, with her hair up in a straggly ponytail, she looked almost girlish.

They sat in silence.

Maddie said, 'I'm sure she'll come back. I mean, why wouldn't she?'

'Why would she?'

'You're a nice guy, David. Honestly. There aren't that many nice guys around. She's probably just feeling restless.'

'Well,' said David. The rhythmic orange beat of light in the bush was giving him a headache. It had been nearly a month since Harry and Alice's dinner, since the mess of his life had gone public. He felt tired of trying, of putting on a show. There were times when fatigue alone was enough to propel a man into risking something.

'What would happen, do you suppose, if we just said what was on our minds?'

She stared at him in the darkness. Little puddles of shadow fell beneath her eyes. Maddie Ridgeway had lived some kind of life, too. At forty, she'd had long enough to accumulate surprises, sadnesses. Everyone had a story to tell. The realisation made Maddie suddenly lovely.

'Maddie, how would you feel about having sex with me?'

'David, I'd feel fine about that.'

David pushed the lever and his seat back reclined. He stretched back and unzipped. With an almost unseemly skill, Maddie pulled off her sweat pants and knickers. She climbed over the gear shift and sat astride him. David ran his hands up and under her top, undid her bra and felt the soft pendulous breasts. David had forgotten what big breasts felt like, how comforting. It was seventeen years since he had felt big breasts. He could actually remember the last time: a freckly big-boned girl called Kathy on the university ski trip. They'd been playing Yahtzee during a blizzard and one thing had led to another. That was right before he and Molly got together.

A car passed them travelling in the other direction, its driver seemingly oblivious.

It was fucking great to be fucking Maddie Ridgeway. It might have been awful. It might have been awkward, but somehow it wasn't. He had slipped right into her. Somehow she had been ready for him, ready for how long? Seconds? Years? He shouldn't flatter himself. But there was an imperviousness to Maddie that made everything seem manageable. She wasn't a bunny-boiler, a neurotic. She was just a squash-playing mum with a hitherto undiagnosed capacity for both kindness and adventure.

Maddie was tilting her head towards him as she slowly moved up and down. It was hard to say if this was intimacy or just a matter of avoiding banging her head on the car roof. She leant down low. Her blonde fringe fell over his face and he felt the sweep of her breasts on his chest and he started to cry for the softness of them and the pleasure rising up through him. Pleasure could be moving after so much pain, it promised the start of something. Very slowly, she squeezed her muscles around him and without speeding up, he came.

Maddie moved gently over the top of him, her fingers reaching down, touching herself without letting him go. She tensed up, moaned softly and collapsed on top of him. He held her. She kissed him and he tasted her, minty and warm, and he felt an incomprehensible rush of love, the receipt of kindness. He bit her lips gently, traced them with his tongue, kissed her face and, as he did so, allowed Maddie to become all women, all women, herself included, all women, even Molly. If he waited long enough, the pain would eventually go. It was going to be all right.

Over Maddie's hair, in the side mirror, David could see the little Noddy light of the RACV vehicle proceeding towards them along Mountain Road.

Maddie pulled herself off and flung herself back into the passenger seat, stretching back to pull on her pants. David opened the car door, levered himself out and did himself up. The RACV van pulled up behind Maddie's car and the serviceman got out.

'Evening.'

'Evening.'

'I think it's a battery problem we have here,' said David.

Maddie moved over to her own car's raised bonnet.

'It just suddenly stalled.'

'Let's take a little look.'

The serviceman walked around to the driver's seat, his orange plastic vest glowing in the dark. He sat in the car without closing

the door. The anxious chug of a motor not quite turning over rever-
berated through the bush.

David looked at Maddie beneath the shadows of the eucalypts
lining the road. She smiled at him.

'I don't want you to think I make a habit of this,' she said.

'That's *your* story,' said David.

nineteen

'Grace, we only want to know *why*.'

Alice was hovering with her arms crossed. Grace sat at the table, head bowed, Harry next to her. Alice was trying to keep her voice low and uncritical, but Grace's refusal to elucidate was frustrating her.

'Why did you choose to ride to Deptford? What got into you?'

As she said it, Alice could hear her own mother's voice. There was a horrible echo, the reminder that each and every parent was foredoomed to ask the same questions, to berate, cajole, criticise, punish with the same tight-throated desperation.

'What got into you? I mean, *the highway*!'

Grace spoke without looking up. 'I *survived*, didn't I?'

Alice sighed noisily, threw her hands in the air and walked around the kitchen counter to put the kettle on.

Harry said, 'Grace, you know that your mother and I are

shocked. We're disappointed. We thought you were sensible. We thought we could trust you.'

'People screw up.'

Alice was glad there was a kitchen bench between them or else she might have slapped Grace, just let her hand fly out and thwack her. Really, these children were genetically pre-packaged souls. Alice and Harry had spent the first three years of Joe's life attempting to gather him up into some elegant arrangement of taste and conformity until they finally admitted he was beyond their grasp. By the time Grace was born, they had all but given up.

Alice realised the best parents didn't make too much of things. Three square meals, the odd trip to the dentist, an occasional appearance at the school musical and a steadfast refusal to react against, towards or otherwise much acknowledge a child, this was what gave children the best chance. They had raised Joe in the shadow of vast expectations. It pained Alice to read Joe's lovely face, endlessly perplexed by the world, irritated by his inability to solve it, know it, order it. She and Harry had been something other, once, way back when Joe had hatched, before they knew the frightening truth that planning anything, least of all *a life*, was entirely deluded. Grace, by contrast, had grown up in the light of her parents' capitulation to impotence. She was reckless and un-dimmable, intoxicated by freedom. This bike ride was one more example of it.

'You're not "people",' said Harry. 'You're our daughter.'

'*This is our family*, Grace Louise Haskins!' Alice could feel herself getting emotional.

'We take care of our family. That's our job,' said Harry.

'Oh *right*!' said Grace. 'Oh, *yes*!'

Harry looked at her perplexed. 'What's that supposed to mean?'

'*Family*!'

Alice and Harry looked at each other.

'David and Molly and Justin were a family!' said Grace, finally looking up.

Alice felt the anger fall away from her. So *that's* what this was about.

'Is a family a good thing? Is it something we *want*?'

She was too much, thought Harry. They really should have tried harder to get her into horses. Something normal. Riding lessons. Big pony posters. Little girls were supposed to belong to pony clubs. Once again, they had not been *prescient*. Grace looked at Harry sternly.

'I rode because I *felt* like it! *I felt like it*! You can lock me up, you can give my bike away, you can tell me over and over what to do and how to think, *but it doesn't make you right*.'

Harry was downplaying it but really, thought Alice as she brushed her hair before bed, there was something not quite right in the way

Grace viewed things. Ever since the last parent–teacher evening, Terry Polhurst's words had been prickling away in Alice's brain, like the time she got fibreglass on her hand, a horrible electric feeling, only this time inside her head. 'Grace needs to just enjoy things more,' he had said, emphasising that she was only eleven, still a child, but there was nothing childish about her. Alice had insisted Grace be punished for riding to Deptford, so Harry had agreed that she was not allowed to ride her bike for two weeks. But instead of running to her room and throwing herself on the bed like any normal child, Grace had remained stoic. She'd said, 'I expected that.' She had wheeled her bike into the back shed and locked it with such dignified acceptance that Alice wanted to scream.

Alice slipped into bed beside Harry. She realised that part of her insistence on Grace being punished was an attempt to suppress her own feelings of guilt. She should have been home. She could not divest herself of this irrational self-importance, that her own vigilance was what kept her loved ones safe. So long as she was on the plane, in the car, standing on the cliff alongside them, the family would be all right. The moment a child moved away from her, disaster loomed.

After all the fuss had died down, after Grace had been collected from the police station and the Serious Talk had been had, it was left to Alice and Harry to work out exactly why Grace had chosen to ride from school all the way to Deptford. It was some kind of strange reaction to David and Molly or the way things had been not quite normal lately. But no-one went to Deptford unless it could be avoided – no-one, not even eleven-year-olds. Grace had told them it was just because she felt like it, but frankly, there were a million other places she might have gone, all nicer, all better rides. She could have ridden in the other direction to the Sunnyside oval, or gone for a bush ramble through the reserve. Something was not right.

In an instant, Alice's irritation moved into the spasm of intolerable relief, the relief that came from registering what might have been. Harry encircled her with his arm, pulled her head into the crook of his neck. Alice felt the tide of love, the full, urgent tide of love and in its measure, *terror*, which pushed past the debris of mundane disappointment and confusion elicited by children. Images of Grace, crumpled, crushed on the embankment beside the highway, moved swiftly into a collaged aftermath of grief, a lifetime absence. How did they survive, the parents of dead children, living always in the shadow of one tiny but indelible bracket of a life: a backyard pool, a faulty toaster, a reversing car?

Alice cried silently, the tears of the spared.

'What would have happened?' said Alice, words caught tight in her throat, then floating above them in the darkness.

'It *didn't* happen,' said Harry.

Scarlett had watched the room come alive, as if slowly the oxygen had seeped in. For hours the tables had just sat there, discs of pressed woodchips. Then the cloths had gone on and they'd laid them with silverware and potted blue hyacinths and Mrs Bailleau had shown up in her mauve velour tracksuit and given them the once-over. Scarlett had been in and out of the kitchen for hours, drying, polishing, chopping parsley, and then the first party goers had arrived, sheepish anticipation on their faces, looking too clean and dressy. Within twenty minutes, the room had filled up and those who feared they had overdressed for the annual yacht-club dinner-dance feared no more. Sunnyside women liked any excuse to glam up, liked to tan up, sparkle up, get even blonder. The cul de sac down the end of Ocean View was crammed full of Beamers and four-wheel-drives and, through the far windows, Scarlett had watched the dinner-suited rich men patting each other on the back and moving towards the yacht-club entrance.

All night, Scarlett had tried to get perspective. As she pushed through the swing doors from the kitchen into the dining room, Scarlett looked over the heads of the patrons to the moon. It hovered over the bay, a spacious globe, lighting tracts of flat sea in long oily triangles. There was Sunnyside Yacht Club and then there was the universe.

Scarlett moved from table to table, clearing away the main course plates. She had turned her mind from the moon to the cash she would get at the end of the night. Only the thought of the notes being stuffed into her dressing-table drawer could compensate for the indignity of the black polyester dress with white Peter Pan collar she had been forced to wear by the club's catering committee. Mrs Bailleau had made it clear that members of the Sunnyside Yacht Club 'expected certain standards to be upheld'. When Scarlett had pointed out that polyester was unhealthy as well as unattractive, Mrs Bailleau had remarked that she could always seek alternative employment where the uniforms were made of organic cotton, though where *that* might be she did not know.

Scarlett wanted to travel after final year. Her mother would buy her an air ticket, she'd promised, if she got straight As. But as to living expenses, these were up to her. She had heard Mr Moorcroft tell her mother that on his recent trip to London, an ordinary apple cost the equivalent of three dollars. Three dollars for an apple! And probably not even organic. England was the most expensive place on earth, despite the fact that on most British television shows everyone looked dirty and had bad teeth. There was *British Vogue* Britain and there was dowdy, chip-eating Britain and then there was *Hello* magazine Britain with its footballers' wives and stately-home couples posing by the maze in their personal tartan. All of it was expensive.

The annual yacht-club fundraising gala was held every spring, to boost funds for pre-summer maintenance. The season was 'almost upon us', Mrs Bailleau had said in the prepatory staff talk the week before. The clubrooms had been renovated, repainted Naked Dawn, donated by the Vintners, and the club boxes, which ran around the central lawn, had all been stripped and repainted as well. The annual dinner-dance usually covered costs, and this year the event had proven a major drawcard since it featured the reunion of the Lifesavers, a successful seventies rock group whose members came originally from Sunnyside. The Lifesavers were Sunnyside's own celebrities.

Scarlett placed chocolate pots in front of the diners. 'Careful not to wobble or the raspberry coulis will end up looking like a Jackson Pollock,' Mrs Bailleau had warned them earlier in the evening, tempting fate by wearing a pale-blue chiffon cocktail frock in the kitchen. Now Mrs Bailleau was pretending to enjoy the conversation of her neighbour on table ten. Scarlett tracked her attention across to the Lifesavers, assembling themselves on the stage constructed specifically for the evening at one end of the clubrooms.

The Lifesavers had not aged well. The four original members had spent the intervening years on the fringes of showbiz, MC-ing charity variety nights, hosting the odd lifestyle show and running suburban talent schools. Now they had applied blond highlights to their hair and squeezed themselves into jeans so tight that their penises appeared to be shrink-wrapped. Forging a fashion first, the lead singer had teamed a 'Mad, Bad and Dangerous' T-shirt with grey slip-on shoes. He boomed the opening words to their number-one hit from 1979 into the microphone. The diners all clapped and cheered. Two couples from table twelve leapt to their feet, the women tugging the men onto the dance floor. One of the women was wearing a long sequinned cream dress. Her husband's bow tie had been made from the same fabric. The women were obviously tipsy and couldn't wait to cut loose. Cutting loose in Sunnyside, thought Scarlett. *Boomers.*

Scarlett couldn't look around the room without wondering what it cost her. Somehow, between the ages of seventeen and forty, *this* became something a person *wanted*. It was hard to believe, but buried amongst these luxury vehicle junkies there had once existed heartfelt intentions to overthrow governments, save pygmy possums or hang Greenpeace banners from the Eiffel Tower. Where did it go, that rampant idealism? At some point it was unceremoniously bequeathed. They were probably not bad people, underneath the dinner suits and frou-frou spaghetti strap dresses and YSL body-glitter. They were probably not bad people, but they were limited. These men and women had forfeited any small stray instinct for originality. There were no artists here. No policy makers for a better world. No humanitarian aid workers. Scarlett could not, would not allow this place to dictate to her what she might expect.

The news that four of the regular yacht club staff had come down with spring flu at the last minute had left Mrs Bailleau with no choice but to recruit some untrained waiting staff from the work-wanted noticeboard outside the newsagency. Scarlett realised that one of these was Justin McClelland, *the* Justin McLelland, looking handsomely notorious and fashionably dishevelled in his white school shirt with cheap black bow tie and pants. He was only fifteen, but he looked older, with his long hair parted in the middle, seventies surfer style. Cool. Justin McLelland would know who she was from babysitting at the Haskins, but that was about it. He probably wouldn't even remember her name. It wasn't like she *liked* him or anything. Not in *that* way. But there was something interesting about him, and kind of mature. She wanted him to know that she was not a million miles away from him. She didn't just *accept* things, either. She didn't go dumping her mother's Daiwoo into large water reserves, but she had *thoughts*. She wanted Justin McLelland to know that she experienced life deeply, that she wasn't just an airhead like those girls who filled their days with calisthenics competitions and trips to Brazon, Sunnyside's tanning salon. It was hard to know how to let a guy know anything, since guys, generally speaking, didn't speak. Vague mumbles amongst friends, maybe. It wasn't like you could just throw something into a pre-existing conversation. She couldn't even send him the right message wardrobe-wise. She would have liked to show him that she didn't do midriff tops and tight jeans and high heels like the wannabes at school. If she wasn't wearing this stupid waitressing garb she'd be wearing something cool and baggy that said fuck-off instead of fuck-me.

While she cleared the dessert plates, Scarlett practised inside her head some straight-ahead comment to Justin that didn't require an answer. *Hey there, I don't know if you remember me, I'm Scarlett, my name's Scarlett, I heard about the car and I just wanted you to know that I'm with you, I'm right behind you, I'm fully there with you, I really get you.*

If life were a movie, he wouldn't be two years younger than her, to begin with. And he'd smile and say thanks and then they'd say something rude to a scandalised Mrs Bailleau and run out of the ridiculous party, ripping off their uniforms and laughing hysterically until, puffed, they found themselves on the cliff-top path above the beach where they'd sit and talk until the sun came up and discover that they both liked Beth Orton and swimming naked in the rain. But life was not a movie and Justin McLelland was now being told to leave the dessert plate on the table by an irate woman in a sweat-stained purple satin shift returning from the dance floor.

Every time Scarlett passed Justin, she tried to make eye contact but Justin seemed like he was on remote control. He was making money, just like she was, but he wasn't letting it get to him. He was floating like the light on the bay, just drifting over the whole thing. Scarlett wished she could do that. Being judgemental had a cost.

By midnight, the Lifesavers had played their final encore and the couples were leaving. Car lights switched on in the darkness, bullbars kissed, silk dresses dragged over pine needles and the kitchen staff polished the stainless steel benchtops ready for the next week's disco. Mrs Bailleau told the staff that once the chairs had been stacked, they could leave. She handed each of them a small envelope with the night's pay. Scarlett stuffed her money in her bag and threw on her coat. Her mother had made her promise she wouldn't walk home, but Scarlett wouldn't get in a car with any of the other waiting staff, whose parents had come to collect them, because she didn't want to make small talk. It would be good to walk anyway, with the full moon, and nothing bad ever happened in Sunnyside, even though it could.

It would be great if Justin McLelland was walking home the same way and *if* Justin McLelland *was* walking home it *would* be the same way, since Boronia Crescent was on the way to Carringdale Road. They could walk companionably in silence and Scarlett would let him know that silence was more than okay by her. She wasn't one of those girls who couldn't shut up, couldn't keep her mouth shut, was frightened of a pause.

But just as Scarlett walked out of the back door of the clubrooms, she saw Justin taking off on a pushbike. *Bummer*.

The thought of climbing the huge hill up to Carringdale Road depressed Scarlett. If she walked along the cliff-top path and then up Waratah, the slope would be gentler on her blistered feet. She pulled her bag over her shoulder and walked onto the dirt path. Along the track, high fences prevented walkers from looking into the front gardens of the sea-view properties. On the sea-side of the path, bushy ti-tree created a buffer from the sea winds. At certain points, small rocky tracks lead down the cliff onto the sand. In the moonlight, Scarlett could see the derelict beach box she and Grace sometimes visited. The high tide was lapping at its edges. It was hard to believe that in a couple of months these same coves would be full of children and nagging mothers and those ridiculous beach shelters that no-one knew how to curl back into their bags. Scarlett looked out across the water. Sunnyside seemed removed, the punctuation point to the curve of lights that spread from the city skyscrapers and encircled the bay.

Up ahead of her, where the cliff track turned at a right-angle, was a corner viewing platform. Scarlett stopped, suddenly, when she realised that a dark shape hovered over the platform, a moving human shadow. Scarlett listened but could not make out any sounds above the rhythmic lap of the water. She moved forward, careful not to snap any twigs underfoot. Two shapes, leaning against the railing, not facing out to sea but into each other. They were making love! It was enough to restore Scarlett's faith in the world that, at the very least, two human beings were lovemaking in the light of the moon and the grasp of the bay. She knew that she should turn away, should skulk back along the track or even race past the lovers before they noticed her. But there was something beautiful in the sight of them, something raw, and she could not draw herself away. Softly, she moved forward until she could hear the sounds of their breathing over the waves. A small woman, her back curved over the railing, and embracing her, a tall man, moving gently, almost gracefully into her. The outdoors and the stillness of the night leant the act itself a kind of elegance that surprised Scarlett. Sex. Which had always seemed so crass. And here, under a wide sequinned sky, it seemed almost an act of faith.

Suddenly, the woman gasped and the two bodies came apart into separate silhouettes. The cloud that had crept halfway across the moon cleared. Scarlett looked closer and studied the faces of the lovers who had now turned to face the bay. Justin's mother! Justin McLelland's mother! And the pool man, the one with the dreadlocks from Magnificent Swim, the one she'd raced off despite being forty-something and a wife and a mother and a publicist! Scarlett turned and ran back along the path towards the yacht club, not minding the noise she made, desperate to get away from the sight of Molly McLelland and her toy boy. *Thank God Justin had not seen.* Justin would be well home by now. But as she made her way up the hill, her blisters rubbing against her Campers, knees sore from the effort, eyes streaming, Scarlett felt incensed on his behalf. For just a moment, Scarlett felt two sides of the same story simultaneously – Justin and Molly *both*. All at once, Scarlett understood what it was to be Justin, abandoned by a woman and her illegitimate desire, and what it was to be Molly McLelland, compelled towards ignition.

Joe woke to the muffled repetitive sound of something unknown. Still dazed with sleep, he tried to make sense of it. Could it be a bird? Did birds make noises in the night? A possum in the trees outside his open window? Whatever it was, it was too *present* to be ignored, he had registered it. Joe pushed the doona back and got out of bed. Foggy with sleep, he reached out his arms to feel for the door and, grasping the handle, opened it. The sound became more distinct and clearly human. It was coming from Grace's room. Joe padded down the hallway and stood at the open door. He looked across the room to her bed. Grace was crying! For a moment, Joe refused to believe it. It had been over a year since he had heard Grace cry. Grace only cried when in severe physical pain, like when she had one of her headaches. Other girls used crying to get what they wanted, but Grace was more strategic. She used words.

Now, in moonlight, Joe could see her body softly heaving under the cloud of doona. This was what happened when things went whacko. They created a domino effect. First Justin and the car.

Then Grace and her bike ride. Now his sister was becoming something other than what she used to be.

Joe stood still, wondering what to do. He turned to walk out and then stopped, caught by some small, flickering memory of what they had once been to each other. Years ago. United in the back seat of the car, united in the circle of relatives and holidays, of family *ways*. Whatever had happened since, they would always somehow be bound by the way their parents acted or failed to act, by what they said or failed to say.

Without thinking, Joe walked over to Grace's bedside and hovered there for a few moments. He sat down on the edge of the bed. Horns tooted in the distance from down on the highway. Other people's lives were speeding past Sunnyside, on their way to somewhere else. Sometimes Joe forgot that this was not the whole universe, this town. There were roads leading to other towns with other families. The thought of this was comforting. Grace had not stopped crying, but when he sat down, she shifted her body closer to the wall, making space. Joe lay down on the bed, next to her. Grace kept crying softly beside him, but her hand reached out from under the doona and he took it in his.

twenty

Tess loaded the shopping into the back of the car. When she looked up, she saw Alice on the far side of the car park. Tess moved a little to the left, hiding behind the lifted boot. How to avoid Alice? Alice might not see her, but she'd almost certainly see the twins, trying out their new rollerblades in the square, their high-pitched exclamations could be heard from quite a distance.

Tess peered around the corner of the car and saw Alice waving at her and heading in her direction. She tried to think, but she couldn't. She was going to have to submit herself to the moment. It was strange, she thought, how at times you divided yourself into the person who watches and the person who acts. Tess had no idea what she was going to do: she would just have to wait and see.

'Hey,' said Alice.

'Hey.'

They kissed cheeks. Alice was wearing a blue cashmere sweater and jeans, effortless, lovely.

'I called you a few times about tennis,' said Alice. 'Is there something wrong with your machine?'

'Busy,' said Tess. 'Work's been crazy. Sorry. But yes, I have Tuesday morning off.'

'How are things?' said Alice.

'Good,' said Tess.

'Jim fine?'

'We're all okay.'

'The girls look well.'

'New rollerblades. Over-indulged.'

Alice paused, waiting for the customary return inquisition, but Tess couldn't bring herself to do it. She could ask Alice how Harry was, but the thought of inciting naivete seemed repellent.

Alice said, 'Grace rode to Deptford without telling us.'

'Why?' said Tess.

'No idea,' said Alice. 'Things are feeling a bit strange at the moment. The kids are a little weird. You know how Joe is living inside his head, only more so. I worry about him. And Harry's . . . I don't know. Distracted. It's like the moment you enter our property, the ground is just slightly tilted.'

Tess could feel Alice willing her to ask her more, to collude, but Tess was resistant because she could not bear any more alteration to the known world. One friendship had already collapsed into itself, lost in its own catastrophe. Not Harry and Alice, too. Better not to know. Better not to tell.

Tess jangled her keys.

'Have you seen Molly?'

'No interest,' said Tess. 'Over it. Sick of the whole thing. She can fuck off to Tuscany and pick grapes with sexually riveting adolescents if she wants to, but I don't want to know.'

Alice raised her eyebrows. 'That's very un-PC, especially for a Do-Gooder. Aren't we all supposed to withhold judgement these days?'

'I know,' said Tess, 'it's very unfashionable to hold unequivocal moral positions, but I'm leading the pack.'

'You're brave, Tess. You've always been brave.'

Tess looked at her. 'What are you talking about?'

'Remember up at Mary Slide? You used to jump right off the edge and go. We'd be snow-ploughing our way down in a little line, and you'd be this steadily diminishing speck of black in all that white. Fearless.'

'That's different,' said Tess. 'I was on skis.'

'No,' said Alice. 'Actually, no.'

Tess closed the boot with a thud. It was a moment to leave, but Alice wasn't going anywhere. Over the tops of the cars, Tess could see Georgia had fallen, hunched over and clutching a bloody knee.

'You say things that ordinarily aren't said. That's the beauty of you,' said Alice. 'You make the truth bearable, because that's all you deal in.'

'No,' said Tess, 'in the end, I'm selfish, Alice. I look around and nothing stays the same. Everything's moving. Time. Allegiances. Politics. Children. Even the planet. Every time I turn around, I have to catch up. The newspapers stack up. The shoe sizes get bigger. Someone's got cancer. Some country has invaded some new country. It's all moving. And I look at you all and I just want you to stay the same.'

'But we can't stay still,' said Alice, 'can we?'

'I'm not looking for news,' said Tess. 'Do you know what I'm saying?'

Alice looked at her steadily, then turned away.

Joe was alone in the house and bored. The football season was over. Boring cricket was starting. He'd eaten three crumpets. Saturday morning music video was stupid and boring. He missed Justin. After the last time they'd played the cumquat game, Joe had called Justin a few times, but he never called back. And when he actually turned up at school, he always seemed too busy to talk.

It wasn't that Justin was unfriendly, exactly. It was just as if he was . . . drifting. Joe had suggested he come over and watch a DVD this afternoon, but Justin had pleaded homework. Homework! At first Joe thought that if he pretended not to care, he might actually train himself into not caring. That had worked before with things. He kind of brainwashed himself into the desired state. The trouble was no-one could take Justin's place. Something just worked between them, Joe couldn't explain it. How could Justin just walk away from that?

Maybe this was one of those times when you just had to act, stand up for something you believed in. In American movies, friends seemed to take friendship more to heart. American movies were manipulative crap, everyone knew that. They kind of twisted your feelings and used big music soundtracks to make your heart jump, but once the credits rolled you came down with a thump, you realised you'd been had. But every so often you wanted to go with the movie, go where it took you, hold onto what it was saying. Sometimes you had to believe that the movies were telling you the right way to live your life. Just because studios made a shit-load of dough from them, didn't make them wrong. Maybe Joe should not give up on Justin. Maybe he should try to haul him back.

Joe found his trainers by the back door, pulled them on without undoing the laces. He left a note on the kitchen bench, grabbed his hooded windcheater and closed the door.

With its overcast, windless sky, the morning felt moody. Joe could smell the smoke from the open fires in the neighbourhood, already lit. Carringdale Road had so many holes in it, it was like a real country road. But when he turned the corner, it was full-blast suburbia, all those neat Colorbonded roofs and whipper-snippered driveways. There was something interesting about the way people gravitated to sameness. He could feel that in himself.

Joe turned right into Boronia Crescent. The track above the road was littered with pine needles. They felt weirdly spongy under his trainers. The McLellands' garage door was open, but David's car was missing. There was no sign of it or Molly's car. It was hard to know who was living where. Molly seemed to be coming and going. Joe had heard Alice tell Harry that Molly's stuff was still in the house, even though she'd paid the bond on the rental place and moved some of Justin's stuff in there. It sounded like no-one had really got used to the new situation, it was all up in the air. Still, it was a relief that neither of them were home; Joe hated seeing them these days. He didn't want to know why a marriage came undone, or what did it up. Really, a marriage ought to just be there without needing to have attention drawn to it. Marriages were other people's business.

Joe walked up the paved path to the front door and knocked. There were no sounds inside the house. He squashed his face into the frosty glass beside the door and tried to make out any movement. It looked as if no-one was home. On the other hand, if Justin was home he'd be just as likely not to answer the front door. In Sunnyside, there was always someone coming to the door trying to get money for Horse-riding for the Handicapped. There were also those weird people trying to sell neon house numbers 'so ambulances can find your house at night'. Like, *right*. Whatever.

Joe walked around the side of the house. He could smell smoke. The back gate was shut but Joe could climb the ti-tree fence. He pushed his feet into the corner where the fence met the house and levered himself up and over, landing on the grass. There didn't seem to be anyone around. He peered through the French doors into the family room, then turned back to scan the garden. There was no-one by the pool, but down the back of the block, smoke was rising in a plume. Someone was burning off. Joe walked around the pool, which had its cover removed. Clean and cold blue, waiting for the first dive of the season.

At the far corner of the garden, a bonfire was burning, tendrils of flame reaching towards the sky. It was a big fire. Beside it stood Justin.

'Hey.'

Justin looked up. 'Hey.'

'Whatcha doing?'

'Burning stuff,' said Justin.

Joe's words had lost themselves inside his head, run for cover. Just *being there* was going to have to do. He would trail Justin, follow him, be his shadow in order to persuade him of something. What? That he could not be budged, he, Joe Haskins, would not falter.

Justin poked the fire. Joe could smell something intense and acrid. Between himself and Justin was a can of kerosene. Joe looked at the fire for the first time. There were sticks there, twiggy dead branches from eucalypts and ti-trees, and leaves too. But mostly, it was shoes. Justin was burning shoes and there were lots of them. There had to be thirty or forty. The colours were changing, but there were still smudges of pastel in the flames, and the strange curve of soles and heels melting. And now he came to think of it, they were all *women's* shoes.

'Soon it will be fire-ban weather,' Justin said.

Joe nodded. Justin turned back to the flames.

'Best to get this done now.'

Grace and Scarlett had walked for nearly a mile along the beach. Scarlett recognised a couple of older girls from the high school sitting smoking, their shoes and socks off, feet buried in little piles of sand. Scarlett pretended not to see them. And there were two old ladies in elastic-waisted trousers walking their Airedales. There was a certain kind of old lady who only had big dogs. They must be the *smart* old ladies, the ones who looked old but were young inside their heads. They looked so dignified, these dog walkers. They had made peace with being old. It was now their time to walk dogs. Or maybe they *hadn't* made peace with it and while their Airedales chased crabs into rock pools, they silently twisted themselves up with rage . . . about bad husbands, or dead husbands, or cruel children or lost opportunities. Maybe getting older was just about *disguising* rage, think of that!

Grace said, 'Justin McLelland burned his mother's shoes. In a bonfire.'

'What?'

Grace felt the thrill of being the bearer of tidings.

'In the back garden. He burnt Molly's shoes. Like, *all* of them. And Molly had *expensive* shoes.'

Scarlett looked shocked. 'How do you know?'

'Joe saw him. *Doing it.* He was *there*. One pair cost *seven hundred dollars*.'

Across the bay, the skyscrapers of the city were like the little blocks that kids played with, only made from shadow. It was funny the way the city would be so close if you could walk across the water. It felt a million miles from city life down here on Sunnyside beach. The rock pools were full and exposed, since the tide had just gone out. As they walked past, little crabs hurtled towards crannies. Scarlett and Grace always combed the beach as they walked, looking for the smooth pieces of worn glass, like jewels on the sand. They were hunting for the brilliant blue pieces that were rare currency.

As Grace walked beside Scarlett, she felt a tremor of happiness. It was fantastic that Scarlett had said yes to the beach. She had proven her worth by telling Scarlett about the shoes. And things could be back on track with Scarlett, because their friendship had not been so good for a while. Scarlett had been weird and distant. Last summer, they'd come down to the beach looking for the glass jewels almost every day after school. Grace had got so tanned and she used to tease Scarlett, because Scarlett always made sure she was covered in clothing, she never used sunblock 'because it was full of chemicals'. They'd had fun. Grace knew that sometimes it was kind of a drag for older girls to have young girls hanging around. But she knew, *she just knew*, that Scarlett had liked her company on those afternoons. Then, when summer moved into autumn, Scarlett had started to make excuses, the weather or homework or 'My mother the Nazi'.

Scarlett moved up the beach towards the beach boxes. Once upon a time, Granny Beaufort had owned one of these, before the cliff rained rocks down on it and it was crushed. There were only a dozen or so left, paint peeling, mostly abandoned. The front doors of the blue beach box were locked with a rusty lock and chain, but it had loose timbers at the back and if you were thin or small, you could wedge yourself between the cliff and the wall and squeeze through to the inside, which was full of old beach gear like hats with towelling pompoms and piles of old *Women's Weeklies*. Scarlett and Grace had discovered it a year ago, and whenever they walked to the beach they'd go inside for fun, and to see if anyone had answered their stupid note.

They'd brought pens and paper down at the end of last summer and written a letter together to 'Person or Persons Unknown'. They'd put in it all kinds of things they believed in. It was a couple of pages and they'd left it there, curled up inside an old Coke bottle, bidding any reader to respond. Grace had mostly left it up to Scarlett, but every so often, Scarlett had included something of Grace's. They joked about round-the-world solo sailors stumbling across it. Scarlett had said, 'That's the way things happen. You put something out there and it might just lead to something.'

No-one had answered the letter, but Scarlett and Grace sat on the sandy floor and ate some organic almonds and raisins that Scarlett had brought from home. Grace didn't really like them, but it felt good to share stuff with Scarlett, it felt special. The thing about Scarlett was, she had *exacting standards*. This singled her out. This made her *right*.

So while Scarlett ate her almonds that weird way – lining them up on the timber slats and then nibbling them individually, making them last for *hours* – Grace told her about the Female Bat.

She started at the beginning, with riding her bike to the campus, and then went all the way through Harry driving her into Deptford and the touch, that touch on her arm.

Scarlett listened without saying anything. She suddenly took Grace's hand in her own.

'You can watch. Or you can act.'

Grace nodded. It felt good to have told someone. It felt good to share this with someone *honourable* and *smart*. Joe would have listened, but Joe wasn't smart enough. She was a whole two years younger than Joe, but she was already smarter than him and *they all knew it*.

'Men are suggestible.'

'Uh-huh,' said Grace. She was trying to commit the word to memory. It was a good word. It was one of those words she really ought to try to work into her impromptu speech in the public-speaking competition. *Suggestible*. Grace knew exactly what Scarlett meant. It was like when Alice said to Harry, 'Are you comfortable wearing that tie with that shirt?' That was all she had to say, and minutes later, he'd be wearing some other tie. He *was* suggestible. So what Scarlett was saying was that if it worked about a tie, it could work about other things. More serious things.

'What do I do about her, Scarlett?'

'There are two possibilities, Grace. One is that Harry sees through her and deals with her himself. The other is that this girl knows how to manipulate him, how to flatter him, and that's a problem.'

Grace waited.

'She could make herself feel necessary to Harry. He could start to see her in his future. Suddenly she makes Alice seem old and familiar. Harry's not a bad person, not at all, but he's vain, like all men, and she plays on this. Harry starts having coffees with her, pretending to both of them he's just her teacher. Then a beer after class. The girl starts dressing in a certain way. Harry wants to be strong but it's hard. When he's with her he feels better about himself: smarter, funnier, younger. He loves his family but he loves the way she makes him feel. Suddenly the idea comes to him: *he could start again*. Be new! *Undo* things.'

'What things?' said Grace, scared.

'You. Joe. All of it.'

'But he loves us,' said Grace.

'He *does* love you,' said Scarlett, 'but he also loves excitement. *Everyone* does.'

Grace was getting that tight feeling around her head. 'Then what happens?'

'He comes home one night and he stands in the family room doorway and he speaks in a quiet voice and you're painting your fingernails and Joe is watching TV and Alice is chopping zucchinis and he says: "I'm leaving. I'm leaving you."'

'*No*,' said Grace.

'He goes to the dressing room and puts some clothes in a suitcase and throws in the old photo of you and Joe skiing and he zips up the case and walks out the door. And somewhere, out there, she's watching and waiting.'

'I don't want him to go!' cried Grace, eyes welling up.

'Then don't let her win, Gracie. Don't let her win.'

twenty-one

Harry was sitting alone in one of the windowed seating areas of the staff club bar, enjoying a quiet glass of wine after the interdepartmental staff meeting. Not for the first time, Harry stopped to savour his place, his position, the view across the expanse of drinking and dining areas, the portraits of the be-gowned Vice-Chancellors lining the gallery, the staff in their black and white *in the service of the academics*. Was it Harry's imagination, or was there a palpable sense of admiration amongst the staff, a rather lovely *gratitude* to be servicing the relaxation of people *who thought so damn hard* for the benefit of mankind?

Harry only had half an hour before he needed to be home to collect everyone for the first round of Grace's public-speaking competition that evening. Half an hour. Enough to mentally debrief from the weekend. It was a relief to have it over. With Grace's ride and then Justin's bonfire, *normal* life was not what it ought to be.

Stress. Harry was always warning his students about this word, another buzz word, overused. But all weekend, Harry had felt the word insinuate itself into his head.

Kathleen Monroe waved from her own little table by the far wall, under the portrait of Mackintosh Felty, the Vice-Chancellor who had famously chopped down the ancient fig tree in the law quadrangle when Harry himself had been a student. Kathleen Monroe. Wearing something unflattering in mauve tweed *with pleats.* Incomprehensible how a ninety-kilo dame could pleat herself. She seemed to have survived the child-care inquiry fiasco somehow unscathed. In fact, someone told him recently that she was a contender for the Chair of her department. Some people just fell upwards.

Harry missed Howard Woodbridge. He had been a convivial and cultivated colleague. Cultivation was not a given any more in the ivory towers, now that tertiary institutions taught Mickey Mouse subjects. Harry heard the other day that the university was considering offering a course on disc-jockeying. *A degree.* Harry suspected that Howard was now grovelling for a tutorial position at some B-grade institution up north and didn't laugh much about anything any more. The Ethical Standards lot had really fucked him over.

As he looked through the window, Harry saw Olivia walking past the staff club with the girl who had done the interesting paper on subliminal bisexuality in Balzac.

Olivia was not, as he had first suspected, without hope. Harry had worried that Olivia might be incapable of rising above her own insecurity, but at the risk of blowing his own trumpet, he seemed to have been able to get to her. Okay, she had not yet handed in her third-term assignment. But there she had been after class, on the grass outside the Krappford, waiting for him. He had looked up and seen her rise to her feet with her long black hair, her short kilt, her beguiling youth. She had told him that she had thought about what he'd said. She realised that she did want to make something of herself. She wanted to be given another chance.

Harry, consciously avoiding being too congratulatory, had nevertheless wanted to show her some support. She asked him if he could drop her off in Deptford, and this gave him the opportunity to extend the patronage he had been cultivating. He wanted to show Olivia she could trust him, that some men could be trusted, that certain men (of which he was one) appreciated smart women and wanted to help them discover their own uniqueness. Was that wrong? Alice would say that women didn't need any help from him to discover their uniqueness. But it seemed to Harry that it was the least men could do, give women some navigation as to what they might find if they cared to look. He had told her that while he was not going to do her any special favours, he was excited by her abilities and conscious that her home life was not doing her much good. In the car she had told him about her father's drunken brawls, her mother's hopelessness, how depressing it was to go home to a shambles but that she knew she could not sink to their level. She had said, *I will single myself out*. He had said, *You have every chance*.

Harry had felt moved to think he had played some small part in liberating this Olivia from the foul-mouthed persona she had been carrying around all year. While not exactly demure, there was now something almost ladylike about her. She had been grateful for the lift. Harry found himself touching her lightly on the arm, finally breaking the spell of antagonism that had existed between them for months. *Olivia, I have faith in you*. And then she was gone.

From the side of the stage, Grace could see the left-hand side of the auditorium. Close to the front, Alice, Harry, Scarlett and Joe were sitting in the same row as Mr Polhurst and Miss Pressfield. Scarlett looked bored, but she looked bored most of the time. There was no work at the yacht club tonight, so Grace had nagged her into coming, hoping that she would realise how exciting it was once she got here. Typically, her parents were nodding warmly as Tabitha made her points, going out of their way to be fair. Behind them, Tabitha's parents and sisters were watching Tabitha with frozen smiles. There had to be at least six hundred people! Tabitha was the second-last Junior to speak and then it would be Grace. On correctly guessing heads on the flip of Mr Polhurst's coin, Grace had chosen to go last since last meant you had a better chance of staying in people's heads.

Until they had actually arrived backstage and been shepherded into their dressing room, which had been made available for them to compose themselves in, Grace really *had* wanted Tabitha to do well. In Mr Polhurst's car, they had seemed friends. They had even giggled with nerves about what lay ahead. But only twenty minutes later, a weird silence had just happened.

Grace hoped that the judges would not have switched off by the time it was her turn. She could feel the heaviness in the air, a dusty hum of boredom. It was going to fall to Grace to wake up the whole auditorium. They had been listening for nearly an hour, with that teacher from Warrington who had gone on and on about young people engaging with their wider school community. Everyone had just wanted to get on with the show. When that first girl from St Brigid's had first spoken on Photosynthesis (*bad choice!*) her voice had sounded so fresh and new after the hubbub of the auditorium. After that it had been the Design of Modern Cities (*wow!*), Pet Care, The Dangers of Dieting and now, as Tabitha was winding up, it had just become a wall of sound.

'After the games, Australia could truly believe in its sporting greatness, a greatness forged by skill, diligence, self-belief and an unswerving commitment to fair play. I, for one, am proud to know that we can call ourself the greatest sporting nation on earth without being at all delusional. I thank you.' *Delusional*. Also rehearsed.

The auditorium erupted into applause. Grace could see Mr and Mrs Arbuthnot waving to Tabitha like a couple of maniacs. Grace hoped that Alice and Harry would not see fit to behave like that. Tabitha took a bow and walked to the far side of the stage. The teacher from Warrington walked to the podium.

'And now, as our final candidate in the junior section of this year's inter-school public-speaking competition, we have Grace Haskins speaking on "Earth's Place in the Solar System".'

Grace walked out onto the stage as the crowd clapped politely. She stood up on the small stand and tilted the microphone so that it sat at the right height and took a sip of water from the plastic cup that had her name written on it in black pen. The lights were so strong, it was hard to see out. *Here we go. Here we go. Here we go. Here we go.*

'Distinguished guests, ladies and gentlemen, girls and boys, the first thing I would like to say to you all is that we do not specifically belong to this peninsula. We do not specifically belong to this state. We do not even specifically belong to this nation. We belong, ladies and gentleman, to planet Earth.'

Grace looked up. Harry had told her to look up occasionally and make the audience feel *noticed*. Grace took a moment to scan the room.

'This planet, Earth *(that wasn't necessary, repeating the name of the planet, but it's too late now)*, was formed with the other planets four thousand, six hundred million years ago. In effect, the Earth is the Sun's leftovers.'

Grace looked down at her notes. It was a stipulation of the competition that you could not read, you could only use small cards with short, handwritten notes. These notes were inspected by an official before the start of the competition. Grace had written INTRODUCTION, followed by ORBIT.

'One of the really great (*maybe too casual*) things about the Earth is its atmosphere, and by this I do not mean the indirect lighting and music.' A ripple of laughter circled the room *(thanks, Dad!)*.

Grace could feel that her delivery was working. It was very important to sound as if you yourself found what you were saying interesting. Harry had said this. Mr Polhurst had said this.

Grace looked down at the next card. It read: SENSE OF WONDER. This had been Harry's idea.

'It is truly *extraordinary* how well designed this planet is. We have life because we have water, this is what separates this planet from anything else in the solar system.'

Grace listened to the words spilling out of her. The more she spoke the stronger the sensation that they had their own life, distinct from her. She had to grab the audience and hold them. *Grace, you can do this. You can do this.*

Scarlett, wedged between Harry and Joe, could smell the musty dampness of the audience. She was trying to focus on Grace, but all she could think of was what Grace had told her about Harry.

Grace was only a kid and could not be expected to take action. She was a good kid, smart. But she was *young*. A person could spend their whole lives wondering: *What if I act?* Her mother could have taken action with her father, could have poisoned him with weed-killer or even run him over. Instead, she had tried to banish him through a new house, a doll collection. *Pathetic*.

All over the place were phony families, families like her own, like Justin McLelland's. Justin McLelland had every right to sink his mother's car. Everyone said he was crazy, but the fact was he was saner than any of them. There was no way for children to make their parents better. Better people. Parents revelled in their own authority. They got a charge out of doing as they pleased. They were so busy being adult, they couldn't see past the paperwork, the tax statements, the council by-elections, the children's school reports, their gym assessments, the car repayments, the newspaper with its thousands of ads and lifestyle suggestions. No wonder Justin had to sink the car in the reservoir, burn the shoes. Only children could fight for families, adults didn't know how.

'The design of the planet is so magnificent that it has encouraged human beings to argue about the existence of God. It is in some people's *belief systems* that only a supreme being could have possibly come up with something that works so spectacularly well.'

The words were coming easily now to Grace. She wished she could pace the stage, could move across it, because it was beginning to feel her own.

'On the other hand, some scientists or atheists validly argue that no one thing, or person, or spirit or whatever could come up with something so complex. Nature itself is the ultimate authority (*great phrase, thanks Dad*), since at its foundation is a guiding force that creates and shapes according to the impulses of *life itself*.

'Once upon a time, human beings believed that our solar system *was* the universe. It's easy to lose perspective and think that your own small world is the only world.'

Something was happening. Something was moving inside her, an energy all of its own, something swift and gathering and electric was moving through her blood. Grace was not going to go with her measured finale. In this ordinary auditorium, Grace had a grip on the extraordinary. She *was* the universe. Inside her, she felt constellations of purpose and meaning and faith shimmering in the blackness. She felt as if she had a thousand little stars whirring around in their own constellations inside her stomach as if the solar system was *within* her, some miraculous force of energy and light.

'But the universe is more mysterious than our own brains can handle and we should not be threatened by this but look upon it as an invitation to discover. The universe has other concerns, bigger than we can get a grip on. And frankly, this is a good thing. We should embrace its mystery, accept the adventure of finding out. We must try to be good and curious. Try to make a difference! Let us not forget that while the Earth shines brightly in the solar system, we may shine brighter still. Thank you.'

Harry pulled the doona up over Grace and turned off the lamp. The moonlight was so bright, it illuminated the room. In the car on the way home, Grace had said that it had been a full moon just for her talk, *as if it knew!* Now, finally, she was asleep, worn out, it seemed, by the exhilaration of her own celebrity. There had been a moment, just before the applause began, when Harry had caught a look of absolute defiance on Grace's face. She was shoring herself up . . . For what? The competition? Adulthood? Grace would never attract the tender love that belonged to those for whom success was elusive or somehow *not central.* Harry had felt in that moment that Grace understood what she was forfeiting in her triumph, the sweet pleasures of ordinariness, of regular expectations and results. People might respect you, admire you, even envy you, but no-one loved you for your ambition. If Grace was going to embark on this life, running circles around opponents, feeling glorious, then she would have to accept what would be forever lost to her. It seemed to Harry that she had made that deal. Afterwards, in the foyer, with all those uniforms and parents and wafting programs, Alice had asked Grace how she felt. She said, *I made it my own.* Harry found it depressing to speculate on where she had found this phrase. But yes, to be fair, Grace *had* made it her own. No-one but Grace could have found such passion for a public-speaking competition.

They had eaten pizza afterwards at Vinnie's, the family place on the highway approaching Deptford, with chunky wooden tables and laminated menus and celebrity photos of the owner with President Clinton, with Kylie Minogue. *President Clinton!* The shouting cooks and screaming kids and blaring pop music had given Harry a giant headache. They had margheritas and garlic bread and he and Alice had a couple of white wines, which tasted as if they'd been mixed up out of powder. They had offered Scarlett wine, but she only wanted mineral water and barely ate a thing. She had been unusually peppy though, talking about the university courses she was thinking of applying for and keeping some running gag going with Joe. Grace was quiet. It seemed that victory, being hers, did not need elaborating on. Harry had been grateful for this, since there was never a child more difficult to compliment than Grace. She was so greedy for admiration. That way she looked, post-race, post-performance, post-school-report, nettled him. *How could he say that?* It shocked Harry that a father should feel this way.

This was his daughter, in her pink flannelette pyjamas, her long eyelashes sloping over those huge sockets, protecting them from the exhaustion of consciousness. It made Harry instantly fatigued to think of the way Grace launched herself at life, unable to let it wash over her, to waste time. Sleep was an escape for Grace, removing her from the relentlessness of her What If mind . . . or was it? Sleeping there, silent, unavailable, was she still absorbed in the peculiar, layered itinerary of her ambitious dreams?

In bed, Alice had already turned off her lamp. Harry switched off his own. The moonlight showed him Alice's alert eyes, questioning in the dark. What was she thinking, this woman he got into bed with every night? Sometimes he felt he knew her so well. Other times she seemed not just unknown but unknowable. Things had gotten so complicated lately. Molly had started it, with the pool man. Then Justin had responded, with the car. Justin, that small, curly-haired boy who had grown up with his own urgent sorrows. Justin, who was probably at home right now hacking into NASA.

Harry felt the sudden need to make love to Alice. It would be good to seal the night united in the face of their offspring, any or all offspring, real or phantom figures of perpetual love and sorrow. Making love would be some kind of antidote to them. But those same offspring were so prominent in his head, it was hard to push them aside in search of that ancient desire, the core of a turn-on. Children got in the way of desire. It was hard to believe how great was the chasm between the making of children and the having of them. All of one's selfness went into the physical act – perhaps a man was never more truthful than in that moment of orgasm. But the end product, if you could name a child thus, was so unerotic, a lust-killer. There was little room for desire in parenting, partly because the relationship between parent and child introduced the concept of profoundly platonic intimacy along with overwhelming exhaustion and responsibility. The result was that children did nothing for a man's desire for his wife. They were obstacles to be dodged. Even now, with Grace and Joe asleep, they bobbed up with all their inexplicabilities – Joe's reading problems, his reserve under which God only knew what was festering. And Grace's strange dislocation from childishness.

Harry pushed Grace aside for a moment and summoned the image to which he often returned – Alice at the wedding of someone they once knew. A ritzy tennis club. A trophy room. The two of them wedged up against a glass cabinet, Harry's trousers comically down and Alice inviting him into the sliver of space where her long black dress split elegantly up the middle. She looked French that night. She had that aristocratic call-girl look, simultaneously impeccable and available. That had to be sixteen years ago. He felt himself harden, turned to her and pushed her gently away from him, slipped his hands under her nightie and felt her skin, up and over her hip. She wasn't saying no. He moved his hand slowly up the velvety rise of her thigh. Alice's hand moved to his, held it fast, stopping it. Harry felt the full, fast tide of sadness rising up in him, a sadness he had been holding down for a year. He wondered how Alice would feel if he masturbated next to her, but the thought made his desire vanish. Harry closed his eyes.

twenty-two

Molly said, 'Well, you know what, I can't take it back.'

Alice had to agree. It was their usual Tuesday morning coffee in the village, only these days there was nothing much usual about it.

'Whatever is done, that's the thing. And now we have to make a reasonable go of dealing with it. Like them?'

Molly straightened her leg and Alice leant over the table and looked at them: new, Italian soft brown leather, flat-heeled ankle boots.

Alice raised her eyebrows.

'You know, he only burnt one of each pair.'

'What?'

'I came home and found one left. From each pair. Remember the Jimmy Choos? I found the diamante buckle in the ashes.'

Alice said nothing.

'He left one shoe of each pair to remind me.'

Alice and Molly sat still in the thick of it: the summoned smoke of Justin's bonfire. Around them, cafe noises swelled and ebbed in unison, the breathy spatter of the coffee machine.

'Is Dan worth it, Molly?' Somehow, in saying his name, Alice felt complicit. 'Is he really worth it?'

'Is *he* worth it? Oh, Alice.' Molly leant back in her chair, defeated by Alice's *obviousness*. 'Of course *he* isn't.'

Over Molly's shoulder Alice could see Jenny Arbuthnot splitting a hazelnut muffin with the woman whose name Alice could never remember, the one with the fake folk-art shop.

'It's not about Dan, Alice, for fuck's sake. It's about *me*. He's reminded me of who I am alone. I'd forgotten that. It's *powerful*.'

What she meant by that, she explained over their caffe lattes, was that she was not after diversion. She was after a radical shift in her *life map*.

'What was wrong with the old life map?'

'I don't need to tell you, Alice. You know stuff. You read books. You're not an idiot. I thought at first that Dan was going to remedy something, fix it. Like throwing a few sacks of salt in the pool, he'd get the levels right in me. But that's not what happened.'

She took a sip of her coffee. Molly was looking post-holiday – is that what adoration did to you? Smoothed your skin, made you young? Around them, Sunnyside mothers were deep in conversations, who knew what about. Alice figured there was more than one story happening in here. Women counselling other women to take action, to cancel it out, to go forward, go back, stay still, surrender.

'I guess that's the risk you take. That one small action may not stay small. And he woke something up in me and now I feel as if there's no choice but to keep going.'

'What happens if you wake up one day and realise that nothing compares to David?'

'Then I'll be very very sad. But I'll have to know that I did the only thing I could do at the time.'

'Is it the only thing?'

'I think so.'

'From the outside it looks as if you have a choice, Molly,' said Alice.

'That's *always* how it looks from the outside.'

She lowered her voice a little, hunched herself over the duralex glass full of skinny sugar sachets. 'He uses words. Real words. *Fuck and cunt and suck and cock*. David never used those words.'

Out on the street, Molly walked Alice to her car. Alice thought about the last time she had seen Justin, a glimpse as she was driving to tennis, but enough to register that uninterested look that distressed children assumed, as if behind glass.

Alice said, 'Molly. What about Justin?'

Molly stopped walking. She grabbed Alice's hand.

'I love that boy. But this is the thing, Alice. Where is it written that *their* life is more important than *yours*?'

Alice stood still, shocked.

'Tell me where it was written when we signed up for mother-hood. Where did it say that *they* win, always and inevitably?'

Alice found that she was crying. It was jumbling up inside her: Grace and Joe and Justin, the years gone and the love and the misery, too. Those odd yearnings that Molly had made concrete and named. The fallout of doing nothing and the fallout of action. Where *had* it been written? Molly was right in this much: there was no contract.

'When all is said and done, he'll survive me,' said Molly.

'At a price,' said Alice, pushing her own tears into her temples.

Molly straightened up, let go of Alice's arm, tightened her voice.

'But everything we do and don't do has a price, Alice. *Everything*.'

Driving home, Alice thought about Justin, trailing in the wake of his parents' fear and courage. How did human beings survive childhood? It seemed extraordinary that most of us survive that extravagant induction only to revisit it from the other side. There had been moments in the months following her two births when Alice had been suicidal with the voluptuousness of love. To love something so much, this small, unknown infant, this suckling hanger-on, was to shackle yourself forever to the ferocity of your emotions.

Even in Sunnyside, to be a mother meant living every day inside some shifting elemental structure, an invisible Greek tragedy.

The streets of Sunnyside were quiet at this hour. Children were in school doing their presentations of homemade projects, small cars made out of icy-pole sticks and corks. Everywhere Alice looked there were liquid ambers breaking into life, the hot tree of the genteel suburbs.

Alice turned into the driveway and pulled up near the front door. She let herself in, dropped her bag on the kitchen table and started to tidy up. The breakfast things were still lying around, the kids didn't help as much as they ought to at this age. But it was more work reminding them to do things than to do it herself. They were being dropped off by Monty's mother after the school play rehearsal. The afternoon spread out, unpunctuated.

The sun had come out. Maybe she should just forget about the house and head into the garden. It was nice the way you could spend an hour there and feel as if something was accomplished. It wasn't like that in the house. Every time she did something in the house, something else came up that needed doing. Whereas, in the garden, she could complete her work section by section and there was beauty *everywhere*. The first rose had come out by the tennis court, little-girl pink. Soon the others would emerge and the climbing roses too; it was like having another family living with you, silent but alive.

She pulled the latches at the top and bottom of the sliding door and slid it. From the top of the slope, you couldn't see the whole of the pool, the bottom was sunk below the grassy rise leading up to the house. Alice walked down the lawn, taking care not to slip since it was really more moss than grass, the surface dank and slippery. The sun was warm, almost the first warm sun, a harbinger.

Alice stood above the pool and looked in. Smooth, concave, white. It looked like a giant shell, fallen, like a meteor, from space. The sun set the white floor of the pool alight. Alice walked around the edge of the pool until she came to the steps. She climbed down to the lowest and then slid down the slope, surprisingly steep without liquid, to the bottom. She could feel the sweat trickling down her ribs being blotted by her silk camisole. She pulled off her cardigan and walked the length of the pool. Fifties pools were so deep, they didn't make pools this deep any more. The sides of the pool created a heat trap.

Alice sat down on the bottom of the pool. The cement seemed hot from within. Everything was crowding her, the sheer belligerence of other people's actions. And those actions required responses. Why should she be drawn into the aftermath of other people's dramas? Was that her role? To always be the witness? Was it Alice's role only to survive other people's choices?

Perhaps it was her stoic reliability that gave other people leave to rebel. Women like Alice kept the planet spinning properly. What would happen if the good, dependable people decided to go mad? Would roofs fly off houses? Would giant elms crack down the middle? Did she want to turn into one of those old ladies interviewed by students about what *other* people of their generation had done?

Alice pulled off her shoes and felt the warmth beneath her feet. It felt so exotic after winter. She had a sudden desire to feel the heat all over her body, to banish the chills she had felt with Molly, talking about Justin. *To be naked!* How long had it been since she'd been naked beneath the sky? She pulled off her pants, her camisole and underwear and lay down on the floor of the pool. The heat pulsed up from under her and the sun bore down from above, filtered through the green boughs of the elm tree.

Alice thought about Harry. Somehow, he seemed different now, in the wake of Molly and David. Perhaps disaster, especially other people's disaster, could serve a purpose. Perhaps Molly's infidelity was responsible for a new piquancy in the way Alice saw Harry. It was strange how his self-containment made him attractive. He had his own systems for survival, silent systems that kept him going, in and out of family life, through the ups and downs of work. Harry, who had married her and seemed, then, entirely known. Now, years later, he sheltered his own small mysteries. Something within Harry had furnished him with the ability to accept things as they came to him, to make small adjustments, to be content. He had had made peace, somehow. He had worked his way through what had been lost and gained. He had made peace with Sunnyside.

Alice moved her hand down across her flat stomach and gently touched herself. The sun felt like a lover. Stirrings of pleasure flitted through her like little moths. It was enchanting to be exposed and yet hidden below the lawn. Alice closed her eyes. She felt delicious and strange, a surge of desire, so long buried, was returning. The white light of the sun made the inside of her lids luminous. Alice felt herself undoing, unbeing, falling open, letting things go, Molly and her words, those words that David never said. There was something fantastic in the contradiction between the privacy of a pool and the exposure of it. Removed from the planes of ordinary life, of lawn and house and street, Alice laid herself bare to the future and the sky.

Scarlett stood about two metres from the edge of the pool. She could see the whole of it. Lying on the white surface of the empty pool was Alice. She was naked. Scarlett realised that her footfalls had been absorbed by the moss. She was clutching her English assignment that she had wanted to run past Alice, but now the thought seemed ludicrous. Alice Haskins was lying naked at the bottom of the pool, white and lovely, like marble, touching herself. Her thin body stretched against the white concrete, small round breasts spread but still rising upwards towards the sun, taupe nipples, jutting hip bones.

Around them, small birds flew and leaves fluttered. Scarlett didn't move. Alice raised her hips slightly and cried. Her hand fell to her side and she opened her eyes.

Grace and Joe, arriving home after rehearsal, helped themselves to large quantities of salty snacks, since dinner didn't look as if it was coming any time soon. Alice was in her study. Her fingers were moving over the keyboard and words were pouring through them like water.

twenty-three

It had arrived in Alice, suddenly, without any kind of warning. Lying on the bottom of the pool, the heat surging through her, the sudden clear comprehension that *this* was her novel. After eighteen months of struggling to find a story that did not feel contrived, the story had finally come to her. In the cul de sacs and crescents, amongst the pittosporum and ti-tree, amongst summer houses and tennis courts, in the secret lives of ordinary citizens on acre allotments. *Sunnyside* was Alice's story, the story she had to tell.

Hot white cement beneath her, open sky, the whiff of clematis. There it was: a tide of words already gushing to the surface, a simultaneous rush of ideas and sensations. Here it was again, the erotic union of words and feelings, the understanding of what story she had to tell, fingers to clit, heat rising through her, *the story of us*.

Alice had opened her eyes with the irrepressible shock of a real idea. And there had been Scarlett. Scarlett, with her long red hair, standing by the side of the pool, *studying* her. Scarlett, with her pale earnest face. *Scarlett* was Alice's story. Scarlett, with her curious resistance to the tight thread of biological bequest. Scarlett, whose very bearing indicated the willingness to battle, the refusal to give in to the inevitable, ordinary tides of an ordinary life. Scarlett, with her quiet yearnings, filled with a kind of rage. The ultimate warrior.

Harry had virtually had to prise Alice out of the study in order to give her enough time to get ready. He'd had to remind her about tonight, had to jog her social memory for the first time in a long time. Recently, Harry had woken to find the bed empty. The light shone out from under her study door. In the mornings she was up before him, working again before the kids woke up. She gave off that sense of pleasurable secrecy, nursing a world that no-one else had access to. Working Alice, who carried with her some vague and lovely sense of *efficiency*. It was back.

Something had altered Alice, but Harry couldn't work out what it was. Was it just that she had finally capitulated to Sunnyside, stopped resisting? Had this freed her? Or was Alice getting cosy with their pool man, the neighbour, the handsome guy from the bottle shop who insisted she'd won the electric bottle chiller even though she'd never bought a raffle ticket. There was a lightness about her he hadn't seen for a year and a half. The house seemed to function better when she was working. He wouldn't say it, of course, not out loud, but he hoped she was writing something *commercial*.

Now they were on the way, but there was something vaguely disturbing about driving your Saab to a nightclub. It hadn't been that long ago since he and Alice had gone to clubs in taxis, crawling from bars on into the night, unencumbered by European vehicles. This evening, Alice had had some difficulty deciding what to wear before deciding on tight black pants with pointy boots and a swirly coloured Pucci top. When Harry had put on a fifties shirt, his only funky choice in a wardrobe of sober classics, Alice had looked at him askance. He had swapped it for a plain black John Smedley. Last time they had been to a nightclub, Alice complained, she had been perfectly qualified to be there. Now, they weren't the young people any more, they were the spectators. How had *that* happened? This had made Harry faintly depressed.

It was Tiffany Beaumont-Smith's twenty-first and as Harry said to Alice, it would not do to piss off Tiffany's father, the Vice-Chancellor, by not attending. Only a handful of the staff had been invited and Harry had felt himself to be distinctly on the fringe of that handful and almost certainly included because Rohan Beaumont-Smith liked Alice.

Harry took the freeway turn-off at the last moment. Even after eighteen months in the sticks, he still could not grasp the intersecting roads which crisscrossed the badlands. New housing developments were spreading like a rash over the flat fields, bare asphalt crescents in the shape of question marks punctuated by electric light poles, waiting for their houses, eerily anticipating life. Soon the country-side would segue into the suburbs and then into the city, with barely a hillock between them.

Approaching the south side of the city, Harry turned off the freeway and pulled up at the lights. The Vintners were in the lane beside them. Harry turned to Alice, 'Hey, we hale from Santa Barbara!'

Alice looked over and waved to Rita, who returned the wave extravagantly before Colin's Mercedes four-wheel drive surged off.

'A four-wheel drive!' said Harry. 'Because their pebble mix driveway is so challenging. I mean, *fuck off.*'

The doorway was down a back alley behind the last inner-city factory outlets, poised to become warehouse conversions the size of mouseholes. Door bitches had glammed-down since Harry's clubbing days. The girl outside 'Glove Box' looked like she'd just been shimmying up ropes at an indoor rock-climbing centre, in her green cargo pants and vintage Metallica T-shirt. She ran her pudgy finger down the list and crossed their names off and the big guy stood aside to let them through. But not much else seemed to have changed since the eighties. The strobe lights still spun, the decor was still industrial chic. Metal walkways surrounded and crossed over the centre of the space so that watchers could look down on the dancers. On small podiums, go-go dancers were shaking and spinning sourly. They wore short skirts and matching white vinyl boots and they had their hair up, Stepford-style. Harry reflected that these professional minxes had been Grace only minutes ago. He could quite easily have forgone conversation and just watched them, more out of curiosity than sexual interest. It would be so nice to be able to *look* at women. It had been outlawed for so long, all women-watching had become so covert. That would be a great idea for a club, thought Harry, glass boxes with women sitting inside them, just reading magazines or doing crossword puzzles or grating carrots, wearing anything at all. Just to be able to circumnavigate them without being accused of anything.

On the other side of the dance floor, in a dark corner, was a conversation pit decorated with tea lights. In the shadows, Harry could make out Rohan and his wife, Moira, who looked frighteningly similar to Cherie Blair, with that mousy little face and those big fawn eyes and the terrible dress sense. She was wearing a brocaded pants-suit with huge draping sleeves, exactly the kind of thing Cherie would wear to a dinner with the Ghanian ambassador. There looked to be around sixty people, generally dressier than the other club-goers, with a noticeable component of geriatrics. The go-go dancers stopped suddenly and the DJ changed the music. Harry's heart jumped up and down to the base beat. The music was that unappealing syncopated thump that had replaced the sexy pizazz of Madonna and Grace Jones of his own clubbing days.

Harry and Alice made their way around the raised dance floor, which appeared to be morphing from purple to white. Waitresses in cut-off shorts and fishnets were circulating with trays of champagne, beer and purple cocktails.

Tiffany was towering in her white stilettos. She had a blonde bob and classy make-up, all neutrals and gloss, so that she came across as clean and fresh as a tube of toothpaste. Dazzling in an air-hostessy kind of a way, she was wearing white pants and a gold top in a style Harry remembered as a 'boob tube'. According to Alice, boob tubes were back, a welcome relief, considered Harry, from the German semiotician look that so many women were into. Black, black and more black. Recently, he and Alice had gone to an art opening in the city where every woman appeared to be dressed as a remote-control unit. Alice handed Tiffany their gift, a day-spa voucher, and Tiffany yelled across the throng, 'Mum! Mum! Look! *The Retreat*!' Moira made an 'O' shape with her mouth.

Harry allowed the crowd to swallow him up. There had to be a thousand kids here. There was something so magical about *night*. He remembered seeing a nightclub in daylight once, when he'd been interviewed about youth culture for a television show. They had shot it inside a place like this and it had been sad to see it in its prosaic ordinariness, the shabby upholstery, gritty bar, worn carpet. But now, under the pulsating lights and decorated in youth, the most sublime of accessories, the club had a wanton joy to it. He understood why kids wanted to come and lose themselves in that beat, in the volume of people, to lose their individuality with all its tiny traumas. Harry scanned the crowd for someone to latch on to, but joyfully, at that very moment, Tiffany landed in front of Harry as if he had just conjured her there.

'Do you dance, Harry? Is it okay to call you Harry?'

Tiffany's eyes twinkled with an intensity that Harry suspected could only be chemically induced. Maybe she could slip him some ecstasy. The thought of taking drugs again was confusing. Before they'd had Joe, Harry and Alice had occasionally done a little coke, or danced the night away in an ecstacy-inspired frenzy. It had been fun because they had been signed up members of Reckless Youth. The last time he had taken drugs was an impromptu line of coke several years back, when his sister's boyfriend had offered it to Harry as the most available survival strategy for enduring family Christmas. Hector someone, an art-mover. He and Hector in his mother's bedroom, snorting coke off her glass-topped dressing table with a collage of family photos staring up at him. Alice had been furious and not out of prurience. She had demanded to know how he could get high without her. 'I'm over forty,' said Harry gaily, 'I'm in no position to decline life-enhancers.' But Harry had to admit it wouldn't be quite the same popping an E knowing that tomorrow you had promised yourself you'd do some serious leaf-blowing.

Harry took Tiffany's hand and allowed himself to be pulled onto the dance floor. Tiffany Beaumont-Smith had asked *him* to dance! Harry could feel good fortune surging towards him. At the very least, this would remind Alice of his sexual currency, that after years of marriage, he was still something of a catch. With astonishing good fortune, the DJ had segued from some nasty rap track into a remix of a Gloria Gaynor classic, and Harry found that magically he and Tiffany had something going, a little thing happening when two separate but sympathetic physiological units hummed together. His body effortlessly grooved to the beat. Not too shabby, thought Harry. A little move, a little groove, a little edge. *He still had it.* Some did, some didn't, but now he came to think of it: *he'd always had it.* Harry looked up at Tiffany, hair skimming her bare shoulders, breasts bouncing splendidly. Was that admiration Harry detected in her gaze, a glazed druggy acknowledgement of Harry's *je ne sais quoi*?

Over Tiffany's shoulder, Harry could make out the faculty faces, many of which, it seemed, were turned on him and Tiffany. Harry Haskins dancing with the belle of the ball and *numero uno* offspring of the Vice-Chancellor. Harry Haskins doing a little rhythmic hip-shaking with the lovely Tiff: nothing sleazy, just a convivial display of appropriate revelry, two young people having fun. He *was* young. Maybe not in actual chronological years, but in his nifty funk-ridden boogying, his cool soul *heart*. Tiffany was smiling. Deliciously fun youngsters swayed and dipped around them, including Harry in their dance floor action, accepting the fact that he, Harry Haskins, despite being a middle-aged white academic, was a psychic resident of the nameless, invisible Kingdom of Groove. Things were actually pretty good! *Life* was pretty good! You could take everything so seriously, too seriously, and sometimes a man just needed reminding of his own spontaneous *him-ness*. Harry-ness.

Gloria Gaynor started to fade beneath the intruding boom of something else, something ominously hip-hoppy. Harry could feel fear rising up through him, dislodging his mellowness. The final boppy bars of the disco classic were drowned out by the aggressive pounding of a track that was, to a man of his taste and age, completely undanceable. *Fuck, no.* Wasn't sulky rock in? Wasn't pop music now all about girls so post-feminist they were virtually pre-feminist, playing guitars and singing about failed relationships? Wasn't motherfucker music over *yet*? Harry looked up at Tiffany hoping that she might indicate fatigue but instead she shouted, 'It's Poopy Snog Captain!'

'Who?' yelled Harry.

'It's Poopy Snog! Captain Snog! My favourite!'

Tiffany closed her eyes in simulated bliss and started jerking her body to the beat. Harry could make out certain words – 'black bitch' and 'cocksucker' – but his body had deserted him. If he just threw himself into the music surely his body would surrender to it of its own accord. He just had to stop trying, stop thinking about it. Over Tiffany's shoulder Harry could now make out familiar faces looking in his direction, but with slightly furrowed expressions as if they were . . . *worried* for him. Amongst them was Alice's cool, pale face, beautiful even at this distance but unfortunately tainted with a faint, distancing frown, the frown of *bafflement*. On being left to their own devices, Harry's limbs had devised their own bizarre choreography, an apocalyptic expressiveness that even he understood to have no identifiable relationship with the magnetic moves of Tiffany and her friends. Harry was feeling *conspicuous*. Harry glimpsed a girl in a blue halter top pointing at him from the conversation pit and Enid Prescott, Rohan's PA, doubled over in an attack of either laughing or vomiting, it was difficult to say which.

Harry mimed taking a drink. 'Thirsty!' he yelled.

'Okay!' yelled Tiffany, moving effortlessly across the dance floor. By the time Harry had escaped into the general non-dancing throng, he noticed she was locked in some chic synchronised move with a shirtless boy sporting multiple piercings.

Harry, consciously avoiding his audience, decided to circumnavigate the dance floor. Presumably he could escape for ten minutes without anything seeming amiss. It was amazing how one moment you enjoyed being violated (the music, the sound levels, the heat, the crowd) and the next moment, it seemed, it was hell. Middle age. Still, it was great that you naturally outgrew youth culture, that your body sent your brain the necessary signals that it was time to bid it adieu. There was something frankly annoying about youth, about its narcissism and over-confidence. There was, in fact, something outright *pompous* about it, with its little cults, its derision of the past. Here they all were, the inheritors, his inheritors, so hilariously, obviously the same as every youthful incarnation from the Byronic poets through to the Beatniks and the Punks: absurdly determined to be original.

At home, he was missing sport on TV. Which sport, Harry wasn't exactly sure of, but some kind of sport *had* to be televised from somewhere in the world, even if it was go-cart racing in Winnipeg. Right now, he could be lying on the sofa with a nice glass of cab sav, watching well-toned individuals trying to win something. *Motherfucker, don't look at me that way, Today is your judgement day, Motherfucker don't put your bitch down.* Really, was it *necessary*? Not that he was a prude, but there was something depressing about people striving for decades to be politically correct so that they could celebrate black youngsters *motherfucking* their way through popular culture.

Harry walked up the stairs onto the walkway overlooking the floor. Hopefully, none of Tiffany's guests would glance up there. It was pleasant being somewhere unfamiliar, didn't happen too often any more. It wasn't the club itself that was so unfamiliar, it was the brazen beauty of youth, of his own past, that had receded from him without warning. There must have been a night some years back that marked his farewell, a final hurrah, but he couldn't remember it, couldn't even remember the year. Life had graciously evolved without markers. As he surveyed the dance floor from which he had just escaped, Harry cast his eye over his own youth, less with nostalgia than with the curiosity of someone who realises that something has been lost to them without it being noticed.

Beneath him, in the corner, Harry could see Alice in conversation. What was it she was wearing? Some swirling pink and mauve thing, like giant magnolias. Something that would have seemed kitsch if he hadn't been told better. Gucci, Lucci, *Pucci*.

On the dance floor, girls in chunky boots with untied laces were jumping up and down. If you really wanted to stand out these days, you'd dress like Gidget. One of the girls had loose golden hair framing a pale, angular face. For a second or two, Harry confused her with his sister Rachel, forgetting the swag of years that had passed since she had looked that way. Did Rachel catch sight of young men and think instantly of Harry? Did siblings always have trouble recognising each other in the present, when they lived so much more vigorously in the claustrophobic past? It had been ages since he'd spoken to his sister, not since the probate had come through. He said he'd pay off his mortgage. She said she was going to plough her share of their mother's modest estate into her art. Not so long ago, thought Harry, smart people who didn't know what to do went into catering. Now they got themselves video cameras and called themselves artists.

Harry felt a finger slide up his spine. He swung around and there, with her black locks piled high on top of her head, was Olivia.

'If it isn't Professor Harry Haskins at a club.'

'If it isn't Miss Olivia Mathers with a new hairdo.'

'Perving on the girls?'

'Absolutely.'

She looked different with her hair up. It was fixed with random pins, birds-nest like. She was wearing a heavily ripped top that was strategically held together with safety pins.

'Run away from your wife?'

'It's the V-Cs daughter's twenty-first and we happen to be invited.'

'Boots Beaumont-Smith? That fucking princess.'

'Boots?'

Olivia took a swig of beer. 'She's famous for wearing her boots in bed. She also has the IQ of a cutlery drainer.'

'With a body like that, she may not need much of an IQ.'

'Didn't you know sexist pigs have been made redundant?'

'I'm a preservationist.'

Olivia smiled. For just a moment, Harry felt a wave of envy. How nice it must be to be on the *other* side of authority. To feel the benevolent gaze of someone, *anyone*. Middle-aged men had no guides. Fathers were dead. Loved teachers from years long past were dead. They were on their own.

'How's that assignment coming along?'

'It's coming,' said Olivia, with a little secret smile. 'Don't worry about me.'

There were cars banked up right along the middle section of Carringdale Road and Joe could hear the amplified din of music in the distance. He skirted the cars, climbed over the wooden fence and took the short cut across the vacant block. Joe had told Scarlett he was just picking up a homework sheet at Monty's and she'd seemed cool about it, but if he was too long she might come checking. He had called Justin at just the right time. Usually on a Saturday night, he'd be out skateboarding or graffitiing, but David had told Joe on the phone that Justin was grounded. Justin was bored enough to agree to hear Joe out.

Joe rounded the corner into Boronia Crescent. As promised, Justin was waiting for him, sitting on the stone ledge beside the letter box. The coach light illuminated half of his face, making him look small, and for an instant, Joe could see Molly in him.

Joe said, 'Hey.'

'Hey,' said Justin.

Justin looked at him, waiting. Joe tried to find the words. Justin did not look exactly hostile, but he didn't look normal, either. Every time Joe saw him now, he had the feeling that Justin was doing him a favour. Joe resurrected the memory of Justin playing Mr Ratchett's Toothbrush with him when they were seven or eight. *That* Justin was somewhere inside this stranger.

'Remember how we used to play Dead Zombies when we were still living in the city?' Joe faked a laugh, trying to make it casual, trying to break the ice.

'Yeah,' said Justin.

'That was so dumb,' said Joe, making patterns in the driveway pebbles with his trainers. 'And Mr Ratchett's Toothbrush. No-one understood it except for us.'

'It's getting cold,' said Justin.

'What are you grounded for?' said Joe.

'Nothing. Just. Crap. He's pissed at Molly and so he's taking it out on me.'

Joe nodded. Justin hugged his arms around his body. He was only wearing a Quiksilver T-shirt and shorts, bare feet.

'Okay, well,' said Joe. 'Here it is. Okay, so. I don't see you much any more and that's cool.'

'School,' said Justin.

'That's cool. But even if you don't think the same way and it's okay if you don't but even if you don't I feel like you know me better than anyone else and somehow it's hard to explain but somehow when I tell you things they don't seem so bad after I tell you.'

'Like what?'

'Like *everything*.'

Justin looked at him, waiting. Joe could see David, in lamplight, looking at them through the front windows.

'Okay, well, small stuff like the literacy tests.'

'The literacy tests are crap. They're just another way to label you.'

'And big stuff,' said Joe. Justin was staring at him. 'Like the terrorists planning even now to blow us up.'

'The Americans want us to believe that, so they can pretend to be the good guys,' said Justin. 'Joe, you have to learn to think *critically*.'

'Like this bird flu they say is going to kill millions of people.'

'*Bird flu?* You got me out here to talk about *bird flu?*'

The pftt of the sprinkler system erupted out of the silence. Justin had a look of incomprehension on his face.

'Okay,' said Joe, *fuck it, fuck fuck fuck*. 'The sheep on the boat.'

Justin looked at him.

'Justin, *they're still on the boat*.'

Justin stared at Joe in silence. He had said it and even now, already, there was relief in revealing himself to Justin; relief and shame.

The front door opened and David walked across the lawn towards them, his shadow elongated across the grass.

'Joe, do Alice and Harry know you're over here?'

Joe said, 'I better get back.'

'Want me to drive you?'

Joe shook his head and turned into the darkness.

Alice looked around for Harry. He had wandered off, obviously embarrassed by that display on the dance floor and feeling no obligation to stand around and make the best of it. Sometimes Alice was impressed by Harry's instinct to follow instinct. She felt constrained by expectations but every once in a while Harry shied away from the unbearable with disarming ease. Alice looked over the shoulder of Kathleen Monroe, the feminist theoretician, the one everyone said had fudged the facts on the child-care inquiry. Casting her eyes upwards, Alice caught sight of Harry on the industrial walkway that crossed the dance floor. He was leaning backwards on the railing, drink in hand, talking to an attractive young woman. Alice had not seen Harry talk to an attractive young woman for a long time, not since *she* had been an attractive young woman. He looked, for a moment, like another person, a handsome middle-aged stranger. It was exciting to think of Harry as a stranger, as someone *strange to her*. The girl was beautiful in a disarming fuck-off way. Harry had turned to the side and Alice could see that he was laughing with her. Harry, the husband, laughing. She felt an odd sensation, a flowing of blood. She hadn't made Harry laugh for a long time, she had been so caught up in her own tight pain.

'Which one's your wife?'

'She's down there in the swirly sort of top talking to Kathleen Monroe.'

Olivia's eyes swept over the crowd.

'The one that looks expensive.'

'You got it.'

'How does an academic afford to keep his wife in fancy clothes?'

'She's a kleptomaniac. I don't pay for anything.'

'Is it so bad having a wife?'

'I have a thing for kleptomaniacs. Them and vegetarians.'

'She doesn't look exactly like the ball and chain.'

'You should see her in curlers.'

Olivia laughed.

Harry leant against the railing, already imagining the headline: 'Adored Prof dies in club accident'.

'What are you doing here? Is this your usual hot spot?'

'*Hot spot*! Actually I came with a guy but I'm trying to lose him.'

'Not your type?'

'He's a Nick Cave wannabe.'

Harry thought that at least he wasn't that. The fact that she said it implied that he was one step up from Nick Cave wannabes, at the very least.

Harry said, 'Clubs haven't changed much. Same old same old.'

'This?' said Olivia. 'This has just been redone. Hilarious retro. It's *eighties*.'

Harry nodded as if this was no surprise to him. *Retro?* It was frightening to think that his own club days were not just last century, they were last millennium.

'Can I meet her?'

'Who?'

'Your expensive wife.'

'You just want to crash Boots' twenty-first.'

They made their way down the stairs and past a couple of go-go dancers drinking cocktails. They were smiling now. The crowd parted as they crossed the space, immediately reforming behind them. Harry enjoyed the sensation of crossing this room with

Olivia, pretending for just a moment that they belonged together. Harry remembered back to the conversation he had had with David on the way to collecting Justin from the police station. David had said that the pleasure of marriage was *snugness*. But here, in this pulsing palace of hedonism, Harry resisted the idea that this was the delightful promise of marriage. Harry had no time for snugness, not here, not now. He was walking across a room with a young woman who was just a little bit *bad*. And that was, in its own way, thrilling.

'Alice!'

Alice turned to him. 'You were a long time.'

She took in Olivia.

'Made a friend?'

'This is Olivia Mathers. Olivia, Alice Haskins.'

'The wife,' said Olivia, smiling.

'The troublemaker,' said Alice, also smiling.

Harry downed the last of his beer.

'So what's been happening here?'

'Harry just called this a *hot spot*,' said Olivia.

Harry could have sworn that Olivia winked at Alice. Alice laughed. A trifle ostentatiously, thought Harry.

'Just getting us some refills,' said Harry, moving off.

There was something oddly disturbing about seeing Alice and Olivia together. Usually each was his own special little secret. Next to each other they came dangerously close to eclipsing him. What had he been thinking! Him and Olivia! A ridiculous fantasy. He was a teacher. He was a *guide*. The pleasure of the association was in how it accentuated his *nobility*. It suddenly occurred to Harry that the right thing to do would be to invite Olivia home, to have a family dinner, to demonstrate to her that people could *behave well*. There was a tradition to maintain, the tradition of educated patronage, of *To Sir with Love* rescue missions. If Olivia felt *embraced* by their family then perhaps she might have something tangible to aspire to: a nice life.

Tiffany Beaumont-Smith was on the dance floor with Quentin Trilby, who had some surprisingly cool moves. Tiffany's narrow hips were swivelling, and she was raising her arms in the air, revealing hair-free armpits. He had a sudden image of her with nothing but patent-leather boots on.

Harry saw Tiffany notice Olivia. A look of annoyance swept over her face and she started to search the crowd for her father. Rohan caught his daughter's eye and Harry could see her mouthing something. She was shiny with sweat.

'Will you check that out!' said Olivia. 'Florida Barbie goes for a twirl.'

'She's very attractive,' said Alice.

'Apparently she asks you if your tray table is folded before she gives you a blow job,' said Olivia, turning back to Alice.

She was much more attractive than Harry had led Alice to believe. That slouchy beauty, that seemed all the more luminous for its owner's refusal to celebrate it. Darkness of this kind always made Alice feel as if her own attraction was ephemeral. Dark-hued beauties seemed so much more compelling than blondes.

'He's a lovely man. Your husband.'

Alice let that sit there, between them.

'How is university?' she asked.

Olivia shrugged. 'I have an attention problem. How is marriage?'

Alice laughed.

'I have an attention problem, too.'

'You're a writer.'

'Intermittently,' said Alice.

'But writers need *oxygen*, don't they? They need to be *surprised*.'

Alice felt strangely slighted. Why was she agitated by this young woman? Was this the beginning of it, the capitulation of status the old offered up to the young?

'Marriage doesn't rule out surprise.'

'She says, a touch defensively.'

'She says, a touch impertinently.'

Olivia smiled. 'I don't mean to be rude. Excuse me. I'm not being flippant.'

Alice studied her. Was she being sardonic?

'What makes a young woman like you so interested in marriage?'

'It's not marriage I'm so interested in. It's love. We're led to believe there is someone out there, someone to love and be loved by, something permanent. But who lives that life? There's hardly any evidence that such a belief has any grounding in reality. Nobody stays in love.'

'That's not true,' said Alice. 'The problem is that people have the wrong idea of what constitutes love.'

'*What* constitutes love?' said Olivia.

'If I told you, I'd have to kill you,' said Alice.

Olivia took a gulp of her drink. 'What worries me about marriage is how to stay interested. What happens if one person in a marriage wants to, like, *change?*'

Alice looked at her. How could she know that? Alice suddenly felt the same desire to confide that she had felt with Maddie Ridgeway. Sunnyside had made her vulnerable to such feelings, the loneliness. There was something about this girl that made her a more likely confidante than Maddie, but it was still ludicrous. Alice was feeling not quite in control. The champagne was edging up on her, smudging her orderliness. She broke off. This was a student. She couldn't be saying these things to anyone. She must be drunk. She tried to focus on a go-go dancer in the background, get a fix on things.

'Harry works with ideas. The books we read, the depth of life. You know, we do the full gamut from Austen and Eliot to Safran

Foer. Sometimes I get exhausted thinking of Harry the teacher having to be able to *process* that amount of experience.'

'That's his job,' said Alice.

'Yes, but if your inner life is so stimulated, how do you keep your actual life interesting? And for you, well, everything's kind of material, right? I mean, you'd always have to be *alert*.'

'Well,' said Alice, 'you need to be sensitive I suppose.'

'You have to feel intensely to be a writer. *Passion*.'

'I suppose passion is a name for it. For being sensitive to experience.'

Olivia nodded. 'Right.' She looked at Alice squarely. 'So, how do you hold onto passion when you're married in the suburbs?'

Passion. The word itself, floating from between the contemptuous lips of this young woman, daring Alice to remember what had evaporated. Who was the Harry who responded to *instinct*? Alice tried to think, but she couldn't. The room seemed to be breathing, the walls moving in and out like giant black lungs. Harry was coming back through the crowd towards them, carrying two beer bottles and a champagne.

'I've got to go,' said Alice to Harry as he returned.

'Absolutely,' said Harry, 'if we can sneak out.' He turned to Olivia. 'Maybe you'd like to have dinner at our place one night?'

'Sure.'

Harry looked at Alice, his eyes bright with a good idea.

'Absolutely,' said Alice, hijacked.

'What about Thursday?' said Olivia. 'After our tutorial. I could get a lift with you?'

twenty-four

At first Scarlett thought someone had accidentally called on their mobile, hit the automatic number button. There was a *swish, swish* sound, like someone didn't know their phone was on. But then she realised it was whispering, someone's whispering alternating with a hand over the mouthpiece. It was Grace.

'She's *here*.'

'Who is?'

'*The Bat! The Bat is here! She's standing in our sitting room right now!*'

Scarlett hung up the phone and pulled on her sneakers. She opened the back door and ran along the path to the hole in the fence. It was not quite dark and the lawn stretching across to the plate-glass windows of the Haskins' house had a metallic glow like a beetle's back. A tall, beautiful, dark-haired girl was standing in the room, gazing out. Behind her, Grace was hopping up and down near the family-room door, looking past Olivia and across the garden towards Scarlett, unnecessarily attempting to point her out. For a moment it looked to Scarlett as if the girl was staring right at her, but that was impossible. She was surveying the garden, *like she owned it*. Into Scarlett's head came the sudden vision of Molly McLelland on the cliff top, Justin's mother in the grasp of another interloper. Grace was right, they *were* everywhere. Scarlett knew girls like that, girls who sought *to make themselves important*. There were a couple of them at school, pushing into other people's territory, claiming things in order to illuminate themselves. Grace was right to be afraid.

Harry and Olivia were talking loudly in the sitting room while Alice set the table. Every so often, Alice could hear Olivia's laugh. Harry was in a loquacious mood, the bon vivant. As she laid the mats on the table, Alice wondered if she was wrong to believe him immune to the diseases that other people caught. Maybe Harry had become someone other than who he had been without her even noticing. At university, Harry was known to be convivial, smart and independent. He could be very funny, drolly even-tempered even in the face of undergraduate provocation and the cacophony of egos which splintered, eventually, into a future population of politicians and lawyers and novelists and journalists. He had a sureness about him and this had characterised him, even when the word was not in currency, as *dignified*.

Alice had carried this version of Harry with her, even this far, even into this house, this life. But did it still hold true? *Could a wife let a husband be something he did not start out to be?* Surely it happened all the time, with men whose humble beginnings transformed into grand middles: the prime ministers and presidents, the concert violinists and QCs, the arctic explorers and the Jude Laws. Their wives and lovers had seen them move into new versions of themselves, had witnessed or encouraged, had approved, disapproved, celebrated or sabotaged them as they became new. Or was it just that men only became what they always were destined to be? Youth disappeared softly, softly, but the seeds were there, only to bloom in middle age. Had Alice given Harry that chance?

The night at the club, the young woman now sitting in their house had raised something frightening – the suspicion that Alice, or marriage, had stilled something in her and Harry, or poisoned it. Had they stalled each other? Or dulled each other, as Olivia insinuated? Perhaps Alice willed Harry to be only what he had once declared himself to be and no more. Perhaps wives did this more often than not.

The cliché was that women always aided and abetted their husbands' ambitions because they enjoyed the vicarious success and its spoils. But it was possible that women insidiously undermined their husbands, fearful that those husbands might outstrip them, or that their husbands' flourishing demands on themselves might trigger their own unrequited murmurings. It suddenly seemed possible to Alice that she had doomed Harry to Harriness, to be what he was long ago, nothing more. Could she be sure that he didn't hate her for it, hate her in a way that was so fierce and complex it lived only deep below the surface of dedication?

Grace hovered in the doorway, her face fretful, then disappeared again. Alice carried the wine glasses from the cupboard and set them down.

But then again, had Harry given Alice leave to become all she might become? Alice suspected that potential was not the same thing for men and women, although the feminists would despise her for thinking this. Women, by virtue of their bodies, were compelled to follow an imperative that rendered occupation, career, fame and riches as covetable but essentially non-essential. Women were trapped, not so much by men, as they had so tirelessly advertised, but by biology itself. The relentless itinerary of the female body, its sexual appetites, its maternal stirrings, its birthings and tendings, these took up the space of choice that men had available. Most women did not have the luxury of asking, 'Who might I be?', not after a certain age, and maybe never. They were caught in the grip of their own astonishing beauty, the beauty of fertility. The elegance of inevitability. A woman would do well to remember that, thought Alice, when she is drowning in the fear and exhaustion of motherhood. That knowledge must be her reward.

Alice took a mouthful of wine. In the background, Nina Simone sang about love.

What might she, Alice Beaufort, have been? An Isabel Allende? A Doris Lessing? Who cared? Least of all Harry. Harry was her husband, a loving husband, a loyal husband. They had lost each other but they would come back. He loved her, she knew that. She was all he wished for. Surely, she was enough.

The fire was blazing in the formal sitting room. Why had Alice decided they'd sit in this room, it wasn't like the Female Bat was a proper adult. The room was supposed to be admired or walked through but not actually inhabited, thought Grace. The Female Bat was wearing a denim skirt sitting on her hip bones, with no tights!, and a tight black top that made her breasts look disgustingly *there*. She was wearing so much eye make-up you could hardly even see her eyes. Grace knew that Alice would hate that, Alice hated lots of make-up.

Grace had been hovering in the doorway from the family room, but now Harry was forcing her to come in. She walked over to the fire and pretended it was interesting to look at.

'This is Grace, Olivia.'

'Hello.'

Grace stared into the fire, used the poker to poke it.

'Hi,' she said, without turning around. This was definitely rude, but she knew Harry wasn't going to say anything. He wasn't going to make a fuss about it, because he wouldn't want to come across as the heavy dad. It was part of that phony thing that adults did sometimes for the benefit of visitors.

'Olivia is one of my students.'

'Wow,' said Grace. '*That* must be a thrill.'

'Our real daughter was stolen last night by aliens,' said Harry. 'Unfortunately, this is the one they sent in her place.'

'You're hilarious,' said Grace. 'You're the funniest person I know.'

Olivia stood up.

'I'll see if Alice needs a hand.'

Harry said, 'I'll open some wine. I've got a very nice pinot I think we'll all enjoy.'

'I can't wait for some *pinot*,' said Grace. '*Pinot, pinot, pinot.*'

Scowling at her father, Grace followed Olivia to the kitchen door.

In the kitchen, Alice was draining the pasta into the sink. Olivia was tossing the salad with the tortoiseshell salad servers.

Grace wondered if this was the moment to stand up and say

to Alice that the Bat had been in *their* car, had been touched on the arm by *their* husband and father? They were everywhere, these people. They came into people's houses. They seemed fine to begin with, they seemed as if they brought nothing along with them. Just a handbag or a tumbler of chemicals to set the pool right.

Alice said, 'Let's eat.'

They sat around the table in the family room. Harry was still fussing about, pouring wine for the Female Bat.

'Oh yummy, *pinot*!' said Grace.

Harry's pouring paused, the bottle hovering over Olivia's glass. Grace willed him to meet her stare, but instead he resumed pouring. *You win*, thought Grace.

Alice put the huge red platter of linguini with clams on the table.

Grace said, 'That looks disgusting.'

Alice said, 'Thank you, Grace, for that.'

Alice handed Harry two separate bowls with ordinary linguini in Napoli sauce. He set them down in front of her and Joe. In the middle of the table, a large glass vase was full of spring blossoms from the garden. *Fancy*!

'Olivia, help yourself to salad, bread . . . Grace, could you please pass Olivia the bread?'

Grace slid the bread bowl hard in Olivia's direction. The bowl swivelled down the table until the Female Bat's hand stopped it from sailing any further.

Harry looked at Grace. She put her head down and stuck her fork in.

'Joe's quite a footballer,' said Harry.

'I can see that,' said the Bat. 'He has a footballer's body.'

Joe blushed. 'I'm not that good.'

'He's very good,' said Alice. 'Next year he'll be playing for the Sunnyside under-fifteens.'

'I'm not that good. There are lots of kids who are better than me.'

'He's always been very fast,' said Alice.

'I'm not that fast. She thinks I'm fast, but she doesn't actually know,' said Joe, looking into his linguini.

Grace watched as Joe looked up, embarrassed, and the Bat winked at him. Joe turned back to his bowl. Alice passed Olivia a steaming bowl of pasta. Grace wished that it was just a normal night, just the four of them. Normal nights seemed so boring, but actually, once you had an un-normal night, you missed the normal ones.

'Grace just won the first round of the inter-school public-speaking competition at her level,' said Alice.

'Really?' said the Bat.

'The final is on Monday night.'

'Isn't that something?' said Grace.

Alice stared at her.

'And what was your subject?'

'Space,' said Grace and shoved a forkful of linguini in her mouth. She slurped it up as disgustingly as possible. She could feel a big ring of tomato sauce around her mouth. The napkin was on her lap but she wasn't going to use it. 'Space. You know, it's big and it's black and it's up there.'

Grace tilted her head back in her chair and faced the ceiling. 'Up there!' she said.

'That's enough, Grace Haskins,' said Harry at last.

At last! Grace turned to the Bat. 'Up there, only *above* the ceiling!'

Joe kicked her under the table.

Alice chose to ignore her. The way her mother ignored her was very powerful. Alice was brilliant at it, forcing you to disappear inside your own annoyingness.

Only two students had ever been to dinner before, as far as Grace could remember. And they'd been from Austin, Texas, on some kind of exchange, so it was different. They'd come because Harry had felt sorry for them, because Americans were so friendly and Australians weren't that friendly. Americans said Australians were friendly because they wanted them to be. So Harry had invited them home. But what was it with the Female Bat? She wasn't from Texas. She could just as easily be having dinner in her own scummy house in Deptford with her own stupid parents.

After dinner, Grace and Joe were excused while Olivia and Alice and Harry sat in the sitting room again, having coffee and some revolting-looking coffee cake. Grace stationed herself near the kitchen door and every so often checked to see exactly what the Bat was up to. It was ten o'clock! *Didn't she have a home to go to?*

Alice was laughing, perched on the edge of the armchair, drinking her coffee. Alice was too *trusting*. She thought that just because she did things the right way, that's what other people did. She didn't realise that some people were just born bad and did bad things, because they were frustrated by other people who did good things and were happy. Grace knew this from personal experience. *Her goodness and her intelligence turned other people bad.*

Grace turned back to Joe, who had his arms clasped around his knees in the armchair and was watching a movie about aliens. Grace wanted to tell him that the aliens were in *their* house. *Right now.* Joe with his sleepy soft eyes. She loved Joe, even while she pitied him. He missed Justin. It was hard to talk to Joe, but Grace knew that, even so, they were in this together. Everything that had happened, was happening, these events that had snuck up on them – they were happening to *both* of them. Now, things kept disappearing from them – the certainty of things. Nothing seemed safe.

'We have to do something,' said Grace.

Joe looked up. '*What?*'

'We have to do something. About *her.*'

'I'm watching a movie in case you hadn't noticed, Grace.'

'*Olivia.*'

'What are you going on about? Shouldn't you be doing homework or something?'

'*Joe,*' said Grace. He turned to her. Finally, she had his attention. Grace could feel the will welling up in her, the will to push past Joe's stubborn *aloneness.* 'You're my brother. We're supposed to trust each other!'

'Okay,' said Joe. 'I *trust* you.'

'Remember when we moved and we didn't want to and they made us? Remember when Dad stopped the car in summer and made us get out and drove off. Remember that? And we were standing there and there was just dust where the car had been and it was getting dark and we were alone.'

'He came back,' said Joe.

'When things go wrong, we're *both* in trouble.'

'What's gone wrong?'

Grace stared at him. *What's gone wrong?* Grace had a sudden sense of the complete impossibility of reaching him. They would go through life on parallel tracks, never actually crossing over. What was the point of sharing blood when human beings worked so hard to keep each other out?

'*Fine,*' said Grace. 'Just don't blame me afterwards!'

Joe shrugged and turned up the volume. Typical. The person who knows the truth is *never* listened to.

At last the Bat stood up and said she'd better be going and could they call her a cab and Harry offered to drive her home and Olivia said no, no, no, like she meant it, which she didn't, and then Alice insisted! *Alice insisted*! And before Grace could do anything, Harry was putting on his coat and grabbing the car keys.

Grace yelled, 'I'll come too!'

And Harry said, 'No, you won't, young lady, it's school tomorrow, get yourself into bed right now.'

'Please, Dad! *Please*! Dad, I'll do *anything*!'

'Grace Haskins, what is wrong with you?'

Grace pleaded and cajoled and nagged, but Harry refused and Alice threatened and the Bat yawned. It was no good.

Olivia thanked Alice and she and Harry went out to the car. Grace stood by the window beside the front door and watched the headlights go on and the car crawl around the driveway towards the road. You could see things happening, but you couldn't always stop them. It was like you had X-ray vision, but what good did it do you when you were a kid? There were so many things you couldn't do. You couldn't have a dinner party. You couldn't follow the news properly. You couldn't speak French (unless you were a French kid). You couldn't own a gun. You couldn't even drive.

Alice was there, suddenly.

'What are you waiting for?'

'For Dad to get back.'

'By the time he drives into Deptford and back it'll be forty minutes. It's time you got your pyjamas on and brushed your teeth. Dad will tuck you in when he gets home.'

'Mum.'

Alice was carrying the cake plates into the kitchen.

'Grace, I mean it!'

'Mum.'

Alice put the plates down in the kitchen and came back out to the front door where Grace was still standing. She sighed and looked at her.

'Listen to me!'

'Okay, I'm listening.'

'She isn't a good person!'

'Who?'

'That girl!'

'Olivia?'

'*She wants things*!'

Alice laughed.

'Listen to me, she didn't have things you had. She didn't have such a nice life as you have. And she's making an effort to fix herself up and Dad is helping her.'

'That's her cover!' said Grace, but she could see Alice wasn't listening. It was terrible to see the outcome of something and not be able to persuade people that it was on its way. It was like those movies where the hero is trying to persuade everyone else that the killer/virus/gorilla/meteorite is on its way, and everyone is too busy taking meetings to believe him.

'What have you been reading, Grace? Her *cover*?'

'Okay. Fine,' said Grace. 'Okay. Fine then. *Fine*. Don't worry about it. But later, later, you'll say: *She tried to tell me*! And you'll realise that I *knew* things and you wouldn't listen because you're an *adult* and I'm a *kid* and you had your chance but that chance is over because *now* I'm going to put on my pyjamas.'

Thank God Grace had gone to bed. She had gone to bed, at last. She'd been driving everyone *nuts*. Everyone was acting a little strangely, it seemed to Joe, but this was not such a bad thing. The focus was off him. His mother seemed preoccupied by something *other than him*. Now Grace was in bed and his mother was on the terrace and his father was driving the girl home, the girl who was kind of cool. She wasn't *overly cheerful* the way girls could be. Why did girls want to be so likeable? At least Olivia had not *chatted*. The alien movie had finished and now Mister Fun Furniture was trying to flog a really ugly bedroom setting from one of his showrooms. Now there was a newsbreak and the newsreader with the purry voice was talking about something that might mean something about water on Mars.

Suddenly the television changed to an aerial image of the cathedral in the city.

Joe hit the volume button and the commentary boomed: '. . . *has not claimed responsibility for the act which police say was a calculated act of vandalism. The vandals struck some time this evening while worshippers were inside attending a late service . . .*'

Joe couldn't believe it. In huge, red, spray-painted letters across the side of the cathedral was written: FREE THE SHEEP.

'*The daring graffiti is believed to refer to the fate of the diseased Australian sheep which have been on the* Cormo Express, *a Dutch vessel in the Persian Gulf, for seventy days. The Australian Government has attempted to find a home for the sheep after they were refused entry to their original destination, Saudi Arabia. Over fifty countries have refused to take the sheep. A government spokesman declined to confirm or deny that approximately six thousand of the sheep had perished. Church officials say the graffiti will be removed tomorrow and security cameras installed.*'

Joe leapt off his chair. As the news music played, the camera moved from the weather chart back to the images of the graffiti. There it was, for all to behold. A simple plea. A plea in huge red letters, letters written in a hand Joe knew so well, it could almost be his own.

twenty-five

For the first five minutes, neither of them spoke. It was so dark. Surely daylight saving would be starting soon. Dinner had gone pretty well, considering. He had been right. It was their duty to help when help could be offered, to show some benevolence. There was something about Olivia that was distinctive. Maybe one day she would be someone and would give Harry credit for saving her. *Harry would really, really love to save someone.* But it wasn't really something you could engineer.

There were so many dangers, an opportunity would surely present itself. Husbands should have no shortage of chances. Only last month, Monty's father had rescued his neighbour's dog when their house had caught on fire from an ordinary TV set exploding. Who knew that old TVs just blew up by themselves? How could you protect yourself and your family when a turned off television just decided to blow itself up? As if there weren't enough *obvious*

hazards, seemingly benign objects were potentially and unpredict-
ably lethal. Just thinking about modern life, all those wires and
cylinders and pipes full of different kinds of rampant, disorganised
temperaments . . . Inanimate objects were actually so frantically
animate, their insides silently masterminding all kinds of devasta-
tion. Once a year or so, the premier handed out bravery awards.
The papers told the stories, something heartwarming between the
reports on childhood obesity and hospital waiting lists. Harry
always devoured these stories: the fisherman washed off the rocks,
the electrocuted toddler, the farmer who'd been run over by his
own tractor, all of them saved. Things came from nowhere and
everything changed for these people. But sometimes there were saviours, incidental saviours, whose own lives were transformed by
doing. It was all very well teaching but it would be so different and
electrifying to *act*: to run, to leap, to smash, to drag, to hold!

As they began the descent of Freeman's Hill, Olivia said softly,
'Hey, the lights.' Harry pulled over onto the viewing area overlooking the bay and across to the city. Some local visionary had
persuaded the council to move the streetlights onto the central
median strip, leaving the view alone. The lights of the skyscrapers
looked like tiny, luminous tracks in the night sky.

In the old days, places like this were called Lover's Leap. Harry
didn't think he'd ever stopped here before although he'd often seen
tourists with campervans parked here, cameras ready. Beneath

them, the lights of Deptford stretched out. Night disguised its character. The town almost looked pretty.

Olivia turned to Harry. She took his hand and slipped it under her skirt so that it rested on her cool flank.

The dazzling rightness of the cliché appeared before Harry. The prof and the naughty student, maturity paring off with faux naivete, each searching for its little thrill, the thrill of the forbidden. Age asserts itself, tilts towards the glorious delicate pull of innocence, unable to deny itself one last flutter. The menace of a cliché . . . its irresistibility. Surely this was why middle-aged men were always getting into trouble, believing that something this unoriginal couldn't really be bad. A man was just taking a role in a myth, the myth of the teacher and the student, the hand on thigh, the eyes meeting in darkness, the ordinary wickedness. Could anything that *predictable* really be wrong?

Putting the ludicrousness aside, it wasn't every day that something tremendous offered itself, something that might be truly *altering*. Molly's experience seemed to demonstrate that the ramifications of infidelity were not exclusively dictated by the depth of the adulterous relationship. She didn't seem to feel very much at all about her pool man, and yet three lives at least were in chaos, and if you counted the vague chest pains, the insomniacal nights of their friends, many more besides. Olivia offered more than herself. She offered the quick electric bite of change, the *kaboom*! that set things off. Harry had finally reached the age where such a thing had its attractions again. It wasn't that he was unhappy – far from it. But sidling up alongside his contentment were the belligerent little reminders of mortality. Just lately, he had summed himself up against his youthful expectations for the first and probably last time. He had achieved some, but that was not much consolation, since he now knew that most of those expectations were not all they were cracked up to be. Okay, he had tenure. Some of his students had expressed a genuine appreciation of him, had lead him to believe that he was not too bad. It wasn't a bad life. There was something cosy about the way his life looked, like a board game, with the campus and its staff club, the Sunnyside village, the tennis club, the yacht club, it was all laid out and not too shabby. He had a family, a *good* family. But there were shadows everywhere, shadows to his thoughts, that did not bear examination: the baffling lack of conjugal love-making, the burden of child-having, the anxiety of home-owning. Every so often came that sharp pain of regret. That things had not somehow worked out to be more . . . *dazzling*.

It would be nice to have a *tiny taste* of dazzling . . . a small sense that one had exceeded taste or decorum, what was circumscribed. To unleash the wild man, that was the sense of it, the wild man within Harry. The upkeep of a conscience was exhausting.

Harry looked at Olivia. Her glassy eyes were looking into his, sending a message loud and clear: *Available*. Harry felt the charge of her. Olivia, the distinctive package, the girl with the dark-rimmed eyes, the clever girl, the one he saved.

He turned away from her and looked out to the ocean. A small boat light shone between them and the lights of the city, night fishermen. The fact remained that the only dazzling thing in Harry's life was Alice. Not that she couldn't be annoying. But most of the time, she was the most exceptional person Harry had ever known . . . He couldn't say how, exactly. Her beauty came and went. But when he caught sight of Alice – at a party at the end of a working day or reuniting in a shopping mall after they had gone separate ways (her to buy underwear, him to buy a rake) – the glimpse of her made him nervous with pleasure. In her face he saw himself as well. He had invested so much of himself in her, and in her pale eyes he saw reflected his own relentless struggle to survive, to endure, to continue. It was all there in Alice's face, not just her beauty, but *their own* haphazard beauty, the beauty of chance.

Something had occurred between them. Not only the children. Some combination of synchronicity and difference, a complicated, satisfying blend of shared outlines and impenetrable distance. A marriage had to have those moments when things could go unsaid, because the silence was so articulate. But it also had to allow a cold, sizeable gap. The gap that reminded you of the limits of a singular point of view, gave you the thrill of knowing there was a different way of seeing things, something intense and foreign.

Even when he hated Alice, he treasured this. That she reminded him, through the gorgeous dullness of domesticity, of a great chasm in his own understanding. She could go to places inside her head that he would never know, could never know, and the thrill of this was in part the substance of his desire.

Harry turned to Olivia and touched her hand.

'Thank you. But I've got to get home.'

Olivia pulled her hand away and stared at him.

Harry tried to read her coolly impassive face: pride or contempt? It would probably be wise to care, he thought, but he could not manufacture caution. Instead he felt the intense desire to farewell his own pretentious What If and be home again, inside his tender life.

'You can't go back, not now,' said Olivia. 'Not in the same way.'

'Perhaps,' said Harry, and turned the ignition.

Alice sat outside on the terrace in the cold. It was so dark, the empty pool was invisible in the sloping lawn. Through the trees, Alice could see that the lights next door were off. Scarlett and her mother were asleep. Since Scarlett had seen her on the bottom of the empty pool, a strange equality had insinuated itself between them. When

Alice had opened her eyes and seen Scarlett looking down at her, she had the distinct sense that nothing would quite go back. Not that Scarlett knew, but from that moment, she became the subject and Alice her interpreter. The words were flying out of Alice. Fixing Scarlett in print, curving her into the shape of Alice's imaginative itinerary. The roles had changed: mother and sitter. They had been seen for what they were, diversions from the heart of things. Scarlett was no longer just the sitter. And Alice was no longer just the mother. Alice had seen Scarlett, seen her with the full flourish of her imagining life. And Scarlett had seen her! *To be seen!*

Alice tried not to think about Harry, about how long it took to drive to Deptford, to farewell, to drive back. The thing about fidelity was, you couldn't demand it. The more you demanded, the less likely it was to assert itself. The ultimate Catch 22. The shivery truth passed over her: that illicit passion could wake two people up to licit passion, could set nerve endings alight. If Harry moved towards Olivia, something would happen. Maybe something was always better than nothing, maybe nothing was a marriage's worst enemy.

It was all about Molly and David. It only took one theatrical bust-up to make people think again – of choices made and not made, of things forfeited, of small pleasures, of what they had lost. Over Sunnyside, in its treasured cul de sacs, the white goods were rattling with the breezes of uncertainty. Those things that were the foundation of civilised lives – love, children, shared history – were turning cloudy. Alice herself had wondered, *what would I be?* What would she be without Harry and the children, without the house to fix her to the earth? A family gave you instant name, purpose, a future composed of graduations and twenty-firsts, of themed anniversaries and surprise birthdays, of family Christmases with their hothouse arguments and festive nibbles. What marriage gave you was a calendar. And now . . . and now . . . Molly had committed this folly, nothing all that amazing really, but in this small community, an act of vibrant self-assertion. If thoughts were words, Alice thought, one might hear the whispering across the suburban lawns: *Do I dare, do I dare, do I dare?*

twenty-six

Alice pulled up in the parking lot outside the Krapp. It was two-fifteen and students were picking themselves up off the raised lawns, tying sweaters around their waists, dropping glass juice bottles into rubbish bins. A general pace was setting in, a return to class, the increase in beats as they stumbled up, high on dope or youth or sunlight, collecting up messenger bags and backpacks. Friday afternoon and just one more class before hitting the pub. Alice had once lain there too, back flat against lawns. But she had been on the city campus. This campus, built in the nineteen seventies, lacked the elegance of the city campus. It was all squat, red-brick buildings surrounded by straggly gum trees and a few beautiful elms and oaks that had survived that decade's mania for natives. But in certain ways, all campuses were alike, little islands, sunny no-man's-lands between childhood's pasture and adulthood's ravines. The young thought they had freedom ahead of them, not knowing that they were never freer than now, innocent of three a.m. wakings, tax audits and dead parents. Really, that was what made youth so beautiful, not the smooth physical features, but the refinement of innocence. No amount of Botox could eliminate the attrition of sorrow.

Harry was in the final moments of a tutorial and his mind was wandering. Where was he going to get a bushy moustache on his way home? Tonight was the whips and spurs party and his cowboy suit needed some choice accessories, although he didn't want anything too gay. A second-year student was giving a dissertation on *Flaubert's Parrot* with less than riveting impact. The air in the room felt dead. He was going to have to give him a good mark or there was a danger he'd repeat the subject and Harry would have one more year of his unctuous application. *Young people.* It used to seem poignant to Harry that the young had no concept of how fast youth vanishes. Now it seemed merely annoying. Olivia had not handed in her assignment and today was the day. She had not even mentioned it at dinner last night and now that they had had *a moment*, it was difficult to know how to approach it. The tough-cop routine wasn't going to work. The casually-benevolent-professor routine was not going to work. It *would* have, what with inviting her to dinner *with his family* as a solicitous act of encouragement, if it had not been for the drive home and the unforgettable whiff of another life. Another life for both of them.

Now he was going to have to flunk her and what might that elicit? Behind those huge dark eyes, what plans might Olivia be nurturing? The vague thought of the Ethics Committee crossed Harry's mind, with its dour, recently circulated mission statement. And then the picture, unable to be dislodged, of soft pale thighs peeking out from denim in the darkness.

For a moment, Harry was distracted by a shuffling noise. A small white envelope appeared under the door. Happily, the young man's presentation was coming to a close. The other students were propping themselves on their fists, waking up in anticipation of the end. Harry casually stood and walked over to the door. The student paused a moment then, on catching Harry's glance, continued building to his conclusion. Harry picked up the envelope and sat again. The front was unaddressed. Using his finger to unstick it, he unfolded the white notepaper inside and read the typed message.

DEPTFORD MOTEL 4 PM
ROOM 17

Harry pulled up in the parking lot of the Deptford Motel. He locked the car door and walked along the concrete path to room seventeen.

He tapped quietly and pushed open the door.

The motel had recently been renovated and the black and pink carpet with tiny black triangles on it had a frosty sheen. There was a king-sized double bed, a TV hanging from the wall and a large mirror above the desk. Two towels sat folded on the bedspread, quilted apricot with palm trees on it. One small window looked onto the Deptford creek, another to the car, but the timber blinds were lowered.

Alice was sitting on a desk chair. She clicked on the bedside lamp and pulled back the cover. Harry watched her take off her coat. She was only wearing a black bra and underpants, the way it was in the movies. He walked over to her and pushed her onto the bed and knelt down and pulled off her underwear.

Alice had to push away the overview, get rid of it. *Be* this woman, this woman in the underwear in the motel. *Make* Harry strange, make him different, create a story.

Alice felt Harry kissing her lightly, skirting her thighs, tracing her belly with his mouth and then, suddenly, thrusting his tongue into her, tasting and nibbling sweetly and she was moving into the rhythm of it, beginning to forget what she had left behind, the life at home, only a few kilometres away up Freeman's Hill. Why was it that women had to create stories to get high? Was it that they had to compensate for life's inadequacies? Men, barely noticing imperfection, had no need to embellish. Women noticed everything. Their stories inside their heads: these were their improvements.

As Harry moved beneath her, tasting her hungrily the way, say, a white Lenny Kravitz might, Alice wondered . . . who was she? Momentarily an empty vessel, a collection of nerve endings and a pumping heart, a wet cunt, a receiving thing. And Harry was . . . not himself, and for the moment this was a good thing. Was he the young Harry, the one in the rain fixing the tyre, wanting sex all the time and funny, funny in a way he hadn't been for years? Or was he the pool man to Alice's Molly? Was it Molly that she was becoming, defiled and defiler, fucker-upper of kids, deserter of husbands, good girl turned bad, a repository of mean, pure, sexual light? Was that who she was here, here at the Deptford Motel with its featured movies of Big Busted Ladies ('no title appears on the bill') and tiny cakes of soap? What excited her more, Molly or the pool man? Or was it Harry, Harry removed from his woollen sweater and his shoes kicked under the bed and his piles of tax receipts and his black felt-tip pens, here somehow new?

Then he was up and pulling her to the desk and unzipping himself and bending her over and pushing into her, watching her face in the mirror, which she could not watch, had to avoid, because if she saw herself she might be reminded of Alice and now she wanted to remain faceless. But she saw him and he *was* someone else. He couldn't care less, was there for what he might get out of it, which was perfect and exciting. She was being *used*. There was no etiquette here, no sense of decorum. The Deptford Motel welcomed those who had felt their desire dilute in the officiousness of sexual politics, in the structures of home and family. It all disappeared, all of it, as Harry pushed into her. Here they were new to each other but removed from the sinister risk of real foreign encounters, the chance that one of them might bludgeon the other to death. There was something in this reinvigoration that was sacred and truthful, as if they had lost their way, become phony, and finally recognised it. How strange to have to come here to do that. A few kilometres undoing what ten years attrition had fucked up. The truth was not so bad, this truth, of badness and selfishness and elevated desire, the absence of tenderness, the realness of wanting . . . there was a tenderness in *this* because it was true. Alice felt there was a giving here that had not been offered in years, a giving over. *They were so much better together when they were less nice.* It was if a wall had been smashed in the sealed compartment of her brain, like that plane over Hawaii that was busted open some years back. Life had been sucked from it. Inside Alice, life was flying out: the bill for the pool and the cereal packets and homemade crab-apple jellies in the pantry, the wardrobe she hadn't sorted through, the contents of the linen cupboard, the pots and pans sailing though the air, the old cheeses in the fridge and the furniture that needed recovering and the tax records and the artwork of the kids and the photos unfixed in albums and the children, *there they went*! Joe sucked through and away, Grace following, sucked into deep space and leaving her free and empty and unencumbered. Alice and Harry at the Deptford Motel, where Molly had had her way with the pool man and within whose unlikely walls they would rediscover what had once convinced them that they deserved each other. Alice felt high, separate, alive. She opened her eyes and in Harry's face Alice saw what she had not seen for so long – a plain, raw *want*. It sent her higher, sweeter and there, in his face, in the reflection, she felt her muscles spasm and thrill again and again and again.

Tim and Minnie Staunton had dropped off an invitation to their party at the bookshop and David had accepted out of plain gratitude, a gratitude that felt precariously close to desperation. All week the feeling of panic – social, marital, sartorial – had been building. Minnie Staunton had not indicated if they had *taken sides*. Which meant that David didn't know if Molly would be at the party and he wasn't absolutely certain that if Molly *was* there he wouldn't smack her in the face. It was ironic that David had nursed a horror of physical violence all his life, had avoided little boys in primary school who had *intent* in their small, savage faces. He had detested places of alcohol-infused aggression, bars and pubs and campus parties, where civility had no authority. Now, fully grown, even *overgrown*, David felt the swift, solid temptation to *use his body*, to give it flight.

For this reason, he had decided not to go. He would stay home and do his accounts. He would light the fire and open a bottle of wine and try to enjoy his own company. Justin had gone to the skateboarding championships in the city with Will. Will's dad had agreed to drive them and pick them up again afterwards. Justin was temporarily safe, he was *contained*. David believed that this meant he should be able to stay home and not worry that life, *his* life, was over. What did it matter that Molly and other people who were not damaged, who were the damagers not the damagees, were cracking whips and jokes up on Orchard Circle at the Stauntons' fake colonial, no doubt lit up prettily with bud-lights, dozens of four-wheel-drives looking on?

The papers lay before him on the dining table. It was the same old quandary every year: you paid an accountant to do the work, but there was so much work to do before you could hand it over to the accountant. Little piles of receipts were in stacks with yellow post-it notes: travel, stationery, postage. Diaries were spread out before him and coloured pens. But every time David looked down at the numbers, the numbers became some other language, blurred by the thought that *everyone else in Sunnyside was happy*. Obviously, this was not strictly true. Other people had problems. But they weren't *his* problems. And there were large numbers of people who were not sick in the stomach at the idea of donning a cowboy hat and making small talk with Tim Staunton about foreign policy or house renovations or the Italian film festival. It wasn't that David especially wanted to be at the party, it was more the growing desire, the desire that could not be dislodged or supplicated by alcohol, the desire to be amongst the many for whom life was not an especially intense experience.

At around eleven, David gave up. He put on his favourite jacket, the warm corduroy surf shop one that Molly insisted could not be seen within a fifteen-kilometre radius of the central business district. He pulled on his beanie and the striped scarf Molly had bought him at the Henry Bucks sale. He closed the front door behind him, not bothering with the alarm. *Fuck them. Let them take everything.* Only last winter, the Arbuthnots had come home from the snow to find that a truck had backed into their driveway and loaded up *the entire contents of their house*. Neighbours had seen the truck but no-one expected burglars to arrive with a large removals van.

If he walked the fast way, he'd be in Orchard Circle in twenty minutes. It felt fine to be out. Winter seemed to stretch into spring the last few years. The cold was sweet and tight at the same time, blasting off the dull morose feeling of the fire and the wine. He was *doing* something. His arms were moving, his legs were striding, he was out in the world.

It was a clear, still night. Lights were on in most of the houses. A couple of twenty-firsts were happening on Fairmount Parade, marquees overlooking the bay, and small, bad bands playing popular classics. As he climbed the hill towards Toorangi, he could see in through the transparent plastic windows of one of the tents to the twinkling disco lights. Girls in straightened hair and sequinned tops, their small pert breasts peeping out, stood in driveways smoking.

David turned into Orchard Circle. The Stauntons' house shone bright with lights and flaming torches. Along Toorangi Road, sparkling clean vehicles were banked up, spilling out of the cul de sac. David stood in the centre of the asphalt circle and watched. He wanted to catch a glimpse of what he had once had. Through the windows he could see them all, the significant faces of a single suburb. The population of one man's lifetime. There was something moving about the smallness of it. The tug of knowing that a man's sense of wellbeing and order could be contained in a house full of tentative women in dominatrix outfits and weak men in cowboy hats. A house was a neighbourhood unto itself. There they were: the Arbuthnots, newly depleted of props, the McAllisters, the Wheelers, the Forsythes and Baraldis. Harry and Alice were there, eating tiny barbecued corncobs or mini-hamburgers. In a corner of the room, Ted Mayhew was riding the mechanical bull and Rita Vintner, in a black plastic catsuit, was pretending to whip him. It wasn't much of a life, come to think of it, but it was his life.

'Going in?'

David turned around and there was Molly, Molly in a fitted pea-coat and beanie, no make-up.

'No.'

'Neither am I. I just thought I'd walk on over and have a look.'

'That's what I was doing. It's a nice night.'

The feeling of wanting to hit Molly had disappeared at the sight of her. There was something about seeing a woman without make-up in a winter coat and beanie that made you love them. The two of them stood side by side looking in at the party. After a few minutes, Molly spoke.

'It's not him, you know.'

David studied her face, waiting.

'No,' said Molly.

'You're not seeing him?'

A tiny flicker started up inside him, the start of something frightened.

'That's not what I meant,' said Molly. 'I just don't want you to think all of this was a diversion. That I was just *diverted*. It seems to me that's belittling.'

David looked at her, puzzled.

'You can't undo the weight of it, of all of it, that's all.'

'All of *what*?'

'A marriage. The whole thing. Meeting and marrying and the

trip to Barcelona and kissing outside the Picasso museum. The house at Meadow's End and then the house at Bedford and then the house in Rockspurr and then Boronia Crescent. The dying of parents, the birth of a son, the movings and stayings, the renovations and holidays, the fights, the sex. The whole thing.'

'Why would you *want* to undo it?'

Molly looked pale.

'It's exhausted me.'

'And me, too.'

'Yes.'

Silence hung between them, draping the trees with the pauses of reluctant comprehension.

'I thought it was about a deepening,' said Molly. 'Love.'

David nodded.

'But I've come to the conclusion what's intoxicating is a lessening. A *lightening*.'

'We had that,' said David.

'Long ago,' said Molly, stamping her feet in the cold. 'But too much time together, you and me. It *kills* lightness.'

'I don't know,' said David. 'I'm lonely.'

'I'm going to wait until the school year finishes. Then see if he wants to stay or come with me.'

'Where?'

'I'm not sure. If I'm near you, I'll come back to you.'

'Come back to me,' said David.

The Stauntons' door opened and Minnie Staunton came out and fixed one of the flaming torches that had tilted over. She called out behind her, 'Oh *you*!' and laughed and went back inside, closing the door.

David could feel the breeze come up off the bay and riffle through them, the two of them, standing there in the middle of the cul de sac. And then Molly pulled her coat tightly around her, touched his arm, and walked away.

twenty-seven

Classes were winding up for the year. Slowly, the days were coming back together, helped by the changing season. It was cocktail hour, Harry's favourite time of day. Harry could hear the distant drone of the financial news on the TV in the family room. Westcom was up. They'd make some dough after all. Tomorrow, he'd put a thousand down on the fucking sound system and be done with it.

Down on the tennis court, Joe was kicking his football. He could spend hours there. There was beauty in Joe. Sometimes Harry watched him and saw in Joe things he had once possessed and then jettisoned – a feeling, a capacity for love that made life unfathomable. Harry had once wrestled with unkindness, with the cruelty of things, and with injustice. But he had realised that a certain degree of numbness was necessary in order to get on with things. Perhaps Joe would be more courageous than he had been. Perhaps Joe would hold on to his sensitivity and use it to wield some kindly influence over the world he was inheriting.

Next to the front door was the cowboy outfit, complete with whip. He'd take it back to the costume rental place tomorrow, there was no hurry. Harry poured them both a vodka tonic, opened the sliding doors and surveyed the lawn. The air was soft and smooth, the calm before the storm. Later tonight was the final of Grace's public-speaking competition, and then they could all relax. In a matter of weeks, school would be finished. All over Sunnyside, the residents were planning Christmas menus and de-rusting their barbecues, fishing out cardboard boxes of fairy lights, trying on the previous year's swimsuits and trying to book holidays on the internet. Harry would go on-line later and do the same, try to book something up north on a beach, near those theme parks for the kids with the giant slides and the performing marine animals. It would be good. It would be hot. Harry held Alice's hand. In a week, Magnus would be back to fill up the pool, back the way it had been only better.

If Grace didn't win, the world would cave in and *they'd all pay*. In ordinary circumstances, Joe would rather be *anywhere* than at the competition. But Joe was feeling generous. Things looked like they were turning around. Things were becoming *lighter*. The sheep had finally found a home in, of all places, Eritrea. Eritrea was such a loser of a country that they'd agreed to take the sheep that no-one else would have, in return for one million dollars in aid. Fourteen thousand sheep were already on land and the others were being unloaded while Joe had to listen to his sister make a dumb speech that wasn't going to change anything. *Like Sunnyside mattered*!

'He's right there,' said his mother. 'Right over there with Molly and David.'

'Justin's *coming*?'

Joe couldn't believe it. As they had pulled into the Beddington Academy car park, Alice had casually said that she had seen Justin with his parents over near the hall entrance, sheltering under the canopy from the rain flurries.

'Molly said they were all coming to support Grace. Despite everything.'

Joe slammed the car door, telling his parents he'd see them inside. The crowd of parents and siblings were swarming through the glass doors of the school hall, frantically closing down umbrellas in the crush. Joe could just make out Justin in the foyer. He pushed through the crowd, stepping on feet and getting glowered at. He didn't care. Justin was moving towards the doors into the main theatre. Joe lunged across a gaggle of blonde girls to tap him on his back. Justin spun around and on seeing Joe moved sideways through the crowd. Molly called out that she'd save him a seat.

Now that Justin was in front of him, Joe's strenuous effort to locate him seemed melodramatic. Around them the crowd was dissipating as it filed into the auditorium. The volume of sound seemed to be shifting from the foyer and away, thinning out the air.

Joe opened his mouth to say the words, but it was hopeless. He could never say what needed to be said. Joe wished that he and Justin were birds, that they were flying, flying over Sunnyside and out to the ocean. Birds didn't have to talk. If you could escape that easily, words wouldn't be necessary. Wings. They needed wings, all of them. Joe and Justin and Molly and David and Alice and Grace. Everyone except Harry, who seemed happy here. His father was the only one who didn't seem to need wings.

The image of the big red letters on the side of the cathedral sat between them. Judgement Man.

'It worked,' said Joe.

'Maybe,' said Justin. 'Something worked.'

They thought about it for a moment, gave pause in honour of the sheep. Joe could see Molly through the throng of people over Justin's shoulder beckoning them into the hall. He pretended not to see her.

'You're scaring me,' said Joe.

'I'm scaring myself.'

Joe looked at him steadily. He saw tears on Justin's face.

'Come back,' said Joe.

Suddenly Justin hugged him. They held each other tight. Around them, the foyer emptied of people until only they were left, then they separated and walked into the hushed theatre.

The lawn was becoming slick with the light grease of raindrops. Scarlett wiped her feet on the mat and turned her key in the lock. One low lamp was on in the sitting room, but the rest of the house was dark and she left it that way. She sat there for an hour, watching it get dark outside, the colours of the garden fading into monochrome under the drizzle of rain. If only she could light the fire, sitting ready in the grate. But that was something Harry would do when they all got home. Light the fire for the family, make it cosy. The Haskins' *home*. It *was* a home. Scarlett knew she would never really belong there. Biological destiny was the ultimate prison. You could never get out from under it. Her mother was the product of her mother and so it went, the long line of ordinaryness full-stopped by Scarlett herself. But this was something worth fighting for, this family with its simple, perfect symmetry: mother, daughter, father, son.

People made something of themselves even if they were not born to it. Yes, it happened. But Scarlett knew that, as long as she lived, success would feel phony to her. It could be agitated for or even earned. But success would never belong to her, the way it would to Grace. The sadness of this overwhelmed her.

In Scarlett's head, it was recorded as 'the pool incident'. For a few days after 'the pool incident', she had avoided the Haskins. She didn't want to see Alice because then she'd have to think about Alice. Alice lying there, nude, naked, *like that*. Just the thought of it was enough to make her feel peculiar. She was too beautiful, it shamed Scarlett. And it had given her something she was not sure she wanted – too much knowledge. Scarlett felt the insistent tug of war inside her head between her hunger for Alice and her need to hold her clear, separate, superior. It probably wasn't right to feel this strongly. She couldn't ever tell anyone. She didn't even know what to call it.

But then she had found that she could not stay away. Grace had told Scarlett that Alice was working again. Scarlett had come over at least three times in the last week and, each time, the study door had been closed on Alice. Scarlett had hung around to see her, but hours had come and gone in the waiting and she had eventually gone home.

What was it that Alice wrote in there? Almost certainly something amazing. To be a writer! To be so on top of things that you could *record* them! Scarlett felt as if she was flat out just trying to keep her head above water, she had so many private worries, so many things wrong with her. Writers had this way of staying above things. Just putting life into words meant that somehow it could not *get* to you. Scarlett would do anything for that.

She walked down the hallway to Alice's study. She turned the handle on the door and pushed it against the thick carpet. Alice's laptop sat on the desk, surrounded by pages of type. Scarlett sat down in Alice's chair. She pushed the mouse and the screen came alive. In its reflected glow, she could just make out the pencil annotations on the paper pages lying on the desk in a muddled heap. Turning back to the screen, she scrolled through page after page of Alice's words, words about what it was to be Alice.

. . . hair the colour of chestnuts. She gave the appearance of plainness, but on closer attention, there was a kind of beauty in her pale, stoic demeanour. None of her teachers recognised that she ran on private fuel, a stirring energy. She would not become like them or her classmates, those lazy girls who would fall into their futures rather than choose them. She would not become the women of Willowdale. She would not become her mother, with her resentments and loneliness, her Princess dolls lined up like small, plastic soldiers in her war against loss. 'My genetic stumbling block,' she had said, brutally, of her mother . . .

Scarlett stopped. *Hair the colour of chestnuts. Princess dolls lined up like small, plastic soldiers.* But this was . . . *her.* Scarlett scrolled back, trying to find her name but the name of the girl on the screen was Stella. *Willowdale.* The details were different, but this was definitely her. *Alice Haskins was writing about her, about Scarlett Kornhaber!* At last someone had seen her, had noticed her. And no less a person than Alice, Alice with her award-winning talent, her beauty, her taste. *This* was proof that Scarlett was not ordinary! *Ordinary* people were not the subject matter of great writers. Scarlett felt a wave of dignity and righteousness flood through her.

This was Alice's next novel, a novel eagerly anticipated after the last. And Scarlett would be in the starring role. To be immortalised in ink! It suddenly became clear. Scarlett could not believe this thought had eluded her until now. *This* was an escape, an escape from the life next door, a life of certain mediocrity – to be written about, to be cared for in the secure embrace of Alice's imagination. Escape, thought Scarlett. *Escape*!

Suddenly, Scarlett heard the sound of crunching pebbles. The Haskins couldn't be home already! Grace's competition would only be halfway through. Scarlett jumped up from the computer and moved quietly through the dark house to Harry and Alice's bedroom. From there she had a clear view of the front door without being seen. Maybe they'd come home early for some strange reason? The possibilities ran through her mind at a lightning pace: Joe had crunched his hand in the car door, Grace had one of her headaches, they'd been carjacked, the competition had been cancelled because the school had been attacked by arsonists . . . Scarlett started thinking of excuses just in case. She'd seen smoke. She'd urgently needed to borrow something. She'd seen a prowler.

Scarlett carefully pulled back the sheer curtain. Standing under the light at the front door was that girl, the one Grace called the Female Bat. The Troublemaker. She was wearing a tartan skirt and a white T-shirt beneath her army jacket, bare legs in unlaced boots. She was holding something in her hand, sheafs of paper. The Troublemaker had come to the house, *uninvited*. Grace would be horrified. Scarlett could see Grace's face inside her head, her look of anguish. Scarlett would not stand for it! A steely fury surged through her. She, Scarlett Kornhaber, was the only weapon the Haskins had against people like this, something Alice *had* to know. She needed to reward Alice, reward her for her faith in her, for seeing what others had not.

Scarlett walked to the front door and opened it. Olivia's face was pale, but for the two vast black rings of her eyes. Sinister.

'Yes?'

'Is Harry home?'

'*No.*'

Scarlett closed the door hard and stood still behind it. She could feel her heart beating faster. This was exciting! To be useful! To guard the Haskins' home, to guard *goodness*!

There was a knock. Scarlett was thinking fast: *what to do? What to do? What to do?*

Another knock, louder. Scarlett opened the door.

'When will Harry be home?'

'I don't know,' said Scarlett.

'Can I wait?'

'*No, you can't wait!* My God! No!'

The Female Bat narrowed her eyes and stared at Scarlett. 'Who are you?'

How dare she! How dare she ask questions!

'You're Olivia, aren't you?'

Olivia looked surprised.

'And you are . . .?'

'The Haskins don't want you to come here.'

Olivia stared at her. Scarlett saw, with satisfaction, that she looked confused.

'Are they here?'

'I told you,' said Scarlett. *'They don't want you here!'*

If Alice and Harry knew, if they only knew, they would thank her.

Olivia paused for a moment under the porch light and then stepped into the shadow. She was walking around the house, not back along the driveway, not the way out! Scarlett stepped out after her, but she could only just make out the white of Olivia's T-shirt, a moving beacon in the dark. It edged around the side of the house, making use of the table lamplight spilling through the sitting room windows, but as the light fell away, so did Olivia, moving into the darkness.

Scarlett followed, then stood still, listening for Olivia's footfall, breaking twigs.

The rest of the house was in darkness, so Olivia would not see her way in, would not find what she had come for. It gave Scarlett satisfaction to see the house as a stronghold against this girl, with her sex and her smell and her *intention*.

Alice looked at Harry in profile. He was watching Grace with a mixture of pride and horror. She herself had occupied that peculiar place: part claimant of children, part renouncer. Even the way Grace stood on stage had an edge of hostility, as if to insist: *I am part of your world*. But interesting people were not always the easiest people to have around. There *were* good things about Grace. A refusal to be defeated. The most useful of all traits. Harry forgave Grace more than Alice: he was softer. This was something Alice would always love about him. He was forgiving. Modern life was an inventory of disappointments: a calendar of self-improvement programs, cynical dismissals of marriages, religions, warnings. And yet, Harry did not make a religion of disappointment. Sunnyside seemed, at times, a place under siege, populated by those who had renounced the wider world, closed in on themselves. This was what Harry found so beautiful about the suburbs, and so poignant.

Harry embraced this. He accepted the way suburbia marketed itself, he had faith. Who wouldn't love such a man? Alice felt a stirring, a pair of wings, the quickening of love. Something was changing. Amidst the calm green lawns and opal beds of hydrangeas, human beings still lived their own dramas, found a future, just safe, just dangerous enough. Alice had been wrong about Sunnyside, after all. You could be a writer in Sunnyside, and a lover. Fear and love, both were necessary, and there was fear and love everywhere, perhaps especially here.

How young people can inherit the future? *How young people can inherit the future.* Okay. All right. It's a big topic and big topics are good. They're like pop songs. They make people feel things. They get people interested. They're *elegant* and *stirring.* And I *am* qualified to answer this question, because I *am* a young person and I *will* inherit the future.

Grace felt something switch on inside her. Words flowed out of her mouth, but her mind was running elsewhere. Somewhere out there in the auditorium were Alice and Harry and Joe. Scarlett had made an excuse which had been hurtful, but next to her family were Molly and David, together again just for this event, bignoting themselves as friends of the Haskins family even if they couldn't hold their own family together. And Justin. Grace knew that Justin was there under sufferance, but he was there, even so. Somehow sandwiched between his parents, Justin had to go on being a child for some time longer. Grace knew how he felt. He didn't know she knew, but she did. She could feel the horror of suspension that fell over Justin. They were stuck. Grace thought it was a joke the way childhood was supposed to be safe and comfortable, with its brightly coloured toys and its stuffed animals and its Disney on Ice. The reality was that *nothing was more dangerous than childhood*. If you survived childhood, you could pretty much survive anything.

Justin never chose his parents. And parents, despite talking all the time about what they wanted for their kids, did pretty much what they wanted for themselves. *You could not trust parents.* They were full of bad impulses that they could not or would not control. They were always making decisions that were in their own interests and then jazzing them up to sound as if they were in the best interests of the children. Kids not only had to survive these adults, they had to see their way clear of them, understand what was happening, get some perspective. Otherwise you just went nuts, like Justin had. Families could be good or bad, you couldn't depend on good. Kids had to wake up to themselves.

On the table, the red light flashed at Grace three times. She needed to pull her speech in, tidy it up and find a conclusion. She lifted her mouth until it was directly in front of the microphone and allowed the thick white lights to envelop her. She would not struggle to see out, she would allow herself to stand alone on the stage, to *feel* alone. She would be the one, the only one, the one that mattered.

It was just a public-speaking competition in a small part of a small state of a small country (importance-wise), so *get hold of that thought*. Grace played over this in her mind, but it wouldn't take hold. The thing was, she might only be eleven and a half, but she understood that *everything started small*. This wasn't about making front page of the *Peninsula Times*. This whole thing was about finding the fire inside herself and running with it. The fire that touched people, that lit things up.

'We are, all of us, made from the past and makers of the future. (*Fantastic start, where did that come from?*) Recently, an ordinary Australian man found a fossil of the earliest known vertebrate that is five hundred and fifty million years old! That makes it five hundred and forty-nine million, ninety-nine thousand, and eighty-nine years older than me, and yet, that small fish-like thing with a backbone is my ancestor. I am made from that fossil, as is everyone here tonight! From that point on, until this very second, life on earth has grown and adapted and we are all the product of that amazing process. In modern times, human beings have made advances in medicine and science, in exploration of land and space, in culture and a whole bunch of things which has lead my generation to this moment in time. Those influences cannot be denied. From the back-bone of that little fish fossil right through to last night's episode of *The Simpsons*!

'And yet, one of the most interesting things about life is that human beings want to discover things for themselves. We want to get credit for *making a difference*! Not all of us, obviously. There are losers who just benefit from the courage of others. But for most people, something wills them to go to places that have not been gone to before, to find answers, to discover new things. It's not enough for us just to be *recipients* of the past. For our sense of our-selves, we need also to feel as if we are shaping the future.'

Something had happened. That's how life was, thought Grace, surveying the audience. Everything went on the same for the longest time, and then little explosions happened to remind you that things could change, were changeable. That's what Justin was doing now. He was making the explosions and Grace knew it wasn't really for Molly and David. It was for himself.

'Young people have to face the challenges, not only of their soci-ety, but of their personal circumstances. Sometimes this seems really hard. Sometimes, it might seem like everything is against you. But guess what? It's sink or swim. Being young is a *privilege* not just a right! Like most privileges it must not be taken for granted. Young people see things in new ways. They are not tired yet! Tiredness is a bigger problem that a lot of people might think it is. (*Getting off the track*.) Not being tired is a major advantage that young people have and we can use it to good purpose.'

The red light flashed, but Grace felt herself reaching a climax. The timing was right. It was just *perfect*.

'Speaking personally, I believe I see the world in a way that is different from every other person. And the same goes for you and you and you! *(Bring it back to the topic.)* People are strange creatures. We need to combine our *excitement* with our responsibility and use this as rocket fuel. *(Bring it back full circle!)* We have to be *not afraid*. We can make a difference *and we will*. This is how young people can inherit the future.'

Up near the family room window, the pale shape of the Female Bat was still for a moment, and then started to descend the garden slope towards the pool. Scarlett stood silently watching at the end of the path, beside the giant camellia.

She suddenly felt fury. If anyone belonged here, Scarlett did. Not some slut from the university campus! Girls like this took things away from girls like herself. These were the ones who stole possibilities, who insinuated themselves into stolen lives until they merged with them. They had the daring. Scarlett did not have the daring to become what she wanted, to transform herself. In the back of her mind was the eternal discordant whine that she was a fake. But now Alice was making Scarlett real. Alice was writing about *her*. If anything bad happened to Alice, it would undo her as well. *It would undo everyone.*

Scarlett could see the pale dot of white material moving over the ground. Scarlett ran towards it, colliding with her.

'Hey!' yelled Olivia, putting up her hands and backing off.

But Scarlett felt hollow urgent desperation willing her on, a sudden unshakeable need to inflict harm. Through the darkness, she pushed ahead, slapped at the Female Bat, darting her arms through space towards her head. Olivia, pushing back, tried to disentangle herself.

'What are you doing? *Stop*!'

Olivia was surprisingly strong and Scarlett felt herself buckling for a moment as the girl butted her with her body. *I'm stronger than she is*, thought Scarlett, her fury lending her strength. *It's me Alice is writing about*! But Olivia refused to fall. They were struggling on the sloping lawn and Scarlett was trying to keep a foothold. It was hard in the dark, since you could not see the gradient of the slope. As Scarlett launched herself towards Olivia again, the Bat's leg hooked under her calf and tripped her up. They both stumbled down the slope, caught up in a flurry of limbs. Scarlett regained her balance and threw herself at Olivia, pushing against her weight. Whatever happened, Scarlett was not going to let this go. Grace depended on her. Alice depended on her. Harry's vision had become impaired. When Harry and Alice found out what Scarlett had done, they would embrace her, hold her, make her one of their own.

Suddenly, Scarlett felt the mossy ground beneath her give way. Her arm swung out to save herself but it was too late. She skidded towards the pool, her feet hit the crazy paved surround and she flew upwards, wavering in the air. She heard herself yell, an almost inaudible cry over the music of rain and insects and the distant highway. And then she felt herself falling beneath the earth, falling down, down, down through air, through cicada songs and whispering trees, through night.

Olivia walked through the rain to the side of the pool. The girl lay stretched out strangely as if she'd been sunbaking. She was so still. The cloud shifted across the sky and the light made her pale face shine, like a small human moon.

twenty-eight

Maddie Ridgeway was cruising the streets of Sunnyside, dropping off the burgundy envelopes enclosing the invitations to her and Angus's anniversary party. The printers had stuffed up the first lot and Maddie had insisted they do them all again. This meant they were late going out so Maddie had decided to hand-deliver the local ones. At the last minute, she had decided to invite David McLelland, and then because she wasn't too sure who else he'd know, she invited the Haskins. She'd only seen David once since their little interlude. They'd been polite. He had smiled rather sweetly at her, but neither one of them indicated that anything might be deduced from that night. Everything had fallen back into the same old grooves, although every so often Maddie could flip herself back there, in the superior position, feeling him inside her. The memory had made things more interesting with Angus, at least from her point of view.

As she turned into Carringdale Road, a cloud of dust enveloped the car. Dirt road. Pretty, *but messy*. She slowed as she approached the Haskins'. Maddie hoped no-one was home. She didn't really want to see Alice Haskins, but she enjoyed the vague sense of benevolent patronage she felt at inviting her to their expensively catered do, when she really didn't have to. The Haskins had never, not once, had *them*.

Maddie pulled up on the side of the road and got out, minding to duck her head beneath a dangling limb of ti-tree.

Things had settled down after the terrible business. Everyone in Sunnyside just referred to it as 'the terrible business', since naming names made it all worse. A young girl had died and it was nobody's fault. Just bad luck that the pool had been empty and it had been such a dark night. Why a young woman was walking around the neighbouring property when none of the Haskins had been home was not something that anyone could answer definitively. Some said she had a 'substance issue'. Some said she had a crush on Harry. The *whys* were really not the point.

Maddie opened the timber lid of the letterbox. Maybe the party would be a kind of healing thing for everyone. A resurrection of the community feeling that was a hallmark of Sunnyside life. Strife had come and gone. Maybe it wasn't such a bad thing, since it reminded them all of what they had. What they had and what they risked when they travelled too far.

Just as she was slipping the invitation into the box she noticed the sign. Wilson Fenwick Real Estate: For Sale. Maddie peered through the ti-tree then slowly crept along the driveway, searching for signs of life. Surely they couldn't have left already, from one month to the next, a family here then gone? Surely word would have reached her if the Haskins had moved? Mind you, it was summer. Book club had been suspended, the tennis circuit had broken up at the start of December. Sunnyside women were with their families, playing Pictionary in beach houses. The Haskins must have been desperate to leave since everyone knew it was too late in the season to be *selling*. But then, Alice and Harry Haskins had always thought themselves that bit too smart for Sunnyside. Which meant there were certain things they just didn't *get*.

Maddie moved gingerly along the driveway until she had a clear view in though the huge windows of the sitting room. The long glossy floorboards stretching from the rock fireplace to the central hallway shone in the final light of the day. The furniture was gone. Maddie followed the path around the house, pushing back the white azaleas. There was the pool, the infamous pool, full again and glistening in twilight, a jewel.

Maddie walked up to the family room wing and peered in the windows. Everything was gone. The house was suddenly a thing again, a thing composed of timber and slate and rock and glass, of nails and putty and wires, a thing to buy or sell, nothing more.

Maddie was suddenly seized with sadness. Most of the time, she saw the houses as the families they housed. In the suburbs, that was how things were. People *were* their houses, defined by the tilt of a roof, the choice of a turret, the shape of a portico. The houses took on the tempers of those within, assembling a character from the fights and the couplings, the odd domestic incidents, the tender compositions of men and women and their young. A vacant house was somehow unnerving, in limbo between the past and the future, tempting new life, promising something it might never deliver. Maddie shivered. Houses should never be empty.

acknowledgments

My thanks go to the wonderful Bryony Cosgrove, for the original response to *Sunnyside*. Bryony's engaged, enthusiastic and accurate observations gave me the impetus to make it better. All her suggestions had her usual remarkable clarity and intelligence.

My marvellous Penguin editor, Belinda Byrne, made a tremendous contribution to the finished book, with her detailed, respectful and accurate eye. Her graciousness and intelligence made the editing process creative and exciting, the book much stronger, and it was my great good fortune to work with her.

Clare Forster was a passionate advocate for this novel. Clare's faith and commitment in getting the book to publication were remarkable. I am greatly indebted to her for her encouragement and resolve. I have been blessed by her professional guidance and, most particularly, by her friendship. I look forward to working together again in the future when the small feet running through our lives have grown bigger.

Bob Sessions makes me want to write. I thank him for his infectious joie de vivre, his creative decisiveness and his great loyalty. He might not know it, but the latter is my weapon that overcomes the empty page.

Thanks also to John Marsden, who lit the fuse to an idea.

Finally, I thank my family, my mother Nita for instilling in me a love for words, and in particular, Raymond. His love for the book and the writer gave creative conviction to both and his brilliant editorial eye sparkled over it. To my darling boys, Sam and Charlie, who lived with me so good-naturedly while I lived in Sunnyside. And also to Lucy – never has a writer had a happier deadline than the birth of this beautiful girl.